MAKING PROGRESS

"Hey lady, watch it!" Will said as Lucy Maud turned quickly, nearly poking him in the chest with the point of her umbrella.

His smiling green eyes melted the ice around her heart. He pushed aside the umbrella, caught her in a tight hug, and kissed her nose. His body felt lean and warm. He hugged her tighter, then bent to kiss her . . . really kiss her. His mouth was hard and warm and searching, his arms held her tightly against his body, and he rocked her slightly in a sort of loving rhythm.

"Hey," he said, between kisses. "I believe we're making progress."

Lucy hid her face against his jacket, knowing only one thing clearly: she'd needed him, and he'd come. Then he was kissing her again . . . and again.

"This 'prelude' stuff has to end," he said huskily. "It's nice, but it's like a classy *hors-d'oeuvre*. It makes you hungry for . . . something substantial. Right?"

Did she answer? She really didn't know. When he left, waving good-bye, all she could remember was the length of him pressed against her, the smile in those green eyes, and her own heart thumping in her breast . . .

WATCH AS THESE WOMEN LEARN
TO LOVE AGAIN

HELLO LOVE   (4094, $4.50/$5.50)
by Joan Shapiro
Family tragedy leaves Barbara Sinclair alone with her success. The fight to gain custody of her young granddaughter brings a confrontation with the determined rancher Sam Douglass. Also widowed, Sam has been caring for Emily alone, guided by his own ideas of childrearing. Barbara challenges his ideas. And that's not all she challenges . . . Long-buried desires surface, then gentle affection. Sam and Barbara cannot ignore the chance to love again.

THE BEST MEDICINE   (4220, $4.50/$5.50)
by Janet Lane Walters
Her late husband's expenses push Maggie Carr back to nursing, the career she left almost thirty years ago. The night shift is difficult, but it's harder still to ignore the way handsome Dr. Jason Knight soothes his patients. When she lends a hand to help his daughter, Jason and Maggie grow closer than simply doctor and nurse. Obstacles to romance seem insurmountable, but Maggie knows that love is always the best medicine.

AND BE MY LOVE   (4291, $4.50/$5.50)
by Joyce C. Ware
Selflessly catering first to husband, then children, grandchildren, and her aging, though imperious mother, leaves Beth Volmar little time for her own adventures or passions. Then, the handsome archaeologist Karim Donovan arrives and campaigns to widen the boundaries of her narrow life. Beth finds new freedom when Karim insists that she accompany him to Turkey on an archaeological dig . . . and a journey towards loving again.

OVER THE RAINBOW   (4032, $4.50/$5.50)
by Marjorie Eatock
Fifty-something, divorced for years, courted by more than one attractive man, and thoroughly enjoying her job with a large insurance company, Marian's sudden restlessness confuses her. She welcomes the chance to travel on business to a small Mississippi town. Full of good humor and words of love, Don Worth makes her feel needed, and not just to assess property damage. Marian takes the risk.

A KISS AT SUNRISE   (4260, $4.50/$5.50)
by Charlotte Sherman
Beginning widowhood and retirement, Ruth Nichols has her first taste of freedom. Against the advice of her mother and daughter, Ruth heads for an adventure in the motor home that has sat unused since her husband's death. Long days and lonely campgrounds start to dampen the excitement of traveling alone. That is, until a dapper widower named Jack parks next door and invites her for dinner. On the road, Ruth and Jack find the chance to love again.

A SECOND SUNRISE

MARJORIE EATOCK

ZEBRA BOOKS
KENSINGTON PUBLISHING CORP.

ZEBRA BOOKS are published by

Kensington Publishing Corp.
850 Third Avenue
New York, NY 10022

First Printing: June, 1995

Printed in the United States of America

To Helen Wright,
Pat Dobbins,
Rita Burbridge, and
Sandy Henry—

who all *know* what a good library
is like, because they run one!

One

It could have been—no, no, it *should* have been—the best day of Lucy Maud Marshall's life. It wasn't. It was the worst.

And it was really her own fault—an error compounded of neglect, then forgetfulness, then an unfortunate, smug sense of her own growing self-importance. Of such complacency are disasters made.

In short, she asked for it.

The day started off deceptively well. She opened her eyes at six, with the bright, cool, October sun glinting through venetian slats and barring the bed with gold. For a moment, in that halfway time between sleeping and waking, she lay very still, content to see familiar things again, to be back in her own place. The annual clandestine trek to a distant hospital had once more dispelled the haunting possibility of devastation—if only for a few more months. She knew it was only for a few. She'd lived with the fact of her radical mastectomy for thirty-five long years, yet one never knew. One just never knew if—or when—the horror would start again . . .

Years ago she'd even visited a psychiatrist once at

that same hospital—on a whim perhaps, or more likely because her mama's carping had bothered her more than usual. The woman had been very pleasant, very kind. Since Lucy Maud hadn't mentioned the horror on Howard Lewis's face when he'd heard of her surgery, nor the alacrity with which he'd taken back his engagement ring, she had gone straight to the obvious point. "Lucy Maud," she'd said, "you are heading for serious trouble if you don't stop burying your feelings and come to grips with them. Because of this mastectomy you feel inadequate. Because you feel inadequate, you've shut off every other joy in your world but your library and your library work. That's dangerous. Get out more. Move around. Smell other people's roses."

Lucy Maud, of course, had thanked her politely and said she would—and hadn't. Howard was long gone from her life, Mama died shortly after, and the only thing she cared for was the library and her library work.

And it had paid off.

Whoopee!

Hadn't it just!

Today was the dedication of the new library building, and in that building was a private office for Lucy Maud Marshall, Head Librarian! Her own desk, her own files, her own Andrew Wyeth prints on the walls!

Without turning her head, she could see herself dimly in the gilt mirror over her chest of drawers. Lucy Maud had never been one for watching herself in bed. There'd never been much to watch but a tired, aging lady trying to sleep—although as far as age went, sometimes at fifty-five she looked younger than her children's librarian, Pam, who had three teenaged kids, a mortgage, a sputtering car, and dental payments tall as the Sears Tower. Sometimes Pam looked a hundred. Lucy Maud pretty much always appeared the same: nicely curled gray hair, bright blue eyes, a figure that would never see size twelve again no matter how many chocolate shakes she didn't drink.

She examined herself, kicking down the covers. She'd had her hair done Monday for today's festivities. It was tousled, but the line was there; it would brush just fine. She'd forgotten to cold-cream her face again, but arriving home at two in the morning precluded a number of rituals. She still had nice legs, she thought smugly, and a good thing, since besides chunking up a bit around the middle she was also one of those thousands of women afflicted with short waists—which meant her hipbones almost met her ribcage and she looked fat even when she wasn't.

Her long, willow-waisted mama had had another thing to chalk up to Lucy Maud's shadowy, never-glimpsed-but-always-maligned father. "Just like him!" she'd snap, wrestling with belts and sashes around her humbled daughter's middle. "You could hang his navel on his nose! Stand still, damnit. You don't have to breathe—unless you want to look like a toad!"

"And now," said Lucy Maud aloud to her image in the rather tatty and faded nightie, "now you are an elderly toad. But a successful one! Thirty-five thousand dollars a year, as of today! Whoopee!"

Thirty-five thousand dollars a year in the relatively small town of Millard, Illinois, was princely—or princessly, if one liked. Its anticipation had already bought

a freezer that would hold a whopping backlog of frozen dinners, a video cassette recorder to film all the
National Geographic and Smithsonian TV shows while
she worked late at the library, and joy of joys—partly
paid for a new Oriental carpet for her apartment living
room. To walk across it in bare feet was, Lucy Maud
imagined, almost like experiencing an orgasm—although having never had one, she wasn't technically
sure about that.

Suddenly aware that the hand curled beneath her
cheek was numb, she sat up, flinching at the sharp
arthritic twinge in her left shoulder. As she massaged
feeling back into the hand, she looked through her bedroom window into the luminescent scarlet and gold of
the last tattered leaves on the maple trees. Above was
an immaculate blue sky, pierced only by the sharp nee-
dle of the Millard Episcopal Church spire, and two
gliding birds, riding the swift autumn breeze. One of
them suddenly turned, and, with gracefully whipping
wings, soared upward.

"That's me," she thought happily. "That's me, today.
Not just today. My day! Onward and upward! A new
library building, room to expand, to grow . . ."

It would be worth it to put up with the speachifying
inanities of an elderly mayor whose only virtue as incumbent, his wife said, was that he looked good in a
suit, and it kept him out of the cathouses. Nothing
could dim the culmination of three years' planning,
conniving, working, scheming—that gorgeous new
building, with its sturdy, clean shelves, its bright,
gleaming glass, its wide double doors—doors opening
to Millard, doors opening to the world beyond—and

doors through which one Kathryn MacClane could now pass outward on her way back to the state capital, hopefully never to be seen again in Millard.

It was not that Kathryn, guardian of state-dispensed funding, hadn't been of assistance in achieving their goal of a new library. She had, of course.

"I just want," Lucy Maud acknowledged wryly, "her to go away and leave me in my new kingdom. We don't need her now—if we ever really did."

And we don't like each other. We've never liked each other.

It was then that the telephone rang.

It was also then that the roof fell in on Lucy Maud, but she didn't know it immediately. Realizing she'd been out of touch for two days, and probably a thousand last-minute things had arisen, she answered cheerfully with an easy heart.

What could go wrong today?

Fred Simmons was seventy, and president of the Millard Library Board. His voice fairly scorched the telephone line: "Lucy Maud, where the hell have you been?"

Fred was also a retired army colonel, and, his wife Mildred said, just now realizing that mail carriers and milkmen didn't salute. Lucy Maud merely held the telephone a bit further from her ear and considered swiftly. Truth was not a necessity in point. In her thirty-some years in Millard, no one had ever known of her mastectomy. Perhaps her reticence was silly, but she'd never had to argue the issue and wasn't starting now.

She answered mildly, "Out of town. I'm back. What's up?"

"More than you bargained for, missy. Why didn't you ever tell us you—oh, well. Get decent. We have to talk, I'll be there in five minutes."

She shrugged. Fred got excited over paper clip orders. "Coffee?"

He barked, "For me. For you, hemlock, you idiot!" and hung up.

That startled her. Hemlock!

Thanks to the more subtle benefits of a college education, she remembered some Greek had drunk hemlock to commit suicide.

Suicide!

That moved her out of bed.

Her pink robe was still folded on top in her open suitcase. She pulled it on over her head instead of the faded, threadbare duster she usually wore, brushed at her hair, and only had time left to shove two cups of water into the microwave oven before Fred was buzzing her apartment door with one hand and pounding with the other.

Good God! Hemlock? Suicide?

What had happened over the weekend? She knew the new library hadn't burned down. She'd driven by it on her way back into town at two, going three blocks out of her way just to luxuriate in its being there—and saying, *Mine. Mine.*

She almost ran across the Oriental carpet, partly in sudden anxiety, and partly because it wasn't yet seven o'clock and her neighbors were not going to be amused.

She undid the chain and snapped the lock, saying, "All right, Fred, all right, I hear you!"

As the door opened, he charged inside, almost bowling her over. He threw his British tweed walking hat on a chair and yelled, "Why didn't you tell us?"

She deliberately made her own voice quiet, having learned years ago with noisy library children that a low tone makes most people stop yelling to listen. "Tell you what?"

She'd closed the door and turned around, so he got her full face as he blustered, "That you didn't *have* a library science college degree!"

That was when she recognized the falling roof—banging her head, crumbling about her feet—the bureaucratic roof of red tape and inflexible nonsense that pursues the finite letter of the law beyond common sense and shelters the governmental "goblin that will get you if you don't watch out!"

She hadn't watched out. She hadn't *thought* of watching out. She hadn't even *remembered* her lack of a degree for at least thirty of the years she'd been librarian at Millard Public Library. She hadn't needed it to get the job; the previous incumbent had been a retired history teacher. There'd been no money to finish school, even if she had needed it. Her surgery had taken care of that.

Then there'd been money, but no time, At least, no time she chose to take.

Then she'd simply forgotten.

Until now.

She sat down limply in the uncomfortable old armchair by the door that no one ever sat in. Her heart was going boom-boom-boom, her blood pressure surely soaring sky-high as she stared at Fred Simmons with the stricken cornflower-blue eyes of a child just torn from her most precious dream. She almost whispered, like a child, "I—I forgot."

The glare faded from his eyes and turned them sorry beneath tufted brows. He reached down, awkwardly patting her clenched hands, and now his voice was only gruff.

"I figured that," he said. "Years ago no one required it. Recently no one around here even—thought of it. You're—you're like the courthouse clock, Lucy Maud—you've been here forever. But—"

She cut across him: "But someone did think of it. And checked. Why? Why?"

Yet even as she said the words, she was already realizing who the someone was—and why.

The "why" Fred was offering in his answer was not her "why." He was saying forcefully, "State funding, Lucy Maud. State funding! That long green stuff you worked your tail off to get for the Millard Library. We should have known, we should have seen it coming. Any time anyone gets state money, state rules come with it!"

"And state people."

She said the three words in a barely audible voice, raising those wounded blue eyes to his unhappy face. "She looked it up. Kathryn. Didn't she?"

"Yes. Yes, she did. It was a fluke, an accident. She called me Friday night after you were gone—she called everybody. She was in a real panic—"

"Bull," she muttered bitterly. "Bull, Fred. She didn't

just look it up. She knew. I'll bet she knew three years ago when she came to Millard. She just waited until she got all the work she could out of this old horse— then she zapped me. When *she* was ready. Because she wanted my job. Because she's always wanted my job. And now she's got my job. Hasn't she, Fred?"

He swallowed. He grimaced. He nodded his distinguished old head.

"Yes. She has."

She made a sound almost like a sob, closing her eyes before he could see the depth of the pain. He bent, putting his hand on her shoulder, patting it awkwardly. "I can't say I don't think you're right about her, Lucy Maud. But there's no point. The board met Friday night with Kathryn and the senator."

"Her boyfriend. She's his mistress, you know."

"Does that change anything, Lucy Maud?"

She acceded grimly to his realism. Fred was nothing, if not a realist. "No. Not a thing."

"All right. Quit bringing in apples with my oranges. We met with them—all of us, except Charlie, who was out chasing loose hogs, and he voted with us later. She had us in a cleft stick, particularly with the dedication and the grand opening today and you unable to defend yourself."

She thought dimly, Against what? The truth? I had no defense, even if I'd been here, and she knew it. My absence just made it less sticky for her. Wasn't that good of me?

Fred had turned and was pacing her new Oriental, scattering cigarette ash nervously as he looked for a place to put them. He wore the uniform of the male retiree—slacks and a cardigan sweater. The sun came through her living room window, casting his shadow like a long, black shape across the stylized pattern of her antique Heriz. Parking-lot gravel was trailing off his shoes. He didn't notice and she was too limp to care. He discovered an old porcelain pin tray, ground out the cigarette butt with the brute force of despair, and swung to stand over her.

"Now listen. You've got the assistant's job. Do you hear that? Is it registering? The assistant's job, Lucy Maud. It's the best we could do on short notice—and surely it's enough to hang in there until we can work out something else!"

Like what?

But she didn't say that out loud. He was trying. He had tried—and the rest of the board probably had, too. Besides, the inescapable fact was that this hoohah was her own fault. Nobody else's.

He added, shaking another cigarette from his pack, "And Kathryn says she'll help."

It seemed to Lucy Maud that Kathryn MacClane had already helped quite enough—helped herself to Lucy Maud's job, and Lucy Maud to oblivion. Because that's what it was, and she may as well face it. She was out of a job, out of a career, and down the tube.

And getting on to sixty. Seven years until social security kicked in.

She got up wearily, picking up the tail of her pink robe with one hand. "Come on in the kitchen, Fred. We can talk there. If there's anything left to talk about."

"Damn it, Lucy Maud—"

"Damn it yourself, Fred! It's not your fault! It's mine. It's hell not to be able to blame someone else, and I can't! Come on, before I cry."

The tiny kitchen was bright with sun. On the window ledge the geranium blossoms glowed like ruffled scarlet balls. As he sat down, Fred touched one with an arthritic finger and was astonished to find it wasn't silk.

"My God! They're real!"

Lucy Maud was getting the hot cups from the microwave. "The coffee's not. It's decaf. All I have. Sorry."

"Don't be. Decaf is all Mildred lets me drink."

He spooned from the jar, accepted the milk carton, shook his head at the sweetener, stirred. As she joined him at the little table, he said, "The assistant's job is yours. I told you that."

Her own cup had a beaming piggy on the side, with the logo "Hogs are Beautiful" and "Millard Pig Day" printed beneath. She put both hands around it for the warmth and took a sip. Over the rim her eyes met his and found them so concerned and so unhappy. He added, "She can't do a thing about it."

"Except make my life a hell. Which she can do— and probably would."

"But you've worked together three years!"

"We're both professional. We both had a goal. I just wasn't smart enough to realize it was the same one."

"So you won't take it—the assistant's spot, I mean?"

"No."

"So what the hell are you going to do? We're your friends. Lucy Maud. Tell us, so we can help you."

She turned around, shoved her mug back in the microwave, and gave it thirty seconds more. She'd always had an asbestos stomach; it made up, her mama had said drearily, for a cold heart.

As for Fred's question, what was she going to do? Curl up and die? Not practical. Nor realistic. Except for the blood pressure, she was strong as an ox. Pull out her Grandfather Hauser's Colt .44 and shoot Kathryn MacClane dead on the new library steps before the opening-day crowd? That had its appeal, but some serious drawbacks. She knew there were libraries in prisons, but one probably had to have a degree there, too.

Suddenly, in the bottom of her limp, cold, frightened soul, a small core of anger began to glow.

That bitch That young, smug, confident bitch—with her master's degree and her eighteen-inch waistline and her tailored suits and her gentle, "But Lucy Maud, dear, don't you think"s, and her superb assurance that when Lucy Maud got screwed, she would be too much of a lady to make a stink!

Well, was she?

Unfortunately, yes. But there were other options. There had to be!

Help me to find one, God, she thought. She retrieved her coffee and sipped it, avoiding Fred's worried, basset-hound eyes.

The Millard townspeople had received their tour of the new facility last week, along with a Styrofoam glass of Kool-Aid and the remainder of the somewhat

crumbly cookies the Library Auxiliary ladies had frozen after Christmas. Today at one o'clock was the formal dedication on the front steps, where the mayor
made a speech to the WGEM-TV cameras and offi-
cially handed the key to the head librarian who then
opened the doors.

Lucy Maud had a new dress for it, with shoes dyed
to match. Blue.

She should have saved her money.

After that, the high school and junior high children,
each with his slip number from the transfer system on
which Lucy Maud had worked for weeks, would as-
semble at the library. Then they were to pick up their
assigned stack of books from the old, shaky shelves
and march in orderly fashion down the blocked-off
street to the new building where staff persons would
put the volumes in their new places according to book
number. The TV cameras were going to cover that, too.
It had been extensively publicized and the kids were
really looking forward to it.

So had she.

If she took the assistant's job, she would still be
there, at least to watch.

If she didn't take the job, then she would be about
as useful as tits on a bull, as her old grandfather used
to say.

She became aware that Fred was speaking. She said,
"I'm sorry. What?"

"I said Mildred was afraid you'd see the papers—
before I got to you, I mean."

"I picked up my mail when I came in, but I didn't
even look at anything."

She reached back to the top of the microwave, brought the bundle to the table, and unfolded the front page of the local newspaper. First to meet her eye was a blurred photograph of herself, ten years ago, and caught in the act of eating so she looked like a munching cow—then a studio picture of Kathryn MacClane, eighteen-inch waist and all. "New Librarian and Assistant" the headlines said. Beneath, the story ran, "Kathryn MacClane announced today that Lucy Maud Marshall, even though her lack of a degree in Library Science precludes her going on as head of staff, will assume the post of assistant and—it is hoped—will continue her high degree of efficiency in the new building."

The paper was dated yesterday. Kathryn hadn't missed a beat!

Fred was saying, "I don't know about the other girls on your staff; they weren't asked to the emergency meeting Thursday night. But I do know the schoolkids are livid. My grandson wants to set fire to the place."

Lucy Maud almost smiled. She'd known Gary Simmons since he'd smuggled his pet hamster into story hour and it got loose in the air conditioning vents. That had been a lively day. At fifteen, Gary still bore watching.

But her eye was caught by the "will assume the post" phrase. A self-saving gambit if she had ever seen one! Kathryn MacClane knew damned well in her own soul that Lucy Maud Marshall wouldn't take that job under pain of death!

And what Lucy Maud was going to do was not her problem—as long as it *wasn't* trotting around Kathryn's new library, frowning over her shoulder, undermining her authority, and stirring up all the shit a dissident staff member could stir. Of all things, Kathryn wouldn't like that.

Nor would Lucy Maud. She had too much personal pride to do something so demeaning, That's what Kathryn was counting on. In three years they'd grown to know each other pretty well . . .

Yet—yet! How costly was personal pride? Lucy Maud had less than two hundred dollars a month income from a small property of her mother's. There would be that seven-year hiatus before she could draw even early social security. And there would be no chance of unemployment compensation because she wasn't being fired, she was quitting.

There were other things, too—things such as eating, and paying apartment rent, and gas—and buying an Oriental rug on the installment plan.

Who would hire an inexperienced old woman? And for what?

Lucy Maud hadn't been scared in a long time. She was scared now. Spitless.

That sun hadn't been coming up this morning. It had been going down!

Two

Anger faded into pure dismay.

Lucy Maud began shuffling through the rest of her mail simply to avoid Fred's sympathetic eyes, chucking away the coupons, sweepstakes packets, supermarket flyers, and the cheap burial plan brochures. Fred salvaged the "You, too, can save your Loved Ones sorrow" envelope and grinned.

He said, "I thought we were the only ones who got those."

She managed a half-smile. "As soon as you turn fifty. Then they quit trying to save you and start trying to bury you. More coffee?"

"Sit still. I can get my own water."

He was trying to kid her. She responded, "Poor baby. If you want it brewed, go next door to Betty Gillam's."

"No, thanks. It's been so long since I had it brewed I'd probably go into cardiac arrest. What did you find—something interesting?"

She had stopped thumbing suddenly and was staring at a letter with a Crewsville realtor's address.

"Maybe."

She knew what the letter was about. Her Aunt

Martha had died in Crewsville last spring, leaving Lucy Maud her small house, New Neighbor Realty was writing for the third or fourth time, asking her to please come sort out the place so they could put it on the market.

Crewsville. Her hometown. She'd been born there, gone to school there, been jilted there, and left there willingly, long years ago. Yet, suddenly, the glimmerings of a rather punitive scheme was forming inside her angry, wounded mind—a scheme that might take her back. Temporarily. Until she could get her head together.

"Fred—"

He was up, drawing water from the tap. "How many minutes? What?"

"Two, to get it really hot." Then as he sat down again, she began, "If I said—*said,* mind you—I was taking the assistant's job, would pressing family business give me some time off—right now? Today?"

He shrugged, puzzled. "You mean, not even going down to the dedication high jinks? Missing the mayor's 'pointing with pride'? The high school band clarinets squawking on the top notes of 'the Star Spangled Banner'? The dinner this evening with curdled creamed peas on tired patty shells and watery sugar-free Jell-O?"

Strange, how points of view differed. She loved to hear the high school clarinets squawk, and had been looking forward to the banquet, prepared so willingly by the auxiliary ladies.

She only nodded. "That's what I mean."

"Then, sure. I can fix it. The library board members really feel bad about this. How much time off?"

"I don't know. I've rarely taken any; I have a bunch accrued." She handed him the letter. "Would that be a legitimate enough reason?"

He fumbled inside his sweater, perched half-glasses on his thin nose, and scanned the realty firm's plea. Then he glanced back at her over the half-moon lenses. "Yes. I'd say so. What are you up to, Lucy Maud?"

She'd reached back and retrieved his cup of hot water, grimacing as her shoulder twinged. She handed it to him now, shoving the coffee jar closer. "Revenge," she said simply. "Of a sort. If I accept the job then promptly take a leave of absence, one, I get paid and I'll need the money until I find something else, and, two, if I'm simply on leave, then Kathryn can't replace me with whoever she has waiting in the wings from upstate—and you can bet your bottom dollar she has someone."

"Which means what?"

"Which means that for a while, since Mona's work-load in research is going to be so enormous that she can't help Kathryn with hers, and Pam can't possibly work upstairs away from the children's section because it's too popular, poor, pitiful Kathryn will have to handle the main adult routine herself without money to hire another minion. And believe me, Buster, it's a chore, because I've done it a few times."

"That's dirty."

"Bingo."

"How long?"

"How long will the traffic bear?"

"Two months. Three. I can get you that—I'm sure. But then you won't come back here? You're certain?"

"Not if I have to take a job in a car wash."

"Don't laugh," he said, suddenly sober. "Some folks do."

That hit home—more than he'd meant.

She bit her lip. "You're right," she said. "I'd better not say I won't. I might have to eat the words. I guess what I'm asking you to do is help me buy time, Fred, time to get myself together. If you can do that, I'll be eternally grateful."

Her voice shook a bit despite herself.

He looked at her sharply. "Damn. You're going to cry. I knew I should have brought Mildred."

"I'm not." She blinked hard, and didn't. "I'm angry and I'm hurt, but mostly I'm—numb, I guess."

"But I have to go and then you'll be by yourself." He half rose, gulping his coffee. "I'm going to get Mildred over here, anyway. She wanted to come."

"No, Fred!" There was no point in saying she'd been by herself for most of her life, even in the middle of a crowd. He wouldn't understand. And Mildred was a sweet lady, but a hand patter. Lucy Maud knew she didn't need that! Quickly, she got up also, saying in the most earnest voice she could muster, "I'll be fine. But I will have to pack and be out of here in a hurry before more people find me. It's up to you to make my story stick, Fred."

"Oh, I'll do that, all right. No problem."

He picked up his tweedy hat, jammed it on his head, then bent and swiftly kissed her cheek. "I just—hate this, Lucy Maud. It's a damned shame. A crime."

"But I did it to myself, Fred. By not finishing my degree."

"How long would it take?" He was grasping at straws and they both knew it.

She said gently, "Too long. I'm fifty-five. I'd only have a few more work years anyway—seven at the most."

Opening the door to the quiet hallway, she held out her hand. "Thank you. For coming here this morning. For everything. You've been a good friend and I appreciate it—more than I can say—and especially now. Oh, especially now!"

"Damn! You *are* going to cry!"

"I'm not," she said again, and blinked back the hot tears. "I'm just so grateful for what you've tried to do for me. Good-bye, Fred. My best to Mildred."

"Be in touch. From Crewsville—or wherever. How can we reach you if things change?"

Fat chance of that, she thought ruefully. "There's probably no telephone. When I get one I'll let you know."

He nodded. "Shit!" he mumbled in lieu of farewell, and tramped off down the hall.

Lucy Maud closed the door, then turned around and leaned against it. She wasn't going to cry. She wasn't!

The hell she wasn't

When it came, it was a terrible, frozen, painful sort of weeping. If she only could have bawled, loudly, with hysterics and abandon, it might have been cathartic. But she couldn't. She could only make this agonized panting sound through clenched teeth, fisting futile hands. Leaning against the door with her eyes squeezed shut and hot tears coursing in wet rivulets down her cheeks to drip on her collar, she suddenly realized she hadn't cried this way since Mama died. And the manner of crying had not been *for* Mama, but because of Mama. Knowing her daughter was in tears had subtly pleased her mother, and due to this, perversely, even Lucy Maud's emotions had become covert.

They were covert now because someone else might hear. No one, ever again, would be able to say they had heard Lucy Maud Marshall cry!

And, of course, even though she fought it helplessly for five minutes, it still got her exactly nowhere. She ended up with puffy eyes, a soggy nightie beneath the damp collar, and brains just as scrambled as when she'd started.

With a last, pathetic hiccup, she opened eyes no longer clear crystal blue but more of a mauve, and stared blindly around her apartment living room. It was the desperate stare of someone needing reality to grasp. The desecrated pintray caught her glance. A conditioned response made her move, pick it up. A sense of numbness made her put it down again. Who cared? If the original owner was spinning in her grave at having ashes yellow the delicate porcelain, so be it. At least she knew where she was and why she was spinning.

About herself, Lucy Maud wasn't so certain. If she did know one or two things pertinent to her present situation it was because she'd been told but not because she'd assimilated them yet. She was just good at precut answers, socially acceptable therefore automatic responses—the ones people expected: Yes, she was out of a job; yes, she was fifty-five years old; yes, she must quickly make some reasonably intelligent moves to keep from becoming a burden on society.

"A burden on society!" That was her mama's phrase, along with "Sharper than a serpent's tooth" on those not infrequent occasions when Lucy Maud had been judged ungrateful, and "Never mind; I'll soon be dead," an event for which Lucy Maud hadn't actually wished, ever, but had felt a guilty relief when it had finally transpired.

Mama had been gathered to her reward after twenty-five years of martyred invalidism, but her influence was still rather awesome. Her daughter was feeling it now, hearing her mother say, "There you go, hotsy-totsy, never looking before you leap! I just don't know how you'll do without me!"

Yesterday Lucy Maud would have said she'd done very well.

Today was another matter.

One thing she did recognize inexorably as she looked around her comfortable apartment was that the prospects of being able to keep on paying rent on this place were, at the moment, dim.

Yet, this was her *home,* the nest she'd made for herself, and the unfairness of it caused the tears to well again. Gone was the unbearably cute "kitsch" that had filled the other apartment with Mama—the awful ceramic kittens that had poured salt and pepper from their heads, the satin pillow proclaiming "Remember Pearl Harbor," the plastic dolls with insipid smiles, hiding Kleenex beneath their crocheted skirts, and the unusable ashtrays masquerading as outhouses, souvenirs of their one vacation to the Ozarks where Lucy

Maud had promptly come down with the measles—
and had never been allowed to forget it. What Lucy
Maud had here, besides some very good refinished
pieces of pseudo-antique Queen Anne furniture and
some sturdy Sears & Roebuck, was that incredibly ex-
pensive, already laid and walked on but not paid for
Oriental rug!

Damn! How was she going to handle that? Send the
bill to Kathryn MacClane?

Come off it, Lucy Maud, she told herself swiftly.
This is too serious to get silly!

Although her checking account was, as usual, precarious, her rent was paid for four more weeks. Her
car was elderly, but it ran—at least sufficiently well
to get her the hundred or so miles to Crewsville.

So, simply, what she had to do, thanks to Fred Simmons, bless his heart, was tell her landlady she'd be
gone a while, close the apartment, and get herself
there!

What alternatives were there? Did she really want
to mope around Millard while more large pieces of
her life fell away—or batten off all the "Lucy Maud,
I am so sorry's" until everyone got weary of cosseting
a useless and mournful old lady?

Also, being cut out of using a library was like cutting out her life support system—yet the idea of going
into the new building and standing on the wrong side
of her own desk, having to work while attempting to
endure the patronizing eye of Kathryn MacClane—she
couldn't hack that. The very idea made her skin crawl,
silly or not.

So she'd take everyone off the hook. She'd leave, at

least for a while, and if she seemed like a mouse scuttling into a hole, so be it.

She felt rather like a scared mouse, anyway.

She even looked like one, she thought miserably as she caught a glimpse of herself in the mantel mirror. A hunchy, tatty mouse out of a Beatrix Potter drawing, all eyes and huff.

She put up her spread fingers for whiskers and nodded. Right. Only thing lacking was a tail coming from beneath the pink housecoat.

At that juncture, before she descended into another bout of whimpering, the telephone rang.

Lucy Mouse shed her digital whiskers and went back to being Lucy Maud—to the benefit of herself and whoever was calling.

The portable was still in the bedroom. She trailed there and answered it, braced for more disaster but never once considering not answering. Response to a telephone was social; one simply did respond and took the consequences—although, if by some incredible stretch of happenstance the caller was Kathryn MacClane, she really couldn't guarantee a socially acceptable response!

Fortunately, the voice pouring into her ear was Pam Wales, the children's librarian: "Lucy Maud, thank God—I've called and called, the last time was midnight, where have you been? The most awful thing—"

The calm in Lucy Maud's own voice surprised even her. It was probably what one read about in Victorian novels—the "calmness of despair." "Pammy—Pammy, dear. I know. Fred Simmons just told me."

"Oh! Bless him! I was so dreading—but we knew

you had to hear before you simply walked into it! Oh, God, Lucy Maud, what are we going to do?"

How easy it was to slip back into the role of mentor, or friend—of senior staff member. Would she ever get used to not doing it—of being, once again, a nobody whose opinions mattered nowhere?

To Pam she said soothingly, "You're going to go right on doing what you're supposed to do—be the children's librarian! She'll let you alone, Pam; there's no glory in kids and you know you need the job! What about Mona?"

"She quit."

"She what?"

"She quit. She told MacClane to stick her research department where the sun didn't shine and walked out yesterday morning. She can, you know; Clyde has a good job. She says she'll go back only if you do."

"I'm not." Then she qualified it, telling the girl her plans, and heard Pam's brief sigh.

"You're right," Pam said. "You can't work for that bitch; she'd keep cutting you down until you were just a scrap in the back files. How about your degree? Are you going to get it? Quincy television referred to Kathryn as 'interim librarian' yesterday, and she didn't care for that—so look out for those boys. They know the sounds of a good fight when they smell it. Also, they've got a handle on the fact that Millard loves you, not her. That's another reason I've been trying to call."

"Oh, my," said Lucy Maud in sudden panic. Going toe-to-toe with Kathryn MacClane on live TV would get no one anywhere! "And my car is parked right out there in plain sight! Listen, hon, I'd better get at it!

Thank you. Love to everybody—I'll call from Crewsville."

She put the phone down, peeked out her window, saw nothing in sight but the neighborhood squirrel burying a walnut in the Gillams' bulb garden, and the landlady's bored Doberman watching. Good. Running outside, she started her car and drove it into the Caswells' garage stall, since they were in Florida. Then she closed the door, ran back upstairs and down the hall, ran into her kitchen, and ran out of gas.

Whew!

Rummaging, she found a stale bagel and a dab of cream cheese, then collapsed back into her chair and munched. The odd thought struck her: what would Crewsville think of bagels and cheese for breakfast? The last she knew, they were still eating good, hot, nourishing oatmeal.

The bagel, however, was really stale, She reached back, shoved it into the microwave, and that caught at the trailing edges of her disorganized mind: had microwave ovens found their way to Crewsville yet?

One thing she knew for certain: hers was going!

While the bagel freshened, she reached for the kitchen phone, dialed her landlady, and was guilty of her first lie. Well—not really. If Mrs. Hutch got the idea Aunt Martha had died recently rather than a few months ago, she simply hadn't listened closely. That certainly wasn't Lucy Maud's fault. What *was* her fault was that she'd hit two minutes instead of twenty seconds on the timer and her bagel was now a rock.

Oh, well. She'd eat on the way—somewhere safely beyond Millard.

What was she going to pack?

She stilled that new surge of panic with the thought that Crewsville was only a hundred miles away.

But she'd better make a list.

The Mastercard billing envelope from the morning mail would do fine. Beneath the heading, "Kitchen," she firmly wrote "microwave." Undoubtedly Aunt Martha had left a facility sufficient to sustain life, but if it wasn't microwaveable, her niece didn't buy it.

Beneath "Bedroom" she wrote "electric blanket," it being October and consequently coolish, and "heating pad" for the occasional ache in her shoulders.

Then she looked at the envelope, grimaced, and tore it up. If the kicks in her life had really deteriorated to food and comfort, then she was in more trouble than even Kathryn MacClane knew!

However, the packing—predictably—snowballed, and by the time she was ready to go, she probably could have made it to Outer Mongolia. Her landlady's husband helped her load the microwave into the back seat of the car, grunting and shoving. He laid the electric blanket in its plastic cover on top and stepped back.

"Hate two-door cars," he said. "And the older I get the more I hate 'em. Is that everything, Lucy Maud?"

"I think so. Tell Caroline thanks for offering to water my flowers. I left the plant food on the counter by the misting bottle. 'Bye. I'll see you all in a week or so."

He raised the garage door and stepped back. As she started the car, the Doberman charged inside and hoisted his leg against her back tire. It was a morning ritual. She didn't like dogs, and he knew it.

The landlady's husband yelled, "Rowdy! Bad dog!"

which was also ritual. Rowdy sat down on massive haunches and showed them both two yards of wet tongue. Lucy Maud backed her car out, narrowly missing the syringa bushes, which was also a ritual, turned it around toward the street, and waved. The man waved—then his wife waved from her window.

How civilized we are, Lucy Maud thought as she drove away. I know I got screwed out of my job. They know I got screwed. But we all smile and mumble idiocies.

I'd love to scream and curse—and they'd probably love to hear me. But I won't; besides, they'd be embarrassed, because we are all such nice people.

I wonder if it's possible for a nation to "nice" itself into oblivion?

Probably not, she concluded. I suspect the percentage of Kathryn MacClanes outnumber the rest of us. What a great way for a country to survive!

This brilliant bit of philosophy was interrupted by the sight of the WGEM-TV mobile van coming toward her. Panic subsided as it went right on down the street and turned into the driveway she'd just left.

She thought wryly that it was probable that no one had told them Lucy Maud Marshall was just another gray-haired old broad driving a Ford two-door.

The light was with her. She drove cross the familiar intersection, looking neither to the left at the old building that she loved so well, nor right at the new one for which she'd worked and planned so hard. She didn't want to see anything, or anyone, or do anything she might regret, such as separating Kathryn MacClane's head from her knees at her eighteen-inch waistline.

The queen was dead. Long live the queen.

She was ten miles out of town headed northeast before she realized she'd forgotten the key to her Aunt Martha's house.

Three

The trip to Crewsville, if not interesting, was certainly varied.

Part of the time, Lucy Maud was angry and resentful and cursed aloud, saying words that would have puzzled Mama, since her generation hadn't had the educational advantage gleaned from reading current best sellers. Part of the time, Lucy Maud wept—that same strange, spastic sobbing in which she'd indulged herself earlier. Most of the time she stared straight ahead with the fixed glare of one of those robots of whom the children in Pam's story hour had been so fond—programmed to start, stop, and speak only when spoken to—which would certainly be her ultimate fate if she went to work as assistant to Kathryn MacClane.

How could she have been so obtuse, so stupid, not to see it coming?

She'd always thought she was reasonably bright. Apparently being top dog in the Millard Public Library for almost forever had really done a number on her. She should have known three years ago—as Kathryn had undoubtedly known—that the state wouldn't hand over control of that much funding to a non-degree person! It wasn't competency on the line, it was requirement!

The fact that she *had* been around forever, like the feed mill and the Civil War Monument, had cut no governmental ice. So now the governmental representative had checked on Millard employees' credentials and found a bonanza. But then she'd kept it quiet. That part, Lucy Maud Marshall would never forgive. How easy it would have been to say, "Hey, Lucy Maud, you're short four credits for your degree. Why don't you pick it up while we're building?"

Would she have done it? Then?

Damned right.

Now?

Too late. Too late, and she knew it.

But someday, somehow, she'd get Kathryn Mac-Clane. She was that much her mama's girl. Mama always got people back.

"Oh, my God!" cried Lucy Maud suddenly.

She had sworn so many times she'd never, never be like Mama! And listen to her now!

Was she going to turn into a second Verna Marshall in her last years—self-righteous, tedious, martyred, a tired old black spider in a dusty web?

All the things she had hated in her mother—were they finally coming full circle in her?

There was a small roadside park ahead, a leaning picnic table anchored beneath stark trees, the circle drive carpeted in gold. She pulled into it and got out blindly, gasping at the sudden crispness of the air. A cocky bluejay, on a leafless limb above, contested her intrusion and she said crossly, "Oh shut up!"

"And I am not," she added into his coarse jabbering, "going to turn into another Verna Marshall!"

It was only recently that she'd been able to look back and see her mother's life as pathetic, and been able also to understand the causes for her bitter strictness, her fierce desire that her only child have the things she never had, be the social success she hadn't been. The shadowy, never-discussed shape of a husband disappearing into the mist after Lucy Maud was born had taken more form with Aunt Martha's whispered, "She really loved your father, dear." The painfully acquired savings from the thin salary of a grocery store clerk had sent Lucy Maud away to college, blissfully happy to escape, totally unaware of how financially vulnerable it left her mother—and, frankly, not caring that much.

Verna had never questioned how her daughter had become engaged to Crewsville's most eligible young man; she'd only been dizzyingly ecstatic with its social ramifications. But Lucy Maud had known why: Howard Lewis really thought a diamond ring would finally get her in bed with him. And it might have—he was passably good-looking and drove a 1955 Ford convertible—had not the awful surgery that cost a twenty-year-old coed her left breast also cost her her fiancé.

"I'm sorry," he'd gulped, green-faced, backing away from her hospital bed. "I can't—I couldn't!"

She'd told herself for all those ensuing years alone that she'd been very lucky without such a poor excuse for a man. But as though it had been her fault, her mother had never forgiven her. For a few brief months Verna had allowed herself to dream of being the parent of the richest, most fashionable young matron in Crewsville. The end of the dream had been more than she could bear—one stroke followed another. The same twenty-year-old girl, struggling to regain her own self-esteem, had been left for thirty more years with a complaining and unrelenting invalid.

She thought about her mother, now, as she took a few idle steps, scuffling windrows of crisp leaves before neatly polished, leather-shod feet. One hand unconsciously touched the left, Dacron breast form with its liquid fill that still gave her the required twin peaks.

She was used to it. No one else had ever gotten close enough to know any different. Certainly every other man's tentative advances had been firmly turned away. Lucy Maud Marshall had been badly hurt once. Once was enough. Why take a chance, why put herself through such a cruel experience twice? One didn't need men in a library career. If one used the proper social strings, they weren't needed outside, either. The stereotype of the "old maid librarian" had been very useful. Without shame, she'd used it again and again, until—until last year . . .

Remembering, she was still not sure whether to laugh or cry. She shook her head ruefully in the cool autumn air, making it fan her round cheeks, sliding the soft gray fringe of hair across her forehead.

Twelve-year-old Cindy, newly arrived from a larger city, had come hesitantly to the front desk of the library. "Miss Marshall?"

She'd taken off her glasses and looked up with unseeing eyes. "Yes, dear?"

"Are you a lesbian? If you are, my mother says I can't hang around here anymore."

And so had the modern world come to Millard!

She'd managed to say the truth with reasonable

firmness. "No, dear. I am not. Nor is Mrs. Wales, nor Mrs. Patterson."

"Oh, I know that. They have husbands. But my mother says you don't even have a boyfriend."

Ancient mores compel strange answers: "I did, dear. One time, long ago. But he—died." Certainly she'd killed Howard Lewis many, many times in her mind.

"Oh. I'm sorry," said the child, and she'd wandered away, satisfied. Apparently her mother had been, also, as Cindy had continued to "hang around."

Now, suddenly, standing beneath bare trees and being roundly jeered by an annoyed bluejay, Lucy Maud thought directly of Howard Lewis—and realized with something of a shock that he was probably still there—in Crewsville. Three or four engagements later, he'd married a bottle blonde whose father owned an apple orchard. She'd heard later that he'd bought the local bank.

Startled, she felt an acorn hit her head, and realized the jay was resorting to bombardment.

"All right, all right, enough!" she said crossly. She stretched, exposing a bit of chubby midriff to the cool air below her heavy gray sweater and above her well-cut gray skirt. Then she cleaned the bits of leaf mold and gravel from her shoes and got back into the car.

Onward to Crewsville!

They could keep the fatted calf for somebody else. She'd be satisfied with anonymity. Being financially precarious, out of a job, and getting older were hardly reasons for rejoicing.

There was a restaurant at the turn-off, the dash clock said eleven-thirty, and her stomach growled; the mere fragment of morning bagel had departed some time ago. Besides, she needed to get on the phone and call that realty outfit, hoping to God they had the extra house key. It seemed preferable to climbing in a window—rather undignified, especially if the neighbors noticed. And she didn't want to go to a motel, although she vaguely remembered that Crewsville had one. She was a bit short on cash, having forgotten to stop and get any. Nor did she want to use a credit card, having also indulged a bit more than usual over the previous few days. That had to stop, anyway. Obviously.

However, sometimes she had thrown the odd dollar or two into the glove compartment . . .

She hadn't recently, but in ascertaining this she did notice a scrawled note on the car floor, apparently blown off the dash.

It was from Fred Simmon's grandson, Gary. It said simply, "Watch the WGEM six o'clock news."

For heaven's sake. Why?

But the note didn't answer, nor the jaybird.

Shrugging, she put the car in gear and drove on to the restaurant.

The sign said "Cafe 107." She parked her automobile next to two red farm trucks full of shelled corn and a muddy pick-up with a patient black Labrador in the back.

His velvet ears pricked as she got out.

"Sorry," she said. "You're very handsome, but I don't like dogs."

The fact was that she'd never had one. Dogs made messes, Mama said, shed hairs, dug unsightly holes, and dribbled. Besides, they did—you know—in full view of everybody, and—worse—seemed to enjoy it.

Lucy Maud opened the cafe door and walked into a warm smell of hamburgers, the sound of men's voices, and a haze of smoke. The voices didn't stop, but they slowed. Aware of the attention, she sat down in the first empty booth and scooted across cracked vinyl to the warmth pouring in from a calico-draped window.

A friendly voice inquired, "What'll you have?"

Looking up, Lucy Maud saw an ample female figure in a sweatshirt that said "Busch Light," topped by a smiling face beneath well-sprayed and outrageously orange ringlets. The voice went on, "Our special today is a fried brains sandwich, tater tots, and a bowl of chili, two ninety-five. With coffee. Coffee's fresh; I just made it."

Well, Lucy Maud thought, I am definitely back in Pike County.

She declined the brain sandwich, opting for the coffee and a burger with everything.

"No lettuce and mayo," she called after the retreating sweat-shirt. "Leave off the lettuce and mayo, please."

"God, lady," said her waitress. "We ain't no Hardee's!"

She shouted her order to an unseen factotum in the kitchen, slip-slopped back in her plastic shoes, and poured the coffee from a shining glass carafe. Her other hand was scrabbling deep in her pants pocket, then tossed a packet of sweetener and one of powdered cream on the table. "Can't leave 'em laying out," she said by way of explanation. "The senior citizens take 'em by the dozens. Carry 'em home, I guess. It's fierce. Your burger will be up in a minute."

"Fine. No hurry." Quixotically, Lucy Maud appreciated not being lumped in with the larcenous senior citizens. "Is there a telephone I could use?"

"Local call?"

"Crewsville."

"Sure. Over there on the counter by the register. Charlie, get off the phone! With two kids ten months apart, if Patty doesn't know you love her now, she's a slow learner! Lady needs to make a call."

Charlie, a lanky young man in a John Deere tractor cap, turned a bright red, grinned, and hung up. "Baby's got a cold," he mumbled, and sat back down on his stool to a bowl of chili covered with crumbled crackers.

Digging in her bag for the number of the realtor she'd scribbled on the back of a sales slip, Lucy Maud said, "Go on talking if you need to. I'm not really in a hurry." I probably have the rest of my life, she added to herself bluntly.

He shook his head. "No, s'all right. Thank you, ma'am. I just had to tell her I'd be late."

A voice from a distant booth called, "How far are the trucks backed up, Charlie?"

"Shit. Pardon me, ma'am. Clear 'round the elevator and on to the highway. And they're out of grain barges to load into. I'll be there until midnight 'fore I get my corn off."

Charlie left, carrying his chili. Lucy Maud hoisted herself up on his vacated stool and dialed slowly. It was a disk dial. She'd gotten so accustomed to punching numbers she almost didn't remember what a dial phone was like. Then it all came back to her: disks ate fingernails.

Smoothing the fray on her index finger, she waited while the digits clicked in. The ring began. Once. Twice.

Then a tinny voice said, "You have reached New Neighbor Realty. We are sorry. All our agents are busy at this time; however, if you will please—"

Well, some advanced civilization has reached Crewsville, Lucy Maud mused in disgust—she was also within a fraction of hanging up when suddenly a deep male voice said, "Goddamned gadgets! Hate this sucker! Hello. Hello! Vic Bonnelli, here! May I help you?"

Lucy Maud laughed. "I hate them, too," she said. "And yes—I think you may. This is Lucy Maud Marshall—Martha Hauser's niece. Will you see if you have a key to her house, please? I'll be there in half an hour and like an idiot I left mine in Millard."

"Oh. Just a minute."

She could hear him mumbling, "Hauser. Habford, Hartford, Hackton, Hauser—shit. John, where the hell is the Hauser file? Oh. Here it is."

Then he was back at the phone, "Yes. We have a key, Mrs. Marshall."

She didn't bother to correct him. Who cared?

"May I pick it up?"

"I'd be happy to drop it by."

"That's kind of you."

"You said half an hour. I'll be there."

She hung up, went back to her table just as her sandwich was being served. She said, "Thank you," and tied into it. Surprisingly, she was hungry, and even more surprisingly, it was good—a genuine, thick, juicy, non-prefab hamburger, pink in the middle.

Bonnelli, she thought, absently eating a french fry— which *was* prefab. Bonnelli. It rang no bells. Wait a moment—hadn't there been a football hero at Crewsville High when she was sophomore? Sure. Vic Bonnelli. He made All-State. God! Just what she needed today—an aging athlete!

She finished her sandwich, looked for the restroom, found it was unisex, and decided to wait for a gas station. The tab for so unexpectedly good a meal was minimal—but then, as she opened her wallet, she found that so was her cash. The cheery "Thank you, come again," from the waitress left her exactly three dollars and some odd change. Good move, Lucy Maud . . .

As she put away her wallet, one of the young farmers yelled, "Turn on the TV, Dottie! We need some weather reports. Buck, here, says it's going to rain."

Dottie reached upward, releasing a massive scent of deodorant over the general aroma of fries and smoke, and adjusted the small set on the shelf with the gum and the Red Man chewing tobacco. "Channel 10 okay?"

"Fine. God, who's that? Bet she can spit a country mile!"

Lucy Maud was meanly appreciative of the young man's observation, as *that* happened to be Kathryn MacClane, speaking directly into the camera, and its relentless eye made her usually cosmetically minimized buck teeth quite obvious. Appreciation, however, dimmed rapidly. Kathryn was speaking from Lucy Maud's office, sitting at her desk, beneath the

Wyeth print she had chosen. Also, brightly, without a shade of guilt, the bitch was claiming Lucy Maud's scheme for the children's book transfer as her own!

"Hell," said Charlie from the booth. "Try Channel 7, Dot. We don't need no yammer about libraries; we got as good a one as she's got. They even bring books out to the place for my old man; keeps him off my back. Whoa—there's the guy on St. Louis—he'll do fine."

But not for Lucy Maud. She'd already turned and left them all, not even hearing the little bell jingle on the door as she closed it.

The black Lab got to his feet and watched as she groped her way to her car. His brown eyes were concerned, but she didn't notice. She slid beneath the wheel and beat on it with an impotent fist. That bitch! That thieving, opportunistic bitch!

And who was to know? Mona and Pam, but they had no clout. The kids—but few people really listened to children!

All that work, all that planning, those hours and hours of typing out slips, of rehearsing the kids!

Perhaps she shouldn't have gone. Perhaps she should have stayed!

And done what? Created a scene?

No. She wasn't articulate enough for that. She'd only look like a jealous old broad, courting applause—which, of course she would be. Face it.

This way was better, bitter as it was. The people she wanted to understand, did. The rest—the hell with them!

As she backed around, Charlie came out of the cafe, threw away a toothpick, and tousled the ears of the Lab in the pick-up. He also waved at her, and vaguely on the cool wind came the words, "Have a good day, ma'am!"

She nodded, giving him her social smile, and turned right. A good day! It had been a dandy, so far. At least she couldn't imagine how it could get worse—forgetting, of course, that it was only noon.

Four

The neat black-and-white sign with its Federal pediment read: "Crewsville. Founded 1820. 1200 smiling people and a few grouches."

"Also one elderly loser," Lucy Maud thought dismally. "At the end of her line."

Where else was there to go? That talk about another job was probably sheer smoke. She'd been too inverted, too turned away from other people to make more than superficial impressions. To be coldly practical, somehow she had to exist until she was sixty-two—and if she couldn't swallow her pride enough to be Kathryn's assistant, then something had to turn up somewhere. And "where" was the problem. She had no connections here anymore, either, especially with Martha gone.

When she was away at school and gave her hometown as Crewsville, some smartass always responded with "Who's ville?"

Perhaps that had been prophetic. To all appearances it was still "whosville." God, Lucy Maud said to herself, two hundred miles to the Fox Theater in St. Louis, fifty to a mall, and heaven knows how many to a decent restaurant. I'm back in the land of twenty-four hour TV and brains on toast! How did Aunt Martha stand it?

Truthfully, she knew that answer. For almost fifty years Martha Hauser had been the cheerful, competent secretary to whoever had been Crewsville's water commissioner at the time. She'd known everyone, loved everyone, and they'd loved her. Even after retirement she'd stayed active with church, clubs, and community activities until her sudden death of heart failure.

What a contrast to Verna Marshall!

Probably, Lucy Maud thought ruefully, the best thing that happened to Martha was the sisters' falling out and our moving away. Martha bloomed. My mother shriveled.

Perhaps someday I'll learn to feel sorry for my mom. But not yet. Not yet!

Depressed and glum, she drove past the four blocks of relatively neat tract houses with plastic tricycles in their square front yards, turned right again away from the distant line of river bluff, and went slowly west down the main street. It was still bisected by a row of tall light poles crowned with birdhouses and interspaced with hardy, breeze-swept beds of yellow marigolds. She noticed that the elderly and handsome old brick storefronts hadn't changed but their contents had. There was a plumbing shop beneath the elaborate pediment of the old bank, and the hardware store now sold groceries. Swing sets stood on a grassless plain where the lumberyard had been. Through the leafless sycamores of a side street she glimpsed the dark brick of the high school, and beyond that the pink and gray logo of Bunny Burger. Well. One ray of culinary hope. They usually made good chili dogs and a pretty fair quiche.

Quiche in Crewsville? Hardly. The management had

probably renamed it something more appropriate to local cuisine: Cheese-Egger? Eggs Velveeta?

Granting that she was being an awful snob, and not fighting it at all, Lucy Maud also observed that what had once been the small, frame library was now a barber shop. But Charlie had said they had a library. Okay. So it had moved to a smaller hole-in-a-wall. That was predictable, since as she remembered the local reading level, it was about on a par with *Roy Rogers Meets the Bionic Cookie*. No wonder Aunt Martha had never wanted her and her mama to come back here, had always preferred to visit them! It had probably been an adventurous escape!

There was a fat, elderly spaniel sunning herself in the middle of the street. Lucy Maud slowed and tooted her horn. The dog rose slowly, wagged her plumy tail, and moved over just enough to let the car by. Then she lay down again.

Typical. No leash law. Doggie-poo all over the place.

At the end of the double street, a cluster of pick-ups and cars surrounded some sort of eatery, a blue-clad postman was working his way down a row of apartment house boxes, and suddenly a three-wheeler bike roared around her, kicking up dust, with two young boys on board.

My thrill for the day, Lucy Maud told herself grimly, glad she hadn't followed her first impulse, which had been to climb the steps of an obviously new bank building without leaving her car. It was probably Howard's bank.

Was that teeth-grating, lemon-colored Cadillac convertible also Howard's?

And was he still putting the moves on the local ladies? Good Lord—he was sixty! He'd probably worn it out!

Although she and Mama had lived on the other side of town, she did remember Aunt Martha's street, but she'd only seen the house once, years ago, when Martha had bought it. She turned right for the third time and slowed to a crawl.

A double row of giant sycamores arched tattered branches over nondescript houses with weather-beaten verandahs. Here and there the random ceramic bunny rabbit, gnome, or full-sized dusty deer dotted lawns edged with faded coleus gone to fall seed, sprawling spirea bushes, and mossy, sealed-over well curbs that hadn't drawn up water for seventy years.

At least, she thought nastily, there don't seem to be tricycles or swing sets.

And that must be Martha's house! That little one, with the weedy driveway, the leaning chimney, the dangling eaves trough, and the putty-shedding windows with yellowed shades drawn. Yes. That was it, all right. She remembered vaguely the peony bed and the old-fashioned rambler rose clutching the porch rail.

Welcome home, Lucy Maud. You have arrived.

She drove into the rutted, pigweed-covered driveway and stopped the car. Suddenly, the sun went behind clouds and the whole world turned gray. Thanks a lot, God. Is that an omen?

Her entire body felt as though it had taken a beating. She opened the door and swung her feet out. Pointing both leather toes, she was stretching her legs wearily when she heard a second door clunk shut. Behind her, a deep voice said pleasantly, with just a hint of accent, "Good morning. Or afternoon, as the case may be. Mrs. Marshall? Welcome to Crewsville."

Surely you jest, thought Lucy Maud. Turning, she saw a short, wide man walking toward her. He had a broad, Slav face beneath a tangle of gray-black curls, and his gait was curious—a stride with a hitch in it. Behind him, in a rather dirty Toyota, another Labrador, a cream-colored one, sat upright on the front seat and observed them both. A mauled chew-bone stuck from one side of his muzzle rather like a cigar, giving him a whimsical look.

She dropped her feet to the weeds and stood up. She was aware the man had been admiring her legs, and was briefly sorry the rest of her didn't match.

He only held out a large hand. "Victor Bonnelli."

"Lucy Maud Marshall."

They shook hands rather neatly—a brisk clasp, then disengagement without awkward clinging. She mentally congratulated him; proper hand-shaking was a good trick.

He repeated, "Lucy Maud. Lucy Maud. I haven't heard that name in a long time."

"It's after Lucy Maud Montgomery—an author my mother liked."

"Sure. *Anne of Green Gables. Magic for Marigold.*"

To her slack jaw and absolutely stunned blue eyes he added, grinning, "Lady, I had seven sisters—all of them older than me."

Then as a sudden breeze swept by, rattling leaves as she shivered, he said, "Come on. No need to stand out here."

He preceded her with that curious gait, went up on the sagging porch, and produced an old-fashioned door key. Over one massive shoulder he advised, "Watch the bottom step; it looks like it could go."

It did, indeed. In fact, to her dismay, the entire house looked like it. Behind him, she said, "I probably should have come sooner. I had no idea the whole place was so run down."

"Oh, well. Martha was a sweet lady, but she got older and her knees were bad—you know—things sort of get out of hand—"

No, she hadn't known, Lucy Maud was thinking guiltily. In the past decade, her contact with Martha Hauser had been the duty phone call and the odd letter . . .

Vic Bonnelli had propped open the rusty screen and was wrestling with the door lock. Grunting a little, he went on, "It was pretty well kept until Frank died, though."

"Frank? Who was Frank?"

She asked it idly, until, moving further out of the wind, she caught sight of Vic Bonnelli's abashed face. Her voice turned incredulous. "You mean—my Aunt Martha lived with a man?"

He straightened and—unexpectedly—grinned. "Is that outrage I hear, or discovery?"

"I—I—I don't know. Aunt Martha?"

"He was a grand old man, Mrs. Marshall. They thought a lot of each other. That's the bottom line, isn't it?"

And she'd thought that in Crewsville she'd be the sophisticate!

She swallowed, saying faintly, "Yes—I guess."

He shrugged and turned again, putting one suede-coat-covered arm against the door framed. "It's swollen a little. Hang on. I don't want to splinter anything."

He pushed, grunted once more, and pushed again. "Now. It's coming. Anyway, the roof appears to be solid; that's a big item. Hopefully, the interior is still okay. Our instructions were to leave the power on so nothing would freeze in case you didn't get up here. I could probably have the water running this afternoon if you'd want it. Ah—there we are."

The door opened with a creaking protest. Damp air poured out with a dank smell of must and mildew. Repelled, Lucy Maud made a repugnant sound, and he said swiftly, "Now, now—give it a chance!"

Reaching around the door frame with a practiced hand, he found the light switch and turned it, adding, "I know. But closed-up places always smell like this. I could have aired it out this morning if you'd called earlier."

"I didn't know, earlier."

Despite herself, the day's pain showed in her voice. Vic Bonnelli swung around, looked at her sharply, and she was suddenly aware of velvet black eyes, lash-circled and young, in an older face.

He asked, "Are you okay?"

She grimaced and half-laughed. "It hasn't been a good day. Never mind. What if we opened some windows?"

"Good thinking. Wait here."

He disappeared inside, leaving a curiously empty

vacuum behind him. No getting around it, the man was short—but big!

She heard him sneeze, then window sashes squealed. She opened the screen, stepped inside, and realized why. The small front room with its sheeted furniture was deep in dust, even powdering the festoons of spiderwebs hanging from the chandelier. Vic could be glimpsed beyond, in a tiny dining room, opening another window. Its shade went rattling to the top. He said, "Shit," briefly, stretched, and got it down again. "There's been construction two blocks north and the trucks used this street," he said over his shoulder. "That's why everything is so deep in the stuff. Is that better yet?"

She took two steps inside, ran into a cobweb, and fought it off, saying, "Ugh—nasty things!" and decided "better" was a moot point. The raised shades and open windows improved the air but not the view. Beyond the webs and the dust, wallpaper was peeling, mice had made mosaics on the dirty floor, and to Lucy Maud it was nothing but spiritless decay. Her heart sank to her toes.

This was awful. She must have been out of her mind even to come here! She'd gone off half-cocked, as usual, as Mama had always said she did—when surely, if she'd thought about it rationally, there would have been some solution besides running to Aunt Martha's!

Well. Too bad. She was here, now.

The massive realtor was simply standing there by the window being quiet, dust on his tangled curls and across his shoulders and a quizzical look on his face.

But as she looked across at him, he suddenly raised one finger. "Listen."

"What?"

"A cricket. Hear him? The Chinese say that's good luck."

That was not what crickets meant to her. Nasty, jumping things! She passed on the Chinese philosophy, asking instead, "Is there any hope? I'm a novice at this."

"Hell, yes," he answered calmly. "The old girl is sound. A little chimney work, a bit of putty, a few boards on the porch, and some paint; that ought to do it. What you're looking at is the dirt. That's superficial. If you like, I can have a couple of ladies I know come in and have it all cleaned up in a day—if that's what you want."

"Want" hardly entered into it. What Lucy Maud *wanted* was to be back in Millard, head librarian of the public library with an Oriental rug that she could pay for.

Instead, she could only shrug helplessly. "I meant to move in and clean it myself."

It was his turn to shrug. "Okay. Then the first thing to do is get the water turned on."

He started past, brushing dust from his coat sleeves, and stopped to look at her. It was a considering look. He asked slowly, "To live in, or to sell?"

"I—I'm not sure."

"Well, then—as I said, structurally I'm pretty certain she's sound. Fixing the windows and the porch won't be much of a job. If your husband is any sort of a guy with tools—"

"But I haven't—I don't—"

Good God! Would you listen to her! Fifty-five-years old, and she was about to apologize to this over-sized pasta for not having a husband!

"I'm not married," she said, her voice flat. "I'm afraid as far as fixing is concerned, I'm very much on my own."

"No problem," he said calmly. "There's a number of locals around here who do odd jobs and won't rob you. How about the water?"

She reached out and with one finger traced a clean streak in a quarter-inch of gray dust. "It might be," she answered, "useful."

He laughed. He was still laughing as he went off the porch to his car, and she realized it was a deep-chested chuckle and a happy sound.

He reached inside his Toyota, briefly smoothed a cream-colored canine ear, received a lick up one cheek he didn't seem to mind, and talked crisply on a car telephone.

"Thirty minutes," he said, coming back toward her as she stood in the door. "Which means sixty—or eighty—but today."

"Thank you. I appreciate it."

"Service of the firm. Look—I have an hour or so. Let's take the tour of the rest of this place so you can decide where you want to start. There's a sweeper sitting in the kitchen. I'll see if it works, while you change out of that tootsy sweater and skirt. Deep cleaning takes old clothes. I hope you brought 'em."

"I brought 'em." At least she'd brought what would have to do.

"Good girl. Okay. *Voilà:* the kitchen!"

He saw she was not precisely thrilled, and he grinned.

"Early functional," he said.

"Yeah." There was a stove and a refrigerator, a single sink with an ancient drainboard, a scant row of cupboards, and four passable chairs at an old wooden table whose top displayed an interesting frieze of mouse droppings.

Lucy Maud, thinking of the lovely, sunny, modern kitchen she'd just left, said grimly, "Be still, my heart."

"And there's more!"

"I'll bet there is."

And there was. She saw a fair-sized bedroom with a double bed—for Frank?—another designed for a midget, and a connecting closet, mercifully empty of all but a few jangling wire hangars. The bathroom had a rusty tub at which Lucy Maud, a shower person, stared in dismay. There was an eight-inch clearance between the john and a cupboard into which, in a sitting posture, a tall person would obviously have to insert his knees, and cracked linoleum of the Pleistocene Era.

There was also a small medicine chest containing one lonely tube of Dento-Grip and a can of powder for jock itch. Frank. Unless there was something else about Aunt Martha that Lucy Maud didn't know.

Hastily, she closed the chest door again. Because there was no room for two, Vic Bonnelli was standing in the doorway, brushing off more dust. He sneezed and said, "And for my next thrilling moment, the back porch—"

She interrupted, "I'll pass. Right now, all these

thrills are giving me indigestion. Besides, I really can't take any more of your time."

"You didn't listen. I repeat: no problem. Can I bring in a bag for you? You need to change—and while you do, I'll tackle that sweeper. Once we can walk without choking to death and get the dust off the furniture covers, you'll make it. I promise."

He was being very kind, even if it might be costing her by the hour. It was worth it. Lucy Maud was beginning to feel desperate again. Assuring him she could get her own bag, he said, "Then watch the step."

She nodded. Even as she went carefully down the weather-rotted stair, holding to the shaky railing, she heard the vacuum start up.

"He probably smiled at it," she thought, and was startled at herself.

A small girl with tight black curls and skinny legs encased in pink, shiny tights was standing on tiptoe at the Toyota, nuzzling Vic's dog. A bit sharply, Lucy Maud said, "Should you be doing that?"

The child grinned, showing a complete absence of front teeth. "Sure. It's Baron, He wikes me. Is Vic in that house?"

"Yes, he is—but—"

The "but" was already directed to thin air. Lucy Maud shrugged. As she opened the trunk and pulled out the weekend bag not even unpacked from yesterday, she heard Vic Bonnelli's cheerful voice above the sweeper.

"Hi, sweetheart! What are you doing here?"

His child? Surely not. She was too young. A grandchild, maybe.

As she carried her bag through the door, the little girl was telling him, "Mom got off work at Bunny Burger and brought me to Grandma's from school. She heard my dad's in town."

"Oh," said Vic, and his voice sounded a little grim. "Dandy. Miss Marshall this is Tina. She's in first grade, this year; how about that? Her mom and I are— friends."

I may be obtuse on some things, but I caught *that,* Lucy Maud thought rudely. So here's another guy with a floozie on the side.

But the little girl was cute as a button, and it wasn't Lucy Maud's business anyway. She said, "Hi, Tina," and went on into the bedroom to change, a project in itself. There wasn't even a decent place to put her suitcase.

The corner of the bureau would have to do. She pulled down the elastic waist of her skirt and her half-slip, careful not to let them touch the filthy floor. Then she folded them in the case, struggled out of her sweater, added it to the top, and was suddenly caught by her bleary image in the dusty mirror.

What other great sights had that mirror seen? Aunt Martha—with a man?

That was so hard to assimilate. Sweet, dowdy Aunt Martha, under her mama's thumb for so long. Gentle, blue-eyed Martha, like a plump little pigeon, cooing over the neighborhood kids, starching and ironing the church altar clothes, secretly rinsing her hair with something called Exotic Mink, clandestinely feeding every stray animal in town . . .

In fact, that had caused the ultimate split between

the sisters. Martha had nursed a ratty old tom back to health in the woodshed; coming home unexpectedly one day, Verna found Mr. Thomas ensconced in the house, in her chair, eating spoon-fed bits of the very best salmon from her Sunday china.

The hoohah must have been magnificent. When Lucy Maud came home from the house of the neighbor who kept her while Verna worked, both Martha and the cat were gone forever.

The quarrel had been ultimately patched up, after a fashion, but when they'd moved to Millard, Martha had slipped farther and farther away.

Had Mama ever known about Frank?

Shaking her head, unable to believe that, Lucy Maud pulled on the older of the two pairs of slacks. They'd have to do, as well as the sweatshirt she'd bought last weekend for Pam's eldest boy and providentially, hadn't had a chance to give him. The unfortunate fact that it said across the front in blazing letters "I'm Tired of This Shit!" was something she'd just have to live with. At least it wasn't as rude as a few others she'd seen, and it was certainly far better than ruining a good Pendleton sweater.

When she emerged, tying a blue scarf around her head, Vic had finished the living room rug and was dumping dust covers out on the porch. The youngster was gone, and his face was sober.

But as he read her sweatshirt, he grinned.

"Me, too. I wasn't cut out to be a housemaid; my knee won't take it."

She didn't notice that he said "knee." She was looking at the uncovered couch and chairs which had turned out to be a depressing shade of mauve velour with crocheted tidies pinned to their backs.

"My God," she said, before she thought. "I didn't know people still did that."

"Did what?" He was bent over, tinkering with the bulky old television console.

"Stick doilies on everything."

"My mom doesn't anymore, She used to—until one of them snagged Father O'Malley's toupee and kept pulling it up and down like a lid every time he moved his head. My dad said he'd never enjoyed a visit from a priest so much in his life. Aha. *Voilà!*"

Before Lucy Maud could decide whether or not he was serious about the priest, he straightened up stiffly and pointed at images fast appearing on the TV screen. "Communication. Of a sort. If you want cable, I'll call them."

"I don't know. Not yet."

"Right. No problem."

She suddenly realized that he'd taken off his coat to run the sweeper. It hung on a doorknob, topped by a paisley tie, and the sheer breadth of his chest in shirt-sleeves was amazing. Lucy Maud had very little experience in buying men's clothing, but the way that shirt fit it had to be custom tailored—or he knew a gifted tent-maker.

He was asking her something, and his words finally penetrated: "Want it left on? Hey! Lady!"

She had one moment of sheer panic before she realized he was speaking of the TV, not his shirt! Her knees went weak! What might she have said? What would he have thought of her?

"Oh!" she answered, and gabbled, "No—no, not now. I'm—I'm going to be too busy."

"Right."

He'd hoisted his chin and was fastening his collar, covering up the handful of graying Brillo that had escaped during his labors. Looking down his nose at her, he went on calmly, "The stove works. And the fridge, although I suspect it's marginal; I wouldn't put in much frozen stuff for a day or so. What about the furnace? If it rains, it's going to get pretty chilly in here tonight."

"What—what do I do?"

"Nothing. I'll turn it on if you're sure you're going to stay here."

She tried to match his calm. "If I can find the grocery store, it would seem silly to go to a motel."

"Probably couldn't get a room, anyway. Duck-hunting season's on. All the loonies are in from Chicago."

He reached out a grubby big hand to push the thermostat on the wall. They were rewarded with a groan, a whush, then a hum from the utility room beyond the kitchen.

Vic listened a moment, then said, "It sounds okay. I'd have it checked tomorrow. There's your water man parking his truck. And I have to go."

"Wait for the water and you can wash up."

He waited, then splashed in the yellow water, scrubbing the dust from thick arms with her soap and saying, "Whew! What is this? I'm going to smell like a cathouse!"

So much for ten dollars' worth of especially milled and scented beauty bar!

She handed him a wad of paper towel. "I really appreciate the time you've spent—and what you've done. May I pay you?"

"If you put the house on the market, let me handle it."

"Of course. In a minute."

He was looping his tie over his head, pushing up the knot. She got his suede coat and held it for him. "Did you grow up here in Crewsville, Mr. Bonnelli?"

"Vic. In a way. Nearer the river, really. But I went to high school here before the war got me. The big war," he said, and grinned. "The one I was in. Korea. Did you?"

"Fight a war or grow up here? I was born on Elm Street. My mother clerked at Bloch's Grocery—if you remember where it was."

"Sure. My old man sold Bill Bloch his hooch for years. Red wine, mostly. Are you certain you'll be okay? You haven't got a phone, you know—although Mrs. Murphy, next door, she'd let you use hers in a minute. A nice lady."

"I'll be fine. Thank you again."

Through the smeary window she watched him as he let his big dog out briefly near an adjacent sycamore tree, and wondered idly about his wife—if she knew about Tina's mom. Probably. In a small town, as everywhere else, women made choices: live with it, keep the man and the support; or throw him out and start a different sort of struggle.

But what the hell. It wasn't her problem. She shouldn't be judging. She didn't know Mrs. Bonnelli, and she certainly couldn't say she knew him. However, she was very grateful for his help this afternoon.

Very grateful, she repeated to herself, and went to the door to sign the paper for the water meter.

The man from the city department was thin and neat, and held his tractor cap in his hand. It startled her. Few men took their caps off for anyone anymore.

He was frowning. "Ma'am—have you got a pet tied up somewhere?"

"Me? No. I have no pets."

"Neither have the Murphys. Nor the Johnsons. But I thought I heard—" He stopped and shrugged, adding, "Thank you," and put the cap back on. "Have a good day."

"You, too," she replied, and thought no more about it. Pets were not in her scheme of things. No cute, cuddly kittens, no chirping parakeets throwing seeds all over the rug, no dogs. Especially no dogs. Beyond inheriting her mother's attitude, she'd seen the agony her friends had gone through at the death of a family dog—and she certainly wasn't going to put herself through that! Not for any animal!

She had troubles enough. She was getting old, she was out of a job, short on cash, and had damned dismal prospects. What else could happen?

Five

The answer was, of course, "a lot." And it didn't take long before it started.

Her first magic trick was to wrestle her microwave into the kitchen. The oven had been one of the first things she'd bought after Mama's death; recently, she'd considered buying a larger one. As she managed to slide it onto the only counter space near an outlet before her arms gave out, she thanked her lucky stars she hadn't done so.

Gratitude was well placed but premature. She plugged in the cord, drew water in a Styrofoam cup for coffee, punched thirty seconds, and blew every fuse in the house.

She was quite ready for this day to be over, she thought grimly to herself, struggling through dusty stacks of indefinable trash in the utility room to find the fuse box. That was, of course, only if tomorrow promised to be better.

And the fuse box was not in the utility room.

So where the hell was it?

She peered out on the ramshackle back porch, heard the eerie wind moan around the corner, saw a few cold splashes of rain begin to pelt the unpainted steps—but no fuse box. She went back to the kitchen, quite audibly snarling. A belated brainstorm led her to stand on a chair and peer into the webby upper right hand corner of the highest cupboard.

As Vic Bonnelli would say: *Voilà!* Fuse box.

Old-fashioned fuse box. No breaker switch. Also, no extra fuses.

That was about par for the day. So far it had been a real winner.

She teetered dangerously as she got back off the chair, grabbed at a cupboard corner, ran a splinter in her finger, said a very socially unacceptable word, and suddenly realized she was so tired she was dangerous.

Also, she'd forgotten to take her blood pressure tablet and her water pill. By tomorrow she'd probably be the color of a beet.

If she didn't fall off the chair and break her neck today.

Gingerly, she stepped down, squeezed the finger to make it bleed, and ran rusty water over it. If she got blood poisoning, it would just serve them right, although who was to be thusly served was obscure.

At this point the heavens opened and sent cascades of cold rain through every open window on the southwest side of the house—which, naturally, was all of them.

Drat! The car windows!

Three leaps, like an aging gazelle, got her onto the damp car seat. Rolling up the glass, she then simply sat there staring through gray sheets of rain at the battered, shabby house to which she'd come—*come down* was a better phrase—felt very sorry for herself, and did some more pseudo-sobbing.

As at all other times, it didn't help. She just got soggier.

Shit!

She said the word with emphasis, waiting for Aunt Martha's ghost to strike her dead. Nothing happened. She never got simple solutions.

Grabbing the electric blanket, she scooted back into the dim house again, slammed the door, sat down in the nearest mauve velour chair, rejected sternly the idea that because it smelled like mice, it contained mice, and took counsel with herself.

She'd been acting, to use Mama's country phrase, "like a chicken with its head cut off"—a grisly metaphor but succinct. She well remembered the first time she'd seen a decapitated hen flopping wildly in their back yard while her mother took her axe to the second.

She had, in many ways, had her head cut off. But she also was one ace up on the chicken. She could survive!

She'd survived major surgery, Howard Lewis's jilt, and those years with Mama—all of them pretty devastating. So she sure as hell could make it through this thing!

But only if she wanted to survive. Did she?

What a damned fool question! Of course she did, if only to get back at Kathryn MacClane!

So much for meritorious goals.

A more practical one was to go to the market for fuses and food, make a clean spot in the kitchen to eat, and somewhere else to sleep.

So, Lucy Maud. Off your butt and get going!

The rain had slackened a bit, and over the peaked shingles of the neighboring house a patch of light sky showed, a pale, shining piece of opalescence. Looking through the window at it, Lucy Maud suddenly realized that below the peak was also a window, that in the window was the small child named Tina and Tina was waving.

She waved back and turned away, not only thinking that next door was "Grandma's" house, but also of the solid, curly-headed gentleman who had tried so cheerfully to ease her burden—but who, in addition, was fooling around with Tina's mother.

Talk about May and December! Vic Bonnelli had to be at least sixty—and Tina's mother could be only— thirty?

The exquisite egoism of the male animal!

Rolling her eyes upward, she wrapped the plastic cover from the electric blanket around her in lieu of a raincoat, locked the front door, and ran back to the car.

Three-thirty in the afternoon was a slack time at the market. Not *market,* she reminded herself, *grocery store!* You're back in Pike County now. There was a parking spot at the curb almost in front. She pulled off the bandana, ran a hasty hand through tousled hair, abandoned the plastic, and ran for the door.

It did not open automatically and she almost broke her nose.

"Sorry," said the young clerk in the red jacket just inside, trying to look sorry instead of amused. "The opener is screwed up. It always is when it rains. You hurt?"

"Only my dignity," she answered, then suddenly realized that his amusement was not directed at her nose
but her sweatshirt, and made the remark about dignity
rather redundant. Oh, well . . .

She took a cart and started down the aisle. For an
elderly lady uncertain of the worth of survival, her cart
filled rapidly. It was apple harvest time, and she took
six satiny scarlet beauties that had never seen cold storage. Cauliflower was only ninety-nine cents a head.
With a carton of dip, she could munch forever! To her
further astonishment not only was there a slot on the
shelf labeled Perrier, but there was one lonely bottle
left on it.

"Big wedding last weekend," said the clerk, pushing
a broom around her. "We'll have more in tomorrow."
Over his shoulder he added, "Banker's daughter got
married."

The astonishment at finding Perrier in Crewsville
suddenly took second place to the last piece of chat.

Howard's daughter? Curious. If she had married
Howard, it might have been hers, also.

Between the cleaners and the mousetraps she tried
to envision herself in floating mother-of-the-bride chif-
fon instead of a sweatshirt that said "I'm Tired of This
Shit," almost got the giggles, and felt better.

Then as she was halfway through the check-out, she
remembered the state of her wallet.

She said, "Oh, dear," in dismay as she looked at her
three dollars and thirty cents.

The balding man in the apron behind the cash register said, "No problem. I'll take a check. Besides—
don't I know you from somewhere?"

It was moot whether Lucy Maud was more startled at the question or at the offer. She stammered, "I'm—I'm Martha Hauser's niece."

"That's it! Those blue, blue eyes. Lucille. You're Lucille. Verna's daughter. I was your paperboy, over on Elm Street. You remember—Tommy Burkiser."

Gnome-like little Tommy Burkiser, skinny legs pumping a ratty bike, and a dirty ballcap on carroty hair! This bald man with a paunch and bifocals!

"Oh, I'm sorry," said Lucy Maud humbly. "I didn't—it's been a long time ago—"

He grinned. "Sure has. I got a kid in college now. You just passing through?"

"No. Well—not exactly. I'm here to get Aunt Martha's house ready to sell."

"Is that a fact? Well, now. We sure do miss Martha and old Frank; they used to come in here all the time. Go on, write a check. Conrad ain't in no hurry, are you?" The latter was addressed to another man who'd come up behind Lucy Maud with a two-liter jug of soda, and he pronounced the name "Coon-rod," a second thing that took her back to her childhood.

She hurriedly scribbled a check. Tom Burkiser scooped up her sacks and carried them out to the car for her, calling over his shoulder, "A dollar sixty-nine for the sody, Coon. Put it by the drawer if you're in a toot."

The quiet streets were shining wet, but the rain had quit again and swallows were swooping in and out of the birdhouses overhead. The grocer said, "We need the rain but it sure screws up the grain harvest. My other boy's fit to be tied; he's got both corn and beans

still in the field, and they're sayin' frost by Friday."
He was carefully loading her groceries into the back
seat. "There you are. Come again. Nice to see you,
Lucille."

"Thank you," said "Lucille." She drove away in
something of a state of shock, although she wasn't sure
whether it was for being recognized for her blue eyes,
or being allowed to write a personal check without
signing a long-term mortgage.

As she pulled back into the driveway, Tina—apparently waiting—waved again. Lucy Maud returned the
salute, hefted her grocery sacks, and made it to the
porch before the box of crackers fell out.

Oh, well. Better than eggs. Perhaps her day was im-
proving.

As she unlocked the door and it groaned open, mul-
tiple flashes of gray-brown fur caught her eye. Dozens!
Thank God she'd remembered traps!

Fuses, first.

Back up on the chair.

A minute's inexpert fumbling was rewarded as the
lights went on once more. Whoopee!

Whoopee lasted, however, until she tried the microwave again.

The fuses blew.

Damn.

The fact finally penetrated that this house was not
exactly wired for microwaves. Unless—

She went all around, turning off the lights. Then she
punched the microwave.

It worked.

Lovely. So she'd do all her cooking in the dark.

Or she wouldn't cook. Somewhere in the dim catch-all of her memory she'd recorded seeing the perky pink gray of a Bunny Burger sign. Sure. Over by the high school. Dandy. Unlike Mama, Lucy Maud was never averse to fast food. Tonight she'd dine with convenience, and tomorrow she'd ask somebody about the wiring.

As for now, she better concentrate on cleaning enough to make Martha's little love nest habitable.

But even as she thought the words, she shook her head in bewilderment. It had to be true. Already she'd heard the name "Frank" from Vic Bonnelli and the grocer, both in the calmest of language. He was real. Or had been real. Yet she could not recall any conversation between her mama and her aunt about a "Frank." What had Aunt Martha done—picked up and succored a stray man much as she had every dog and cat in town?

Lucy Maud found herself smiling. It really did sound so like her aunt.

Martha Hauser's wishes had been that after her demise, the "dear ladies of the Episcopal Church" should make whatever use they could of her pots, pans, dishes, silver, linens, and clothing, "the residual money to be placed in dear Father Morgan's discretionary fund." As Lucy Maud filled a rusty foot tub with water and carried it over to heat on the stove, she figured that request probably and effectually eliminated whatever tangible was left of "Frank."

While she waited for the water to heat, she tackled the kitchen windows—somewhat an exercise in futility, as the outsides, though streaming rain, were dirtier than the insides. Realizing then that no one could peer in at her if they wanted to, she recklessly ripped down the limp, fly-specked curtains, wheezing as she did so. This disgruntled more than a few spiders in their webs and also displeased another mouse who'd spent weeks gnawing an exit through the bottom sash, only to have this jessy in the funny sweatshirt poke it full of Brillo.

By the time the water hissed, she was as greasy gray as the heap of curtains, and her shoulders ached from reaching upward. However, at least one cupboard had to be cleaned in order to get the few staple groceries off the top of the microwave.

The fingernail she'd weakened on the telephone dial broke in scrubbing the cupboard. Damn. Lucy Maud knew she had the typical veiny hands of an older woman, but they were nicely shaped, and she'd taken care with her nails especially for the dedication today, using strengthener faithfully, and being careful not to file too far down the sides. Somehow the sight of the ragged stub typified everything.

Tired, aching, discouraged, and frustrated, she climbed back off the chair and shoved up the groceries, not really caring how they went in. The label on a pepper can sitting back to front on a shelf was certainly not going to change the course of things in Millard right now—and once again it seemed outrageous that the proper head librarian of Millard Public Library should have to be here in this disgusting kitchen worrying about a back-to-front pepper can!

Also, having to acknowledge that ninety-nine percent of the fault was her own was not guaranteed to make her feel dandy.

In Millard, by now, the parade was over, the kids'

book transfer was over, the mayor had spoken his inanities, that bitch had opened wide the new library doors, and everyone had gone home to get dressed for the banquet.

She should have been home, too, in her nice, clean apartment, soaking in her peach-colored tub, looking down the length of gleaming, scented water at basking toes. Nice toes, readying themselves to join good legs in brand-new panty hose beneath the silky sweep of a really smashing blue dress.

Where the holy hell she'd wear the dress now was a good question. The most fun she could remember in Crewsville was a half-dozen fellows picking bluegrass music on thee steps of the Masonic Temple.

It didn't bother Lucy Maud that she was being ignorantly unfair to Crewsville, or a horrible snob. At the moment, she didn't mind being unfair; and as for being a snob, snobbery was about all she had left of her own shattered sense of importance.

"Goddamn everything all to hell!" she announced in a loud voice, threw down her wet scrub rag, kicked at the empty grocery sack that had fallen on the still-dirty floor in a muddy puddle of slopped washwater, and marched past the peeling veneer of the dining room sideboard into the parlor. In passing, she snatched off a piece of dangling wall paper, balled it up, threw it to the ceiling and cried inexplicably, "Happy New Year!"

The whole thing was rather a hard act to follow. She settled for plopping into the mauve armchair, glowering at the silent television, and working her lower lip in and out—a defiant leftover from childhood. Quite early she'd learned Verna's threat of nailing the lip to the wall was not feasible.

The television had no lip to thrust back in mock imitation, either. The end result of this furor was that heavy silence settled over the little house again, striated by the dismal sound of rain.

And something else. Something distant. Strange.

From outside?

She listened.

Nothing.

But the clutch of the black spell was broken. Even a little ashamed at her juvenile outburst, she went soberly back into the kitchen, picked up the scrub rag, and started in again.

She even reached up and reversed the offending pepper can.

By six o'clock, it was dark and still raining. Despite, the thrum of the furnace the house had an overall smell of damp. However, she'd finally made definite inroads, gone through three cans of Lysol spray, reduced a steel wood pad to shreds, emptied the sweeper twice, accumulated five bags of assorted trash, and reassured herself completely that there were no colonies of mice lurking beneath the old couch where she'd decided to sleep.

She collapsed in the armchair again. Glancing at her watch, she remembered Gary Simmon's admonition, reached out for the remote control, grimaced, hauled herself painfully erect, walked over and turned it on manually. More than one thing in this house was antediluvian, but the TV might head the list if she didn't.

She was halfway back to her chair when Kathryn MacClane's dulcet tones reached her.

She wheeled around and almost turned it off. It was the same clip she'd seen at the restaurant, and she'd had about enough of that. But before she could reach the switch the camera turned on the children, beginning the actual book transfer. There was Gary in the front row, and Pam's Susie, and that cute Haskins youngster and Monica Parks in a new Millard High School jersey—it seemed she knew almost all of them. The band was playing, the parents were cheering, and the children were marching down the street before the TV cameras, carrying their number slips and their stacks of books and beaming and laughing and having such a good time she couldn't be anything but glad she'd tuned in.

Good God!

What were they doing?

She asked it out loud, in dismay, grasping the chair arms, almost lurching to her feet: "Kids! My God! No! What are you doing?"

Even then, she knew. She didn't need Gary Simmons to dart from his place and give a "thumbs up" sign directly into a camera. Helplessly she watched as each participant discreetly passed two or three or more of the books in his armload to someone else who also was randomly passing on two or three of his. On their way down the street to the new library, they were completely scrambling both the alphabetic and Dewey Decimal System order of the library inventory as efficiently as though they'd piled it in a single, enormous, muddled heap.

It was simple, gleeful, calculated sabotage of the highest order. Being done for Lucy Maud. Their way of saying to her, "We're sorry."

And not one single adult was paying attention! As the cameras panned inside the library, Kathryn was shelving those shuffled books row by row according to the child's printed slip as he handed them over—not even glancing at the volumes. It was a complete disaster, and no one had discovered it yet!

"Oh God," said Lucy Maud, this time quietly in simple horror. She groaned. She held her head. She looked through her fingers.

She laughed: unkind, punitive, and satisfying laughter.

What a mess! What a diabolic, stupendous mess! Every book would have to be pulled out, categorized, alphabetized, and reshelved in its proper place. It would take a month. Months!

And Kathryn MacClane had said on public television that the system had been developed by her own clever little hands!

Lucy Maud told herself severely that she shouldn't be laughing, she shouldn't be enjoying the debacle, she should be ashamed of her *very* non-professional reaction!

She would be—tomorrow. Maybe.

But today—bless their hearts! Love those kids!

She giggled rudely all the way through the rest of the local news, which was merely *standard* disaster, and the weather forecast which was predictably, wet, and the stock market, in which her mama's investment had gone down half a point. In the empty, echoing, little house she sounded like an idiot—which she probably was.

But when she bent, her back creaking, and turned off the TV to resume her domestic labors, something else came to her ears which was not funny—which was, really, a little frightening.

She heard that sound again—and it wasn't the furnace. The furnace was already running. It wasn't the fridge. Its steady hum was providing a counterpoint to the furnace.

It was a sound of pain—of hopeless despair. And it was coming from somewhere beneath the house.

Six

For one moment she froze, one hand still on the TV switch. Visions of horrendous headlines danced in her mind's eye: "Woman Finds Corpse Beneath Aunt's House! Murder Was Done—But Lucy Maud Marshall Maintains She Knows Nothing!"

Then common sense took over. A corpse doesn't make noises. If there was something under the house it was alive. A cat, perhaps. Stuck on a nail. Cut by glass . . .

"Oh, why me?" Lucy Maud grimaced as the noise came again—a hurtful keen of agony. She couldn't just do nothing. She was, after all, humane. But—what could she do? There was no phone, she knew no one to call anyway . . .

You can go look, you idiot! she told herself reluctantly, and pulling her coat on over her sweatshirt, she opened the front door to the cold, wet wind, fished in her car glove compartment for her small flashlight, took a deep breath, and knelt on the soggy dead grass to shine its beam beneath the sagging porch floor. Nothing. Just the dirty detritus of years, augmented by a few soda cans.

But she was not allowed relief. The noise came again,

louder this time as though whatever it was sensed her presence. And it came from beyond the crumbled brick of the house's foundation. Grunting, Lucy Maud went flat and extended her flashlight into the nearest hole. Nothing again. Just fallen brick and—

Wait! Two eyes glowed. Back there. In the corner.

If it's a skunk I'll scream, Lucy thought grimly as she wriggled forward under the porch and refocused her flash.

What she saw then was heartrending, even to a non-animal-lover. A heap of matted, bloody, black-and-white fur lay in disarray just at the edge of her light beam. One tousled leg stuck out at a strange angle. And two pleading brown eyes were fastened on her.

For ten seconds they both were transfixed. Then the dog tried to move toward her, and this time the pain was transformed into a howl.

"Oh, shit!" mumbled Lucy Maud, and never meant the rude phrase more in her entire life.

What the hell was she going to do?

She couldn't get it out herself. Heaven only knew how badly the thing was hurt, and she had no phone, knew no one—

"Stay!" she rasped, the single command coming from somewhere in the depth of a Susan Conant murder mystery where her dog heroes always took her to the final clue. "Please—stay!"

It must be right. The poor beast didn't move.

Wriggling backward into the mist and wet, Lucy Maud hauled herself erect, glanced around wildly, and took off, stumbling up the neighbor's front steps. There was no doorbell. She pounded.

She was rewarded by lights going on in the deepening gloom, casting a yellow glow across a shabby floor and an idly swinging porch seat. The door opened a crack, framing one slice of an elderly lady in an apron with little Tina's dark head poking around it knee-high.

Tina said brightly, "Hi, lady!" just as behind her another voice asked, "Who is it, Mom—Vic?"

Suddenly aware of her dripping dishevelment, Lucy Maud said, "Please—I'm from next door—Martha Hauser's niece—and I need a phone—there's a—a hurt dog under my porch—"

Tina said, "Wow!"

The elderly lady opened the door and said, "Come in."

A taller, younger woman in a Bunny Burger uniform appeared behind both of them and said, "That's awful. Mom, have her call Will. I'll bet we can still catch him at the clinic."

In ten seconds Lucy Maud was inside with warmth enveloping her, holding a towel to mop the wet, and the younger woman, telephone already in hand, was asking, "Want me to make the call?"

Lucy Maud nodded, suddenly overwhelmed with the simple small-town responsiveness she'd almost forgotten. She said, "Oh, please. I don't know anyone!"

"Will Evans," the older lady was saying. "He's the local vet. He'll come. Tina, what are you doing?" The small child was struggling into a pink coat that matched her tights.

Tina said simply, "I get him. Poor thing—I bet he scared."

"No, honey—if he's hurt he might bite you. Just wait, now. Your mom's got Will. He'll come—won't he, Eileen?"

The young woman in the fast food uniform was hanging up the telephone as she spoke, turning with a smile that showed braced teeth, and nodding at Lucy Maud. "As soon as he can get here. I was going to threaten him with tabasco on his burger but I didn't have to. Will's a doll. Oh—I'm Eileen Taylor. Vic said you were moving next door. We sure do miss Martha and Frank."

"We sure do," the older woman echoed, holding out a thin hand. "I'm Jessie Murphy, Eileen's mom. And you've made your coat all dirty. When you've got your dog out, come throw it in my washer. I'm not sure Martha's is still workin'."

Lucy Maud was so taken with the generous offer, she skipped remonstrating on the "your dog" phrase. She said, "I just kept hearing something—as though it was under the house. Then when I looked—" She shivered.

Mrs. Murphy nodded sympathetically. "This vet'll handle it. Best man with small animals I ever knowed. Not worth a damn with hogs, but that's his son's department. Look out, Leeny; I saw headlights flash."

Eileen peered through the starched lace curtains. "It's Vic," she said. "But Doc's right behind him. Talk about calling out the marines! Tina, honey, you stay inside; it's too chilly for that coat." She was pulling on a shabby denim jacket. "I'll let you see as soon as I can. You can stay in, too, Mrs. Marshall. I can help the boys if they need it."

"No. Thank you—but I'll come." Lucy Maud was also ignoring the "Mrs. Marshall" again. "Thanks for the phone. I'll try to get one into Martha's as soon as I can."

Her last view of little Tina was a lower lip outthrust on a small face peering through window curtains. Shivering again at the cold, wet wind on damp clothing, she followed Eileen down the steps and around Vic's Toyota, a pick-up truck, and a Trans Am she'd been too bemused to notice before.

The bulk of Vic Bonnelli was on its knees, focusing a large flashlight beneath the battered porch while a longer, thinner form in canvas dungarees squirmed its way through the aperture. He said, "Hi," over his shoulder, whether to herself or Eileen, Lucy Maud didn't know and went on, "See anything, Doc?"

Muffled tones came back. "Yeah. Turn it a bit left, Vic. There, there, sweetie, it's okay. It's okay. Stay, now . . . Holy cow! It's Cutie!"

Eileen gasped and said, "For God's sake! I thought they took her to Quincy!"

"Whatever—she's back. Stay, Cutie. You're home. Stay, girl . . ."

Lucy Maud asked, "Who's *Cutie?*"

"Your Aunt Martha's dog. Just a mutt, but a real sweetheart." Eileen was shaking her pony-tailed dark head. "How in the world—is she hurt bad, Doc?"

"Can't tell, yet. I think there's enough room under here. I can sort of sit up. But I need more light. Vic, can you—"

"Only if I lose fifty pounds," Vic answered ruefully. Eileen said, "I can do it. Gimme the light."

To Lucy Maud's amazement, she grabbed the flash from Vic and began to wriggle beneath the porch. The veterinarian's voice came back muffled. "Good girl. Hold it right there. Vic!"

"Yes, sir."

"My bag's by your left knee. Shove it in to me. I need to give her a shot to start with. That leg's either broken or dislocated. And she's banged her head. A car, probably. There, there, sweetie, remember me? It's old Doc—I'm your friend. Eileen, too. You're home, babe; you're going to be all right . . ."

Vic was saying, "Will, I've got a filebox lid in the trunk—it's plywood and about two by four. Want to slide her on to that?"

"Good thinking. We'll give it a try when the shot takes hold. By golly, Eileen, I think she does know us. At least, you . . ."

Vic was heaving his bulk to his feet, smiling down at Lucy Maud, winking one eye as he brushed leaves from his knees. "Another 'save' for Doc," he said. "I'll bet money on it. A good man. Be right back."

He scrunched away. She saw a trunk lid creak open in the early evening gloom, heard him mumble, "Damn—oh, here it is." His massive silhouette came toward her again, knelt awkwardly, and slid a wide board beneath the porch. "Think that will do it?"

"Great. No problem. Help me here, Eileen. Easy, girl. Easy . . . Vic, ask the lady to open the front door for us. That's closest. And clear the kitchen table. Here we come . . ."

No one had certainly asked Lucy Maud if she'd open

the front door—or if they could use her kitchen table. They just—*assumed!*

Acknowledging she was chicken—even more, a chicken who did not particularly care for dogs—Lucy Maud did as she was asked. A careful entourage of veterinarian and realtor carrying a be-dogged slab entered, followed by Eileen, wiping muddy feet before she entered, and then a bemused Lucy Maud, who did close said door against the wet wind. That, she could do!

By that time, the doggy burden had been carefully deposited on the kitchen table, but Lucy Maud didn't care to look. She sank into one of the mauve chairs in the living room and said, "Oh, boy . . ."

Eileen, in the doorway, glanced back at her. "Don't worry. Will thinks everything is minor."

"Worry" was not precisely what Lucy Maud had been doing. Unless it was what in the world she was to do with an invalid pooch she hadn't even wanted! Surely this man—this vet—would take—Cutie—ugh, what a name!—back to his clinic. She needed looking after, obviously.

Eileen broke into her thoughts: "That leg is just dislocated. Doc put it back. That's happened before. Cutie's not young, you know. He's cleaning her off, now—and putting some stuff on her feet—poor baby, her pads are raw. Could she have come all the way back from Quincy? That's thirty miles or so! Frank's cousins took her—we knew she didn't want to go, but they were real nice folks . . ."

Then they may get her again, Lucy Maud thought wryly, seeing a ray of light.

She heard the door to the back porch open, and the

sounds of shuffling. Victor Bonnelli's voice came clearly: "Eureka! I thought I saw it here this afternoon! Now, old girl—your own bed back. What do you think of that? I don't see your pillow but I'll bet that nice lady who lives here now can find you one."

Lucy Maud arose a little wearily, thinking, It's a conspiracy! She went to the kitchen door, standing by a much taller Eileen who smelled of rotted and wet leaf mold. Vic smiled at her, holding out a ratty, rattan three-sided basket thing.

He asked, "What can we use? Any idea, offhand?"

Hopefully, the resentment in her voice wasn't too noticeable. She said, "I'll scare up something."

"It needs to be warm. An old throw rug would do."

That was from the vet, and for the first time she got a good look at him.

She wasn't impressed. He was medium height, medium size, wore ordinary dungarees now soaked down the front under a muddy jacket, had wire-rimmed glasses and thinning gray hair.

Then the furry heap on the table stirred, a black-and-white nose gently nuzzled his sleeve—and he smiled.

And the room lit up. It almost made her blink. Worse, no one else seemed to notice. Vic said, "See—she knows you, buddy."

"Of course she does. But more, even—she knows she's home."

Then those magical, shining green eyes came to rest on Lucy Maud. "You couldn't have come at a better time," he said, wiping off a brown hand and holding it out. "I'm Will Evans."

"Lucy Maud Marshall," she said and took the hand. It was strong, warm, and shook her own briskly.

"Welcome to Crewsville," he went on. "We all miss your aunt. She and Frank were almost our patron saints. Now. Find us a rug."

It took a few minutes. Mostly because Lucy Maud stopped in the bedroom before the seamed old mirror and stared at herself, gripping the edge of the bureau with shaky fingers.

She looked the same. Short, nicely curled gray hair. Blue eyes. A rude sweatshirt, now rather dirty. She hadn't reverted to age twelve, and it wasn't Valentine's Day! What the hell was wrong with her?

Low on estrogen again. That was it. Probably in the next ten minutes, even Vic Bonnelli would look good—tomcat though he might be.

When she rejoined them she found all three sitting around the kitchen table with Cutie as a centerpiece and coffee perking on the counter. (Vic had obviously found her pot.) The only difference was Tina, perched on Vic Bonnelli's knee and petting the dog gently.

"I didn't think you'd mind," Vic said of the coffee, grinning at her. He took the ratty bathmat, added, "Fine," and arranged it in the dog basket with Tina helping.

Will Evans had turned, stretched out denim-clad legs, and put his hands behind his head. "Long day," he said and yawned. "Tim couldn't make it up from the other place, and I think every dog in Crewsville needed shots." He grinned at Lucy Maud, adding as explanation. "Tim's my boy. He really runs both places. I'm supposed to be retired, but it never has seemed to work out yet. I think Cutie's going to be fine. She had a brush with a car, or somebody's boot—but mostly she just seems to be worn out. Let her rest. Put this stuff in the can on her pads—stop by the office tomorrow and I'll give you some more. Yeah, Vic—black, and lots. I'm due to play poker at Buffalo Bob's tonight, and damned if I know whether I can stay awake."

Vic handed him the steaming mug, grinning. "You'd better if Bob Marsh is playing. He'll skin your hide."

"Shit. Pardon me, ladies. He couldn't do it in Korea, and he couldn't do it in 'Nam. You know that. You were there. Cheers, everyone. You, too, Cutie. Welcome home."

Vic started to resume his own seat, then winced. "Dammit. You did a number on the dog, Will—how about one on me? Suddenly this knee isn't fitting right."

"Hmm. That requires taking your pants off. Think we should adjourn to the bedroom?"

"It might be wise."

Taking their coffee and grinning, they left. At the table Eileen smiled across at Lucy Maud. "Vic has a prosthesis for that left leg," she said. "Lost it on an aircraft carrier. But you'd never know, would you?"

"I wove him," said Tina. Perched on the edge of Vic's chair she smiled at Lucy Maud. "I wish *he* was my daddy."

Embarrassed, Lucy Maud dropped her eyes to her cup, but Eileen laughed.

"I know, baby," she said. "But you have a daddy. Maybe some day he'll grow up and be a real one." Then she added to Lucy Maud, "I don't know what

I'd do without Vic. You've seen what kind of guy he is—he and Will, both."

"I really appreciate their coming." Lucy Maud thought that was a safe statement in an ambiguous situation. But Eileen smiled as she rose to dump her coffee in the sink, saying, "Shhh. We make good brew at Bunny Burger; it's spoiled me. Oh, Vic was coming already. My mom was feeding him tonight, anyway. I don't think he has anything in his apartment but a fridge and a microwave—and a cook he ain't. Hey—Mom's got a big pot of stuffed peppers. How about you and Doc, too? I know he hasn't eaten—he was just closing up when I called."

"He—has no family?"

"Oh, yeah. Tim—and Karen. But they live down the road from his farm—and Doc's divorced. What do you say?"

Things were moving a bit too fast, especially for a lady whose security had always been in straight lines with calculated endings. Lucy Maud made a polite but cowardly excuse. "That's really nice—but it's been a long day for me. And maybe I'd better stay with—with Cutie."

At the sound of her name, the furry black and white centerpiece opened languid eyes and focused on Lucy Maud. The plushy tail made a brief wag. Eileen reached and smoothed the supine back.

"Maybe you're right. Next time, then. Hey guys—what took you so long? Two single men—hmmm. Should I be suspicious?"

Vic only grinned and took a mock swipe at her. The

doctor laughed, making crinkles around those amazing eyes.

"First I made him sign a no-malpractice waiver," he said. "Give me a hand, Bonnelli. Let's get Cutie down into her bed."

The dog hardly flinched, and settled into the bathmat with a look of comfort. Dr. Evans patted her furry back gently, and getting back to his feet, nodded at Lucy Maud.

"I think she'll be fine. Like I said, keep her pads moist with this salve and let her rest."

Lucy Maud nodded back, mumbled something banal, then hated herself for her lack of originality. But her next move was worse. Reaching for the purse leaning against the half-empty bottle of bleach, she went on, "What do I owe?" then realized far too late that his fee had best not exceed three dollars!

But he was shaking his head, pushing back the silver hair that had fallen across one eye when he'd petted the dog, smiling at her. "Not a thing. Call it a 'welcome to Crewsville' gift—both to you and Cutie. Am I behind you, Vic? I'd better move along. It's seven o'clock. Bunny Burger may already be out of quiche."

"Come on to Mom's," said Eileen, putting Tina on the floor. "She's got gobs and Dad won't get in off his run tonight until late. Besides, he's not a stuffed pepper freak."

"Come," said Tina, already ensconced on Vic's arm.

The veterinarian shrugged. "Sold," he said. " 'Night, Mrs. Marshall."

Lucy Maud let it pass. Again. Perhaps, she thought ruefully, it's my instinct for survival. She saw all four to the door, closed it on them, turned and leaned against it, eyes shut.

The day had been long. And bad. Surely nothing else could possibly happen—short of the furnace blowing up, or mice in her bed, or the damned dog peeing on her clean kitchen floor.

And those were still minor things when matched against Kathryn MacClane's treachery.

For the first time, she thought wearily, going back into the kitchen, I can almost rationalize an assassination!

The coffee cups were Styrofoam, so the wastecan took care of them. She poured the last of the coffee in her own cup, turned off the pot, and sat down in the chair that had faced the veterinarian.

That was a mistake, too. She could almost see him still sitting there, and suddenly realized that the vision was imprinted on her stupid brain.

Why, for cryin' out loud? He was certainly no male model! Just a—a nice man who'd helped her overcome a bad situation And men were no novelty to her. Of course, most of the ones who'd come into the library got their Clive Cussler or Tom Clancy or Louis L'Amour and promptly left, or buried themselves in *The Wall Street Journal* or the sports page in the reading room. And handed her their check-out card while looking at their wristwatch.

So much for them.

And after Howard's cruel jilt, she'd never really trusted anything male again, figuring all men wanted two boobs instead of one. As far as she was concerned, that was *that*. Let those other silly jessies fall on their faces trying to please, then come moping into the library to take refuge in a bodice-ripper novel.

Not Lucy Maud Marshall!

She was going to be top dog in her small field and live happily ever after!

Except—

Now she wasn't.

What she *was* was sitting alone in her dead aunt's shabby kitchen turning a cup of lukewarm coffee in her hands and wondering what she was going to do next.

To pay her bills.

To survive.

There was hardly room for the complications of a— a divorced veterinarian in that *précis*.

Also, it was almost seven-thirty. Back in Millard, they were all dressed up, milling about the high school gym floor drinking pink punch and admiring each other's clothes. Where she ought to be. In her new blue dress.

Damn!

The "splat" was the not-quite-empty Styrofoam coffee cup poorly aimed and hitting the edge of the wastecan.

She just looked at it—the dribbles, the brown mess.

Then suddenly Lucy Maud Marshall almost smiled.

She was wondering if Kathryn MacClane had discovered her magnificently ill-sorted library yet.

Seven

If Lucy Maud had learned anything about bad days, it was that ending them with a warm bath and a good read had its advantages. She couldn't remember if she'd had any sort of ablution that ill-fated morning, what with Fred and all the phone calls. No matter. Aunt Martha had a tub, and Lucy Maud still carried the new Eugenia Price novel in the depth of her suitcase.

One thing she did miscalculate was the length of time it takes an aging hot water heater to get going. Still, getting out of the damp, soiled stuff and into her warm, woolly pink robe was the nearest to heaven she'd been for some time.

There was an outlet behind the old couch. With extreme caution she plugged in her electric blanket. Nothing blew. Good. She didn't need the TV, just that lamp on the end table flanked by a tarnished brass vase with a cupid on it. Also ignoring the fact the lamp base consisted of two cutesey cherubs embracing each other—Aunt Martha's taste had run to *kitsch*—Lucy Maud settled herself beneath the growing warmth, punched up the lopsided pillows, and settled down to the first actual peace she'd known since waking.

It lasted forty-five minutes.

Then there was the sound of booted feet on the front porch, a knocking on the door, and a voice saying, "Miss Marshall? It's me—Will Evans."

Now what did *he* want?

She kicked off the blanket, said, "Just a minute," and padded in soft, shapeless plush slippers to the door.

Undoing the chain, she opened it and said, "Hi."

She meant the word to be tentative, non-gender, and neutral. After all, it was getting on to ten, she was in her robe, and from what she remembered of a small town, social hours ended with the TV news.

She didn't realize, nor would she have even believed, that the Lucy Maud with softly tousled hair in a pink robe was a whole different ballgame from the efficient, rather blank-faced lady seen earlier in the day. Vic Bonnelli, however, just starting his Toyota, whistled softly to himself and said, "Whoa, Doc. Think it through!"

Will Evans was saying, "I'm sorry. It is getting late. But would you like to have me take Cutie out to do her business? She may be so dehydrated it wouldn't matter—but getting up in the middle of the night is nobody's favorite."

"Oh. Oh, how kind of you. Yes, I'd really appreciate it. I—I'm afraid I'm not really into—pets. Dogs particularly."

He may as well get that straight right now, she was thinking as she stepped back and widened the door.

He was wearing a dark green jacket zipped up the front. As he brushed by, she noticed the back said "Veterinary Clinic" and below that, "Evans & Evans." She also noticed another thing—any man, standing next to the block that was Vic Bonnelli, looked small. Will Evans, on his own, was fairly tall, with good posture and rather broad shoulders—at least in the vet coat.

He was gently cradling Cutie and heading for the kitchen door. Lucy Maud said, "Wait—I'll get it," and hurried ahead of him, almost tripping over her soft shoes.

The damp chill came in like a blast, but he didn't seem to mind. She watched him go down the three tottery steps and kneel, supporting his furry burden. Then he hauled her back in again as she licked his chin.

"Watch those steps," he said, restoring the dog to her bed. "Now, then. She should be okay until midmorning. I think she's pretty dehydrated. It might be a good idea to put a bowl of water right by her—if you don't mind."

"No. Of course not."

Why couldn't she bring herself to say, "Why don't you just take her back to your clinic and do it yourself?"

Why would it sound so crass?

Other people didn't like dogs. She wasn't the only one.

Instead, she turned obediently and filled a small bowl at the tap and handed it over.

He nodded. "Good," he said, "that should do it." Then he placed the water near Cutie's black-and-white muzzle.

He stood up and smiled down at her. "Now I'll git. You're probably tired. Vic says you drove in today."

"Yes."

"And that you're a librarian. I remember Martha

saying that, too. She was proud of you. Of course, I'm pretty proud of Karen. My daughter-in-law. She's one also, down in Penfield. And that's a vastly under-rated job. Karen works her tail off."

He couldn't have said anything to please her more if he'd tried for a hundred years.

"Yes," she answered ruefully, "it is." Or was.

"You're taking some vacation time?"

And how!

"A month," she answered. Maybe more, maybe a *lot* more!

"Good. Then we'll have you around for a while." Now he was at the door and she couldn't see his face— although why that was important she couldn't imagine!

" 'Night, Miss Marshall. I'll see you tomorrow. There's enough salve for one treatment, then I'll get you some more."

She watched him stride across the crumpled leaves of the lawn and swing up into his pick-up truck before she finally assimilated the "Miss." Vic Bonnelli must have told him.

Why? Why should she be important enough that he get her name right? What had they said about her over at Jessie Murphy's?

"Good Lord!" she said aloud in disgust. "I'm suspicious of everybody!"

Tomorrow would be better. It couldn't be worse.

At least she hoped not.

Sleep came slowly on the old couch. It wasn't contoured to the human frame—at least not to Lucy Maud's. The last time she peered at her watch in the streetlight shining dimly through tatty curtains it was three o'clock.

At eight she was awakened by a cold nose gently pushing at the bare arm outside the blanket.

Startled, she opened bleary eyes on Cutie who had one ear up, the other not quite, and for a moment wondered in awful bewilderment where in the world she was! And—worse—far worse—why had she been dreaming such an incredible dream of being held, of being caressed, of nestling warm and loved in someone's arms!

The caress—of course—it was the dumb dog's nose! And she chose with enormous deliberation *not* to think *that* through any further. The dog was Aunt Martha's leftover with whom she seemed to be stuck. And she was in the process of moving temporarily into Aunt Martha's house.

Love nest?

"Oh, surely you jest!" she said aloud to herself. Cutie nosed her again and whined.

Out! the big golden-brown eyes were pleading. *Please—take me out!*

Not even a non-pet person could misunderstand that message, especially as the fluffy black-and-white canine limped to the door, looked back, and pleaded again.

"All right already!" Lucy Maud said crossly, swinging bare feet to the floor and scuffling them into the soft shoes. She shuffled over, undid the night chain, and turned the knob.

Well. It *was* daylight. As Cutie made it down the shaky steps under her own steam and crouched with an audible sigh of sheer relief, Lucy Maud shivered against the sudden chill of an autumn morning, pulled her flannel nightie up around her bare throat, and tried to remember what day it was.

Sunday. That was it. Around eight o'clock. She glanced down at her wristwatch.

At home she'd still be sound asleep—or lying lazily supine, listening to the approaching "thunk!" of Sunday papers hitting a row of porches, and thinking of the frozen waffles in the freezer, perhaps weighing them against going out to Bunny Burger for quiche.

At least she could do *that* here!

Cutie was coming painfully back up the steps, but her furry, banner of a tail was wagging. Nosing Lucy Maud's ankle in passing she went on through to the kitchen, and Lucy Maud heard an audible doggy sigh as the old rattan basket creaked.

Well—at least so far she certainly wasn't any trouble.

Tomorrow she'd cope. With the dog, with—everything. Today she was going to coast. Surely she was entitled to that!

Not sure what constituted entitlement in her world anymore, Lucy Maud closed the door and leaned against it wearily.

And a little dizzily!

You idiot! Take your damned blood pressure pills!

At least that was a sensible piece of advice in an otherwise awful world.

She took them. She also looked into the medicine chest mirror in the shabby bathroom. But she wasn't seeing herself. She was wondering what images had been reflected in that mirror in the past few years—besides the mundane ones of tooth-brushing and eyebrow plucking, and so forth.

Aunt Martha, of course, with her home-permed, home-dyed brown hair that sometimes looked a little green when she'd got distracted during the process. Aunt Martha, with her obviously factory teeth. And her nice, sweet smile . . .

Lucy Maud's mom had said once, grumpily, that Martha Hauser would smile if she was dyin'.

Had she?

Lucy Maud had been miles away at a library seminar when the notice of her aunt's death caught up with her. The body was being cremated, she was told, and Martha's attorney would be in touch shortly. Which he had, delivering the property title to this house, and telling her to do with it what she would.

At that time, living in it had not precisely been Lucy Maud's intention. But—beggar's can't be choosers, she told herself wryly and turned away, not wanting to focus on the real image of herself in that silent mirror.

What had the nebulous "Frank" looked like as he'd shaved or scrubbed, or whatever?

And who the merry hell was he?

Lucy Maud couldn't conceive of her mother keeping to herself the story of her only sister "living in sin." It would have been far too good a story! On Martha's rare visits, certainly no "Frank" had ever, ever been mentioned! And she and her mother had never returned to Crewsville, once they'd gone.

Curious. Really curious. It bore looking into. Just for fun, of course.

In the nonce, food would be nice. Her stomach was growling inelegantly, and there wasn't a darned thing in that tatty kitchen that enticed her. Certainly not last night's coffee—however, that was no problem anyway as it soon became quite obvious there wasn't any.

But the kitchen was neat, with the shabby chairs pushed up to the old table and the empty pot rinsed and up-ended on the sink drainboard.

Who'd done that? Vic? The vet? Eileen?

A little embarrassed at her lack of memory, Lucy Maud pushed the light switch, filled a cup with water, put it in the microwave and, naturally, blew the fuse again.

"Damn!" she snarled aloud, making the fluffy fur heap at her feet cock that one ear. "When am I going to learn? Someone has to do something about this! It's ridiculous!"

Vic Bonnelli. He'd know who to call.

She stood on a chair, reached up with her last new fuse, sighed, got back down, turned off the light, climbed up again, and pushed it into place. There, darn it. And where in hell had she put the instant coffee bags?

She found them; there was only one left.

Oh well. She'd get by.

Punching up a minute and a half on the microwave, she turned and saw something else strange lying on the counter. Oh. The salve stuff. For the damned dog.

Resigned to doing what one had to do, she grunted to a cross-legged posture on the cold, worn linoleum next to the rattan basket and unscrewed the round lid.

Cutie was eying her warily.

"Paw," she said and took one in her hand. The dog flinched, but remained inert. Her golden brown eyes were very wary.

"If you bite me," said Lucy Maud flatly, "you're out of here."

She smoothed on the pink salve gently. The dog whined, but she understood. Those scuffed pads had traveled many a mile—and for what? To get back to this place? To Martha?

Something impelled her to say soberly, "She's gone, dog. Martha's gone. I'll have to do until—until we both can make better arrangements."

Did they have an animal shelter in Crewsville? The vet would know, of course, but somehow she didn't think he'd be too pleased at her asking. Yet—damn it! She had enough on her plate without cosseting an invalid mutt! And certainly she couldn't take it back to her apartment!

Grumpily she put the lid back on the salve and found a pink tongue licking her wrist.

She knew it was a "thank you."

"You're welcome," she said, and struggled up to her feet. "Now what can I feed you?"

She'd heard somewhere that "people food" was not good for dogs. So that meant a trip to the grocery again. She may as well get dressed, and go by Bunny Burger on the way.

Taking the cup of water from the microwave, she dowsed the one coffee bag in it, noted that the morning sunshine revealed definite greasy streaks on the windowpanes, grimaced, and took the coffee into the bedroom.

Her garment bag was still tossed on the bed. Extracting clean slacks and a heavy blue sweater, she performed what morning rituals were absolutely necessary, picked up her shoulder bag, chugged the now-tepid coffee, and went out the front door.

The steps hadn't improved magically, but the sun was showing deep mauves and golds in the aging aster blossoms, and water dripping from the sagging, rusty eaves had an almost musical tinkle.

Next door the Trans Am was just backing into the street. Eileen called cheerily, " 'Morning!" and Tina waved a small hand from her side, flipping the fine beads of a rosary.

Lucy Maud waved back. Eileen reminded her of Vic Bonnelli, and Vic reminded her of last night's disclosure that he *wasn't* married, and she had a momentary flash of embarrassment for the small-mindedness she thought she'd escaped when she'd moved to a larger town.

It never paid to be smug.

"I'll tell the world!" she muttered aloud for that bit of unoriginal observation, and grimly applying it to her personal situation, she slid onto the cold seat of her car.

Her next discovery was that a gas station would be in order. One that took credit cards. She'd prefer to spend her last three dollars cash on breakfast.

She had to get some money. Tomorrow. Her bank account was at its usual end-of-the-month low, especially after her recent trip, but salary checks should have been written on Friday, and a phone call would confirm the usual automatic deposit.

What she must keep painfully in mind was that it
would be her last, not counting the one for this "vacation." Unless the moon turned blue. Or someone
strangled Kathryn MacClane with her own eighteen-
inch belt. Or until Lucy Maud Marshall sat down with
herself and seriously, studiously came up with a more
reasonable solution.

Tomorrow.

Today was to be a three-dollar day with some of it
for dog food. Dog food! That would give the girls at
the library a laugh . . .

Aware that she could use one herself but that the
subject of dog food wouldn't do it, Lucy Maud put
her car in gear, backed over a corner of the marigold
bed, and started down the street.

Bunny Burger. Food.

Oh, yes—and dog salve.

Another chance to see what's-his-name—the vet.

"Oh, be still my heart!" she said aloud for the second time, left-turned into Main Street, and headed for
chow.

Eight

At the neighborhood intersection some strange impulse made her turn right instead of left, and drive the five crooked blocks to the old house she'd shared during those unhappy years with her mother. It was still there, in need of paint, the garage doorless and jammed full of junk, and a pick-up truck parked where the daffodil bed used to be. Her mother wouldn't like that. One thing Verna had done well was grow daffodils.

Strangely, Lucy Maud felt no qualms, only curiosity. She drove by at a slow speed, looking. A lanky teenager was leaning against the truck with his ball cap on backwards. He waved. She waved back, pretending not to notice the cigarette he'd hastily palmed. Kids! When would they learn?

At the next corner was a two-story apartment house replacing the little neighborhood grocery store she remembered where the elderly grocer used to hand out free peppermints to the children on the block. A number of cars were parked in its lot, including a Toyota with a realtor's sticker on the bumper.

Well. If she needed Vic in a hurry he certainly wouldn't be far away—

Although why in the world she'd need Vic in a hurry

she couldn't imagine . . . surely she could handle most things competently. She had done so for almost forty years.

Hadn't she?

What was "competence"? Isolating oneself in a narrow world that when ripped away left one naked and vulnerable—that was competence?

Oh lady, she thought ruefully, turning back onto the main drag, you did think you were so damned smart! You really did think so. And look where it's got you now . . .

Her useless diatribe was suddenly interrupted by a sound she'd hadn't heard in years: church bells! Church bells pealing and jangling and bonging on the cool morning air, from the brick edifice on the corner, the limestone church half a block down, and the old Gothic just at her left with a few bundled parishioners already descending the steps from early-morning Mass, a bare-headed, smiling young priest shaking their gloved hands.

Lucy wondered briefly what had become of Father Mulcahey, then realized with a rueful frown that the poor man would be at least a hundred and ten by now, hardly able to stand in the chill wind blessing the faithful. How time does get away!

As she negotiated the turn toward Bunny Burger, she noted Tom Burkiser unlocking his market door, with what appeared to be the same somnolent spaniel wagging its tail at his knee. Across the street the lemon-yellow Cadillac was gone from in front of the bank building. Had it been Howard's?

I could not, she declared to herself firmly, care less! And drove on into the fast food parking lot.

The only space available was between a battered Chevy—and a lemon-yellow Cadillac.

Lucy Maud hesitated, then shrugged and said out loud, "What the hell!" and parked.

Of all things Howard Lewis would not be expecting was the sight of an old girlfriend he'd cast away thirty-five years ago. Particularly if what he saw was a strange woman with no make-up, barely combed hair, and a baggy sweater. Besides, the place was jammed.

It was also noisy, cheerful, warm, redolent with the smell of hot cinnamon rolls, and tangled with customers crossing each other's paths from breakfast bar to booth to counter to restrooms. Anonymity should be a snap.

Lucy Maud grabbed a half-table as the previous occupant slid out the other side, parked her lumpy handbag on the low windowsill, and reached for a menu. She knew what she wanted, but it might be a cover if she needed it.

Coward! she said to herself, and put the menu down. She was, after all, fifty-some years old, pretty damned successful at what she did—or had been, but no one here need know that!—and didn't need to hide from anyone!

"Welcome to Bunny Burger. May I help you?"

The little waitress had frizzy hair, a big smile, and bunny ears a bit askew. She was also out of breath.

Lucy Maud smiled. "Want me to be slow, so you can rest a minute?"

The girl laughed. "No. It's okay. Sunday mornings

are always like this. Besides, Eileen—the other girl—just came on so I get a break in a minute. Coffee?"

"Please. Black. And I think—quiche, with ham on the side—and—" What the hell! It's only money! "—And a cinnamon roll."

"Right. I'll get your coffee. Hey, Eilly—did ya say a prayer for me?"

Eileen, also in bunny ears, was smiling down at Lucy Maud. "Kook, I said two for you—if that's who I thought it was with you at Buffalo Bob's last night. Hi, Miss Marshall. Kookie got you okay?"

"I think so."

"You're number 82 B. I'll bring it in just a smidge. How's Cutie this morning?"

"She seems to be—better." "Better" being relative to what?

"Good. That's a real sweetie dog. Be back in a flash."

Figuring the "flash" might be a bit longer than described, Lucy Maud settled into the corner of the high-backed seat and surveyed the premises. Lots of people—most of them chowing down in what Pam at the library called "Sunday-go-to-meetin' clothes." No one she recognized. After all, forty years were forty years! Neither was she still the short-waisted, blue-eyed girl with shoulder-length brown hair and saddle shoes most of Crewsville had known simply as "Verna's daughter—you know—the one at the grocery store." That lady by the end booth there, just standing up and wadding a paper napkin—in a kinder light she could look a bit like Miss Warpington, the shorthand teacher in high school. Lots of money, but just loved teaching kids. Or so she said. The kids had never been asked.

The thin, elderly lady turned, and rheumy eyes behind thick lenses flicked over Lucy Maud impersonally. She was reaching back toward a coat being held by unseen hands.

Then Lucy Maud's luck ran out. Again.

The hands were suddenly seen, attached to the arms of a stocky gentleman in tweed. He patted the coat into place, saying something at which the lady smiled wryly.

It was Miss Warpington.

Also, the gentleman was Howard Lewis.

The hair was still brown, although a dead brown, the waves carefully set over one eye. Noses do not change, nor jawlines—even if this one now seemed a bit jowly. And he still favored tweed—projecting the gentleman-farmer image.

It was Howard, all right.

If Lucy Maud had been a bug, she'd have scuttled. Unable to do that, she immediately and involuntarily scooched her fanny as far back into the seat corner as she could. The aisle led right past her; they had to come by. Where was the damned girl with the coffee? Or anything! Anything!

They never even looked. Miss Warpington sailed by, glancing neither to the right nor the left. Howard followed, too absorbed in pushing aside lesser minions to make room for Miss Warpington. They left. They went out the door and were gone!

"Wow!" said Lucy Maud Marshall with a deep breath of utter chagrin, relief, and anger at herself.

How long do conditioned responses last, for Pete's sake! She hadn't sat in that old termagant's classes for years!

But it wasn't only Miss Warpington making her heart thump, and she had to admit the fact. It was Howard. It was seeing Howard while she was clad in an old sweater, with no lipstick on. Because when she met Howard—which, being in Crewsville, she inevitably must—she wanted it with full make-up, fashionable hair, and a dress that screamed "Money!"

The sight of him had done nothing but make her skin crawl. She wouldn't have him on a gold platter with an apple in his mouth. But it was never too late for revenge! And just now she was in a mood to add Howard Lewis to the list!

Eileen distracted her, leaning over to pour steaming coffee in her cup.

It smelled heavenly. Maybe that's what she needed to start making some sense.

She said, "Thanks, hon," and took a sip, looking up to smile.

She hadn't seen Howard Lewis come back in the door.

He said to Eileen, "Did Miss Warpington leave her gloves?"

"I don't know, Mr. Lewis. Let's look."

He followed the tall girl back to the booth, and Lucy Maud strongly considered sliding beneath her table. She simply didn't want to meet the man this morning!

She grabbed up her paper napkin, and as they returned, gloves in hand, she pretended to sneeze into it.

She lucked out. Again.

Howard left.

Eileen stopped at her table, asking anxiously, "Miss Marshall, are you okay?"

"I'm fine," Lucy Maud said, crumpling the napkins and trying to smile. "Something just—just hit me."

"It's the cold wind. Flu weather, my momma says. Drink your coffee. Your order should be up now."

While she waited, Lucy Maud peeked through the slats of the window blind. Howard was handing the gloves in to Miss Warpington, then going around to his side of the Cadillac.

He'd gained a lot of weight, Lucy thought nastily. He really ought not to button his suit coat. And that hair—what a lousy dye job! Who did he think he was kidding?

Uh-oh.

Howard had stopped suddenly, half into the car, and was staring hard right at her window. Surely she couldn't be seen!

With enormous relief, she saw him shake his head as if puzzled, climb in, and drive the car out of the lot into the street.

Eileen was placing a steaming platter of quiche before her, and topping her coffee cup. "The rolls will be out in a minute. We serve 'em warm, or our boss has our hide. Enjoy."

"Oh, I will."

"I'll check back with you shortly. Oh—hey, here's Doc! Hi, buddy, how was the poker game last night?"

Will Evans was shucking off a muddy denim jacket, and he looked so tired his shoulders drooped, but the smile he gave both Eileen and Lucy Maud was the same brilliant one Lucy Maud remembered. Well. Too damned well!

"I never made it, hon. Stupid duck hunters from the city wandered into private land and shot up the Hendersons' flock of Muscovy. I tell you, Eilly, this is worse than deer season! Coffee, sweetie, and I'll see if I can persuade Miss Marshall here to listen to my troubles."

There really wasn't a choice.

Lucy Maud nodded. After all, she could make banal conversation as well as the next person. "So you didn't get any sleep?"

"Is it that obvious? But you're right. I'm dead-ass tired—pardon the expression. I'd go home and hit the sack, but Tim called—my son—and asked me to run out to Don Worth's place. One of his Charolais has a birthin' problem. No rest for the weary," he added, and grinned. "How's Cutie?"

"She seems to be doing fine."

"Great. Here—I stuck some more salve in my pocket. I was going by your house, but this will take care of it. Damn, that quiche looks good. Eileen, put an order in a roll, and I'll eat as I go."

He stretched his long legs, took a cautious sip of coffee, and rubbed his eyes wearily, laying his glasses on the table. "If this is retirement, I'm goin' back to work. It was easier." Then over the cup, he looked at her. "Jessie makes good stuffed peppers. You should have joined us."

"Last night I was the one who felt worn out."

"Bad day?"

"Not one of my best."

"Better this morning?"

"I don't know," she answered honestly. It was a mistake. He was looking at her with those level green eyes, waiting for something. What? She didn't confess to strangers, not even if they had broad shoulders and friendly eyes. She smiled and went on, "I'll have to see. Dr. Evans—"

"Will."

"Will—how soon do you suppose I can get a telephone? I hate imposing on people all the time."

The frizzy-haired little waitress was pouring coffee at the next booth. The vet shrugged, holding up his cup. Kookie grinned, filling it.

"Now *drink* this one," she said, adding to Lucy Maud, "he inhales the first two."

It was his turn to grin, making fine laugh wrinkles around his eyes. "They know me well," he said. "Got all the single guys pegged, haven't you, Kook?"

"You bet," she answered, and moved on down the line. He dug deep into a denim pocket, produced a folded white handkerchief, and began to polish his glasses. His green eyes went back to Lucy Maud. "I'll call a guy I know," he said. "This morning. He works for the telephone outfit. I'll bet we can have you hooked up early tomorrow. Martha's phone is still there, isn't it?"

"Yes."

The voice sounded a bit abstracted. He followed her gaze to his glasses then back. "Want yours cleaned, too?"

"No—no, no," she stammered, feeling like a real idiot. How could she say it had been decades since she'd seen a man with a real, genuine pocket handkerchief? "I—I'm just always astounded at—at how quickly things are done in a small town. I mean—in Millard it would take three or four days."

"That's why I'm here and not there," he answered affably. "Oh, I tried practicing in a big town once. Springfield. No, thanks. It got to be too damned frustrating."

"Frustrating?"

"All those silly women shortening their pets' lives by feeding them people food—a dog's innards are not designed to assimilate chili and fries, for God's sake! And letting them run loose, then come crying to me when the poor things got hit by cars." He was putting the wire-rims back on what she now observed to be an aquiline nose, and refolding the handkerchief. He was also laughing, a rather short, wry chuckle. "My wife stayed," he said. "Found herself a city man. I was lucky with Tim. My boy. He's not a big town man, either. Hey—I'd better roll," he said to Eileen as she passed.

"Any time." She gave his wide shoulder an affectionate pat. "Gonna watch Vic arm wrestle tonight?"

"We'll see how it goes with the Charolais." He was standing up, zipping his jacket. "I'll call about the phone from Worth's, Lucy. Don't fret it. See you, girls!"

"Now there," said Eileen, removing Lucy Maud's plate, "is a prince of a guy. Want another roll?"

In amazement Lucy Maud was assimilating the fact that not only was her plate empty, but the cinnamon roll was also gone! When had she done that? "N-no.

I've had enough. But it was good. I'd better let someone else have my seat."

Her second surprise came when the cashier said airily, "Never mind your tab. Doc paid it. Have a mint."

Lucy Maud took the mint. The cashier said, "Hey—are you Martha Hauser's niece? Gee, we miss her. City Hall just ain't the same without Martha stamping our water bills. And Frank—my momma says no one understood her old washer and dryer like Frank did. Whatcha goin' to do? Sell the place?"

Personal questions from strangers was another thing to which Lucy Maud had become unaccustomed. She mumbled something she hoped was socially acceptable, and went out into a fall morning bright with sunshine. As she unlocked her car, another just pulling in beeped its horn. The driver pointed, she nodded, then backed from her space so he could slide into it.

At least, she thought wryly, heading down the street, they can't say I'm not cooperative.

The yellow Cadillac was now parked at the Methodist Church, its shape a gleam of gold among the somber Chevys and Fords.

Very suitable for a banker, she said to herself, and pondered the next question: Had Howard Lewis recognized her?

Nine

Suddenly Lucy Maud found the anger rising at herself. What was the matter with her? Howard Lewis had been out of her life for almost forty years. She'd hardly thought of him for thirty. And the man she'd just seen, with sloppy fat buttoned into a too-tight suit and dead-dyed hair combed over from a part almost in his left ear certainly didn't ring any bells!

She wanted back at him! That was it. After three decades the hurt was still there. The hurt of rejection. The feeling was childish, petty, immature, and stupid. But Verna Marshall's kid would still like to stomp that cockroach good!

And if she got a chance, she admitted ruefully, she would.

But she wouldn't waste time looking for a chance. She was too smart for that.

Surely she was.

I am! she declared fiercely, and, turning down the main street toward the grocery store, she resolved to get on with her life.

A life she'd handled so well, she added with painful truth, that a stranger buying her breakfast had left her enough money for dog food without writing another check.

Oh, yeah, Lucy Maud, you're a real winner!

Automatically locking her car, Lucy Maud went inside to be greeted cheerfully by the same skinny stock boy. " 'Mornin', ma'am. Bit brisk, ain't it?"

Agreeing that it was, indeed, she found the long row of dog supplies. She also found herself giggling. *Krunchies! Yummies! Goody-bits!* The memory of Will Evan's face as he recounted his city days of succoring pets pigged out on a what he'd called "people food," she selected a relatively sober bag—and only five pounds as she certainly wasn't sure how long-term this relationship with Cutie was going to be. She was also chagrined to discover that even that size sucked up her remaining three dollars.

The stock boy checked her out, taking away her last dollar bills forever—plus fifty-one cents in change—and said, "Then Cutie must be back! Good. I heard she was. Here—take her a dog biscuit and give her a hug for me. Tell her Jimmie sent it."

Lucy Maud looked from the hard-pressed cereal thing in her hand to the smiling face with the hint of adolescent beard. "Jimmie?"

"Yeah. She'll know."

Hers was not to reason why. Lucy Maud said, "Okay," and put the thing in her pocket. "When do you close?"

"One o'clock. Tomorrow we open at seven. Have a good day, ma'am."

It already could use improvement, she thought, but aloud said only a banal word of thanks. The bag of dog food on the seat beside her, she started the car again and hesitated.

Back to Aunt Martha's?

Practicality dictated it. Her gas gauge registered a quarter of a tank and the next fill would have to be with a credit card.

There was a paper rack on the corner by the drug store. Could she afford one? Perhaps somewhere in the want ads they wanted a lady librarian without a degree.

Smiling grimly at that, she scrabbled in the glove compartment, found enough change to make fifty-five cents, got the heavy county edition, and headed for Martha's.

The neighborhood was quiet, she noted. Jessie's drive was empty, muddy ruts the only evidence of previous tenancy. Prickly sweet-gum balls rattled on her car roof in a sweep of breeze as she pulled into Martha's, hefted the dog food, and climbed the squeaking, splintered steps. The sound of the door being unlocked was enough to bring Cutie limping to the front room, fluffy tail wagging. Curious, Lucy Maud reached into her pocket, produced the biscuit thing, and held it out.

She said, "Jimmie."

The dog nosed the biscuit, and glanced upward.

Lucy Maud repeated, "Jimmie."

And she could swear a light went on in that satin head. Cutie emitted a "Burf!" and gulped the thing.

She went into the kitchen, Cutie trotting happily behind, found an old pie tin, dumped dog food into it, and placed the tin near the dog bed. Cutie sniffed, nosed the contents curiously, then began to chow.

"Good for you," said Lucy Maud dryly, "because that's the choice right there."

She'd bought two pizzas yesterday—one of them would do nicely for lunch. And it was sunny enough in the kitchen not to have to turn off all the lights to run the microwave.

We do get thankful for small things, she thought, shrugging, and went back into the living room for the Sunday papers.

Time out, Lucy Maud. Enjoy it while you can.

She plumped the couch pillows, kicked off her shoes, noted a run in her nylon knee-highs, frowned, and put that problem on hold with the others. Then she sat down, resigned herself to black-leaded fingers from offset printing, and opened the hefty edition.

She knew the headlines would be disheartening— negative and argumentative; she'd read those tomorrow. She didn't need a look at the latest fashions designed for bony, boobless tootsies with horse-mane hair. She had no yen for a recipe that made mead from potato peelings, nor did she know a Boston Bull from a nanny goat. She went directly to the book reviews, saving the want ads for last.

The book reviews put her to sleep.

What awakened her was a concerted banging on the kitchen door and Cutie nosing her with patently pro- voked canine bunts of exasperation.

"All right!" she said crossly, blinking sodden eyes, then raised her voice: "Just a minute! I'm coming!"

Two people were standing on the cluttered back porch: Jessie Murphy, hot-padded hands holding a steaming bowl of something or other, and a dumpy man in a tool belt who said briskly, "Doc says you want your phone going."

"For heaven's sake!" said Lucy Maud in pure surprise. "Er—yes, I do. I do, indeed. Come in. And you, too, Mrs. Murphy. I'm sorry I didn't answer—I guess I dropped off."

"Told 'im you probably had. Looked pretty weary last night," said Jessie calmly, putting the bowl on the table. "Phone's around the corner, Cal. Hope you like chicken 'n' noodles. We had plenty, thought you might eat some."

The clock over Jessie's neat gray head said one-thirty!

Amazed, Lucy Maud said, "Oh, thank you—yes, I'm sure I do. This is very kind."

"No trouble. Figured you weren't ready to house-keep just yet. Eat while it's hot, child. I'll pick up the plate later—got to get back. Missouri's playin' Nebraska today."

She was out and gone, the wind floating her apron strings as she trotted through the ragged hedge and up on her own kitchen porch. Bemused, Lucy Maud shut the door and went back to the living room. The telephone man was already dialing the phone.

"Y' hear me okay? Fine. Yeah, that's the number. Who do we bill to, ma'am?"

"Oh. To—to *Marshall*. L. M."

"Right. No problem." Into the telephone he said, "L. M. Got it? Thanks."

Unfortunately, Lucy wasn't listening closely. She was too amazed that she already had a phone. She said, "Marvelous. It's *Sunday!* I can't believe you came!"

He grinned, all yellow dentures and engaging smile. "No sweat. Besides, I owe Doc one. He got my old mare goin' again when everyone else said shoot 'er. Tell you what I would, though. I'd take a bowl of Jessie's noodles. M' wife's at her mom's and I've eaten enough cheeseburgers to own a share in Hardee's."

"Of course. Help yourself."

She found a stack of bowls in the cupboard, washed one off, and handed it over with a battered trio of silverware. Elegance had not been Aunt Martha's thing— at least not recently.

"The church ladies got the good stuff," the man said, correctly interpreting her face as he sat down, making the old wooden chair creak. "I know. M' wife helped. And don't think it's not appreciated. 'Specially when the bishop comes. Sit down, have some, too, or Jessie'll get my hide. Oh—I'm Cal Bonnett."

"Lucy Maud Marshall."

"Glad to know you. You and your mom had left town before we came. But we knew Martha, bless her. And Frank. Saints, both of 'em. A real loss to Crewsville."

It was on the tip of her tongue: Who the hell was Frank?

But etiquette prevailed, and all she did was sit down on the other side of the table and fill her own bowl. Casually dipping noodles, she said instead, "The town has changed a bit. Since we lived here."

"I s'pose. Not as much as it should, probably, but when the economy is based on hogs and apples, life just sort of goes on. The sad thing is, of course, that there's no jobs for the kids so they're leavin'. Oh— some stay. The lumber outfit has its boys takin' over, and the grocery store." He suddenly grinned, wiping a noodle from his stubby chin. "The bank, now— Howard, that blond jessy of his only produced girls. One of 'em's already left, with one to go—and, of course, Howard's lifestyle doesn't leave much room for his turnin' money over to anybody else, anyway. My God, how he and her can spend the dough! Boy, this was good. I do thank you!"

"Have some more."

"Don't want to eat yourn."

"You're not. Help me clean it up."

"You twisted my arm." He went on about Howard.

"Howie's all right. He does a lot of good things around town—among the old folks, 'specially. Takes 'em places, remembers their birthdays, stuff like that. They really appreciate him."

"That's nice." If the words had been printed on glass they couldn't have sounded more brittle—but of course he couldn't know about her relationship with Howard. He'd said he hadn't lived here that long.

He was standing up, patting the belly inside the striped coveralls, and tugging the crumpled old ballcap back down on thinning curls. "Sure do appreciate the chow. Oh—tell Doc while I was doin' your connection under the porch I looked at those risers. He's right. Watch your step when you go up and down. They're pretty rotted. I'd give the lumber company a call, ma'am—especially if you're meanin' to sell this place. They'll treat you okay—bein' as how you're Martha's niece. And it wouldn't hurt to say Doc and me sent you. Hi, ol' Cutie, welcome home."

Cutie, who had been patiently nuzzling his knee, got her satiny ears rumpled, then he was out the door with a cheery, " 'Bye. Have a good one!"

Between his farewells and the sound of a vehicle back-firing as he left, woman and dog looked at each other. The dog was waiting patiently for whatever came next. The woman wasn't sure what that would be.

Neither had much time to cogitate before it came.

The phone rang.

Lucy Maud literally jumped and said, "Oh!"

The dog gave her a puzzled look, then trotted around the corner as if to say, "This way, dummy."

She followed as it rang again, took a good grip on the back of one of her aunt's tacky old velour chairs, and answered tentatively, "Hello."

"Eureka! He got it going! Good old Cal."

Will Evans. She knew it before he said so.

"This is Will. Look, I have Don's problem taken care of. Let me have about three hours' sack time— under a haystack maybe where I can't be found—then why don't we go down on the river to a place I know that does great barbecued ribs? Okay?"

A date. Lucy Maud Marshall, after thirty-some years, was being asked for a date! In her hometown. Where everyone else had been afraid of offending Howard Lewis!

Of course, Will Evans didn't know that. He hadn't been around thirty years ago.

"Lucy Maud? You hang up on me?"

"No. No, of course not. But—Will, I hardly brought any clothes—"

"What you were wearing will be fine! I'm just going to change my pants. They have stuff on them you don't care to hear about. I tried to get Don and Marian to go with us to protect my virtue from a city woman. She heard laughter in the background—affectionate, tolerant laughter—but he's got to take her to catch her plane. So—about six-thirty. Okay? No later. I'm starving."

One scared Lucy Maud Marshall stood off in the shadows hearing a second Lucy Maud in her best librarian's voice say, "Fine. I'd enjoy it."

"Attagirl," said Will Evans, and the line went dead.

No deader than the line Lucy knew connected her brain with her body.

What had she just done?

A date!

Not an engagement with some guy who wanted to sell her a new line of encyclopedias, or modernize the eternally obsolete computer system, or enroll her in a network that activated the genealogy files in Timbuktu.

An engagement with a guy who only knew her as Martha Hauser's niece.

Dinner. Okay. But after dinner—what?

What if he tried to kiss her? Kissing led to other things—in this day and age a *lot* of other things—she knew that.

And then he would discover she only had one boob.

"Oh God," she said out loud, and felt sick. She liked Will Evans. She wanted him to like her.

Then—the obvious. No kissing. Zap. A polite

"Good night, thank you so much," out the car door, and into the house.

She was almost sixty! Surely she could manage that! Couldn't she?

Her track record on everything else hadn't been too great recently.

But—look at it this way. If she bombed with Will Evans—so what? She just met him yesterday. He wouldn't affect her job hunting, or this house—or anything. Not really!

And for a woman with sixteen cents in change, a free meal was a free meal.

Lucy Maud, you are positively crass! she said to herself, and went to take a nice long soak.

Stupid as it seemed, she felt excited.

Ten

What the hot bath really did was dry her out like a prune, but half a jar of cream took care of that, and at least the beginnings of those arthritic twinges in her back disappeared again. While Cutie sat on her plump fanny in the doorway totally bemused, Lucy Maud took great care with her make-up, matching the deep rose tones of lipstick and cheek blush with the sweater she'd fortunately not unpacked from her last foray. So the tweed skirt had an elastic waistband. Beneath the sweater, who would know? And pullover sweaters were the best disguises in the world for short waists!

Her low-heeled black suede shoes would have to do, but she didn't want to be taller than Will, anyway.

How tall was he?

As she'd observed, next to Vic Bonnelli any man looked like a midget.

People certainly seemed to like him, too, she mused, looking down her nose at the clasp on her string of pearls. Had there ever *been* a Mrs. Bonnelli?

Not that it mattered.

And she realized with a sudden, guilty start that she really meant that. She wasn't just repeating useless phrases.

It *didn't* matter. Verna was gone—and after five years perhaps her daughter was finally able to make social decisions on her own!

She could imagine her mother's face, if she had been around to hear Will Evans. His being a veterinarian would have pleased her; Verna had approved of professional men. But she would have had to know his income, what was going to his ex-wife, how independent his children were, if he owned his house, the year of his car, and the names of other women he'd squired. Or had affairs with. Or shown an interest in.

It was what she and the girls at Millard Public Library had called the women's soap opera syndrome—a condition they swore they'd never have!

And at the moment Lucy Maud Marshall was measuring up nicely. What she really knew about Will Evans at that point would make a very small paragraph.

Almost as much as he knew about her, she realized wryly, spraying a nice, flowery cologne.

One thing about Aunt Martha's dresser mirror— Grand Rapids repro though it might be—it was a good, clear one, with no distortions or streaks.

What was it showing now?

A woman in her fifties, nicely dressed—but more than that—a woman about to get some confidence back—a woman who was ready to stop running and deal with her problems?

"You'd better hope so, lady," she said aloud, giving one last approving brush to the obedient silver hair and turning away, snapping off her aunt's circa 1930 dresser lamps. The stripped and rather dumpy double bed caught her eye. She'd make it up tomorrow, she decided. The church ladies had left the sheets, and a small, folded blanket might fill the hole on the middle. If Martha and Frank had slept together, they'd certainly been cozy. Sleeping on the outer rims of that mattress would have required hand holds.

But the old iron headboard was sort of neat, twining in curlicues up to a heart-shaped point.

"How appropriate!" she murmured and made a grimace of continuing amazement. How little she'd known about Martha Hauser after all!

Her wispy memory of Martha was a sad one of continual bickering on her mother's side, and inexplicable patience on Martha's, culminating, of course, when her aunt had gathered up her cat and moved out. Then they'd moved, and Martha had visited them only twice in fifteen years.

Frankly, she couldn't blame Martha. The visits had been brief consisting of Verna's unending questioning and snide remarks. And Verna had never returned to Crewsville, though it had only been a hundred miles away.

"Why?" she'd asked bitterly. "I have no friends there. Backbiters, all of them!"

Well. Her daughter was back. And damned glad to have had someplace to go!

Lucy glanced at the clock to move her mind to something more constructive.

It said seven-fifteen—not its fault, as it required winding and Lucy Maud hadn't done it yet.

After her heart resumed its proper place, she did so,

setting the old brass hands at six. Half an hour before Will Evans was due.

Laying out her windbreaker against the sunset chill, she wandered into the small living room, sat down in one of the awful old chairs, got up, turned on the TV, and sat down again. Cutie ambled in, painfully hoisted herself up into the other one, and put her head on her paws with a comfortable sigh.

From the white hairs on the wine-colored velour it would appear this was not the first time. That chair was probably the one her aunt had sat in. Martha had liked pets on her lap.

So *she* was in Frank's chair—logically, anyway.

Okay. She hoped his shade liked Channel 10 because that was what she meant to watch.

Perhaps tomorrow she'd have enough incentive to inventory the problems on this house, get some repair prices, and consult with Vic about selling the sucker.

She certainly wasn't going to stay here!

Was she?

"No!" said Lucy Maud again, sharply and out loud.

Cutie jumped and looked at her questioningly, one ear half-cocked.

"I can't stay," she said to her in reply, unconscious of talking to a dog. "What would I do here? Besides, this place would drive me nuts! I need a job, and income, and—and I don't need Howard Lewis breathing down my neck!"

She might as well admit it: the prospect of Howard Lewis watching over her shoulder stuck in her craw. There was no rational to it, but that was the situation and she was going to have to deal with it.

Years ago she'd simply run. Now cowardice was going to catch up with her—at a rather inopportune time in her life.

But beggars can't be choosers, she thought grimly, stooping to an unfortunately appropriate cliche. She was here. She just had to deal with him. She knew that in her bones.

Cutie flumped awkwardly down from her chair, trotted to the front door, and looked back at Lucy Maud pointedly.

Time to go out.

I don't believe this. It can't be me . . .

But it was Lucy Maud Marshall, the no-pets person, letting a dog out to do her thing.

At the same time, a pick-up truck with "Evans Clinic" on the blue door pulled into the driveway and honked cheerfully as the door opened to let Will Evans swing to the ground.

"Hi!" he said, stooping to pat a madly wagging Cutie, and then giving Lucy Maud a comprehensive visual sweep as he straightened. "Good God, lady. You clean up nice! And I only put on different pants!"

"I brought a limited wardrobe," said Lucy Maud. But she was very pleased. "Thank you, anyway."

He waved an arm doorward to the dog. "Okay, sweetie, in you go! Your girl and I have plans."

Cutie trotted obediently up the steps and they followed, Lucy Maud aware of the wooden creaks and the vet aware of the dog.

"She's better," he said. "A lot better. Get your coat, lady. I know Martha and Frank didn't allow alcohol on the premises, and with your kind permission I want a nice, cold beer."

Lucy Maud stopped involuntarily. "She—they—didn't?"

"Nope. Well, you know Frank had had sort of a problem."

No, she hadn't known.

But letting it pass, she reached around the corner for her windbreaker and allowed him to help her into it. He had a good smelling cologne and the push back toward the door was friendly, easy-going.

"You're locking?" he said at the audible click. "Good God—what will Jessie do if she needs sugar or flour or something? In Crewsville, hon, that's downright unfriendly!"

"In Millard it's necessary," she answered shortly, and put the key in her purse.

He shrugged, helped her casually down the steps again, and opened the truck door. "Step up," he said, and the palm of his hand against her fanny, lifting, was nothing but impersonal assistance. "I should have brought the car, but hell, it was in the garage and probably needed jump-starting. I haven't driven it in weeks. And I figured you wouldn't mind."

"No. Not at all."

She was breathless because of the exertion of climbing. As he slid in beside her, she said, "Wow. I'd forgotten how high up you are in a truck!"

"That's why us truckin' boys are kings of the hill!"

He was laughing, giving her a grin and a flash of those green, sparkling eyes as he started the engine. "Hey—there's Tina. Give her a wave."

Lucy Maud obediently flipped a hand at the face framed in the lace-curtained windows next door.

She said, "Will—not to pry. Really. But what's the situation there?"

"With Tina? Oh—the usual. Her father's an irresponsible rat. He took off when she was born. He does make support payments. Sometimes. Eileen's a good kid, works her tail off. She and little Kookie were sent up here to help start Bunny Burger." He was expertly backing into the street, cranking the wheel, straightening out. "They're from Penfield. You know—the county seat. She's got a casual thing going with Vic. It's Tina, mostly. He does love that kid." Then as they started down the street, he cut his eyes to her. "You know Vic's problem?"

"He has an artificial leg."

"And most of his genitals shot off in the carrier action. I'm surprised he hasn't told you. He lays it on straight with almost everyone he meets."

She shook her head ruefully. "Poor man. He may have—I've been so bemused it might have escaped me. But he seems like a really nice person."

"He's a prince."

It might take one to know one, Lucy Maud thought. She felt very comfortable with the man next to her. It was going to be a nice evening.

He'd headed the truck east out of town toward the autumn blaze of the riverbluffs, basking in the last golden shafts of the sinking sun. On either side tidy rows of trimmed apple trees marched up gentle slopes.

"Good crop this year," Will said. "Oh. I hope you

don't smoke, lady. If you do, you'll have to ride in back."

She laughed. "No. I never did. Can you believe that? Well—a few in college, but somehow it just didn't get me. I couldn't afford it, for one—even if cigarettes were twenty-five cents a pack then. My mother would have had a fit. Then at the library it just wasn't convenient, anyway. I—somehow gather that you don't, either."

He laughed. "But I did! I was up to four packs a day! Then I had this little stomach problem, and I'll tell you, lady, cold turkey was the only way! But my son will confirm that I was a genuine sonofabitch for about six months! See that side road—that leads to Buffalo Bob's—you heard the girls mention the place. It's a roadhouse where everyone goes. But I wanted something a little fancier this evening—to impress you, of course."

He was laughing, again.

She said, "Well, thank you, sir."

"And Buffalo Bob doesn't do ribs on Sunday night."

Then she laughed, too. "That's really called 'placing your priorities.'"

"Right. I knew you were astute. As well as attractive. You see, I can't take a lady anywhere who doesn't measure up to my standards. I have a reputation to maintain, after all."

It was oral boxing, and she found it a challenge.

"Well," she said, tossing her head, "I also have standards to maintain. I'll give you a checklist at the end of the evening."

And they both laughed. He reached over, patted her

tweed knee briefly. "You'll do fine," he said. "I like a gal who speaks her mind."

To her amazement, Lucy Maud realized she hadn't felt so comfortable with a man since her routine evenings with the copier repairman who spent the entire time showing her pictures of his six kids. She watched with interest as they turned into a crowded parking lot at the foot of a bluff where the silver sheen of the river rippled beyond.

"Looks like a good thing I made reservations," Will was saying, deftly parking his truck between two others. "Here, we do lock up. I have all my vet gear in the back, and they get a lot of transients."

He loped around the hood of the pick-up and deftly swung her to the graveled grounds. "Scoot, lady. That wind's turning cool with the sun down."

As he opened the double doors, Lucy Maud felt a rush of warmth, the sound of many voices talking and laughing, and dark shapes moving in the dim orange lights of a crowded bar. Over it all was the silky nasal voice of someone mourning his lost love against a background of guitars. To their left was a dining room, much more adequately lighted, and a slender hostess in a large black cowboy hat saying, "Hi, Doc! We've got your table, right by the windows where you like it. Good evening, ma'am."

"Good evening," said Lucy Maud, and followed as the woman threaded her way through crowded tables of diners to one set up for a pair against floor length windowpanes. The trip was a veritable forest of similar western hats set far down on mostly male ears.

I feel a hundred and ten, Lucy thought. I just haven't

got used to men not removing their headgear. Mother would have a fit!

She settled into a nicely padded chair that Will held for her, and glanced outside. Beyond an empty lime-stone terrace, the last rays of the sun shot golden spears across the calm river. Tiny twinkles of light laced the blackening bluff on the other side. A bridge span arched its steel lace to the opposite shore and overhead, birds on outspread wings sailed in circles above the molten surface.

Lucy Maud said, involuntarily, "How lovely!"

Will, seating himself, laughed. "Nothing like this in Millard?"

"Nothing like this. We're on the flat plains."

He *had* taken off his cap, laying it on the low window ledge, and smoothing back the gray. The hostess had been followed by a little blond waitress in a western-cut shirt and blue jeans, who stood waiting, pad in hand.

"Hi, Doc. Your usual? How about you, ma'am?"

"Order for me," Lucy Maud said to Will, taking the easy road. She was not going to say she didn't know anything more about alcoholic drinks than what she'd read in novels.

Will shrugged. "Two Busch Lites," he said to the waitress. "And some nibblin's. I'm starved. I think I skipped lunch. Then the ribs, heavy on the sauce."

"You, too, ma'am?"

"Yes. That's fine."

"Baked or fries?"

Obviously she meant potatoes. Lucy Maud an-swered, "Baked, please. And sour cream."

"Okey-dokey. And you guys go to the salad bar when you want."

"First the beer."

"Coming up."

She wended her way back through the clustered tables. Will watched her.

"Damn!" he said to Lucy Maud. "I knew her when she was toddlin'. In tears because her puppy died. Now she's got at least two kids. Time does go on, doesn't it?"

"I'm afraid it does."

"You, too?"

"Just what you said. When the little girl who screamed and yelled because her mother was parking her at Story Hour brings in her own little girl, screaming and yelling, then you know about time."

"So you make the best of what you have."

"If you're smart." She said it ruefully, but he couldn't know that.

He was smiling at her. "I knew it!" he said. "I knew we were a good match! Once in a while ol' Doc lucks out. Hey, Martin," he said to a man in a St. Louis Cardinals hat, walking by. The man patted his shoulder, grinned.

"Hey, Doc. How y' doin'?"

"Fine. You?"

"Dandy." The man's eyes slid over Lucy Maud, and she thought she detected surprise. "Ready for deer season?"

"Don't spoil my dinner."

"Mary says this year we're going to spray the word 'cow' on everything in the north pasture."

"Good thinking. Take care, now."

"You, too."

As he went on, Lucy Maud echoed, "cow?"

"Damn big-city hunters come down here, get likkered up, go out the next morning with hangovers and shoot at anything that moves. Thanks, Judy—" he said to the blond waitress unloading two foaming Pilseners on their table. "—And keep them coming one more time. Golly, look at that river."

A towboat, pushing a long row of barges upstream, was splitting the silver surface into a lacy, foaming vee. On board the tow a white-aproned figure emerged, tossing scraps into the air. They never hit the water. Those same enormous, circling birds suddenly turned into dive bombers, catching their prizes and zooming back high out of sight.

"Eagles," Will said, grinning. "The ones some ecologists say are so scared of people. The ones around here sure aren't. They sit on the end of the grain barges while the elevator guys load, just waiting for spills. How is it?"

Lucy Maud had taken a cautious sip from her glass. She considered. "Not bad."

"This is Busch country. Lord, I'm hungry!" He'd almost emptied the bowl of peanuts. "Good! Here it comes!"

"Has he been gnawing the table?" the slender waitress asked Lucy. She was placing enormous platters before each of them, a ten-ribbed piece of meat on each, lathered with deep red sauce and flanked with butter-oozing baked potatoes. "You guys haven't been to the salad bar yet!"

"We'll get there," Will said. "First things first, Judy. How's your Doberman?"

"My God! Ten foot tall. Charlie didn't tell me he'd be bigger than the kids! Here's the rolls. Now, if I forgot something, whistle."

Will nodded. He was already carving off an enormous chunk of rib. Lucy Maud, minding her manners, said, "Thank you." Will corroborated: "Yeah. Thanks, hon. Lucy, if you want salad, go get it. I'm tackling the main event."

"Not a salad man?"

"Not when there's a choice."

Lucy Maud thought a little coleslaw would be nice. Getting up, she wended her way through the diners to the long, lighted table against the opposite wall.

Picking up a plate, she joined the line of salad fanciers, thinking it looked like a really good selection. It was in reaching across for the cinnamon apple sauce that she glanced directly into the eyes of Howard Lewis.

Eleven

He was looking across at her with a mixture of question and uncertainty. She'd been right about his hair part—it almost disappeared into his ear. And the dull brown strands so carefully combed over his forehead shone with spray beneath the salad bar lights. But his eyes confirmed his identity—still rich brown, still long-lashed.

It was Howard, all right. With one big change—the eyes no longer turned her knees to mush.

She said brightly, "Why, Howard! I almost didn't recognize you!"

He smiled. "We all change. I—I heard you were in town."

"Really? Important news still travels fast, doesn't it?"

"Uh—yes. Yes, indeed. Amanda, dearest, this is—is an old friend. Lucy Marshall. Lucy, my wife, Amanda."

The old phrase "measuring each other" was no joke—at least not on Amanda Lewis's part. The lady's eyes raked Lucy Maud's face, her hair, her pearls, her sweater. The carmined mouth smiled.

She said, "Indeed. I've heard so much about you. Years ago, of course."

"I do hope it was," Lucy Maud answered smoothly. Her own glance had rapidly taken in the facelift scars, the painfully blond hair, the fat roll at the waist—and the bulbous, ample boobs. Oh, yes. The boobs. Two of them.

"You're selling Martha's property?" Howard asked, spooning macaroni salad.

"I'm not certain. It's rather—relaxing to come back to a small town. Once in a while."

Amanda Lewis said, "I suppose. Come, Howie. Our guests are waiting. Nice to have met you, Miss Marshall. Do drop by the house. I'm always home on Wednesdays."

She left the bar, Howard followed. Over his shoulder, he said, "Nice to see you again."

Lucy Maud didn't dignify that with an answer. She got her applesauce, forgot the coleslaw, and went back to her own table.

Will Evans had accumulated six naked bones, and was wiping sauce off his mouth with his napkin as she reseated herself.

"Find someone you knew?"

She was tempted to tell the truth, but she didn't. Instead, she sat, readjusted her napkin, and tackled her own ribs, dismissing his question with a shrug.

"Mmmm. Good," she said, whether about the meat or her sense of having survived a dreaded encounter she wasn't certain. At least she hadn't gone all goosey and blown it! A few years in the library business *had* taught her some rudiments of diplomatic maneuvering.

Will had finished his Pilsener and was signaling to

Judy. One green eye winked at Lucy Maud. "Somehow I sense you don't need a refill."

"I'm fine. It's good, though."

"What a nice little girl. She minds her manners although she's not going to make a beer drinker. One more time, Judy, and bring the lady coffee."

Guiltily feeling she should say *something,* Lucy Maud swallowed and said, "I went to school with Howard Lewis. But I'd never met his wife."

She knew he was about to say, "No loss," but stifled it. Instead he took a deep draught of beer and went on. "Ahhh—just right," he said, adding, "Amanda Krueshank she was. You know—apple orchards out their kazoo."

"Oh—those people! They bought the Smaller orchards."

"Yes. That was before my time, but I've heard about it. Pass the salt, please."

She forebore saying it didn't need salt; his blood pressure was his own problem.

"I've heard the Krueshanks have hit hard times, too," he continued. "Selling out, maybe."

"The apple business slow?"

"No. No more than any seasonal enterprise." I expect they're just big spenders. Amanda certainly is. A good thing she married a banker. Meow," he added and smiled. "What the hell. It's certainly not my business. How about some apple pie?"

"Go ahead. I'll have a hard time getting through what's on my plate."

"Ask for a doggie bag. You'll have lunch tomorrow. Oh—shit."

"What?"

"I forgot to leave the damned thing in the truck."

"What are you talking about?"

"My beeper." He was already hauling it from his pocket and now even she could hear the electronic bray. "All right. I'm here. What?"

Then his face went intent. The transformation was instant: relaxation to annoyance to business. He said, "Okay. No problem, son. Glad you caught me. I'll be right there."

With a wry face, he refolded the gadget and slid it out of sight. "Sorry, hon. I have to go. John Dolper's Clydesdale got tangled up in his electric fence. I'll pay the tab. You get your doggie bag."

Sensing urgency, Lucy Maud caught up her coat and purse. The waitress was already at her side, offering a plastic container.

"I saw Doc with the beeper," she said. "That's the way it is when you go out with him. It's not the first time, and sure not the last. Do come back. We've missed him, with Dottie gone."

Then her face registered an almost audible "Oops!" Lucy Maud, however, was too intent on her possessions to do more than half hear. She snapped the plastic lid, hauled on her windbreaker, smiled at the waitress, and hurried toward the exit.

Will was already there.

The trip back to town hardly warmed the pick-up seats. She could almost see his mind tick-ticking as he drove, and had sense enough not to interrupt his chain of thought. He didn't even pull into her driveway, just leaned across her and opened the door.

"You're an understanding gal," he said. "I'm sorry about this, I'll call tomorrow."

"No problem. Good luck with the poor horse."

She slid to the frosted ground. He said, "Good night!" and lurched away, shifting gears as he drove.

Standing alone at the bottom of the rackety steps, Lucy Maud suddenly started laughing.

And she'd worried about being kissed good night!

For some reason, she thought, unlocking her door and feeling grateful for the surge of heat, she'd never equated the urgent schedule of animal doctors to people doctors. It would appear they might be very much the same.

"Burf?" inquired Cutie, stretching her satiny ears toward the outside.

"He had an emergency," replied Lucy Maud before she realized she was actually talking to a dog again!

She took the plastic container to the kitchen, Cutie trotting behind. The refrigerator seemed to be functioning; at least the milk carton was cold. She stowed the barbecued beef on a shelf, realized another cup of coffee wouldn't be too amiss, and got out the bag.

It wasn't even nine o'clock yet!

Some date!

A couple more chapters of the Eugenia Price novel, then early bed didn't seem that bad an idea. Tomorrow might be quite a day.

While the microwave heated the water she let the dog out, refilled the dog dish, took off her clothes, and cleaned the stuff from her face. She wished she'd brought her old, shabby robe instead of the pink woolly number that tickled her throat, but considering the haste of her departure perhaps she'd been fortunate even to remember a robe at all.

The book had slid from her hands beneath the couch the previous night. She found it, adjusted her back against the pillows, and settled down. Now, if she didn't look at the tacky chairs and had her Oriental rug, it would seem almost like home.

"Home" did not have a dog in it. Particularly a dog with that one ear cocked toward the door again. And there *were* footsteps!

Maybe Will was coming back!

Shocked at the sudden surge of pleasure, she swung her bare feet to the cold floor, patted her hair, and made it to the door as the knock sounded.

It was not Will.

It was Howard Lewis, the yellow Cadillac thrumming regally in the drive behind him.

"My, my," he said, the light from behind her illuminating a grin she didn't care for at all. "And you're alone! What a waste."

"Howard, what do you want?"

"You dropped your gloves."

"They're not mine." She didn't even dignify them with a glance. She hadn't been wearing gloves "What do you want?"

He leered again. And swayed a bit. Suddenly she was aware that whatever the man had been drinking, it had hit him hard. He was looped.

"Jis' give you a piece of advice," he mushed. "You bein' new back in town an' all."

"I don't need advice, Howard." Least of all, yours!

"Yesh y' do. 'Specially if you're shackin' up with the playboy of d' Western World."

"Who?"

"Ol' Doc."

Suddenly the world turned red. She tried to close the door, but his foot was in it. "Good night, Howard!"

"Not yet. Not till I tell you how he's screwed every single bitch from here to the state line—includin' Dottie Mase, but she got smart and went to California. Hell, Lucy, if you're needin' a piece that bad I'll give you one!"

That was when Cutie sank her teeth in his ankle.

He howled, grabbed it with his hands, fell on the porch, and Lucy Maud slammed the door.

Leaning against it, she listened, her breath drumming in her ears.

He got up, mumbling, "Goddammitalltohell, you'll be sorry," and apparently made it back to his car, as she heard the Cadillac roar, shift gears, and screech away.

Slowly, she slid to the rug, her back still against the door. Cutie whined and huddled her warm body against Lucy's knees, nosing her gently.

And Lucy Maud Marshall, turning, hugged the animal with both arms!

"Cutie," she whispered, "Thanks. I really owe you one."

Cutie indicated that there was no problem, wriggling her silky body closer.

They sat there for a long time, Cutie quite contented, Lucy Maud with her mind in a whirl.

Playboy of the Western World?

Kind, patient Will Evans, with the big grin and the green eyes?

Screwing every bitch from here to the state line?

And who the hell was Dottie Mase?

Then she remembered the surprise on some faces at the restaurant. And the waitress saying, "We've sure missed Doc since Dottie's been gone."

It hadn't registered then. It registered now.

Well.

And she'd been worried about being kissed good night!

Slowly Lucy Maud got to her feet, returned to the couch, and tucked herself back beneath the blanket. Cutie hopped up and turned around twice, cuddling between her and the pillows, and she didn't even notice.

As she'd said earlier, she hardly knew enough about Will Evans to fill a paragraph.

Welcome home, Lucy Maud. Welcome home.

Twelve

It was the second night in succession that ranked right up there with having an ulcerated tooth.

The bottom line came to her about three in the morning: from years of being a Millard *Somebody* she'd plunged to being a *No One!* Not only was that hard for her pocketbook to take, it was damned tough on her psyche! The safe trappings of the head librarian position were gone, leaving her naked as a jaybird!

Lucy Maud Marshall wasn't caring for that at all—along with the unexpected ramifications, like Will Evans, who apparently might have been just looking for a quick lay, and Howard Lewis, who was on the make as well.

For a moment it was almost funny. Lucy Maud certainly wasn't a virginal sixteen—she was a gray-haired broad with the beginnings of arthritis! But the funny side faded fast as she pursued the subject. Will Evans she could play by ear, but Howard would probably be something to deal with cautiously—particularly if the neighbors had seen him on her porch.

Damn. Why had she come here in the first place? Why hadn't she thought it through a little better?

Because there'd been no time. Because the best she

could do at the moment was cut a reasonable deal with Fred and the library board for four weeks' grace with a paycheck, using Aunt Martha as an excuse.

So, you damp noodle, she told herself angrily, tossing blankets off and trudging through the dark to the kitchen for some coffee, take advantage of that deal. It's all you have.

You can't work for Kathryn MacClane—you'd have a stroke or a heart attack within a month. You know the insidious ways she could find to make your life a misery!

So. Aunt Martha, bless her heart, left you this one option: her property. Repair the damned place, sell it, and get the hell away from here with enough money to tide you over until—

Until what?

Grimly mulling this, she filled a cup with water, turned on the microwave in the dark, and felt for the coffee bag box.

It was empty.

Damn. Damn everything. To hell!

When the microwave dinged, she turned on the light above the old wooden table and fished in the wastecan for the afternoon's soggy bags. Beggars can't be choosers.

Hadn't she said that before?

Well. It was still a truth.

Two old wet bags made sufficient color in the hot cup to call it coffee. Sort of. She pulled out one of the old wooden chairs and plunked down at the table. Behind her she heard Cutie schloop-schlooping in her water dish. Staring straight ahead, her tired eyes suddenly focused on a small mouse, perched at the edge of the drainboard. He was watching her curiously, ears pricked. But not moving.

That's how important she was right now. Not even a mouse was scared off!

"Shoo!" she said viciously.

He scampered—but he took his time.

His refuge was a small hole where the drainboard adjoined the cupboard. She'd have to remember that tomorrow and fix his red wagon!

Then she thought—Why? Why bother? Let the next tenants cope. She would be gone from here as soon as humanly possible!

Cutie had sacked out in her basket, but one eye opened as Lucy shuffled by, then closed again when she merely tore a sheet from a hanging calendar that said "May," found an old pencil stub in a drawer of bottle caps and wire ties, and sat down again to sip at the coffee.

The blank side of the calendar would do fine to make a list. Number one would be to call Vic and tell him she'd decided to sell.

Number two would be to check with the Millard bank and be sure her salary check had been automatically deposited as usual. She wouldn't put it past the MacClane bitch to try to screw that if she could.

Number three was to sit and think and try to come up with some associate in the state library system who might rescue her with the possibility for a job of any sort—for a non-degree ex-librarian.

Lucy Maud sighed. Wearily. Bitterly. She'd screwed herself there, and she may as well admit the fact.

But surely she could do something! Thirty years of experience must have some value!

And if it didn't? After she'd checked out the book-sellers and vendors and all those people she'd dealt with commercially for years and years and the answer was still "no."

She was a little long in the tooth to go on the streets. Despite what Howard Lewis seemed to think. So. The want ads. Great.

Lucy wadded up the list. She didn't need it. She could surely keep three options in her head. Since three were all she could manufacture. Four, if you counted the want ads.

Besides, it was nearly five o'clock in the morning. And tomorrow she might need a very clear head.

She dumped the rest of the coffee and started to dump the bags—then had second thoughts. The loose change in her wallet certainly wasn't going to buy much of anything until she could cash a check.

Grimly putting both on the counter, she turned out the light and shuffled back in to the couch. The soft pat-pat-pat was Cutie, following.

Well. She did owe her one. She'd said so.

"All right," she said wearily, and let the dog back up on the pillows.

Nothing was making sense, so why should she expect a pooch to understand?

Monday would see the dawn of the old Lucy Maud, she promised herself as she wriggled her shoulders into some comfort beneath the wadded blanket and shut her eyes to sleep.

It didn't work.

One thing she had not dealt with in her cogitation was Will Evans.

So what was the big deal, she thought sullenly, thrashing over and finding her nose on the silky back of a dog. There was no problem, she went on, removing the nose and putting it instead against a musty smelling velour couch arm.

Howard said he was a stud. It doesn't *always* take one to know one. Maybe it's envy. And maybe he *is* a stud. In this town unmarried men were as valuable as rubies when we lived here, she mused. Why should that change? Men don't.

I know he's not my stud. He bought me dinner, for Pete's sake—and I only ate half of it at that! And at least I'm still in charge of my personal life!

The man is nothing to me.

Nothing!

"Methinks the lady doth protest too much."

Damn—that was one of the hang-ups about being a librarian. You remember all the quotes and all the clichés—and they come back on you at one hell of a poor time!

Desperately summoning up all the fantasies about Rhett Butler and Mr. Darcy and Superintendent Alleyn that had lulled her to sleep so deliciously in the past, she finally drifted off to restless slumber.

But it was strange—all the fantasies had a nice grin and green eyes . . .

Seven-thirty found a small, cold, wet nose urgently touching her cheek again.

"You're the one who drank all the water!" she mumbled, but nonetheless hauled herself erect and opened the front door.

Sunshine, unable to penetrate drawn blinds, greeted her in golden shafts through the sparse, falling leaves of the trees across the street. Beneath the trees, cars were pulling from driveways next to small, wooden-framed houses. Lucy watched in amazement as a woman in a print housecoat emerged, bent, took two cartons of milk from a box on her porch, and went inside.

As she paused, looked, and waved, Lucy Maud waved back. She was still gaping. Milk. In a box. Delivered!

They hadn't delivered milk in Millard since 1970!

The phone was ringing.

She almost didn't answer—then she thought acidly. Well, you were the one who wanted the thing going!

"Hello." To her relief, the female voice on the other end said cheerfully, "Hi, this is Jessie. Next door. Need anything?"

You want a list?

But of course Lucy Maud was too civilized to say a thing like that! Instead, she minded her manners and replied, "How nice of you. But no, I think I'm fine." Out of money, out of coffee and probably out of her mind. That was fine? "I do appreciate your kindness yesterday."

"Honey, I'm more than glad to do what I can. Martha and Frank were the best. We miss 'em like you wouldn't believe."

"Mrs. Murphy—"

"Jessie."

"Jessie—it's awful to admit, but Aunt Martha and I had really sort of lost touch. When did—did Frank die?"

"Oh—'bout two years ago. His liver was gone, poor man. Never drank a drop for twenty, but the damage was done. And you know, I really think that's what took Martha. Bein' without Frank."

Lucy Maud had yet to meet a man who could so shorten her life! She answered an all-purpose, "Mmm," then added, "Thanks. I really didn't know."

"I can understand. Your mama feelin' as she did."

Lucy's eyes widened. Her mother had known about Frank? Jessie was going on innocently.

"No love lost, that's for sure. My, my, how people's lives do get mixed up. Anyway, I have to run—this is my volunteer day at the hospital. If I can help, or Eilly—just give a holler."

Bemused, Lucy hung up. Another talk with Jessie Murphy certainly might be in order.

But later. There was enough on her plate at the moment.

Two slices of stale toast later, Lucy was on the phone to Vic Bonnelli.

"So you think you want to sell?" Vic asked.

"Probably." Read that, *You bet I do!* but Vic Bonnelli needn't know. "Either way, there have to be repairs."

"Right. Trust me to round up some guys and get estimates?"

"Vic, you know the people. I don't. I've been away too long."

"Fine. Glad to do it. I'm showing a house down

the road a piece, but I should be back. Shall we say afternoon-ish?"

"I'll be here."

Where else, she asked herself bitterly as she hung up, would I go?

Then, realizing that her clean clothes inventory was reaching the precarious stage, her next project was checking out her aunt's facilities in the crowded little storeroom. This was not a success. The dryer started fine, but the washer was sprinkled with mouse dirt and didn't even try to buzz.

Great. Jessie Murphy had invited her to use hers but she wasn't home. So—had Crewsville progressed enough into the twentieth century to have a laundromat?

There was, of course, no telephone book. But Crewsville was hardly that big.

She put on last night's clothes, loaded the dirties into the same plastic bag that had sheathed the microwave, got in the car, and went looking.

Bingo. Right on the main street, across from the grocery store and the central island of park benches, purple martin houses, and a water fountain, was a laundromat.

It wasn't open.

She only discovered this as she propped up her laundry bag with her knee and tried to open the door.

A whistle made her turn. Tom Burkiser was waving from the door of his grocery store.

"Half an hour," he said. "The lady that runs it, her kids got chicken pox. She'll show as soon as her mom gets to her house to babysit. Come have a cup of coffee."

Lucy shook her head. "Thanks. I'll just drive around a little. It's been a while since I've seen the old town."

There was, she estimated, getting back in and heaving the laundry into the rear seat again, about twenty miles left on the gas gauge—and Crewsville still wasn't that big! When the banks opened, she'd cash a check. There should be at least enough money in her account to cover a moderate amount even without the paycheck—and that would be better than a credit card. Those probably should be saved for an emergency.

Like what? she asked herself and almost laughed, knowing she really didn't want to know.

The north end of town had been the affluent section—and still was, she realized in sudden dismay as in circling the low, sprawling high school complex she turned into a street that had become one-way. The only avenue left was past the "richies," as she and her friends had called them years ago, one of which in all its unchanged Gothic knobs and crannies sported a yellow Cadillac parked by the militant stone gryphons flanking stylized beds of sternly disciplined marigolds.

Obviously that one was still the Krueshanks', Howard's in-laws—unless he lived in it now!

She drove by, not looking and fervently hoping that no one else was, either. She didn't need Howard thinking she was tracking him down!

At the end of the block she gratefully turned left into a normal street heading back to the main one. One goof was enough per morning. The long, low building that once had contained the lumberyard now bore a sign reading "Evans Clinic." There was a familiar pick-up truck nosed to the curb.

Outraged at the involuntary quickening of her heart, she drove by that one, also. Deciding a cup of Tom Burkiser's coffee might keep her out of trouble, she turned left again and almost hit a low wooden fence that hadn't been there thirty years ago.

"Next time you take a tour, walk!" she mumbled to herself angrily, jamming on her brakes.

The neatly painted fence partly encircled a small parking lot which in turn abutted a tall, old Romanesque stone-block building she remembered as being city hall. Now, however, over the wide door was a rather amateurishly painted sign saying *"Library*—Enter here." Half the stone steps were covered by a handicap ramp, and at the top a young woman in a hooded coat was just unlocking.

Like a horse to water, Lucy Maud backed up, parked her car in the first lot slot, and climbed out.

The young woman looked up as she pushed open the door. She was thirtyish, bright-faced and smiling. "Hi. I'm just opening. Come on in."

By the time Lucy Maud made it across the lot and up the steps the woman had lights snapped on and was venting enough slatted blinds to let the warm sun pour over three card tables, twelve chairs, a desk, and four rows of double-sided bookshelves.

"A 'visiting fireman'!" Lucy Maud said of herself. "Is this new?"

"Rather. We're just getting started. The old one burned down in the middle of the night and half the people in Crewsville went into withdrawal. They are *readers,* here. Where are you from?"

"Millard."

"Hey!" It was like a candle lighting the pleasant face. "Then you're the gal Will was talking about! I'm Karen Evans. Tim's wife. Welcome. Let me show you around."

Oh, well, Lucy Maud thought, it was too late to back off. Besides, three more chapters would finish her book, then *she'd* be in withdrawal!

"Lucy Marshall," she said.

"That's it! Martha's niece, Frank's—" then the blaring phone rang across her voice, obliterating whatever else she was going to say. She grimaced. "Excuse me a minute, and go ahead—take a look. We can use all the suggestions we can get. Crewsville Library; may I help you?"

Lucy Maud turned to the nearest shelves featuring new books, and found the selection scanty. They must have a budget of less than a hundred! Behind her, Karen Evans was saying, "No, no, this is Karen . . . Oh, yes, Mabel's doing well, but I'm afraid she won't be back for at least a month. We're just having to make do . . . Mrs. Murphy volunteered last Friday, Mrs. Krueshank, so I can't answer that. But if you'll hold, I'll check the list."

She put down the telephone and turned to riffle through an index file, grinning impishly at Lucy Maud. "Owns half the county," she murmured *sotto voce.* "She's too tight to buy the latest Danielle Steel and give it to us, but thinks she should be first on the rota to read it. Surely you don't have any like her!"

Lucy Maud smiled back in total understanding. "Only about fifty," she said.

Karen giggled and turned back to the phone. "You're up fifth," she said brightly. "Right after Mrs. Lewis. We'll give you a call. Bye-bye."

Lucy Maud was piecing together her memory. She said, "But I didn't think you worked in this one."

"Oh, I don't. I'm the children's librarian in Penfield. Where Tim and I live. But we don't open until one, and they're desperate up here. One lady moved to California, and the other—Mabel, the girl I mentioned to Mrs. Krueshank—she got thrown when her quarter-horse shied, and broke her shoulder."

She had moved from behind the desk and was picking up an armload of books scattered on the shabby tile floor beneath a door slot. Lucy Maud bent to help.

"Good Lord," she said. "Is someone still reading Joseph Conrad? He's good—don't misunderstand me—but with Tom Clancy and Clive Cussler, Conrad has turned into a doorstop in Millard."

Karen said, "We have a lot of Conrads and not too many Cusslers. If you'll notice, three-fourths of what's on the shelf is donated."

"And glad to get it?"

"You're right, there. You know about state budget cuts. What we can *buy* is minuscule. I saw tears in Mabel's eyes last week when someone gave us a complete set of Nancy Drews. And not even the new ones—the old ones, before she had TV and a cellular phone in her convertible. Hey—got a minute? I'll put on the coffee."

"May I check in these books?"

"Oh, lady, be my guest!"

She disappeared through a rear door and Lucy Maud heard a tap running. Sliding her fanny up on a tall stool behind the desk, she reached for the card file and opened a returned volume to the bookpocket and the date card. It would, she mused, be at least the year 2000 before Crewsville progressed to scanning—and she felt a moment of pure pain, remembering the marvelous computerized system at Millard Public.

Kathryn MacClane's system. Not hers

She was twenty books into the haphazard stack when new sunlight and a crisp breeze slanted across the desk and she heard Karen say cheerfully, "The man has an instinct for fresh brew, Hi, Doc!"

And Lucy Maud glanced up to see Will Evans in the doorway.

Thirteen

Outlined by the bright sun, his hair shone silver and his denim-clad shoulders filled the door. Her heart jerked. She hated it. She sure as hell had better have her estrogen checked!

He was laughing, that low chuckle she remembered from last night, and saying to his daughter-in-law, "Hi, hon. Tim said you were up here. Good morning, Miss Marshall. May I remark that you look perfectly at home sitting there?"

"Isn't she a pet?" Karen said. She slid one steaming cup to Lucy Maud, another to her father-in-law, and slipped back out of sight. Her voice carried to them: "Go ahead. Chat. I have to wash another cup."

Lucy took a sip of coffee, and was reminded of one of her mother's sayings—that caution was a virtue. The coffee was hot enough to melt her fillings. Will was still smiling at her but saying nothing. Damn it, Will Evans! Make social conversation! Don't leave it up to me!

Well. She guessed it was her turn.

Brightly she asked, "How's the Clydesdale?"

"Hopefully having learned something about electric

fences. She'll be fine. How did you find this place so early?"

"The homing instinct." She half-believed the statement to be true. He grinned, unzipping his jacket and putting both brown, capable-looking hands around his cup.

"Cold fingers," he said. "I figured Karen would have something to warm me up. I never thought it might be you. Neat."

Fortunately, Lucy Maud didn't have to answer to that as Karen re-emerged, carrying a steaming pottery cup that was emblazoned "Shit Happens."

"The only one I can find," she said, smiling. "Remind me to shove it under something when anyone else comes in. You and Tim get those hogs ringed?"

"Girl! And here I am trying to project a Kirk Douglas image!"

"Sorry." She amended her words, and Lucy Maud got the feeling she and this man had an excellent relationship. "You and Tim get those lions ringed?"

"One of them thought he was."

"Got bit, didn't you?"

"No, he missed—got a snoot full of cement block instead. He'll remember. Hogs are smart. Lions, rather. How's Robby? Tim says he got in trouble at recess yesterday."

"He and his buddy, Poo. You know—Evelyn Cass's grandson. They did, all right. They decided it might be fun to hide Poo's new pet in the girls' restroom."

"New pet?"

"The little iguana Dad and Evelyn brought back from Florida."

"Jeez Louise!" said Will Evans. His daughter-in-law looked at him sternly.

"Don't you dare laugh in front of him. Or Poo. They're both in deep doo-doo."

"How's the iguana?"

"Wow. Once a vet, always a vet! Never mind the two dozen little girls that peed their pants. The iguana's fine, Will. He just isn't going to visit school anymore. Okay, Miss Marshall. I'll finish the books and you finish your coffee. I really appreciate the help. I may ask you again."

Lucy slid from the high stool. "I was going to put in some laundry—I imagine it's open now. Thank you for the coffee." Scalding or not, she drank it down, putting the cup on the desk. "Nice to see you again, Will."

"I'd hope." He was holding the door open for her. "How about dinner tonight? I'll leave the beeper in the truck."

"Call me." That was a coward's answer and she knew it. "Vic's coming by and we're going to try to work some things out."

"Tell him I asked first. He can take you to lunch."

He was standing in the door as he held it; she had to brush by, feeling the swell of his chest, and the rough denim of his shoulder. Was that deliberate?

Damn him. Whatever it was, it worked!

Over her head he was saying, "Oh, hi, Mrs. McCartney. Yeah, they're open."

"Good. Since you're here, is Dottie back?"

" 'Fraid not. She's gone for good. Sure do miss her."

"We all do. She always knew just what books I liked."

As this little byplay continued, so did Lucy Maud— to her car. "Since you're here, is Dottie back?" she echoed sarcastically.

No, Mrs. Whateveritwas. She's not—but there's always a replacement! Does he figure it's me? We'll see about that.

The laundromat was open, but she was so bemused she punched the hot water button before the short little woman at the next machine asked, "Are you sure you want hot water?"

"Oh! Oh, no! Thank you," Lucy Maud breathed fervently. What she wanted was a keeper! "I would have had a mess."

"You're right. When that water says 'hot' it's hot! You new in town?"

"I'm Martha Hauser's niece."

"Such a nice lady. Sure miss her at the water department." But for once, miracle of miracles, she didn't add anything about Frank! "Care for a sody? I just got my daughter's kids off to school and I need a break."

"I just had coffee. Thank you."

The woman inserted fifty cents and the machine clanked out a can of cola. She turned back, popping the top and glancing out the window. "There goes Doc Evans. Nice man. I bet he sure misses Dottie. They went together two, three years. He told my husband it kept the vultures off. Listen—you got something else to do, run along. I'll be here. Nobody'll take your stuff."

"Why—thank you. I do need to run to the bank."

"Go, then. Bring me back a hundred or so."

She was smiling, showing yellowed teeth, and reaching into her big bag for a paperback. "I'll just let Louis L'Amour keep me company."

"Good choice," said Lucy Maud as she went out to her car, slid onto the cold seat, and sat a moment, absorbing the latest piece of information about Dottie. So. It "kept the vultures off"?

I am not a vulture, she averred in silent conviction as she backed out, then drove two blocks to the bank.

The yellow Cadillac was nowhere to be seen. Thank God. She needed to establish her credit, but she didn't need Howard's assistance. Of course, after last night, even his assistance might be dubious. And this was the only bank in town.

"Problems, problems," she muttered, swung out her feet, and went inside.

The business she had to conduct took fifteen minutes—thanks to a FAX and a young teller who'd never heard of Verna Marshall and made no connection with Martha Hauser.

She returned to the laundromat, reflecting wryly on what a few dollars cash in one's pocket does to a sense of security.

The short little woman said, "Hi." She had also put Lucy Maud's laundry in the dryer. "No problem," she went on cheerfully. "Gail Hodges was in here with her two young'uns and it was like tryin' to read in an earthquake."

It was not the time to say she had a dryer at home.

Lucy sat down, murmuring, "Well, thank you. How much?"

"Fifty cents. Tell you what. You watch my stuff while I run over to the library. Since Dottie's gone there's no one to deliver books out to the people stuck at home and my mom is about ready to chew on the furniture. I'll check out a couple for her."

Lucy glanced at her watch. Vic had said afternoon-ish. It was only eleven-thirty. "Sure. Run along."

Glad that Gail Hodges and her kids had disappeared, Lucy Maud sat down in a folding chair by the front window to enjoy the sun and the quiet. She strongly suspected she'd better enjoy herself while she could.

She was right.

A van labeled "Pike County Senior Citizens" pulled to the curb, disgorging three elderly women, one elderly man, six plastic garbage bags seemingly filled with laundry, and a van driver who thrust two more bags inside the door.

"All right, listen, you guys!" he said in a voice cranked up to a volume obviously designed to penetrate failing ears. "I'll be back at twelve-thirty. Okay? Twelve-thirty. And the Center said they'd hold your lunches." He sent a sideways grin at Lucy Maud. "The housing project machines all quit at once this morning. Of course, it had nothing to do with certain ladies overloading with quilts and stuff. Right?"

"Damn. 'Mrs. Neatlies'!" the older man grumbled, chucking socks and shorts into the machine nearest Lucy Maud.

"Now, now, Everett!" one of the ladies chirped, dumping housedresses, dresser scarves, and a chair slipcover helter-skelter into the next washer. "Who was it last month tried to wash two pots and a skillet with his bedsheets? Run on, Herb; we'll be ready when you come back." There," she finished, clapping the lid down with a clatter. "I'm walking over to the library. I see Karen's car."

"You see Doc's pick-up—that's what you see," another lady laughed, and closed the lid on her machine also. "Sure, I'll go."

The remaining women indicated their willingness, also, and they all left, their cheerful chatter dwindling into silence as they crossed the street. The man looked at Lucy Maud and shrugged, sitting down in the chair beside her. His lined face was rueful, the mouth beneath the untidy white moustache only half-smiling.

"Don't fault 'em, ma'am," he said. "They're nice gals. Really. And Doc knows it. He'll joke with 'em, make 'em feel special. Me—I can't do that, yet. I'm too close to having lost my wife. Oh—Mason Willard."

"Lucy Marshall." She shook the old hand, smiling pleasantly and wishing the damned dryer would hurry.

"Sure. Martha's niece. Going to put the place, on the market, are you? Vic called m'boy this morning, wanted some prices on eaves-troughing. I'd sell, t'was me. Seein' as how you're a city lady."

Wondering incredulously if he also had heard the asking price, Lucy nodded, made an ambiguous answer, and saw—with relief—her dryer fall silent. Not really wanting to sort out nightgowns and undies under this old gentleman's eye, she bundled it all back into the plastic bag. "There. Thank goodness that's done. Nice to have met you, Mr. Willard. Would you watch that dryer until the lady comes back?" There was some virtue in a small town, she mused.

"My pleasure, ma'am. Tell Vic 'Howdy'."

"I'll do that."

As she chucked the laundry into the back seat, she noted Will in his truck, just pulling away from the library building. He waved. She waved. The four women standing in the library doorway waved.

Was his departure a retreat?

If it was she, it would be, she acknowledged, starting her car.

The fat spaniel was dozing in the street again. She drove around it, nosed against the curb at the grocery store, and entered. This time the door opened automatically but the wrong way, almost bopping her nose. Tom Burkiser was checking out a young woman with two small children lolloping suckers.

" 'Mornin'," he said cheerily. "Need some help?"

"Coffee."

"Second aisle with the tea and baking stuff. Teddy, dammit, give me that!"

One small boy who had just poked his brother in the eye with a denuded sucker stick surrendered it reluctantly. As she went around the corner, Lucy Maud heard the ensuing battle cries and lingered at the coffee rack until it subsided. Juvenile mayhem was something she had surrendered to Pam's jurisdiction years ago.

As Tom scanned her coffee, he said, "Going to sell Martha's place, I hear."

Her first impulse was to laugh. Her next was to have a sign printed saying "Yes, I am selling Martha's place!"

Her third was a bit more civilized—and compassionate. People in this town had obviously loved Martha.

"Yes. I probably am."

"Hope it gets a fine price for you. Oh—tell Vic to remember: there's a sealed-over well in the backyard there, with damned good running water. It used to be full when the rest of the town went dry. There you go, Lucy. Reckon you can manage a carton of coffee?"

"I reckon."

"Nice car." He was following her to the door. "Ford?"

"Yes."

"Good mileage?"

"Not too bad."

"I remember, Martha sold Frank's. She never did learn to drive. Take care, lady."

"You, too."

I should start lists, she thought grimly, heading toward Martha's house, on what I'm learning. About myself. About Aunt Martha. About Will Evans. And Vic. And Eileen. And Karen Marsh—and the ladies from the retirement home.

I wish they'd let up! I've only been here since Saturday night!

And there are a lot of things I don't *want* to know. Things that could complicate my life, which is the last thing I need.

All I want to do is get some money, get out of here, and get a job! That's all! That's it!

Attention, Crewsville! Will you please get off my back?

As she rounded the corner, she saw some sort of utilities truck pulling out of her drive. It had been parked next to Vic Bonnelli's Toyota, and the block of a man, himself, was standing on the lawn beneath the naked sycamore trees, talking to Jessie Murphy. As Lucy pulled her car alongside, Jessie waved, saying, "Got to go check my oven," and went back up her front steps. Vic waited for Lucy Maud, his graying curls ruffling in the light wind, his tie loosened comfortably. As she got out, he grinned that broad, good-natured Slavic grin.

"Hi, lady. I got around a little earlier. What's for lunch?"

Men! Their very hearts were attached to their stomachs!

"Pizza?"

"Or I'll take you to Bunny Burger."

"Let's eat the pizza."

"Fine with me."

He turned, reached a tree bole of a fist inside his car and ruffled a pair of tan satin ears. "Stay, Baron. I'll be back."

The big Lab took the petting with insouciance, then collapsed on the front seat, his nose on his paws. Vic followed Lucy Maud up the steps. He said, "I got an estimate on your two porches and the window frames."

"How much?" She was unlocking the door.

"You won't like it."

She didn't.

He followed her inside, saying, "Hi, Cutie-pie," ruffling a second set of ears. "It's really not too bad, Lucy. And we can probably cover it with the purchase price. Since the fall flooding, houses are bringing more than their worth—but who are we to complain?"

He took off his jacket, folding it over a kitchen chair

back as she got out the pizza and stripped off the cellophane. "Microwave?"

"I don't even know if the oven works."

"It does. John checked it—the guy in the truck. But that's fine. Got any extra cheese?"

"Sorry."

"Oh, well. Shall I make coffee?"

"There's the new box."

"Right." He put two cups of water in the microwave, and tapped three minutes with a thick finger. "Somehow I suspect we cook alike. Saw your car at the library. Who's running the place—Karen?"

"Yes."

"She's a sweetie. Her dad and Doc and I won the Korean War together." He was pulling out a kitchen chair, testing it before he sat. "Bob stayed in, retired a few years ago when his wife got Alzheimer's. She's dead now, poor gal. Okay. Sit a minute and let's go over these estimates."

It was not Lucy Maud's favorite thing, and she was left feeling more of the world had changed than she'd realized, cosseted in her little library cocoon.

She shrugged and stood up to extract the pizza. "If that's the way it is."

"I'm afraid so. Now you can get by without a new roof. That's a plus item. But these windows are bad news, we have to do the porches, and the whole thing needs paint. Shall we go for it?"

"Is there a choice?"

"You can ask another realtor."

"You'll do."

Was it because she simply didn't wish to bother, or was it that she trusted this man?

Well—why shouldn't she? Everyone else seemed to trust him.

What a long way from Millard, she thought wryly, reaching behind her in a drawer for a knife.

Sitting there across from her he looked like a Sumo wrestler in a tailored shirt. Of course, she'd never seen a Sumo in a shirt. They'd always seemed very naked, floppy fat, and poised to jump. She handed him an enormous slab of pizza on a paper towel and said, "Have at it."

"Mmph. Good."

It was. She wiped a string of cheese from her chin and asked, "What do we do now—start repairs?"

"If I have the go-ahead."

"You have. May I live here while they're doing them?"

"I don't know why not."

"Good. I wasn't looking forward to sleeping in my car."

"No friends?"

"Not anymore. It's been thirty years."

"Okay. I'll have our gal at the office type up a contract. With all these figures, and so on. If it still seems all right, then we're in business. Where will you be tomorrow?"

"Probably right here."

She didn't intend to sound grim, but apparently she did, because he suddenly glanced at her sharply. "Not your idea of a vacation?"

"Something like that." She made herself smile. "Finish the pizza. I'm full."

Cutie had her head on his knee and was obviously waiting. He pinched off a small piece and fed it to her, grinning over at Lucy Maud. "Don't tell Doc. Hey—I meant to tell *you*. I'm glad you two are hitting it off. He's been sort of at loose ends since Dottie left."

She banged her coffee cup down so hard the coffee slopped.

He glanced over at her, startled. "Hey—did I say something wrong?"

She gritted her teeth. "Who the living hell is Dottie? That's all I've heard for two days! Dottie this, and Dottie that! She wasn't his wife?"

"No. Regardless of what he says, Doc really loved his wife. It took twenty years to get over her—and sometimes I'm not sure he has even yet."

"Then who is—or was—this Dottie?"

"I think," Vic said, grinning, standing up, wiping his massive chin, and reaching for his coat, "that you'd better ask Doc about Dottie. If it becomes important enough. After all, I don't want to ruin the man's pitch. We bachelors," he added, heading for the door, "have to stick together."

"You bachelors," said Lucy Maud, shaking her head and smiling back at him, "do."

But after he was gone she still sat there, twiddling the coffee bag in a refilled cup and feeling a bit of an idiot. She hadn't popped off so irately to anyone since those two junior high kids had run off a hundred copies of a candy bar wrapper in the copy machine. With candy bar intact. By the end of a hundred copies, it was melted.

Finally she sighed, got up, and went into the bathroom to see if she'd brought the little vial of estrogen with the rest of her medication.

She seemed to need it.

Fourteen

The estrogen wasn't there.

She said a brief word closely associated with the daily habits of various agricultural denizens and returned to the kitchen. What she needed now were some lists to bring reality back into her life. Some organization. A framework for a daily routine to keep her sane in the suburbs of never-never land.

One of the old wooden chairs sagged alarmingly as she sat in it. She discovered the side spindles pulled from the front legs. Men! Dammit! Why did they have to tilt backward and put their feet up?

Shoving the invalid to the other side, she sat down in another one, scrabbling in the shoulder bag she'd slung from a cabinet knob. The pad she usually used to note down library engagements would do just fine. She certainly wasn't going to need it for the original purpose.

Crumpling up the sheet that said "New Bd mtg Mon nite," she tried to ignore the pang she felt when she realized they were meeting this very evening and certainly without her. Let the MacClane tootsie make the coffee and bring the cookies. At the top of a new page she wrote "Schedule"—then almost laughed.

Schedule, indeed. Stay out of the way of workmen replacing windows and steps, try to do *something* with Aunt Martha's stuff to make the house more appealing, do some telephone job prospecting, and keep her sanity amid all the Docs, Dotties, Howards, and Franks of present-day Crewsville.

She crumpled up that page also.

The one item not on her mental list was the least emotionally demanding: bring in her clean laundry and decide where to put it.

As she stood up, so did Cutie, looking at her questioningly, ears cocked, the left one slightly askew as usual.

She sighed, "Okay," she said. "Come on."

While she pulled the plastic bag from her car, the dog sniffed all four tires, did her thing on the uneven grass, and trotted back up the steps ahead of Lucy Maud. Then she whined and lifted one paw. Lucy Maud saw blood traces on the porch floor and said, "Oh, shoot! The salve."

She dumped the bag of laundry on the sway-backed divan and followed Cutie into the kitchen, digging in her bag on the counter. Cutie had already flumped into her basket. Groaning a little, Lucy Maud flumped down beside her and reached for a paw, mumbling, "This is not really my mission in life, dog."

So what was her mission?

Fortunately that question didn't have to be dealt with promptly because of a tentative knock on the kitchen door.

Even if she was in Crewsville, she still had Millard ways.

"Who is it?"

"Just me, ma'am. John. John Basalti. The utilities guy."

Lucy Maud heaved herself upright, one hand on the table," and glanced out the uncurtained window. Right. The power company truck was back in the drive.

She unlocked the door and opened it. A young, wiry man in a company shirt, with curly dark hair in a tail down his back beneath a St. Louis Cardinals ballcap, grinned at her cheerfully through the battered screen.

"I guess I missed Vic."

"He just left."

"That's okay. I'll ask you. The power pole's down in the backyard where Frank used to have his Cub Scout meetings. A storm took it. Martha, she never had it replaced, but if you're fixin' to sell, it sure would add to the value."

"Oh." Lucy Maud hadn't even really known there was a backyard, let alone what was in it. "I—I don't know. I'll think it over."

"Sure. Just give us a call."

He was almost off the porch when she remembered the fuses. "Young man! Mr. uh—Basalti!"

He turned. "John," he said.

She explained about the fuse problem. He followed her back inside, saying, "Leave me just take a look. Hi, ol' Cutie. Glad you're back."

Appreciative of the ear fluffle, Cutie trailed him to the kitchen corner where, without being told, he stood on a kitchen chair and opened the cupboard door.

Amazed, Lucy Maud asked, "How did you know it was up there?"

His voice was muffled as he peered. "Whole block's like this. Except Miz Murphy's, and we rewired her place just a year ago. Couple 'coons chewed a hole in from the chimney and accidentally fried themselves in the bargain. Oh, yeah. Oh, yeah. I see your problem, ma'am. A new breaker'll take care of it. You goin' to be home this afternoon, I'll come back and fix the sucker." He climbed down again, grinning. "Martha, she never had a microwave. Well—hi, Dillie!" he called to the screendoor meshed image of a young woman standing on the kitchen porch.

The girl said, breathlessly, "Oh, Johnny, it is you! Thank goodness. Will you run me to work? My car shot craps down the street in front of Willard's, and if I'm late again Daddy will have a cow!"

"Sure, no problem."

John was wiping his hands on a swatch of paper towel and opening the screen. "Miss Marshall, Dilanna Lewis. The banker's daughter. Be impressed at the company I keep. The banker isn't."

"Hi," said Dilanna Lewis to Lucy Maud, and made a wry face at John Basalti. "Hurry, Johnny. I just can't be too late!"

"What'll he do, fire you?"

The door banged, and Lucy Maud watched them get up in the utilities truck. That's Howard's daughter? The girl was chunky, her hair too frizzed and her very *avant* suit exactly wrong for anyone but a slender, long-waisted person. Then she caught a brief but explicit glimpse of them in the truck cab locked in a passionate embrace. "Well!" she murmured and closed the door.

So far, Crewsville had certainly held some surprises.

Who had the girl looked like? A brief glimpse had hardly been enough, but Lucy Maud suspected the chunkiness and the clothes from Mother and the genuine sound of panic from an overdose of Father.

Fortunately, it wasn't her affair.

The bottom line was that John said he'd be back to fix the fuse box.

Perhaps this was a good time to inspect the backyard.

She went down the three rickety steps, Cutie at her heels, and realized that "yard" was a proper word and "lawn" denoted lush, well-tended verdure of which that long, narrow, crabgrass-clumped stretch to the rutted alley had very little. A dejected shack ornamented one side, halfway down. Curious, she opened the door and discovered a rusted-out barbecue grill, a sprawled stack of ancient kindling wood, and two ancient bicycles, their tires mouse-chewed.

Bicycles! Aunt Martha and Frank Whoever—as one was a girl's and one a boy's.

Musing on this, she shut the creaking door again as she waved at Jessie Murphy, who was hanging out towels on a long line beyond the ragged privet hedge. Lucy Maud wandered back to the house, noting the leaning power pole, its shattered lamp pieces gathered on the top of a weathered picnic table. Well. She'd ask Vic about the power pole.

In the meantime she'd best put the laundry away and tackle that bed. The divan in the living room did lack a little comfort, although she *had* slept amazingly well.

This line of thought was interrupted by another knock at the door and an accompanying "Hoo-hoo!"

This time it was Jessie.

"I ain't got but a minute," she said as Lucy Maud opened the ratty screen door again. "But I saw you in the back and thought I'd better warn you—that there round depression in the sod by the mower shed—stay off'n it. Underneath is a pretty deep well; I know they capped it years ago but you can't tell me those timbers ain't all rotted. I wouldn't want to come home and find you floatin'."

"Oh. Thanks." Looking over Jessie's shoulder, Lucy Maud could see the vague circular shape in the scraggly weeds.

"Sure. Got to run—school's just a half-day today, and Tina'll be here 'fore I know it."

She waved, and trotted back through the gap in the untended and shapeless line of privet.

"Well," muttered Lucy Maud, shutting the door again, "now the laundry!"

This time she got as far as the bedroom.

The phone rang.

It startled her. Number one, she'd forgotten it had been reconnected; and two, she was a bit leery of who might be calling *her*.

"Hello." Hardly the brisk, "Millard Library, Lucy Marshall speaking" of yesteryear—but perhaps she *was* learning to cut her losses.

The voice on the other end was equally tentative: "Lucy?"

Pam! Pam, the children's librarian. In a rush of relief, Lucy said, "Hi, hon, how's it going?"

Did she detect a giggle? Pam replied, "I'm fine. I may be the only one around here who is, but nonetheless I am fine. How are you?"

Having acquired, in the last few days, a taste for sweet revenge, Lucy ignored the last question and went straight to it. "Tell me about the—the others."

Now it *was* a giggle. "You saw the telecast?"

"Yes. Yes, I did. Is Fred's grandson in trouble?"

"Let's say he's not too popular around this establishment, but no—he isn't. If he were, there'd have to be blame cast on about three hundred other kids and that might be a bit difficult. Especially since one of them would be the senator's daughter, who doesn't like Her Nibs anyway and thought the idea was super."

"How's *she* handling it?"

More giggles "She didn't notice until Monday morning when a patron came in for an American history volume and found three books on gourmet cooking and nine on insectology in the 900 section. Then it hit the fan."

"What's she doing?"

"That's the fun part. She can't do much. Publicly, I mean. After all, she did say the system was hers, right?"

"That's what I heard."

"So did we. Mona about swallowed her upper plate. But I told her to just sit tight, which is what we did— and her ladyship's in a real bind. She can't squawk. At least publicly. We're having to replace Mona and no one will hire on at the money she made. So there's no help to do the reshelving—at least, not on staff. I guess she's bringing two or three people down from

Springfield to work nights, and paying for it herself. Isn't that just a shame? Oh—she's calling it 'reorganization.' Trying to cover her butt, of course. Me, I'm just staying in my department with my kids and trying not to laugh too loud. We do miss you, Lucy. It was going to be so great until that asshole came to town."

"Thank you, hon. I'm still sort of—floating, I guess."

"Are you okay?"

"Oh—sure. My aunt's house needs some work before I sell—and that's legitimate."

"But you're not coming back here?"

"Not if I can help it. Particularly now. The mess must be horrendous."

"Only if you don't like finding Erma Bombeck in the Civil War section."

"She's not taking it out on the children?"

"How can she? Then the next question would be 'Why did they do such a thing?'—with the answer, 'Because they didn't like Lucy Maud getting screwed.' There's too many ramifications. No, no, she's just got to swallow it."

"But you're not taking any flack?"

"Not yet. I think I know too much, and she's aware of the fact. Oops—the other line. Got to go. Keep in touch."

"You, also."

"Will do. Bye-bye."

Lucy Maud hung up and turned to look down at Cutie, sitting erectly at her feet, ears perked, waiting for the next move.

"Well!" she said, ignoring the amazing fact that she

was once again talking to a dog, "that was quite a conversation."

It had told her one thing: regardless of Fred and the library board, returning to Millard—even as assistant librarian—would not be a good idea. It might be, in fact, comparable to jumping off the Empire State Building wearing water wings.

So swallow it, Lucy Maud: you have to have a job somewhere else.

Like where, she wondered morosely, dumping the plastic bags of laundry on the bedroom mattress. Selling this house would augment the $200 a month from her mother's property for a while. But "a while" was not forever.

It was two-thirty. Middle of the afternoon.

Leaving the laundry, she fished her address book from her bag, pulled a chair up to the telephone, and got on it.

By three-thirty she figured she'd run up a long distance bill large enough to choke the classic horse. She also realized that if she heard the phrase, "We'll keep you in mind," one more time she'd throw up on the new mouse turds littering the floor from their nocturnal romping last night. She finally realized that some time ago Cutie had wandered back into the kitchen, appropriated Jessie's relatively empty chicken-and-noodle bowl from the sink, and was lying on the rug before the television, licking out the last vestiges.

Life did go on, whether one was employed or not.

And when her dish was empty, the dog adapted to something else. Perhaps there was a message in that.

But what, for cryin' out loud?

"Oh, you are an idiot!" she said to herself through clenched teeth and took the bowl from the dog, who surrendered it insouciantly, since she was done licking, anyway. "This is all your own damned fault! For being a—a mole! Never looking out at the real world! Well, lady, look now! Take a good look!"

When the telephone rang again she almost bit off the mouthpiece: "Hello!"

"Ooops," said a cheerful, masculine voice. "Shall I hang up and try again?"

Will Evans. The last person she needed, she thought, although she was very fuzzy about why. She calmed her voice and answered, "Sorry. Not a good day."

"Then let's make it better. Karen and my son are going to eat with us. I'll pick you up about six."

She was near to saying "No!" then reconsidered that, also. So what if Karen and whoever were merely protecting Dottie's interests by their presence. Or checking her out to see who the hell their father had picked up this time. A free meal was a free meal.

"Fine," she replied in a civilized voice, "I'll be ready."

For what, she added silently, hanging up. The apocalypse? Personally, she thought she was probably already experiencing it.

Almost blindly, she went into the dismal bedroom, yanked open a middle drawer in the tatty veneer chest, and scooped up a pile of underwear from the bed. Then she stopped. Even in her present vile mood the torn paper liner was too much to let pass. Sighing, she dropped the pile on the bed again, went to the kitchen, tore off a few sheets of paper towel, and returned. The old liner ripped out in a moment, but there was a curious lump in one corner, half beneath the tatters. Her searching fingers found something smallish, square, and flat. For heaven's sake. A little picture album.

Putting the frail old piece on the chest top, she flipped it open. The pictures were black and white, crisp with age, and all of a very small child.

Lucy Maud Marshall.

Tears filled Lucy's eyes, and she felt all anger, all resentment seep away. She sat down on the lumpy mattress and thumbed through it, thinking regretfully of Aunt Martha. Dear, sweet, Aunt Martha . . .

The photos were all carefully annotated: Lucy, three months; Lucy, a year; Lucy, two years—with her beloved teddy bear; Lucy, three years. They stopped when she was ten. When her mother and Martha had parted company.

Yet the album was worn, bent—as though Martha had carried it with her constantly.

"Oh, dear," Lucy Maud said out loud with a terrible sense of guilt, of not having understood, of not even caring. How awful to find someone had loved her so dearly when it was too late to love back!

She remembered Martha with her little box camera, squinting one eye, saying, "Smile, dear." Verna had never taken pictures. In fact, Lucy Maud never recalled even having seen *these*.

With a hand that shook a bit, she laid them on the top of the chest to look at more closely later, and put her underwear in the drawer. She was too bemused to notice that the drawer smelled faintly—not of perfume, but of aftershave.

Fifteen

The rest of the afternoon was spent setting the dozen mousetraps, baiting them with cheese, and putting them in places where, if she was a mouse, she'd incautiously scamper into. At least she used cheese until John Basalti appeared once more.

"Hey—don't waste good cheese. Use peanut butter."

Standing on the same chair, he also installed something he called a circuit breaker, and said he'd give Vic Bonnelli the bill—which was fine with her.

Then, it being five o'clock, he acceded to her snack attack and joined her in polishing off the cauliflower and dip.

Very casually, she asked, "Dilanna Lewis—is she Howard's daughter?"

He had his long legs stretched to the disabled chair, and was absently smoothing Cutie's back. And apparently he found nothing intrusive about the question. "Yeah," he answered. "The oldest. Her sister got married last week. Wow, that was a blow-out! It cost ol' Howard a few bucks—or the Krueshanks—Dillie's grandparents. But she pleased them by marrying a senator's son, or something from downstate. Anyway, he has money—and he'd better; Audrina can spend it faster'n her mom. Dilanna's not like that."

"Oh?" It was a careful, unipurpose sound, but John, wiping the last of the dip with a nub of cauliflower, didn't seem to notice.

"No. Poor kid. She switched her college major to elementary education so she could teach and that wasn't glamorous enough. Then she quit her sorority and her mom had another fit. So they pulled the financial plug, brought her home, and stuck her in the bank."

"Is she happy there?"

"Not really." Then he was looking at the watch on his wiry wrist, standing up, and putting his saucer tidily in the sink. "I'd better get. Thanks a lot, ma'am. You can blow a fuse anytime when you feed me like that. Just holler."

"I appreciate your coming back."

She saw him to the door, looked at her own watch, and realized she'd best get cracking also. Will had said six. It was well past five.

The same rose-colored sweater and the same slacks were going to do it again, although she found herself taking unusual care with the collagen-based anti-wrinkle cream and the soft blue eyeliner. Not for Will Evans, of course! After all, an aging woman without a job had better look her best! Who could know whom she might meet?

Sure, sure, she adjured herself grimly. I'll suddenly engage the eye of some guy at the salad bar, he'll turn out to be the president of the Timbucktu Library

Board, and offer me a job because of the way I cut my lettuce. Dream on, kid . . .

On the other hand, it wasn't necessary to dress like a slob! After all, Karen had really seemed very nice, and wearing her feelings on her sleeve was Lucy Maud's fault, not hers!

She'd just blotted her lipstick when she heard the pick-up truck in the drive, and Will at the door.

"Hi," he said cheerfully and flashed the smile that still dazzled her. "I'm a bit early, but I thought maybe I should have a look-see at Cutie's paws. Hello, old girl. Lie down, and we'll take a glim."

Cutie was delighted at the attention. She stretched out obediently and Will crouched at her side, reaching a long arm up for the salve on the counter.

Watching them, Lucy Maud thought, now is the time to ask about finding another home for her . . .

But for some reason she didn't.

"You're better, sweetie," he was saying to the supine heap of fluff. "Your girl's taking good care of you. I thought she would. We're meeting Tim and Karen at the cafe," he went on, getting back to his feet a little stiffly. "Damn. I've climbed too many fences today; my knees show it. Anyway, this time we won't worry about the beeper. If it goes off Tim can handle it. In fact, he'd probably welcome a chance to skip PTA, anyway. Got a coat? It's cooling down outside."

He was right. As he boosted her up into the cab—again with that impersonal hand on her fanny—she noticed how the wind had turned chill, and the western clouds above the peak of Jessie's house were purple.

"Rain, maybe," Will went on, swinging himself in

on the other side. "But who cares? The beans are in, the corn isn't quite ready, and we don't melt. At least— I don't. Do you? You look nice enough," he added, turning the ignition key and smiling over at her. "To melt in the rain, I mean."

So much for wearing the same pink sweater! Did he even remember?

"Thank you," she answered, and let it go at that.

This time it was a short trip—up what Crewsville called "the main drag," and an expert parallel park job beneath the purple martin birdhouses and between two other pick-ups

"This is Ralph Bleacker's place," Will said, swinging down and coming around to open the door. "He does prime rib on Tuesday and it's mighty fine. Watch the dog doo."

Lucy Maud watched. "Do they know anything about leash laws around here?"

"Oh, Amanda Lewis tried to get one passed couple of years ago. It failed with a boom. I'm not sure whether the reason was that folks just don't want to bother—or because it was Amanda." He was grinning, opening a wide door that—in her childhood—used to admit people to a hardware store. Warmth, the sound of chatter, and the rich smell of gravy caught her nose. "There are my kids—in the back booth."

He led the way, threading through crowded tables, nodding at the numerous "Hi, Doc!"'s, putting off detaining fingers and a query about chicken enteritis with "I'll talk to you later, Bill," and arrived circuitously at a wall booth where Karen had been waving one hand.

"Hi, guys," she said. "I didn't wait. I'm starved. I

don't remember eating lunch today. Gee, I'm glad you could come, Lucy Maud. This is my husband, Tim."

Tim Evans, half standing and extending his hand, was a startling replica of his father—lean, wide-shouldered, and with a similar flashing smile. But blue eyes.

"Hi," he said. "*I* waited for you. Mrs. Smelter fed me at noon after I finished her yearlings and she put enough fried chicken on my plate to choke a horse. Bill Kindle try to nail you, too, Dad?"

"Oh, yeah. I told him to wait. Free advice comes *after* dinner."

Will slid in next to his son. "Have you ordered yet?"

"We have to order? I thought it was set in stone."

"Well, Lucy Maud might have another preference."

"Oh, yeah. An outlander." Tim smiled across at her, but Lucy Maud had the distinct impression Karen had stepped on her husband's boot beneath the table. So. The shadowy but ever-present Dottie had probably been part of that "set in stone" bit.

She would be nice about it.

"Whatever you all order," she said sweetly. "I shared a pizza with Vic at noon, and it does seem rather a long time ago."

No eyebrows at the name "Vic." Just comprehension.

Tim grinned. "I'll bet you're hungry, then," he said. "I've seen ol' Vic eat pizza."

Will had turned to signal a young, aproned waitress with a pencil behind her ear. "And Lucy's not an outlander," he said, settling back again. "Her folks lived here before we ever came. None left now, though. At least—I don't think so."

He was looking at Lucy. She shook her head.

"None that I know about. Aunt Martha was the last."

"That's right. Frank died before her."

The waitress was unloading two more coffee cups from a tray, turning them right side up and pouring coffee.

"I'll tell you, we miss 'em both," she said, smiling down at Lucy Maud. "When my mom's hot water heater goes out she has to get a guy clear from Penfield now. What'll it be—the usual?"

Lucy Maud acceded to custom. "That will be fine."

"Good girl," Will said—probably in the same tone he'd used on Cutie. "Heavy on the gravy. And I assume there's apple pie."

"Is the Pope Catholic?" the waitress replied, and hurried off, replenishing coffee cups as she wended her way.

"So," said Will to his son, stirring two packets of sugar into his own cup. "Busy this afternoon?"

"Oh—you know—routine, mostly. We need to do Bent Bonford's hogs tomorrow. Put that on your list."

"Up the hill at the Crane place?"

"Yeah."

"Bent and Ellie getting married yet?"

"I don't think so. Why hurry? What is Ellie—sixty? She's sure not going to get pregnant."

"Timothy! Where are your manners?" said his wife, but she was smiling. "Lucy, how did the rest of *your* day go?"

This was not the time for truth.

"Fine," said Lucy Maud blandly. "My telephone

works—" she said with what she hoped was a brilliant smile to Will, "—and a very nice young man fixed my fuses so they won't blow every time I plug something in."

"Oh—Johnny? He's a sweetheart," Karen said. "He came here about ten years ago with his mom. She was the Lewis cook before she died."

"Speaking of the devil," said her father-in-law *sotto voce*.

"What?"

"Lewis. Here comes Amanda and Howard and—yeah, Dilly, too, with that wuss CPA from Springfield they're trying to unload her on."

"Dad!" Karen moaned, turning to Lucy Maud and shrugging wryly. "The Evans men!" she said. "They're hopeless. No finer feelings at all."

Lucy Maud had already caught sight of Howard, trailing behind as his wife swept down an adjacent aisle between tables, ahead of her rather depressed-looking daughter and an undersized young man with a receding hairline and thick-lensed glasses.

"We do have finer feelings," said Will, grinning at Lucy Maud. "We just call a spade a spade. Good! Here it comes!"

"It" was a wheeled cart, bearing four enormous platters of steaming food.

"Enjoy your meal," said the waitress cheerfully, sliding them one by one beneath their collective noses. "Holler if you need something."

Lucy Maud couldn't imagine what it would be. The ribs were pink and juicy, the gravy rich and brown, the potatoes fluffy and the stack of green beans high enough to hollow out and sleep in.

The Lewis entourage had passed out of sight, apparently without Howard noticing her. Of course, Lucy Maud hoped, he'd gotten his facts straight the other evening when Cutie'd taken a bite out of his ankle. If he hadn't been too drunk to remember . . .

I'm not worrying about it, she told herself grimly. That asshole is certainly nothing to me.

But—an irritant. Definitely an irritant. Yet, temporary. She must hold that thought: temporary. Until she was able to kiss Crewsville good-bye and start a new life.

Somewhere.

"Poor Dilly," Karen was murmuring, munching a hot roll and licking butter happily from a forefinger. "I do wish Amanda would concede she is *not* Audrina and stop putting her in those fluffy ruffles! In jeans and a tailored shirt, Dilly's a different girl! Try the steak sauce, Lucy Maud. Ralph makes it himself and it's super. Hey, I must tell you how I did appreciate your pitching in at the library this morning. We're so short of help—and you know better than anyone—running a library is a bit more than sitting and checking books in and out."

"Yes," Lucy Maud agreed, laughing. "I do know. How much of a circulation do you have?" After all, if the Evans men on their side of the table could talk cows, she and Karen could certainly talk books. And also—books were safe. She knew about books.

But apparently not much else, she added to herself

in brutal self-flagellation. You've been a bit short on perceiving things in people, kiddo . . .

"I'm not really sure," Karen was answering, cutting a rib. "It's a mess. There's just no one really in charge. I come up from Penfield when I can in the mornings. But with Dottie gone and Mabel out for at least another three weeks, it's a very iffy situation, particularly the program Dottie started—taking books out to the seniors. It's had to be trashed—at least for now—and that's a real shame. A lot of our elders really looked forward to having something to read."

Lucy Maud remembered something about the young farmer in the other cafe saying that his father received books at home—and how it kept him off his back. Now the speech clicked. She said in amazement, "You did that here? A little place like this?"

"We have an aging population. Like it or not, that's a fact. And we were managing pretty well until—you know. Things seem to cave in on us. Don't you do that in Millard?"

"We have a bookmobile through the state library system."

"Wow. Super. We just lug bags. Oh—I almost forgot. Congratulations on your new library down there. Gosh, it must be nice."

Watching sharply for clues, Lucy Maud realized Karen had no guile in her voice, no knowledge of her problems.

She gave a generic answer again: "It's a beautiful facility—really an asset to the city."

"I'll bet it is. In Penfield we're short on space, short on staff, and the head librarian says our computer knew

President Carter personally. Other than that, Crewsville makes us look like the Pentagon. I expect you'll be happy to get back on the job."

To lie or not to lie? Another generic answer: "It is rather like being a fish out of water."

"You're welcome to come 'swim' at our place here anytime. The key is usually in the mailbox."

Why didn't that surprise her? Lucy Maud laughed and said, "I might."

"Okay. If the key's not there, ask Tom at the grocery store. He's got one in his cash register. What, Dad?"

"I said," answered Will in mock severity, "that if you two were done talking shop—"

"*We* were talking shop!"

"Whatever. I was going to ask Lucy Maud if she'd like to accompany me to a movie."

"Dad, get real. The only moviehouse for miles is showing a Ninja Turtle thing. I know. Rob is staying with Boo because of the PTA meeting and Boo's grandma is taking them. It would be more fun going to your house and watching the VCR of last year's cattle show."

"Besides," Lucy Maud said hurriedly, "I do have to get back to Aunt Martha's. I—I have some calls coming in."

Damn. Now she was stooping to lies! But Will was replying in an easy voice, "Fine. My TV's on the fritz. Let's take our desserts with us, and if I'm a good boy perhaps you'll let me watch the old 'Star Trek' on Channel 10."

Tim said, "Great! Let me come, too!" and his wife was saying over him, "*You* are going to PTA!"

"Oh—fiddle," said Tim, grinning and crumpling up a gravy-stained paper napkin. "Grown-ups never have any fun. At least not until they retire—like the old man, here. No, no, Dad, you get the tips. I'll pay the tab."

"Well! If I'd known you were going to do that, I'd have insisted on eating at Romano's!"

"Next time."

They obviously had a good relationship. But Lucy Maud, standing with Karen as the two men settled up at the desk, was a bit bemused at the remaining evening schedule. How did she get herself out of this one? Did she even want to get herself out?

Karen must have sensed her uncertainty. Quietly she said, "Tim and I really appreciate this, Lucy. You, I mean. Dad's been—a little lonely."

Since Dottie left?

But the young woman didn't say that. She went on in the same quiet voice, "When he's by himself too much, he—he starts thinking about Reba. Tim's mom. Then he tends to—to drink a little. And he's not supposed to—not with his ulcers. And you two do seem to have hit it off."

For the first piece of information about the ex-wife, Lucy Maud was tempted to express her thanks. But she didn't. Sometimes it was hell being nice.

All she did was nod. At least "nursemaid" was different from "bibliophile." She was broadening her experience.

And surely she was bright enough to find a graceful way to send the man home—when she wanted him to go.

Tim and Karen said their good nights and left. Will,

finding his arm engaged by Bill Kindle, raised his eyebrows at Lucy Maud expressively and said, "I'll be just a minute."

After five minutes of "enteritis" and "going down in their legs," Lucy Maud went down on hers, finding a padded bench by the entryway. From there she had a good view of the rest of the dining area; a few tables were vacant now, and the street lamps shone in through undrawn red drapes on the remaining diners, relaxed and sipping coffee. A mirrored wall cornered the windows; she suddenly saw the Lewis party in another dining area, Howard and the young man eating and talking animatedly, Mrs. Lewis fingering her fussy, too-blond hair and gesturing covertly at Dilanna who was staring sullenly straight ahead. Not a totally happy group.

Not, also, Lucy Maud Marshall's affair.

There were still some positives in her world and that was one of them, indeed.

What if she had married Howard?

Would that have been her daughter sitting there so unhappily in a too-frilly gown that emphasized her chubbiness and staring from under frizzy, uncut hair?

"Sorry," she heard Will say as he smiled down at her ruefully. He added as she rose, "I ought to send the sucker a damned bill."

But it wasn't until she was in his pick-up and heading to Aunt Martha's house that panic struck.

It was only eight o'clock!

Please, dear God. Don't let the TV go poof!

Sixteen

Between them on the seat was a square plastic box that Will had deposited tenderly before he started the engine.

"Dessert," he said, grinning sideways as he pulled into the street. "Now don't tell me you don't need it—I don't either. But with the kind of half-ass cooking I do at my place, Ralph's pie is a real treat. Jeez Louise. Look at that Caddy! That color is almost as bad as the pink ones you see!"

"That Caddy" was, of course, Howard's, shining a brilliant yellow-gold beneath a street lamp.

"Maybe his wife picked it out." She didn't think so, but hers was not to say.

"I doubt it." Will's voice was dry. "He does a lot of so-called good deeds with that Cadillac, and I suspect he wants people knowing he's doing them."

"Like what?"

They'd turned off into Martha's street, and people idling in shadowy porch swings waved as they passed. Will tooted his horn lightly. "No secrets in Crewsville," he said. "Everybody knows this truck, too. Oh—Howard. He specializes in lonely old ladies. Particularly those with money. Takes them to the store, to eat, to shop—that sort of thing. It sounds real generous until you realize he'd do a lot more good going down into the subsidized housing and giving those folks a ride. Look at that!"

"That" was Cutie's nose pressed against the living room window between the tatty lace curtains.

Lucy Maud said in amazement, "She knows your truck, too?"

"Probably. Couple buddies and I used to play a lot of gin rummy with Frank."

As he swung out, going around to open her door, she noticed the bright lights streaming from Jessie's upstairs and a definite flash of lightning over the peak of her house.

Out of the warm truck, the cool night air made her shiver. It was going to rain; she'd bet on it. What windows were up?

Will corroborated her thoughts. "Rain," he said. "For sure. Your car okay?"

She nodded and fished for her key. As it turned, Cutie's nose disappeared and she met them in the open door. Will stepped aside to let her out.

"Honestly!" said Lucy Maud, watching the furry fanny bounce down the steps. "It's every fifteen minutes! Has she a kidney problem or something?"

He shrugged, hunching his shoulders against the wind. "No, no. She's just putting you on, hon. When Martha was working Cutie'd be in the house six, seven hours at a stretch. Some way I get the impression you've not been around too many dogs."

"My mother—" Then she stopped. "No," she substituted. "I never had—time for one." Will Evans didn't need to hear Verna Marshall's daughter whining.

"One thing about a dog," he answered, letting Cutie back inside, then shutting the door firmly, "is that when everyone else thinks you're shit, your dog still loves you. Pardon my language. Shall we have our pie now, or wait until after "Star Trek"? Hey—I was serious, lady. My TV is out. And your company seemed much more desirable than going down to the Legion hall."

Perhaps if he'd quit smiling she could think straight!

"Let's wait," she said. "Turn on the set. I'll take the pie to the kitchen."

When she returned—after fluffing her hair and repairing her lipstick in the mirror over the sink—he was comfortably ensconced on the couch, Cutie stretched beside him, and from the television the lilting strains of a Lawrence Welk ensemble filled the air.

"Good!" he said to her.

She hadn't done a thing. "Good, what?"

"You didn't shudder. Or scream."

"At what?" He certainly hadn't made a pass. Or waved a gun. Or anything.

"At Lawrence Welk. Tim just rolls his eyes up, but Karen leaves the room. It's a generation gap, I think."

"I like Lawrence Welk."

"Good Lord. Another mutual thing. Like liking ribs. And dogs."

The dog thing was damned iffy, but she didn't say so. She ignored Cutie's blatantly complacent look, and sat down in the chair. There was certainly no diplomatic problem about whether or not to sit on the couch with Will. There wasn't room.

He was saying, "This place sure looks different. You've been working your tail off."

"Thank you."

"Want to come do mine?"

"No, thank you."

"Shucks. Thought I had chance, there. My thing is not dusting doilies. Nor coordinating curtains and hot-pads."

"Mine, either," said Lucy Maud dryly.

"See? Another thing in common. Tim's mom got upset if I wore a red jacket with blue pants. Or if my socks didn't match. Oops. Ancient history. Sorry."

But he didn't seem sorry. Did this man just have an insidious way of letting her know things—about his food preferences? His recreations? His ex-wife?

Then he'd bear watching. The insidiousness might also extend beyond giving information to getting information. And she really didn't think she was ready yet to give anything to a guy she'd only known a few days—even if he did have a dazzling smile. Beyond keeping house, for heaven's sake, or—or matching up her daily costume, *her* thing had to be much more mundane: buying food and finding a job and paying or an Oriental carpet!

He'd stopped smoothing Cutie's ears. She reached out a silky paw, and touched his hand significantly. He said, "Oh—sorry, kid!" and started again, shifting his long legs to make her more comfortable.

Then Lucy Maud saw what he meant about socks. He wore one black and one blue.

He was smiling at her face. "Somewhere at home," he said, "I have another pair that match these."

She laughed. She had to laugh. She'd never met a man quite like him. The few men in her sphere had been three-piece suiters, state officials, or book hawkers—all wanting her business, her approval, or her signature. Will Evans was something she only vaguely remembered as a little girl, waiting for her mother to get off work at the grocery store on Saturday night and watching the local farmers lug out the next week's supply of food. Carry-boys had been unknown in those ancient days, of course.

The Welk orchestra was finishing a medley of show tunes. Will said cheerfully, "I'd ask you to dance but it would wake up Cutie."

Lucy Maud's heart popped into her throat. Cutie! Don't wake up. Please!

She didn't know how she'd handle dancing with this man—particularly in this room. Alone. Touching. The very thought made her catch her breath—and she wasn't sure why!

"Oh, that's all right." She tried to sound easy. "I'd probably step on your feet." That's it, she thought harshly. Put yourself down. Just like Verna always did. He was saying, "I doubt it. But some other time. There's the theme song, anyway. Now—umpteen commercials, then my hero."

"Your hero?"

"Mr. Spock. With the pointy ears. I can see you're not a 'Trekkie'."

"No. My mother—" Damn, she was doing it again! "We usually watched some soap. I don't remember which, now."

"You're not a 'soaper'!"

"My mother was." That mention was acceptable. "She lived with me until she died. A few years ago."

"Whew!" he said, and wiped imaginary sweat from his forehead. "I thought we'd just found a dissimilarity! Hey—in lieu of a beer—which is a dissimilarity I can handle—would you have a soda or something? I guess I'm dry."

"Iced tea?"

"Fine. No sugar."

"No sugar!"

"Remember—we Evans boys are outlanders. Where we come from the only thing that goes in iced tea is the thought that makes it."

"Coming up," she said, and went into the kitchen.

Bless microwaves! Even iced tea could be made in a hurry!

Rain began to patter against the south windows as she reached for a tray of ice cubes. She caught a glimpse of herself in the glistening pane—hurrying. For a man!

But—at this point—a nice man, she protested. He hasn't tried a thing. Nor does he seem inclined to try.

Perhaps I've been reading too many romance novels!

Holding that thought, she went back into the living room.

He said, "Thanks. None for you?"

"I'm still floating in coffee."

She sat back down in the old velour chair she'd decided had been Frank's. On the screen some sort of winged spacecraft was zooming about dodging lightning.

Apparently one hit because the TV went blank.

Will said, "Shit! I mean—shoot! And the street lamps are out, too."

"Then why didn't the lights go off in here?"

"Different circuit, I guess. Oh—there we are!"

The TV was back. Lightning crashed, thunder rumbled, and the house lights went. Lucy Maud gasped. She said in a small voice, "I don't like this much," through the sound of rain hitting the house roof in buckets.

She felt two things: Cutie's nose and Will's arm.

Will said, "It's okay, hon."

Then the lights came on again.

Will grinned down at her. "Shit!" he said again. "And this time I mean shit! Here I thought I could take a little advantage of a lady in distress! I have to talk with the damned power company!"

He gave her shoulders a small squeeze and went back to the couch.

Lucy Maud gave a little laugh she didn't mean to be a giggle. "Those are the breaks," she said. "I think I will have iced tea," she added and escaped to the kitchen.

He nodded, his eyes glued on the man with the pointy ears shooting what appeared to be a pump handle.

What in the wailing world was wrong with her? Ten seconds more and she'd have had her arms around him, and been trying to— to cuddle like a homeless kitten! Good Lord! When the shell on a woman's world cracked, everything fell out!

She made a glass of iced tea strong enough to pass for coffee, then dared herself to go back into the living room, to *prove* she could damned well control the situation!

The lights were on, the TV off, and Will Evans was asleep.

His gray head had slid against the sofa pillow, his mouth was a bit agape, and his breathing was deep and rhythmic. As Lucy Maud appeared, Cutie hopped to the floor, shook herself, and ambled over to lean against her legs.

"My turn?" said Lucy Maud. "Forget it, kid."

Some romantic evening! She *had* been reading too many damned novels!

Rationale said the man was tired. With the demands on his time, God only knew when he'd gotten up, or when he'd gone to bed.

Something latently maternal in her led to adjusting the worn velour sofa pillow beneath his head more comfortably.

Twenty minutes later the TV came on.

The musical background caused Will to open his eyes. He blinked, glanced around, and said in a tone of utter disbelief, "Oh, for Crissake. Lucy Maud, I'm sorry!"

"No problem," she answered, smiling. "Want your pie now?"

He laughed ruefully. "I guess," he said, and followed her to the kitchen.

"Jeez Louise," he muttered, sitting down on one of the remaining solid chairs at the table. "Some red hot date I am!"

She was getting out forks—that matched—and two saucers that didn't. "Ice cream?"

"Got some?"

"In the freezer."

He brought the carton to the table, forked an enormous gob on his, and looked at her. She shook her head.

"Dieting?"

"Let's say I can't afford a larger sized wardrobe right now."

Dumb answer! She knew it immediately. But he only said, "You look great to me the way you are," and sat down.

The pie was really excellent. He wolfed his, and the remaining third of hers.

He said, "Your Aunt Martha made excellent pastry. Frank loved her chocolate pie."

Verna hadn't even allowed chocolate pie in the house.

"They seemed to have been a happy couple," Lucy Maud said.

"You—didn't really know?"

She shrugged. "We were a hundred miles away. And my mother and she had—you know sisters—had their differences."

"But she left you her house. She must have been fond of you."

Tears came unexpectedly to Lucy Maud's eyes as she remembered the battered little photograph album. She swallowed and said, "Sometimes a family just doesn't know—everything."

"That's a truth." He mopped his mouth, crumpled the paper napkin. "Whoa. Ten-thirty. And I still have to go by and check on Bill Kindle's foxhound."

"I thought it was a chicken."

"No, no. Bill raises chickens. He knows I had a minor in poultry management even though I'm a vet—that's the free advice. But he's paying for his puppy's distemper shots."

He was standing, stretching, lean hands almost touching the old discolored ceiling. "Wow! The nap did me good. I feel like batting a hundred now. Shall I come back?"

Those green eyes were on her, and—what—twinkling? That, certainly.

"No," she said. "I have guys coming at six in morning to fix eaves troughing."

He pulled his cap out of his hip pocket. "Later this week, then? I'll give you a call."

"We'll see."

"Cautious wench. Or—disillusioned wench. What if I promise not to—oh, God, I'm still embarrassed—go to sleep?"

"I'll still see. I don't know what the week will bring." That was a truth! She followed him to the door.

Cold wind swept inside, but the rain had passed on, and there was no sound but the sibilance of dripping eaves and the patter of wet foliage in a light gust that made him turn up the collar of his jacket. The orange street lamps made the rainy street glisten. His pick-up was a luminous bulk with misted windows. Water was running in a silver stream from a dislocated downspout across the weedy grass to the nearby sewer, lending its tiny tympany to the harmonious gush inside.

Will took a deep breath.

"Doesn't it smell clean?" he said. "Isn't it great? Everything washed and new. Wow. I wish it really was."

He turned, held out his hand to her in the doorway, took her fingers, and gently kissed the tips.

"Thanks," he said. "More than you could ever guess. See ya later!"

The standard Crewsville departure. The "See ya later" part. About the rest of it, she—she wasn't sure.

He loped for his truck, swung up, and slammed the door shut. The engine purred as the lights came on.

He backed out; she caught a shadowy wave and he was gone, his turnsignal flashing at the head of the street as he hesitated, then went west.

Cutie calmly trotted down the steps to pee, which was fine, because her new owner hadn't moved.

She was holding one hand with the other, that gentle kiss very much in her memory.

Cutie returned, bunted her silky black and white furry head against a very still knee, and went on into the kitchen, making a pattern of wet footpads on the worn carpet. She then could be heard schlup-schlupping at her water bowl.

Almost blindly, Lucy Maud closed the door and followed. To put the two saucers in the sink. To stare at the two saucers as though she'd never seen them before in her life.

She never even caught a glimpse of the long car going quietly into motion down the street, and certainly never saw the glint of street lamps on yellow, turning it to gold.

Seventeen

Lucy Maud literally made herself walk into the small bedroom with its one ratty-shaded window, search among the few sheets the church ladies had left for a usable pair, and put them on the dumpy bed. Finding only flats did bemuse her for a few moments as she wrestled with the shadowy memory of how to secure the corners. But that was momentary. She added one of the two thin, worn blankets, slipped on two unmatched pillowcases and called it a day. In her present numb state of mind she would probably sleep on the edge of absolute idiocy anyway.

What was her problem?

For an aging lady out of a job and evidently out of good prospects also, she could not afford to get distracted from the main point: survival!

Face it, Lucy Maud. Will Evans was a nice man. He was single, so she was violating no local mores. Let things take their course, she chided. If there was to be a course . . .

Cool down, dammit! Look at the good side. He didn't come on to you—which you wanted him to do. Admit it! But he didn't—so neither did he find out you only have one breast! He doesn't know that. Not yet, so he's still good for a free meal or so while you're learning to survive. Right. That's crass. Really crass. That's the way men are, though: they may have a gut that hangs over like Pike's Peak—but you'd better look like a beauty queen!

So call it a game two can play. And play your part. While you can.

Yet—looking at herself in Martha's mirror—Lucy Maud felt a sort of helpless agony she hadn't felt in years. She didn't want to play games. She had wanted Will Evans to put his arms around her in that doorway, to feel his warmth and strength holding her, sapping the loneliness.

And she had almost forgotten what that would ultimately lead to. For the second time.

Disillusion. Revulsion.

And more heartbreak.

Well, she didn't need that. Not again.

A gentle nuzzling at her knee wrenched her eyes from the tormented face in the mirror, taking them down to the furry creature looking upward. And she suddenly heard Will Evans's voice in her ears: "When everyone else thinks you're shit, your dog still loves you . . ."

"Oh, Cutie," she said, and knelt, burying her face in that warm fur, while a tongue softly licked her ear. "Cutie, I'm so scared . . ."

Then in the hall the telephone rang.

Her heart in her throat, she almost ran to answer it, the dog trotting behind.

"Hello."

No answer.

"Hello!"

No answer again, just breathing. Then an audible "click!"

Oh! She hated it when people did that! Why couldn't they just say, "Sorry, wrong number," then hang up?

But the episode did bring her back to reality. Of a sort. Woman and dog continued to the kitchen, she poured more food into Cutie's bowl, and Cutie munched while she made herself a cup of strong coffee.

Then they watched the TV news together and Lucy Maud changed into her nightie and went to bed.

She was bemused to note that Cutie didn't try to go with her. She checked to be sure Lucy Maud was in bed, then calmly trotted back to the living room. Lucy heard the chair creak, and a canine sigh.

Apparently her Aunt Martha had set up *some* rules.

Sleep came slowly, hampered by a brain-wracking to come up with some job possibility that she hadn't recalled so far.

Somewhere between perhaps selling for a book wholesaler or the horror of peddling encyclopedias door to door, she did drift off. The shrill alarm jangling at six o'clock was not totally welcome.

Still, the concept of being stark naked in the bathtub when the workmen came to reset her windows had little appeal also. This time, however, she let the water warm before she stepped into it.

Lucy Maud hadn't really taken baths for years unless they were nice, long, luxurious soakers in her own dainty apartment tub full of suds and lovely, fragrant bath salts. This sitting down and trying to wash was a technique she'd willingly forgotten. Without a shower, how did one get the soap off?

Perhaps it was the fact of bathing, not showering, that found her suddenly, poignantly looking down her chin at her one-breasted chest. Still just one. And just a—a flat place. Hardly any scars. It had been more than thirty years, dammit! It wasn't repulsive, nor ugly. It—it just wasn't there!

She moved the other breast tentatively with a wet hand. She'd never been over-endowed—Verna had reminded her of that many times. But still, what she had left wasn't too bad. For an old broad.

Then the memory of all those romance novels swept over her—how the man would hold both breasts in his hands, stroking them, kissing with a warm, wet mouth. She squinched her eyes shut and cried out in pure pain, "Oh, no, no, no—" and scrambled out to an ungainly, slippery heap on the rough old mat.

Because Will Evans had been the man. She'd been imagining Will—then Will's face, when he—he found out.

A soft pat-pat-pat on the hard linoleum told her Cutie had heard, that Cutie was there, and that the bunt of a cool nose was concern.

She put a wet arm around the warm, fluffy dog and said thickly, "It's all right. I—I was just being stupid."

She stood up, reaching for a towel. Cutie sat, but not far away, and her tail was very still.

And Lucy Maud found herself laughing—which, she supposed, was better than tears—saying aloud, "Good night! Can this really be me? Worrying over a man and apologizing to a dog!"

Wrapping the towel around her, she pulled the plug on the scarred old tub, deliberately making herself notice the rust, focusing on whether a renovated bathroom would be necessary to a sale of the property, making a mental note to ask Vic Bonnelli.

She skipped make-up—she wasn't going anywhere—and pulled on an old pair of slacks from her suitcase. A ratty sweatshirt was folded beneath them. It would certainly do to try to bring some sort of appealing decor to Martha's living room. Buyers had to be attracted. She couldn't stay in Crewsville forever!

The clatter of ladders on the side of the house told her she'd been none too soon. As she opened the front door with its usual teeth-grating squeak to let Cutie out, a young man said cheerfully, "G'mornin'." He was kneeling by her front steps with a tape measure.

"Vic said do your front, today," he went on. "Then we can paint tomorrow and he can show the house without havin' to go in the back door. Hi, Cutie."

Despite herself, Lucy Maud laughed. "Did everyone in town know Aunt Martha's dog?"

"Shoot, ma'am, sure they did. Why, when ol' Frank was Grand Marshal in the fall harvest parade Cutie rode in the convertible with him. Looked pretty neat in that big red ribbon, didn't ya, sweetie?"

Behind Lucy the telephone was ringing. The young workman said, "Run on, answer it. She'll be okay."

This time someone did reply to the generic "Hello." Karen Evans's happy voice identified herself and went on, "Lucy Maud, I am so dumb, dumb, dumb! I don't know *why* I didn't ask you last night! Would you be interested in running our little hole-in-the-wall library up there in Crewsville for a while?"

Lucy Maud's jaw dropped. It was an inelegant motion, but on the phone no one sees. Karen proceeded cheerfully, "Dad came down this morning. He's helping Tim give heartworm shots. And he said, 'Karen, why in the world don't you ask Lucy?' " She giggled. "I think Dad just wants to keep you in Crewsville. Anyway, I understand it's nowhere near the responsibility you have in your library, so be a sweetheart and look on it as a paid vacation. We do pay a little. When someone goes in every day. And I've already checked with the Board up there, and they think it would be grand. How about it?"

Screeeek! went the sound of rending lumber outside as the workman began demolishing steps. Lucy Maud involuntarily clapped a hand on her free ear. Karen, also hearing the noise, added, "And it will get you out of the house."

Lucy closed her eyes and saw that abysmal little one-room establishment with its ancient books, its 1930s checking system—and even the half-typed stack of index cards by an obsolete standard typewriter. She tried not to laugh. Let the girl down easily. She was a darling. But surely Lucy Maud Marshall wasn't that desperate!

"I—I don't know, Karen. Let me think about it. I'm not too certain how much I'm needed here. I'll have to talk to Vic."

"Okay. That's fine. But if you do decide to do it, call me at work." She rattled off numbers Lucy Maud didn't even try to take down, as she wouldn't be needing them. Then she said, "Got to run! See you!"

Lucy hung up, still bemused.

Well. It would be a challenge, that place.

Unfortunately, she already had all the challenges she could handle.

Lucy punched the microwave to heat her first cup of coffee. She had a vague, undefined feeling she was going to need it.

She was right.

The first thing she noticed was that the cheese-baited mousetraps were empty of everything, including the cheese. The three peanut-butter-baited traps had done their duty. With averted eyes she pitched away both the *corpus delicti* and the traps. Then she went looking for the fourth peanut butter trap. And found it. Dragged beneath the cupboard, it had caught on a floor-tile corner. Kneeling down to peer into the dark and cobwebby dust, Lucy Maud saw the remainder of the problem.

A very tiny gray mouse, tail securely snagged by the wire trap, was peering at her with scared eyes. And it made a small squeak of total despair when she reached out her hand.

Lucy couldn't do it. She just couldn't do it. She knew what Verna would have done—she'd seen her, many times. One heavy, brutal footstomp and the problem was solved. For everyone.

But those terrified eyes. And the silky little body heaving with gasps of sheer fright.

Lucy Mad reached in under the cupboard and pulled up the wire.

The mouse was gone—gone in a heartbeat. She was left in an undignified crouch on the floor, feeling like an absolute idiot.

But—damn it! She'd put out more traps. Maybe he'd get caught again. Properly. And killed. That would be his problem. She wouldn't have to do it herself.

Heaving herself erect and going stiffly to rescue her hot cup of water, she hoped that someone else, unknown, would be that kind to her.

After two cups of instant coffee and the last ragged chunk of packaged sweet roll, she felt fortified enough to go take a long look at her Aunt Martha's living room.

She really didn't want to spend any money, but perhaps some sort of throws over that awful velour would perk up the place. Some knickknacks. A plant, or so. Plastic, if she had to buy one. She certainly wasn't in a secure enough position to take living greenery with her when she left.

Maybe in that awful little storage place behind the kitchen . . . she remembered boxes of stuff when she'd been looking for the fuse box.

The boxes were still there, but they were full of old clothes, magazines, and indefinable junk—single gloves, half-spools of thread, buttons, and silent wristwatches. Three were full of receipts and correspondence, dating back to 1969—probably the year Martha had moved to this house. She was just retreating to the kitchen to wash her filthy, dusty hands and sit down for a moment when she heard the young carpenter's voice say cheerfully, "Go on in; I know she's there somewhere!" and she came face-to-face with Miss Warpington.

Behind Miss Warpington was Howard Lewis.

Just what she needed.

"Well—good morning!" Lucy Maud caroled brightly.

And waited.

Miss Warpington answered calmly, "Good morning, Lucy Maud. I assume we're not intruding."

"Of course you aren't. I'm delighted to see you. Please sit down; I'll just wash off these dreadful hands. Try the living room, Howard. It would be more comfortable."

She didn't do an extra clean job on her hands but she didn't rush it, either. Reentering the small front room, she found Howard staring through the curtains at the workman on the steps and Miss Warpington seated in one of the chairs, scanning yesterday's newspaper.

She put it down at the sight of Lucy Maud, saying, "How nice to see you again. It's always interesting to find how one's students have grown and changed through the years."

Now there was a wide-open statement! But twenty-some years of dealing with clubwomen trying to look down their noses at an "old maid librarian" had taught Lucy how to escape most conversational traps. She was not going to reply, "But you haven't changed!", a statement more than usually true as there were still the gold-rimmed spectacles circling piercing blue eyes, the thin body encased in expensively tailored serge, and that sense of detached amusement at a daughter of well-to-do manufacturers finding herself teaching mere children.

Instead, she smiled, nodded pleasantly, seated herself on the coach, and said, "Please do sit down, Howard. Aunt Martha's chairs are hardly what I'd choose, but they serve a purpose."

He blinked. It was fast, and she almost didn't see it; nonetheless, he did, though recovering swiftly. And he obeyed.

"Now," she said. "What may I do for you today?"

"We were just driving by," Miss Warpington said, "after breakfast. Howard is so good to take me about. I've surrendered my license, you see. At any rate, I suddenly remembered that your Aunt Martha had borrowed my umbrella. It was just a few days before she was—taken, poor girl. Would you have seen it?"

"Oh, my!" Lucy Maud answered in genuine dismay. "No, I haven't. But do come and look. It would probably be in a closet somewhere if the church ladies haven't taken it."

"No, no—I needn't look. Thank you, though. Just keep an eye out."

"Oh, I will. Indeed."

"Then we'll go. I know you must be very busy. Such a sad task. Come, Howard."

Howard rose obediently. He had been avoiding Lucy's eyes but also had hardly taken his own from the hall and the far kitchen. Neither had he spoken two words aloud.

Cutie! He was afraid of Cutie!

At that sudden realization, Lucy Maud almost giggled. The slob had no way of knowing the dog was in the backyard helping two workmen replace eaves troughs. And she wasn't going to tell!

"So nice to see you again," she said to the elderly lady as both Howard and the young carpenter helped her down the unsecured frame of the new steps. "I have pleasant recollections of shorthand class."

Miss Warpington half turned. Suddenly Lucy Maud saw the calm, ladylike mask on the old face slip. Just a bit. Miss Warpington said, "Do you, my dear? Thank you. Perhaps when you're not so busy you could—come by and chat a while. I'm still in the house on Elm Street."

Strangely touched, Lucy Maud said, "Why—I will. I'd enjoy it. We'll do some catching up. Good morning, Howard."

"Uh—good morning." If he sounded a bit bemused he could be forgiven. Both he and Lucy Maud glimpsed Cutie calmly trotting around the corner of the house to see what was going on out front. *His* trip around his Cadillac to slide his girth hastily into the front seat was to any comprehending eye more than a bit precipitate.

Miss Warpington waved as they drove away. The young carpenter, fluffing Cutie's ears, said, "Nice lady. I do jobs for her sometimes. What are you growling about, pup?"

Lucy Maud said, "It's okay, Cutie. I guess she's just protective."

"Or a good judge of character." He was measuring lathe.

In surprise, Lucy said, "I thought you said she was nice!"

"Not her. Him. Sorry—I hope he's not a friend of yours."

"I went to school with him. That was thirty years ago. What's his problem?"

He shrugged, unzipping his jacket as the sun tipped the top of the sycamore trees. "I dunno. He just rubs me wrong—the way he smarms around the old ladies in town. But maybe all bankers do that."

"John Basalti doesn't like him either." She was trying hard to get some information while still keeping a seeming detachment.

He grinned. "John's got a reason. He and Dilly are in love—that's the old boy's daughter—and the Lewises can't see John for dust. What they ought to do is run off and get married—I keep tellin' John that. Hey—is that your telephone?"

It was.

"Thanks!" Lucy Maud said over her shoulder and ran into the hall. Perhaps it was one of her contacts calling back. Perhaps they'd found something she could do. Perhaps she had a job, after all!

Perhaps she should have saved her breath.

It was the man who leased her mother's property. The insurance company was requiring new insulation.

So there wouldn't be any rent money for two months. Maybe three.

Stunned, Lucy Maud hung up the phone and stared blankly at the new shafts of sun brightening the dingy hallway.

No rent. No money. For two months or three.

And her library pay wouldn't last beyond the first one.

Now what, Lucy Maud?

She knew.

What else was there?

She picked up the phone again, to dial Karen Evans. To tell her she'd take the library job.

Of course, she didn't have the number.

Eighteen

Lucy Maud wondered fleetingly how long it would take her to come to grips with cold reality and stay there! So far she'd had the staying power of a wet noodle.

There was no regional telephone book to be seen. Going through the operator meant additional cost and she already had a phone bill the size of a moose.

Then it struck her: hadn't she seen a list of 800 numbers jotted down by the telephone in the Crewsville Library? She had! She'd noticed them while checking out books the other day and laughed to herself because they were written with red marking pencil on a stick'em sheet ornamented with teddy bears.

Cutie was a fluffy curl on the front sidewalk, basking in the sun. The young carpenter said he'd keep an eye on her. Nodding her appreciation, Lucy Maud slid into her car, backed out, and headed for the main street.

Where had Karen said they left a key?

In fact, it didn't matter. The parking lot already had a car in it. The door was unlocked, and as Lucy Maud walked inside, Mrs. Howard Lewis looked up in surprise from behind the high desk.

Actually, there was a little more than surprise. There seemed to be guilt in her expression.

Knowing full well that the lower shelf of the desk held new books not ready for the general public, Lucy Maud said calmly, "Hello," and walked around the island to the same side. "May I help you?"

Amanda Lewis badly wanted to bristle, but was thinking better of it. "Oh. You're that—person I met the other evening. An old—school friend, I believe Howard said. What was your name again? I'm very poor with those things."

"Lucy Marshall. And I've agreed to help out here— while I'm in town."

Amanda moved out from behind the desk on the other end. "I needed something good to read. And there's just nothing on the shelves. I suppose everyone else has been in here before me." She had turned and was roaming slowly down the wall of books. Over her chubby shoulder she said suddenly, "You're going to fill in for that—that Dottie person?"

Lucy Maud's jaw tightened, but Amanda wasn't in position to notice. "Whoever."

"Well. I do hope you are more competent than she. All she knew to do was keep her clutch on poor Dr. Evans." And she turned. Her plucked eyebrows were arched. "Do tell me. What's your background? Do you have a degree?"

For this hole in the wall? Surely you jest!

But Lucy didn't say that, and was proud of her restraint.

She smiled, instead—a charming smile. "Dear lady,

I've been head librarian for thirty-some years in a city downstate. I do know a bit about books."

"Oh! Oh, yes—you're the one who—I mean, you're Martha Hauser's niece."

"Yes."

And my husband's old girlfriend.

She didn't say that, but she was clearly thinking it. "How interesting," she murmured. "Perhaps, then, *you* can find me something to read. My husband is going to be gone this evening, I thought I'd just stay home and curl up with a good book."

"Very commendable," said Lucy Maud. Her roving eye fell on a thick paperback. She recognized it as a copy of one recently returned by a patron in Millard who had also remarked wryly that the sex scenes had almost scorched her bedsheets. "How about this? My patrons have found it very—interesting."

Amanda Lewis's bulbous eyes had already locked on to the half-clad, muscular young man on the cover. "Oh, really? Well—if there's nothing else, I suppose it will do."

There was no point asking for this fat bitch's number or her card. She was, after all, Mrs. Howard Lewis. Minions should *know.*

Good Lord, how many of these idiots I've dealt with, Lucy Maud thought wryly, thumbing the card index. Leeds, Lerdon, Leslie—Lewis. There it was.

Just as she inked the date stamp, a cool draft signified the opening of the door. But that wasn't what caught her attention. It was the sound in Amanda Lewis's voice as she said, "Well—hello!" and the rapidity with which the paperback with its male porno cover disappeared into her handbag.

"Will! You saw my car! How nice of you to come in to see me!"

"Truthfully, no," said Will Evans calmly. "I saw Miss Marshall's car."

"Oh. Well—of course. You wouldn't know mine, now. Dear Howard has bought me a new Buick. Oh—you and Miss Marshall have—met?"

"Once or twice." Will grinned at Lucy, a gesture Amanda obviously didn't like at all. And it hit Lucy Maud: this broad has the hots for him! Howard's wife!

Will was leaning on the desk. "Karen said she left me the new Tom Clancy. See if it's still there, will you?" And he winked at Lucy Maud, making a wry face.

Amanda Lewis was touching his sleeve, his shoulder. "Ooo. You're so dirty—you piggy man . . ."

Fortunately, Lucy Maud didn't have time to throw up on her as the door opened again and her daughter appeared, saying impatiently, "Mother! Will you come on? Daddy *has* to have those papers signed before he leaves for Springfield!"

"Oh. Oh, all right. Nice to—to meet you again, Miss Marshall. I'll see you later, Will."

When the door closed on the both of them, Will Evans hid his face in his hands and murmured, "Oh God. I really needed her, today. Tell me she's gone, Lucy. Please."

"She's gone."

Will looked at her through his fingers and said, "Laugh. Please laugh, too. Then perhaps I can."

"How exciting it must be to be so in demand."

"Oh, Christ. Lucy, don't do that! My boy jokes

about it—he says I must throw out a scent like a moose in rut. But it's not funny to me. Not at all."

Remembering that discretion was supposed to be the better part of valor, Lucy murmured, "All right. Hang on, Dr. Moose, and I'll see if I can find your Tom Clancy."

It hadn't been just a dodge! The book was there, with his name on a slip. Now she was caught with the possibility he *had* just come in for it—not to see her.

Stop acting like a damn teenager! she told herself crossly, and straightened up again. "Just a minute. I'll put a date card in."

"No hurry." He'd turned away and was riffling through a lopsided shelf of worn paperbacks. "I'm always looking for a Louis L'Amour I haven't already read three times," he said, but his face was still turned and his voice sounded strange.

"A lot of us have that problem. He's really missed."

The stamp pad needed to be re-inked.

Could they even be bought anymore? Millard had been scanning everything for at least three years.

She opened her mouth to make a mundane remark about obsolescence and closed it again. The sag of his denim-clad shoulders on the other side of the desk did not go unnoticed. Chitchat wasn't the answer. If they were friends, it wasn't needed. If they weren't—then he could just—go. Leave.

He was turning about, and the green eyes looked dark. Almost haunted.

"I'm just—damned tired of fighting everything," he said. "I know. That doesn't make much sense to you. But sometimes I swear if it wasn't for Tim, and the

fact I really like being a vet, I'd—I'd get out. Go somewhere else. Of course—" and then the grin was back,
flashing at her, "—being almost sixty has something
to do with it, too. Pulling up stakes is a little easier
for a young guy."

"Tell me about it!"

The remark came out before she thought. "My problem is a younger woman."

"She wants your job?"

She's got my job.

But Lucy didn't say that. All right. She was a coward. She just shrugged again, and let it go. Will put
out a lean hand, covering both the book and the fingers
that held it.

"Then—can you take this job, here? For a while.
Or must you go back?"

His hand was warm around hers, and safer to look
at than his eyes. She said to that hand, "I am taking
this job. For a while. I—I don't know if I'm going
back."

She wasn't telling it all. He knew it. He didn't ask.
He only answered quietly, "Well—what may not be
good for you is certainly good for me. Look upon it
as a charitable gesture. Because whatever the words
are worth—I want you to stay."

She made herself meet his eyes, then, and what she
saw in them caught at her heart. She answered almost
desperately, "Will, understand—I may not be good
for—for anyone!"

"I'll be the judge of that."

He was taking the hand, loosening it from the book,
lifting it to his mouth again. Giving it back. His tone

low and wry, he went on, "And I'd better get out of here before what is already obvious to me becomes obvious to you—handholding is not enough."

"Will—"

"Hush. Unless my ears deceive me, there are patrons advancing toward the door. Right?"

She swallowed and looked over his shoulder, past those wide shoulders, that erect, silver-crowned head, the senior citizen bus was in the parking lot and at least half a dozen chattering passengers were advancing on the library entrance.

She nodded. "Yes."

"What I want with you, lady, is quality time. Tim and I have a seminar in Jacksonville this evening. May I take you out to dinner tomorrow night—if I promise I won't go to sleep?"

She was drowning in the backwash of her own heartbeat. Frantically trying to control her expression and keep her voice calm, she answered, "Yes. Fine."

Fine! Fine! What a romantic answer, Lucy Maud, you idiot! What a revealing one! There was your chance to say, "No, thank you, but I'm busy. Aunt Martha's house, you know." Or, "I don't think I really care to go." Or the truth: "Will, I'm scared. Give me some time."

But it was too late for any of that. He was already turning around, book in hand showing it to an old gentleman entering, saying, "Sorry, John, old boy, but I got it first. Ask next week. I'm a fast reader when it's Clancy. Hi, Mrs. Adams. How's that handsome cat of yours?"

"Oh, Dr. Evans, he's just fine now. Want to see a new picture? Here he is with my little great grandson . . ."

Will commented on the picture, winked at Lucy Maud, and went out the door. The remaining senior citizens seemed to know where they wanted to look. Three were browsing the paperbacks, two in the old westerns, and two more contending over a hardback Faith Baldwin.

None seemed to need assistance yet. Perhaps now was the time to get her heart rate back to normal, call that 800 number, and tell Karen Evans she was taking the job.

Temporarily, of course.

Karen was delighted. Against a narrative background of children's laughter and someone reading aloud from what Lucy recognized as *Make Way for Ducklings,* she said, "Super! I'm so glad. And that's nothing to what Dad will be. May I tell him? Or—will *you* see him?"

"He was in." One may as well be truthful.

"Why doesn't that surprise me?" Karen giggled. "He was so embarrassed. He told Tim he went to sleep last night. Anyway. Make your own schedule. As you know, people can always use the key. But if you have time, we would appreciate your taking some books out to our home patrons. You know—the ones who don't drive or are incapacitated—something like that. The list should be in the desk drawer."

"I'll see."

Lucy Maud was making no promises. Things were already far enough ahead of her.

What was that she'd promised herself just a few hours ago about taking control? About dictating her own survival?

Anyway, something like that . . .

Nineteen

While the seniors were still browsing, Tom Burkiser came loping across the street from his grocery store, Larry McMurtry's *Lonesome Dove* in his hand and hoping someone had donated the sequel. Someone had, but it was checked out. Lucy finally penetrated the very loose filing system to ascertain that fact.

Tom said, "Shoot. Put my name down for it. Call me if you can. Or my wife. She's cleanin' house—got some old paperbacks to bring over, anyway."

"Romances?" asked an elderly lady with bright eyes beneath frizzy dead black hair.

"Gosh, Roma, I suppose. I don't read 'em. They'd either give me herpes or diabetes."

"Oh, pooh, Tommy Burkiser. You sound just like my first husband. But George—I've *got* him reading them—especially the historicals. He says he's learned a lot he didn't know."

Tom grinned. "Is he better in bed now? If he is, I'll take a dozen."

She hit him with an affectionate swat. "You men! Always puttin' down something *you* don't know! Yes, as a matter of fact, he is. Shall I have this lady pick you out twelve or so? That's assuming, of course, that your reading level has now surpassed the See Dick, See Jane stage."

"Whoa. Never cross swords with your old fourth grade teacher," said Tom, and grinned across at Lucy Maud.

"Okay, everybody, next stop the grocery store," intoned the bus driver from the door, and in the rush to check out, Tom escaped. The little lady cocked her eyes through thick lenses at Lucy Maud.

"Do I know you?"

"Roma, for heaven's sake, you didn't teach everybody!" said the taller woman behind her. "I did."

She was handing over two Hemingways and a Michener to be dated. Lucy Maud took them and, looking her right in the eyes, said impishly, " 'This is the forest primeval. The murmuring pines and the hemlocks—' " She stopped at the woman's pleased laughter.

"Well!" the woman said. "How nice to know something I taught took! I'm sorry—but who are you, my dear?"

"Lucy Maud Marshall, Miss Wilson. Your American literature class. My senior year."

"Lucy Maud! Of course! How nice to see you. Whatever are you doing back here? Oh—Martha. I should have known. Besides, Eleanora Warpington said you were in town."

Checking out the books, Lucy thought one thing about Miss Wilson hadn't changed—she had to be pushing ninety, but her attitude was still as sharp as her linen suit was fashionable. Miss Wilson had been another faculty member with money on the side. Her father had been senator, and her mother one of the

Krueshanks. Good Lord. She was probably related to Amanda Lewis—but Lucy decided she wouldn't hold that against her. She'd liked Miss Wilson. She'd been the only one, in fact, who'd warned her about Howard Lewis long before her mastectomy. With discretion, of course. And Lucy Maud Marshall had smiled politely, laughing to herself. What did an old maid know?

What, indeed? asked today's Lucy Maud wryly to herself.

The bus drove away. The place was empty. Lucy glanced at her watch. What was to be a quick trip to make a phone call had turned into an hour. If she wanted to escape, she'd better do it now.

But she'd checked out over thirty books. There were gaps on the shelves to be straightened, and twenty or so volumes to be checked in and replaced. Cutie would surely be all right for a while . . .

A hesitant throat-clearing turned her from plucking a Max Brand from the mystery shelf and putting it with the rest of the westerns.

Dilanna Lewis stood inside the door. Her blouse was too ruffled and her skirt too tight and the sun through the windows made her frizzy hair turn not gold but brass. Still her smile was tentative but vaguely imploring. Not superior. Not snobbish.

"Yes?"

"I'm Dilly Lewis. I was at your back door the other day. And—you knew my father. A long time ago."

I did, indeed.

But Lucy didn't say that. She was still given to civilized responses. "Yes. That's right. Come in, child. I think there's some instant coffee back there. Would you like a cup? I feel the need to sit down."

Dilanna's smile made her almost pretty. "I'd love it. If anyone comes in, let me check them out. I do it sometimes for Karen."

"Fine. I'll remember that."

Be careful, she told herself, rinsing cups, running water, and reading the dials on the small microwave. This poor child's life is already a mess. Whatever she wants, you needn't add to that.

With coffee bags in hand, she went back into the main room. Dilanna had just finished shelving the rest of the returned books, including those shoved through the door slot into a cardboard box which Lucy hadn't seen.

"Thanks," Lucy said. "I hadn't even noticed those!"

She sat down at the tottery card table, hooking another reedy chair over with her toe. "Drink. While it's hot. I hate cold coffee."

"I never drank coffee until I started at the bank. Everyone does there. We need the caffeine, I guess."

The girl's smile was rueful.

Lucy took the plunge. "I think I heard John say that banking wasn't particularly your first choice of a vocation."

"No." She had nice hands, but they were laced almost painfully around the hot cup. And she sighed. "I wanted to teach. I still want to teach. Perhaps someday . . ." She stopped, then went on quietly, "Teaching isn't prestigious enough for my mother."

"It's all in your point of view."

"That's hers."

"What did your sister do?"

"What she was supposed to do—marry rich."

Lucy laughed. "Perhaps I should have hung on to your father. If 'rich' is the goal around here."

"Father's not rich. Mother is. Or was."

The last part escaped Lucy Maud, as she was suddenly overtaken with the exquisite bad taste of leading this child into unsuitable confessions. Come on, Lucy Maud! You are surely not at the point where you have to stoop to that!

She shrugged, smiled, and honestly tried to turn the tide of the conversation by asking something about this tottering old building. But Dilanna rode right over her:

"You weren't rich. When you were engaged to my father?"

Then he *had* mentioned the engagement! In heaven's name—why?

"Gracious, no! Of course, then, neither was he."

"Then—what happened?" Seeing Lucy Maud's frozen expression, she went on desperately, "Miss Marshall, I'm sorry but I have to know! I'm almost at the end of my tether!"

The girl's voice rang true.

Lucy closed her eyes. "What did your father say?"

"I don't know. They—they weren't talking to me and mother shut the door. But I caught your name. Then she yelled a lot. My mother always does. More, recently. It's—kind of awful sometimes. I—I want out of there. Badly."

The girl's voice shook. Lucy considered her words carefully. "He broke off our engagement. That's true. But it was a—a very personal thing. Not money."

Dilly's eyes opened wide—so wide her artificial lashes stood up like shawl fringe. "You weren't two-timing him? Oh—I'd love that! Were you? Was there someone else?"

"No, child. There wasn't somebody else. As I said—it was a very personal thing."

"You hurt his ego!"

"Yes."

This young girl was astute—or knew her father very well. Lucy nodded, and sipped her coffee. She added wryly, "So that was that."

Dilly's voice was softer now. "Were you devastated?"

"My mother was. More than I."

"Welcome to the club. That's what my mother would be if I ran off with—the guy I love." She was looking down at her coffee cup, and it rattled against the tabletop. "It doesn't seem to have ruined your life. Breaking up with my father, I mean."

Deep water here, also. "I'm not sure I loved him. Looking back, I don't think I really knew what love was."

"I know!" Dilanna closed her eyes, and smiled. "Oh, yes. I really know . . ."

Watching her, Lucy Maud thought in dismay, this is an unreal conversation! I just met this child!

She sipped more coffee, playing for time, and came up with a "safe" remark: "Just don't do anything rash."

"What did you do?"

"Went to college. Found a career."

Grimly Dilanna said, "I've done both. And had them

yanked. Mother wants to be able to watch me. Oh, it's really great at home. I practically have to sign in and sign out." She shrugged. "Of course, I keep hoping my mom will change. She's always been sort of a—a fruitcake—but right now, with all those freaky diets she goes on, she's a real mess. Which reminds me—" She was scrabbling in her shoulder bag, bringing out a half-filled bag of small candy bars. "Have one. Help yourself. I'm a chocolate freak."

Perhaps that accounted for the soft roll around her waist, Lucy conjectured, slipping the paper from a piece. "Thank you."

"Take more than that. I have to leave, anyway. Here."

Dilanna threw half a dozen on the table, getting up as she did so. Then she said hesitantly, "and—thank *you.* I was about to go up the wall. You could probably tell. I appreciate your listening. It helps."

"Any time." Lucy was standing up, looking at her watch, collecting the empty coffee cups. Dilanna had eaten three chocolates, and was putting another in her mouth.

"Sometimes I wonder," she said in muffled tones, snapping her purse shut, "if my father would stay home more if it would help. I mean—all he does is take around his old ladies when he's not in the bank. Oh, well."

She smiled, wiggled her fingers in farewell, and was out the door.

Which, Lucy thought, she'd better be, also. Before anyone else came in. Except—she did need something to read. Perhaps an old Agatha Christie. Something nice and intriguing to take the weird taste out of her mouth. She didn't need any more of other people's problems— especially when she sensed they touched on hers . . .

The great thing about a Christie was that no matter how many times you'd read it before, you still couldn't remember *whodunnit*. She found *Easy to Kill*—which would be just fine.

Then the next problem was where to put the key that was lying on the corner of the desk—although why anyone bothered to lock up at all was getting to be a bit beyond Lucy Maud.

The mail box! That was it.

There were three more library books stuffed in it, but Lucy ignored them. She'd try to get back later in the afternoon. Or early evening. Since she wasn't doing anything tonight.

But she was, tomorrow night. With Will Evans.

Doing what?

Then it came back to her, in a rush that left her shivering. It came back—that speech about handholding not being enough. Also—the look in those green eyes, before the seniors had come pouring inside. And the sense she'd been too spineless to say a simple "no."

She locked the door, clattered the key in the box, threw her book on the car seat, and climbed behind the wheel roughly, angrily, her lower lip thrust out in the way Verna Marshall had deplored.

When the hell was she going to learn? She'd done without a man for thirty years, and very well, thank you! Why was she such a—a pushover for this particular one right now?

Maybe Tim Evans was right about the moose scent, she thought sarcastically.

And why at this particular calamitous juncture in her life had she had to encounter a—a "moose"?

Twenty

The best thing about the next twenty-four hours to Lucy Maud was that one got through them. It rained again, or off and on in brief, torrential spurts which effectively halted the house repairs. She discovered that her aunt's refrigerator, far from self-defrosting, was so iced up that the cube trays were welded to each other. She also found that the mice had tugged the steel wool from the hole beneath the window ledge and were once more trespassing freely. And peanut butter was now passé—or the word had gone out, as no more traps were sprung.

Vic, who came by to see if the basement was still dry after the rains, suggested grape jelly.

"To go with the peanut butter?" she asked, not really trying to be cute, and he'd grinned that wide Slav grin, answering cheerfully, "No, no. That's what my mom uses. Dad, now, he says she ought to leave bottlecaps full of red wine; by the time the trap sprung they'd be so stoned out they'd die happy."

"I like his philosophy."

"So did the mice."

He also said he was bringing a company appraiser by the next day to get a ballpark figure on the sale value of the house. Which he did. Lucy Maud was not totally thrilled at the bottom line, but considering the house itself—and also the fact that she, personally, wouldn't buy it on a bet—she accepted the figure with good grace. When one had so little, any amount of money was an improvement!

Also, hanging over her all the time was the fact that she was being foolhardy enough to go out with Will Evans again. Will would not have been exactly charmed to learn she was equating it with biting down on a sore tooth.

She spent the afternoon at the little library, checking out twenty or so more books, rearranging the nonfiction section so that a donated and not totally obsolescent set of encyclopedias would be more accessible without lying on one's stomach, and typing more index cards on the standard typewriter—which cost her another fingernail.

Will found her there, sticking his head inside the door and saying cheerfully, "Hi! Six-thirty okay? And no formal attire, please. I haven't been home since yesterday morning, and need to do laundry."

"Where are we going?" Surely that question wasn't undue. She'd stood up and was looking at him over the high desk, pretending her dumb heart wasn't going bump-bump-bump at the mere sight of that lean, faintly bristled, and smiling face.

"Back to the ribs place. Okay?"

"Fine." Particularly since she'd finished her doggy bag last evening.

"That's my girl. Oh—hi, Tom."

The grocer was ducking under Will's arm, carrying

a rubber-banded stack of paperbacks. "I said my wife was cleaning house," he said, putting them on the desk. "Say, Doc, what the hell's that rattling around in the back of your truck? It sounded like a load of cannon-balls when you pulled in."

"Oh—my sump pump. It died a week ago, and I keep forgetting to have it checked. Got to run, guys. See you later!"

"Sure never know he's retired," Tom said, chuckling, and pocketing the rubber band. "Of course, it's probably good for him. Doc ain't the sort to sit and rock. Oh—here. I brought you an apple."

It was scarlet and solid and shining and the first crunching bite was delicious. Lucy said, "Mmmm—good!"

"It's a Stark something-or-ruther—from Acles Orchards. Krueshanks have sort of let their trees go downhill. That McMurtry come in?"

She checked, crunching more. "Not yet."

"Shoot. Give me a call."

"We will. Thanks for the apple."

"Sure. See ya!" Echoing the Crewsville standard farewell, he was out the door and gone, also. His parting shot was, "Wow! Looks like rain again!"

He was right. Ten minutes later the heavens opened up once more and Lucy drove home in it, slamming her car door and bolting for the house.

Cutie welcomed her insouciantly, the reason for the insouciance being a note on the fridge, pinned there by Jessie: "Gave dog last of meatloaf. Pot roast to-morrow. Come on over."

Two things struck Lucy: either she hadn't locked the kitchen door, or Jessie had a key.

The door opened to her hand.

So. That solved that. She *was* getting careless in her old age!

Her next magic trick was deciding what to wear on this third evening out with Will. Particularly in light of that speech about "quality time."

Wryly she thought, I could wear the "Shit" shirt—and was momentarily tempted. The sentiments concerning what she was tired of had momentary appeal—and lasting truth.

Just one short week ago she'd received the good news her breast was still immaculately healthy, and had started driving back to Millard in a positive glow of anticipation—head librarian in a new building with a ribbon to cut and a celebration that would put the Fourth of July to shame!

Now where was she? Sitting in a ratty kitchen, being affectionately nuzzled by, of all things, a dog, and debating what to wear on a dubious date with an elderly vet who was probably on the make—and for whom she seemed to have the adolescent hots!

The front door banged, and a green florist's van pulled in behind her car. The young man on the partly-mended porch held what was obviously a bouquet, paper-wrapped though it might be.

"Miss Lucy Marshall?"

"Y-Yes."

"Then those are yours. Have a good day," he said cheerfully, put the bouquet in her hands, and hopped agilely to the ground, heading for his vehicle through the drizzling rain.

She took off the paper, saw she held a half dozen satin-red roses—and a card. No messages. Just a card—signed simply, "Will."

Lucy hadn't received red roses in thirty years.

She found an old iced tea glass—the best she could do—and arranged them in it with shaky fingers.

Still in a sort of daze, she wandered into the bathroom and started getting ready to go out.

Sanity returned somewhere between brushing the partial plate and putting on the eyeliner.

The flowers were lovely. She'd thank him graciously.

But that would be that!

She donned the tailored skirt she'd worn to Crewsville, and in the bottom of her suitcase found a blue silk blouse with a soft-pleated front, packed for the hospital trip and never worn. It zipped down the back. Unconscious of double meanings, she hooked on the new bra with its lovely false contour, donned the blouse, and, twisting in the mirror to see, locked up the zipper with a small safety pin.

If he gets pushy, she thought with a certain strange sense of self-protection, that ought to slow things up.

Until I can decide what I want to do?

There's a doubt?

She couldn't face that one. Or—didn't want to face it. And the image in the mirror was staring at her. So—are you going to zip-lock your pants, too?

Outraged, Lucy Maud grated at the reflection, "No. No, damnit!"

Good God in striped pajamas! She was fifty-five

years old! She'd had *some* experience since Howard Lewis, including that bald computer equipment salesman who'd gotten fresh in the library storeroom and she'd shoved a metal drawer in on his other hand.

"Hi," said Will cheerfully, giving her that familiar grin as he bent to inspect Cutie's paws. "Now the back ones, Cutie. The back ones! Good—good—you're doing fine."

With a final smooth of the fluffy coat, he straightened up, and she saw raindrops on the shoulders of a very nice tweed sportscoat.

"Tim's," he said, following her eyes. "I said I hadn't been home since yesterday."

"Thank you for the flowers."

"Thank you for being here."

Behind him lightning flashed and thunder rumbled, lowering Cutie's ears precipitately and also cracking the different sort of electricity between the two of them that had all of a sudden shot out a message of its own.

Cutie whined, and he said, "It's okay, old girl. Really okay."

Was that for the dog—or for her? she wondered.

Then he said softly, "We'd better—go. Those clouds look like there might be some more wet stuff coming."

She said to the dog, "In! In! No, sorry, you're *not* going!" Picking up her umbrella, she snapped the lock on the door, knowing with relief that he was grinning again.

"Habit," she said.

He shrugged, took her arm down the unanchored framework of the new steps, and boosted her into his pick-up.

"Someday I'll surprise you and show up in the car," he said, swinging into the seat on his side. "Wow! Just in time!"

Pulling on the lights and pushing the wiper lever, he put the truck in reverse as rain pattered on the windshield.

"You look nice," he said, one arm across the back of the seat as he maneuvered out into the street. "Here I thought you might wear that 'I'm Tired of This Shit' shirt. Otherwise, I might have asked to borrow it."

I did think about it . . . she mused, but didn't say it. "Bad day?"

"Let's say I've had better."

They were proceeding down the blearily lighted street, truck tires swishing gently, the wiper blades making their own melody on the spattered windshield.

He glanced at her, and for the first time she saw the weariness in those eyes.

She said quickly, "You didn't need to—to come tonight!"

"I did. I needed your company." Then before new caution lights could go on in her head, he added, "There seems to be a rash of elderly dogs calling it a day. Most of them are old friends. It's hard on the owners, but damn it all, sometimes it's hard on their vet, too. I had to put three to sleep this afternoon—sweethearts, all of them."

Lucy Maud Marshall, who had never even loved a parakeet, heard the emotion in his deep voice and was very touched. She patted his knee gently. "I guess old friends aren't always human."

"And humans aren't always old friends."

With that, he gave her a sidewise smile as they caught the green light and turned south to the highway. "Philosophy of the day. But—damn. We saw some city jaybird in a big car hit a stray today, didn't kill it, backed up and ran over it again! If I hadn't been riding along, I suspect Tim might have run over *him!*"

Then she got another sideways look. "Think Cutie might like a friend?"

"You—you saved it?"

"I hope we did. We think we did."

"Now what?"

"Oh, Tim's on the farm. He's only got two dogs. Maybe three. One more won't hurt."

She was laughing, shaking her head.

"What?"

"In Millard, my apartment hardly has room for a row of geraniums. I was trying to imagine four dogs."

"Then you need a larger place."

She ignored that. The man couldn't begin to know what she needed!

They were nearing the line of bluffs now, with lights twinkling through the early gloom and shining mistily on the silvered water of the river up ahead.

Will swung the truck into the parking lot and nosed it between two others. "Not too busy tonight."

"The rain?"

"Oh—that, and it's Thursday. Tomorrow's payday. The rain's slacked off again. Grab your umbrella and we'll make a run for it."

They made the double doors in fairly dry condition, and once more the sound of chattering voices poured out on the warm wings of country music. They were shown to their same place at the terrace windows by the same waitress smiling from beneath the enormous cowboy hat—but this time Will ordered one beer and a vodka tonic.

"I'm learning," he said cheerfully.

Lucy, who had not seen either a yellow Cadillac or the noxious sight of either Howard Lewis or his wife, relaxed. And also realized she was hungry. The pizza, shared with Vic and the appraiser had been a long time ago.

Also—for some reason, the little waitress assuming they both wanted the ribs failed to annoy her this time. Perhaps it was because the waitress called her by name. Not "Dottie."

"Hey, I really like that Bobbi Smith book. Thanks for recommending it. Got any more?"

At Millard Library, at least ten. At Crewsville, Lucy really didn't know, and said as much. But the satisfaction of recognition remained even as the large hat with the girl beneath it went away.

The drinks came.

Will took his, then wheeled around and stretched out long legs, his eyes on the light-streaked waters beyond the glistening terrace stone. Lucy could almost see his shoulders relax, his neck muscles loosen. He said quietly, not looking at her at all, "I've been thinking about this all day."

She decided to be impish. "The beer?"

"No, you idiot. Being here. With you. And no beeper."

"It's in the truck?"

"Tim's got it. Pay for his retired old man helping

him give heartworm shots today. Remind me, though, to stop by the clinic when we head out. I haven't been there all day either, and there might be something on the damn machine—hopefully that information from the state on llamas."

"Llamas?" She repeated the word in sheer surprise.

He laughed quietly. "You *have* been away. That's a growing industry around here now, hon. And they're sweethearts—big, soft, fleecy old boys. Thanks, Judy. You are a good girl."

"And you look pooped," the waitress said, placing a platter of snacks by his elbow. She smiled at Lucy. "You go on, help yourself over there at the bar," she said. "I just sort of know what Doc here likes."

"No dill dip," Will said, munching. "Lots of cheese." As the girl retreated again, he added, smiling, "There are advantages to being a public character."

"Figure." She was correcting him.

He corrected her: *"Character.* I tend to—speak my mind, anymore—and the hell with it."

She liked dill dip and went for some. Another lady at the buffet table, busily loading chips on a stacked plate, said, "Hi. Nice to see you down here."

Fortunately for good manners, Lucy quickly placed the blue hair and the thick-lensed glasses as the woman who'd checked out three Grace Livingston Hills and a large print Reader's Digest. "Thank you."

"Are you going to take books out to home folks, too? We'd sure be glad to have that going again. My mom's even reading the backs of the cereal boxes. Those Hill books won't last her three days."

Lucy had found the list of patrons needing home

delivery in the desk as Karen had said, and had been appalled at the number. There had been thirty or so people on the sheet!

Cautiously, she answered, "We're thinking about it. I may try. The problem is that I don't know how long I'll be in Crewsville."

"Honey, even *once* would be a lifesaver! Try the coleslaw—they make it good here."

As Lucy recalled, she'd meant to try it last time, but something called Howard Lewis had ruined her selection sense. This evening, she skipped the applesauce and took the coleslaw.

When she returned, Will was mopping an empty snack plate with the last chip. He said cheerfully, "Just in time. Here are the ribs."

Without Howard Lewis, and without a beeper, Lucy enjoyed every bite. Will didn't do too badly, polishing off his rack of bones and two of hers.

"Wow," he said, finally pushing back from the table and mopping barbecue sauce with a crumpled napkin. "That sure made up for no lunch."

"You didn't eat lunch?"

"Shoot, girl—I said we were busy! Karen ran over with some sandwiches, but I think mine's still in the fridge on top of some serum boxes. How about dessert?"

"I'm not sure I can finish my coffee."

"No problem. Let's run by the clinic for a minute, then I'll buy you a shake or something. Will, the High Roller!"

Okay. Another step. But she remembered where

she'd seen the clinic sign, half a block down from the library. That seemed simple enough to handle.

The rain had stopped again and was teasing, with a sliver of moon shining between two banks of clouds. They made the trip back to town in a pleasant silence with the FM radio playing softly. Suddenly Will braked and said, "Look!"

He was pointing. At the edge of the highway, antlers erect, ears up, was a deer. Suddenly he bounded right in front of the truck. Three doe followed, poetry in flight. They jumped the leaning old fence and disappeared into the timbered darkness on the other side.

"Hell on cars," Will said wryly, "if you're not watching. But aren't they beautiful? I guess that's why I'm a fisherman, not a hunter. I've never formed a very close association with a fish."

He stopped at the light, turned right, and right again, parking next to an old Ford with its driver slamming down the hood.

"Bad connection," the man said cheerfully. "Evenin', Doc. Evenin', ma'am. Say, boy, ain't you glad I talked you into buyin' that sump pump a few years ago? If we hadn't had those suckers this morning you and me'd both be swimmin' in our basements."

Will froze. "What?"

"That damn sewer back-up this mornin'. Oh—I remember, you weren't around. But don't fuss. My pump handled it just fine, and I'm sure yours did, too."

"Oh, sweet Jesus!" said Will and bolted for the clinic entrance. "No, it didn't," he said over his shoulder, fitting a key in the lock and throwing open the door, snapping on lights. "Because the damn thing's in the back of my truck!"

Both Lucy Maud and the man with the Ford flew into action. Lucy beat him to the clinic threshold, but he beat her to the basement stairs because he knew where he was going.

Will was already there, gazing downward, muttering, "Shit! Shit! All my files, all my cages, my supplies, my freezer stuff—"

He stooped, threw off his shoes, and peeled his socks. Past him, looking downward, Lucy could see water gently lapping at the steps with at least two of them immersed, their shapes barely definable. Pushing by her, the other man had already shed his footgear; he followed Will into the flood.

"Damn! It's colder'n it was this morning! Hand stuff to me, Doc—we'll get out what we can!"

Lucy said, "I'll help."

"No, no, hon, you just stay right there."

But she already had stripped off her shoes and was stepping gingerly into the water.

The man was right. It *was* cold!

Twenty-one

It also smelled, and had myriad things floating on it. A clipboard sailed by Lucy and an empty dog chow bag, all on a tide generated by the two men's sloshing. She caught the clipboard, laying it on a dry step, and looked around, feeling her heart sink at the row of metal files, their bottom drawers inundated, the instrument cabinets, the stacks of dog food, the soaked cartons, the vast accumulation from years of doing business in this place.

The other man was saying, "Don't open those file drawers, Doc—it jus' lets more water in! Let's try to carry them upstairs, take 'em out there. If the stuff's real wet, we'll spread it out—I got room at my place in the back, if you need it. Here, ma'am, carry this—"

"This" was an armload of dog leads, collars, and tags from the top of a cabinet.

Obediently Lucy Maud sloshed to the stairs and on up, amazed to find her frozen toes still bent, and imagining what Will and his friend's feet were like. Behind her she could hear grunting as the two hefted a file cabinet. "I have to help," she thought, and threw down the leads on a handy chair.

"What the hell's goin' on?"

Two other men stood in the open doorway. The balding one answered himself: "Oh, Christ, Doc's been flooded! Is he down there?"

At Lucy's nod, he loped past, pausing only to turn up his pantlegs and say over his shoulder, "Charlie, run across the street—Bill Wendle's in the cafe, coffeein'—tell him to get a pump the hell over here! I know he's got one in the back of his store. Hey, boys, heft that up to me. Where do you want it, Doc?"

"Anywhere you can put it, Mac."

"Right."

"Anywhere" was almost on Lucy's bare feet. She hopped out of the way, making wet tracks on the carpet, then steadied the four-drawer file as he set it down. A thin stream of water ran from the bottom drawer.

"Oh, boy," the man said. "That doesn't look good." He glanced around. "Doc's examinin' table's back there. Suppose you could spread some of this stuff out if I dump the water?"

"Sure."

She helped him carry the drawer to the door and upend it on the street, then took the armload of soggy files. Behind her another cabinet had made its way up, and she could see three more figures dashing across the pavement. Another pair was slower, carrying what she guessed was the pump. By the time she had every available flat space covered with records, books, and loose papers, the upper floor space was crowded with wet, gleaming metal cabinets and there was the sound of a dull thrumming below her feet.

"God damn," the bald man called Mac was saying

as he came up the stairs. "Wish we'd known this earlier. I thought you had a pump, Doc!"

" 'Had' is the word," Will said grimly, coming into view accompanied by four other men in varying degrees of sog and slime and smelling like sewer rats. "Thanks, guys. I owe you all a big one! Oh, Lucy—you poor girl! And I had to get you into this mess! This isn't exactly what I had planned."

"I'll bet it ain't," said Mac, and everyone laughed cheerfully, poking each other.

Shaking his head ruefully at Lucy's bedraggled skirts and dirty hands, Will said, "Go on over to the bar, guys—tell 'em to set you up for me, I'd better take this lady home."

"If we'd still had Frank, Doc wouldn't have had a pump problem," said one of the men to Lucy, shaking his head as he reclaimed a pair of western boots from the pile. "Sure do miss that man. Jeez, Bill, are those moccasins yours? And I thought the basement smelled bad!"

Lucy, putting on her shoes over run-riddled hose, merely smiled an all-purpose smile. Straightening, she realized her back hurt, but that was small compared to Will. His face was gaunt with fatigue, his pants wet to his crotch, and he was limping as he waved his friends out the door.

She said, "Will, you're hurt."

"No—not really. I just tripped over a cabinet corner. Lord, hon—did you spread all this stuff out? You didn't need to do that—we could have got it done!"

"I wanted to help. We flooded at the library once. I remember what it's like—wow, do I ever remember that mess! Surprisingly—a lot of your papers will really be okay, Will—a little yellow, maybe—but as long as they don't dry stuck together, it's not too bad."

She was gabbling. She knew it. And he was just standing there, a tall, tired man in wet clothes, looking at her. She went on, "And you're right. You'd better take me home and then get there yourself. Will, you're worn out."

"That's not all I am," he answered softly, and the grin was still there, even in those weary green eyes. "Okay. I'm sleeping here tonight. Now, don't hissy-fit, 'Mom,' I do it often when I need to stay with an animal. Would you like to see where?"

"I think not," she replied calmly, belying the sodden lurch of her heart at the look in his eyes.

"Coward," he grinned, and followed her out the door. "Wow! It is cold when you have wet pants!"

"Don't you have anything dry?"

"Oh, sure—I'll get something later."

He swung up into his side of the truck, shivering in the damp night wind. "God, what a night. I am sorry, Lucy. Maybe I'd have been better keeping the beeper. If that skirt will clean, send me the bill. I can see grease on it, and heaven knows what else."

It was starting to rain again, coming down enough that he had to turn on the wipers as they headed toward her house.

The sound of the truck caused the front curtains to waggle, and a canine nose appeared.

"Your watchdog," Will said, pointing.

She was gathering up her bag and her umbrella. "Will! Don't get out. I'll make a run for it."

"Always a gentleman!" he said, limping around, opening the door, and reaching up his hand. "Watch it. The step's slick."

The rain was turning into mist, glowing softly orange in the light from the street lamp overhead. Will had left his wet cap on the seat, and his silver hair lay tousled on his brow like a little boy's. But the steady eyes behind the wire-rim glasses were not a child's as he looked up at her. Rashly, hardly believing her own words, she heard herself speak.

"Will, come on inside. You're going to catch cold. Let me throw those pants in the dryer and make you some hot coffee!"

"No!" he replied almost harshly, as though convincing himself. "Hon, I smell like a sewer, or worse. This is not how I meant this evening to go. And I won't have it this way. But—there is one thing you can do."

"What?" The word was almost a whisper; she was watching his eyes.

"Come here. Hold me. For just a minute. I promise—just a minute . . ."

Almost blindly she stepped down into his arms, felt them close around her, felt his face against her hair, knew that somehow her own arms had found their way to his wide, damp back. He was saying brokenly into her ear, "Lucy, Lucy . . . oh God, I so need someone to hold, to care, to make me come alive again. Is it you? Is it?"

Then headlights swept through the truck cab and sent shadowy bars along the side of Martha's house as a car pulled into Jessie's drive.

Lucy Maud felt Will's chest shudder against her, felt

his breath stop, then start again. Lightly he kissed both cold cheeks and let her go. Into her ear, he whispered, "If this isn't the measure of my whole damned day!"

On the other side of the truck they heard Vic Bonnelli's deep, cheerful voice saying, "Hey, that's Doc's pick-up! Run for the door, Tina sweetie; tell Grandma we'll bring the pizza in a minute."

Blindly, her knees ridiculously weak, Lucy turned toward the steps, then heard Will in her ear: "If you run, I'll smack you!"

Had she been trying to run?

If so, she stopped and turned, finding him smiling ruefully and winking at her. "Next time," he said in a voice so soft she almost didn't hear it, "my luck has to turn!" Then he shouted, "Hey, Vic? What was that about pizza?"

Gravel crunched, and Vic Bonnelli appeared around the bed of the truck. "Hi, guys. You want some? I got plenty."

"Lucy might—I have to run."

"You sure have—to something! Whoo-boy, man, what did you fall into—a hoglot?"

"Ain't it hell to be popular?" Will was swinging up into the passenger side, scooting over. "You tell them, Lucy. I'll see you tomorrow."

He backed out, his headlights casting elongated shadows behind Vic, Eileen, and a more slender figure Lucy suddenly recognized as John Basalti. She explained, adding, "And I'll pass, too. Thanks, though."

"If you change your mind, come on over."

"First I have to change clothes."

"I'd recommend it," Eileen said, and laughed. "Okay. Run, guys; here comes the rain again!"

Everyone dashed. As Lucy unlocked her door, another car turned in behind Vic's Toyota. Glancing curiously over her shoulder, Lucy saw Dilanna Lewis scramble out and join the others, John's arm going around her as they all went inside.

Jessie's door shut. No light remained but the misty orange blur of the street lamp.

Fumbling in the dark, Lucy stepped inside and felt a cold nose. It obviously started in surprise, then began to snuffle up and down her legs.

And Lucy Maud Marshall stood there in the shadowy living room, not knowing whether to laugh or cry. What an evening!

At age fifty-five, she must have developed a split personality!

This simply could not be the Lucy known to Millard—the calm, matter-of-fact spinster librarian, who delighted in TV documentaries, Oriental carpets, and the rewarding discovery that certain hyped bestsellers deserved the title.

This strange Lucy had just stood in the rain in the warm arms of a man she'd known hardly a week, loving the lean, strong feel of him, her heart beating wildly against his chest, her mouth turning, waiting, wanting!

That nothing else had happened was not the point. The point was that she'd wanted something else to happen—and now felt hollow. Shaken. Cheated.

And somehow she had the suspicion a dose of estrogen was not the answer.

At her knee Cutie sneezed, perhaps a comment of another sort. Lucy sighed, an enormous, bewildered sigh, and turned the overhead light on.

Everything was the same—tacky velour furniture, scraggly curtains, worn carpet on which she was now making two muddy prints. Nothing had changed. Except her.

Was she changing?

Even more scared, and scared in a totally different way, she put down her bag and umbrella and reached to feel something real, something graspable in two fluffy soft ears.

"Oh, Cutie," she said, "I need help!"

Then the telephone rang.

She ran for it, stumbling over the end table she'd forgotten she'd moved nearer the door, reeling into the door frame, and keeping herself upright only by frantically grabbing the back of the couch.

"Hello! Hello!"

The voice that replied sounded as though it was coming from an echo chamber. But it wasn't the sound that made her gasp. It was the words: "Well, you big city whore! So you finally made it home!"

Twenty-two

She couldn't believe her ears!

Angrier than she'd over been in her life, she demanded, "Who is this? Who is it?"

Her answer was only a click as the line went dead.

She slammed down the phone and stood glaring at it, fists clenched, street words boiling into her head at a rate that would have shocked Verna Marshall.

This was hardly the manner in which she'd thought to end her day!

The phone did not ring again. Turning toward her aunt's bedroom, Lucy Maud kicked off her damp, smelly shoes, reached back to unzip her blouse, and froze, elbows still in the air.

She almost couldn't believe the smug, self-righteous, virginal frump who had stood before that same mirror just a few hours ago and safety-pinned the damned thing so Will Evans couldn't handily get his fingers on her one bare breast!

Frustrated, angry, cheated, and insulted! How was that for a plateful of goodies? Perhaps other people returned happily to their old hometowns, renewing acquaintances, positively wallowing in maudlin memories of yesterday, but that certainly wasn't happening to her! Then on top of everything else this damned vet comes into her life and screws up the last of her common sense!

That she finally got to sleep at all was due more to total exhaustion than the power of reason. Morning came too soon—or not soon enough, depending on one's point of view.

The bottom line was, she admitted blearily, swinging her legs out of the dumpy bed next morning, that she was stuck here at least two more weeks. And she'd best learn to cope with the whole ball of wax. Stay cool. Occupy her time so fully there wasn't room for idle conjecture—or idle anything. In short, stay so damn busy sleep would be a luxury.

Doing what, smartass?

The library. That hole-in-the-wall morass of antiquated books, 1950 card system, and fusty, tatty paperbacks, needed so much help Andrew Carnegie would blanch in terror. So there's your answer, Lucy Maud Marshall. A Good Deed for Crewsville in Aunt Martha's name. Go for it!

No one was around when she parked her car in the library lot at nine. It was a little later than she'd meant, but she'd had to make a decision on storm windows and what color to paint the new front steps. Those earth-shaking matters out of the way, she delayed herself further by gassing the car and buying a new bag of dog food for Cutie.

If my finances don't get better she may be sharing with me, her disgruntled mind told her as she unlocked the creaky door and almost fell over a staggered spill of books on the floor.

Well. The Larry McMurtry that Tom wanted had returned.

She'd call him after a while.

First she'd check and shelve, then sit down and survey this half-baked operation. There had to be a few cost-free things that could be done to take it out of the literary Dark Ages.

By the time she was done with the shelving, bright sun slanted across the ancient tile floor, warming one card table. That seemed a reasonable place to sit with a cup of instant coffee and scan the local newspaper still stuck in the mail slot, she thought as she settled in.

Then she did get a jar.

Miss Wilson was dead.

She'd been found at the foot of her stairs where she'd apparently fallen, striking her head against a stone jardiniere. Her body had been discovered by Howard Lewis when she'd failed to answer the door . . .

The story ran on, but Lucy Maud didn't read it. She didn't need to know about post mortems and the rest. Miss Wilson was dead. That was it.

What she would remember was the face that had brightened just a few days ago when she had started reciting "Evangeline" right here in this library. How glad she was now that she had!

A shadow falling across the table before her was young John Basalti, saying a cheerful, "Hi!" and handing her a bright-covered Civil War novel. "Can you save this for Dilly? She'll pick it up this afternoon."

"And the note inside, I presume?"

He flushed and grinned. "Shoot. You're sharp. Can

you just think of yourself as Cupid? That's what Dottie always said."

Well, she certainly didn't want to countermand Dottie! Leaning back, she tossed the book on the desk, asking dryly, "Nothing else? No secret blueprints of an escape route or how to disguise herself as Darth Vader?"

"Nope. It's just that all her phone calls are screened, and this seems a simple way to communicate. How are your fuses? Nothing blowing?"

"They're fine, thank you."

"Good deal. See ya!" Halfway out the door, he wheeled, the wind sifting his fine, fair hair across his angular cheek. "Oh—my mom said to ask: if you're going to take books out to the homes again, would you please bring Grandpa a couple of Jack Londons!"

"Of course. If I can find any he hasn't read."

"That doesn't matter. He'll read 'em again."

This time he was gone, and Lucy heard the utility truck roar away. But she was already on her feet, thinking, that's the first thing to do! I'll bag up some books for the people on Karen's list and take them out tomorrow.

It was, however, the classic case of "easier said than done." If there had been someone else to work the desk while she bundled, it would have been a lot simpler. But with the arrival of the senior citizen bus things got a little complicated. Dilly's appearance on her lunch hour helped.

"I'll check out," she said cheerfully, her plump cheeks rosy from reading John's note. "You go on, get the other stuff together. There are rubber bands in that drawer—that's what Dottie always used on each patron's stack."

"Oh. Good idea," Lucy Maud said, checking the next item on the list that said "Mrs. Marples. Front Street. Two paperback romances and a *Better Homes and Gardens*. Code: 'MM'."

"The other 'M' is for Marva," Dilanna said, looking over her shoulder. "And pick sexy ones. I know that lady. She wants them hot enough to start a fire."

Lucy shrugged. Hers was not to reason why. "Where on Front Street?"

"Oh—I forgot. You haven't been back here long. That's the nursing home."

"The nursing home?"

"Yes. Mr. Holt's there, too. The Code 'AH' that says three Zane Greys and a Time-Life history book. Oh—I just checked in this old Jane Austen. Hasn't Miss Warpington been asking for it?"

Lucy Maud stopped rubber-banding some paperbacks and looked at the list. "Right. How did you remember that?"

"I drove her to the store the other day—Daddy got caught up in the Miss Wilson thing, you know—poor lady. I did like her—she was nice. Anyway, Miss Warpington said she'd loaned her own and never got it back, so I said I'd put her down for it. Ten minutes more and I have to run. May I put this pita in the microwave and zap it?"

"That's your lunch?"

"I had lunch with Mom. Two stalks of celery and a boiled egg." She grinned, pushing frizzy hair down her back. "Oh—if you need more book bags, Karen's got them under the desk."

"What I need are more large-print novels!"

"Give her a call. If they have some in Penfield that Crewsville hasn't had, she'll send them up with Will today. Hey—I hear he almost got drowned out at the clinic!"

"Yes." Lucy Maud suddenly turned away as the mental image of that tired face and the memory of those hungry arms holding her swept through her head. "That—that's a good idea. I'll phone her."

Karen was more than willing, delighted that Lucy Maud was going to try to make some home deliveries. "Ask Jessie Murphy if she won't come in tomorrow while you're out. She's done it for Dottie. And hey—have you seen Tim's dad today?"

"No."

If it was a very short answer Karen didn't notice. "He's so hoarse he can hardly talk. I'll send him up early with the books and you send him home. Okay? The man's pneumonia prone, anyway. Besides," and her voice lowered just a trifle, "I want him out of Penfield. Tim's mom is coming to dinner, and I don't need a fireworks display with dessert."

Lucy Maud hung up, struck by the unspoken import of Karen's words. Obviously, Will and his ex were not on the best of terms. Why? All he'd said was that she liked the city and he didn't, that she'd remarried and stayed there. But what had Vic Bonnelli said? Something about "not getting Reba out of his system?"

The "ping" of the storeroom microwave distracted her. Dilanna emerged, holding a pita in a napkin with red sauce on her chin. "Good!" she said. "You see nothing, you know nothing. Right?"

"The story of my life," Lucy Maud answered, grateful this chubby young woman couldn't know half the truth of the statement. "Thanks for coming in."

"No problem. But I do have to go. You should have a little break now until two o'clock or so. Maybe later. This is canasta day. 'Bye. See ya!"

The pita had started Lucy Maud's juices flowing. The young mother with two little girls looking for Waldo books said she'd check herself out. Knowing ruefully that what was in her fridge was mostly Cutie's, Lucy Maud got in her car and drove to Bunny Burger, which reminded her she'd gone through her cash pretty fast. Reluctant to even go near Howard's bank, she wrote a check for fuel at the gas station, had it accepted without a blink, and returned to the library musing on the advantages of small towns.

The place was empty except for one of the small girls sitting at the card table, reading aloud from a Dr. Seuss book, and Will Evans, sitting with her, listening.

"Hi," he croaked. He got up, put his arms around Lucy Maud so tightly she could feel the beat of his heart through the zippered jacket, kissed her forehead and her fluttering eyelids, and let her go.

"I needed that," he said hoarsely and sat down again.

"Karen's books are behind the desk. I'm sitting with Nancy—her mom will be back in a minute. Go on, hon; I suspect Miss Marshall likes Dr. Seuss, too."

Miss Marshall was trying to get control of her senses.

What had *she* needed? Was it really what this man had just set afire in her, sending warm, breath-catching waves through her entire body?

She half turned, coward that she was, ostensibly looking for Karen's books. "Oh. I see them. You—you sound terrible."

"I feel terrible. Damned cold, I guess. Self diagnosis." He was grinning, those green eyes rueful.

The little girl was looking at him solemnly. "Can't you do what you did for my kitty?"

"A couple of shots and a nice warm blanket?"

"And she was all better the very next day!"

"See? By golly, I *am* good!"

Then he was standing up again, putting his cap back on that tousled silver head, saying to Lucy, "I just wanted to see you for a minute. That's all. I am going home, Karen threatened to wreak terrible havoc if I didn't."

"May I—I do anything to—to help?"

"You just did. I'd like more of the same. Lots more. But later."

What was there to say to that? Only an inane, "Then take care."

"Oh, I will. I think perhaps I—I have a reason to now. Have I?"

A pure coward's answer: "I—I'm not—sure."

"But you didn't say 'no'."

He was turning away toward the door, a tall man in dirty jeans and muddy boots. "I'll call you. Okay?"

"Okay. Will—"

He turned, and she had to meet his eyes. A little huskily she said, "Take care."

And he grinned again, saying in a hoarse croak, "You bet!"

The little girl's mother and her other child were just coming back in. Will held the door for them, tousling the child's soft hair. "See ya!"

"See ya!" the girls and their mother echoed. Then he was gone. Through the window Lucy watched him swing up into that familiar pick-up truck and drive away.

The woman and her daughters took their stack of books and left also.

Alone, Lucy turned and put her head in her hands, leaning on the tall desk. Amazed at herself, appalled at herself, she thought, I feel like a sixteen-year-old!

Certainly not like a—a big city whore!

Twenty-three

The obnoxious telephone call was never very far from her mind during the next twenty-four hours. From ten o'clock on that evening she slept only fitfully, waiting for the phone to ring again, but it didn't. After that the impact lessened until she could almost laugh, realizing that whoever the caller had been, calling Lucy Maud Marshall a "whore" was so far off the mark it was ridiculous.

Even forty years ago she'd confined Howard Lewis's attempts at lovemaking to a few wet kisses and blind gropings. Since then, wrestling on a couch or in the back of a car had been pretty far from her agenda.

What she would do if Will Evans came on to her she deliberately blocked out of her mind. The young, innocent girl to whom Howard Lewis had been the rising sun had seen that same sun set with a crash. She didn't believe in second sunrises.

Determined to keep her resolve to stay usefully busy until she could leave Crewsville for good, Lucy got up early the next morning. Jessie had cheerfully agreed to "sit" the library, saying Tina could come there from school as easily as she could walk to her house. No problem.

No problem! That's what everyone said in this little insulated place!

Lucy Maud's impulse was to snap back, "Get real!"—to the old farmer who drove on, smiling when she slid into the last convenient parking place at the grocery store, to the woman who let her take the only package of margarine left in the sale bin, to the young carry-out boy who waited patiently with two huge, heavy bags of groceries while she fumbled with the wrong key to her car trunk.

Unloading her purchases at home, she found her Aunt Martha's minuscule freezer space would not accommodate both the new half-gallon ice cream container and the one that was almost empty.

"No problem," she said out loud, almost smiling, and ate the rest of the old one for breakfast.

Then she went back to the main street, loaded about a ton of books into her car trunk, took her list, and set off. It should be an interesting day, she realized.

The lady at the nursing home wanting sexy paperbacks turned out to be a cheerful soul of ninety-two who thanked Lucy Maud and then said, "Wait just a minute."

While Lucy obliged, she thumbed the first few pages of each selection, then put them by her bedside with an impish grin. "Okay," she said. "If they ain't in a pretty hot clinch by page twelve, I don't want 'em. When you're ninety-some, honey, you may not have the time to read to a hundred and ten to get to the smoochin'. These look good."

"I'm glad. I'll bring you some more next time."

"Yes, do, honey," said the arthritic lady in the next

wheelchair. She was smiling. "It'll keep her from climbin' in bed with Ben Clancy."

Lucy glanced swiftly at the ninety-year-old who only shrugged. "What does Ben Clancy think about that?"

"Oh, he don't mind. But his wife's none too pleased. Ain't it a cryin' shame about Leona Wilson?" she went on without a pause. "We'll sure miss her out here. She used t' play the piano for us on Thursdays. And I hear tell she was well nigh broke—although folks didn't know it until they started lookin' into her estate. How about that? I didn't think the Wilson money ever ran dry."

"There's a bottom to everything, I guess," Lucy Maud said, and went on down the hall. Next on her list was a bedfast gentleman bemoaning the death of Louis L'Amour and inferring one or two of his wife's favorite romance writers would have been much more expendable. That lady reached out from her easy chair and swatted him. The last person proved to be another feisty lady wanting a cookbook using wine. The doctor said she couldn't drink it, but nothing had been said about *eating* it.

"My daughter will cook me whatever I want," she told Lucy. "Isn't it a real shame about Leona Wilson? And they say she was near broke when she died. You'd sure not knowed it the way she dressed!"

Lucy Maud made her escape with a noncommittal nod and a feeling of *déjà vu*.

Far, far from routine, this phase of being a librarian was turning out to be a bit more than she'd expected. With a certain amount of relief she saw that there was only one more name on her list, and a private home at that.

Miss Warpington.

She parked in front of the handsome old brick home, picked up the Jane Austen, and mounted three steps edged in nicely trimmed ivy to ring the bell.

When the elderly teacher answered the door, Lucy was shocked to see how tired and worn she looked. But Miss Warpington said, "Lucy Maud! How nice of you to bring my book. I was just having a cup of tea—won't you join me?"

Truthfully the idea was not high on Lucy's list, but feeling so sorry for the thin, droop-shouldered shadow standing there, she said, "I'd like that. If it's no trouble."

"I'd enjoy it. Actually I probably need someone else in the house just now. The place is so full of—of ghosts. My parents are gone, my sisters, so many of my old friends—and now Leona. Leona! I'm still in shock. She was so well, so—happy, so full of plans on Friday . . ."

She stopped inside a cavernous living room, draped with Belgium tapestry and gestured at one of two deep chairs drawn up to the warmth of a fireplace.

"Please sit down, dear. I'll fetch another cup."

Lucy took one of the chairs and found for all its knobs and ornaments it was surprisingly contoured to the human frame.

"Chippendale," said Miss Warpington, reentering and stooping to pour amber fluid from a delicate pot into frail, saucered cups. "Some idiot said to me the other day, 'Eleanora, what do you *do* with real Chippendale chairs?' And I said back to her, 'Well—mostly I sit upon them.' Such a moron! Thank you for the Austen. Dilanna remembered, the dear child. Sugar, dear? Lemon?"

Lucy Maud shook her head and sipped. It was very good.

"Earl Grey," said her hostess, lifting her own cup to dry, thin lips. "How nice to have someone taking over from Dottie Mase. We've missed her dreadfully, we seniors. Most of us have surrendered our driver's licenses, some of us walk very poorly, and getting about is a problem to such places as the grocery store, not to mention the library. If we didn't have dear Howard, we'd really be in trouble"

"I—I understand the senior bus is—available."

"Oh, yes. And very nice. But it runs on a schedule, you see, and also I'm afraid my—my tastes don't always coincide with that of the other passengers."

In short, Lucy Maud thought to herself, you haven't changed. If you can't lead, you don't play . . .

Behind those thin-wire-framed glasses, Miss Warpington's sunken eyes were on the bright flickering flames of the fire. She said, "I suppose you haven't seen my umbrella."

What Lucy Maud had done was forget. "No. I'm sorry."

"No matter, I suppose. Strange—it had been Leona Wilson's, first. Then she gave it to me because she had a new one. Now—they're both gone."

Suddenly she put down her cup with so much force it clattered in the saucer, and turned those old eyes on Lucy Maud. Her voice was almost harsh. "I don't understand it. I just don't! What they are saying—that Leona's finances were in—in arrears. Why, she showed me her financial statement just last month, and her investments were booming!"

"I—I really have no information." There was nothing else Lucy could say. What she was thinking was that Miss Warpington had got herself into a real state!

"We compared notes," the lady was going on in that same thin voice, "and then I've meant to question Howard. He advised both of us, you see—and my situation was not half as—as comfortable. But with—Leona's death—it hasn't seemed appropriate to mention it. I—I just don't know what to make of it all!"

Then she stopped abruptly, made a wry face, and gave Lucy an apologetic smile. "Oh, dear. What am I saying? This is certainly no way to entertain a guest! I understand you've done quite well, Lucy Maud—since you left Crewsville. How good to hear that about one's students. I always have the somewhat vain thought that perhaps I contributed—if only a little. Heaven knows, I couldn't do so now—shorthand is practically an anachronism and standard typewriters are surely as antique as the chair you're sitting in!"

"But it was the start you gave us," Lucy answered, making a diplomatic effort to please this distraught and aging autocrat. There was certainly nothing to be gained by confessing that all the shorthand she remembered now was the fishing-pole line with the hook on it that meant "Dear Sir."

"How nice of you to say so. More tea?"

"I'm fine, thank you. But it's very good. I just have to go on soon. Is that someone else at your door?"

Miss Warpington leaned forward, craning her thin neck. "Oh—it's all right. That's Howard, and he has a key. Come in, dear. See who I have for my guest."

Howard Lewis entered, shutting the heavy, ornate door behind him, and the look he shot Lucy Maud was startled.

"Well! Indeed. Good afternoon, all. It's a bit brisk out there today."

His move was toward the fireplace, where he stood, his handsomely suited back to them both, rubbing his hands above the warmth. Miss Warpington rose to her full height, catching at the wing of the chair to steady herself.

"A bit dizzy after I sit," she said. "I'll get my wrap. Howard is going to run me over to the funeral home, dear. I'm sure you understand."

"Of course."

As the elderly lady went out, Lucy Maud said sternly to herself, Be in command, you idiot! Take charge!

She wished she were wearing her high heels. They had always made her just a bit taller than Howard. In oxfords they had been the same height.

Of course, now, she thought nastily, he's probably wearing elevator shoes!

She stood up, draining her cup and picking up her bag. "I must go."

"Lucy—"

He hadn't turned around.

"Yes, Howard?"

Then he did so. Under that ridiculous plaster of stringy, lacquered hair, his eyes were glazed with contact lenses but looking directly at her. For a moment. Then they darted away. And came back.

"I'm sorry about the—the other evening. On your porch."

"You should be."

"Can't we be friends?"

"I see no particular advantage in it."

He didn't like that. Not at all. Those eyes narrowed. "If you're staying here—"

"I'm not."

Was that relief in those rat-like eyes? Why? Surely Lucy Maud Marshall, aging spinster, was no threat to Howard Lewis! Or his fat wife. If necessary, she'd tell her so!

"I see. Still—I'm sorry things didn't—didn't go well for—us."

"Some times one gets a lucky break and is slow to recognize it."

"You're still angry!"

"No, Howard, I think the word is more like—like 'grateful'."

"Oh, thanks a lot!"

"Anytime. Besides, you got Amanda. Two breasts. And money. I should think you'd be the grateful one."

"God damn it to hell, woman, you don't half understand what I go through every day—"

His furious whisper died. Miss Warpington, clad in her fur coat, was entering again. "Sorry to be so long. I'm getting very absentminded; it's a real trial. Did I thank you for the book, Lucy Maud?"

"Yes," Lucy Maud answered, turning toward the door, pleased with herself for having handled the bastard very well. She didn't give a tinker's dam what he went through every day!

"Good-bye. Thank you for the tea. I enjoyed it."

She made sure she was in her car and on her way before the two of them entered the lemon Cadillac nosed against the curb. She wanted no more interchange. Not now. It had been a long day. She was tired. Head librarians, as a rule, aren't required to spend their day lugging books from door to door. Her arms ached.

Aunt Martha's living room would actually look welcoming, tatty chairs and all. And Cutie, her warm, furry self nestled up against her side.

"Oh, I don't believe I'm thinking that!" said Lucy Maud aloud in amazement, and drove the three blocks to the library in an almost stunned state.

A dog! She was looking forward to seeing a dog!

Then a rather sobering and poignant thought struck: is this what it's like when one has nobody else?

And—suddenly realizes it?

Twenty-four

Little Tina was on the sidewalk outside the library jumping rope by herself, shiny black curls flopping. As Lucy Maud parked she opened the library door, calling, "Grandma! Grandma! The lady's back!" Jessie appeared immediately and helped Lucy Maud carry the two bags of returned books up the steps.

"I lit the ol' kerosene heater," Jessie said as Lucy felt the welcome warmth. "Didn't figure you'd mind. And I found the Halloween decorations. It's next weekend, and the old folks do enjoy seein' 'em."

"I wike skel-ton," Tina said, laying her rosy cheek against the knobby cardboard knee of a bony personage hanging by the door.

"I feel like one," said Jessie briskly. "Sandwiches just don't hold me anymore. Tina and I will walk home, now—work some of her energy off. But remember—I got pot roast tonight. We're kind of celebratin' as it looks like Eileen is going to get the Bunny Burger manager job. Evelyn Cass, down in Penfield, has recommended her, and it sure will be a lot more convenient for us. So Vic's comin', too—never turns down a feed, that Vic. And I ask Doc." She was pulling on a heavy sweater, buttoning it. "Figured he could use a good meal also, the way he sounds. So come on over. 'Bout six, I reckon. Put your hood up, honey, that wind's chilly."

Tina obediently flipped up the top of her pink jacket. "I got a dog book, lady. Grandma checked it out on her card."

Lucy Maud said, "Fine," almost automatically, her mind still on what Jessie'd just said. Doc. For dinner. Should she go? Or—not . . .

She waved them out the door and turned to the desk, finding it neat and clear, with orange and black crepe paper streamers looped across the front.

For just a moment she envisioned how Pam's department in Millard would look now, with all the ghosts and pumpkins and a bright "Happy Halloween" sign emblazoning the doorway. Upstairs, Lucy always had fat jack-o'-lanterns with smiling faces and a special black vase holding orange marigolds on her desk.

Probably Kathryn MacClane was above such mundane things.

Well, she wasn't. Tomorrow she'd spare just a little cash on something for the front windows, and perhaps a few more Halloween candies for the jar Jessie had set out.

But she wouldn't fill the jar. She'd learned that from three elderly Millard ladies who calmly helped themselves with small plastic bags out of their purses. At her look of outrage one of them said, "Well, our husbands couldn't come today."

Their husbands, to Lucy Maud's knowledge, had the reading level of See Dick, See Jane—besides which, they hadn't even been in the library since opening day in 1924.

But some women were just like that. More women than men, it appeared, Lucy amended to herself, lugging the book bags around behind the desk. There was time to process them before she went home, and besides, the shelves looked a little bare. Jessie had had a good day.

She was just separating the battered old Faith Baldwin novels to put another in its proper place when a brisk breeze announced the door opening behind her. Glancing around, she saw an elegantly clad woman standing there, a surprised look on a cosmetically sealed but very beautiful face.

Lucy Maud asked pleasantly, "May I help you?" A sales person? A magazine rep? she wondered.

The woman put a slender hand with perfectly enameled nails to soft, well-shaped brown hair. "Mrs. Mase. Dottie. She's not here?"

Ah. She *was* a sales rep. Salaries had certainly gone up if she could dress like that! Perhaps, Lucy Maud thought wryly, I ought to pursue that phase a little harder!

"I'm sorry. I understand she's moved to California."

"Oh? Really! Well."

The woman shrugged. "Then you haven't seen Dr. Evans."

Lucy replied a little stiffly, "Not today," very aware that now the woman's eyes were flicking up and down—and were unimpressed.

Who was she? One of Will's earlier conquests? Looking for a rerun?

She was already half out the door.

"Tell him Reba was asking for him," she said, and disappeared, high heels clicking on the steps as she went.

Conscious of soap opera tactics, Lucy Maud nevertheless moved to the window and watched her drive away. She had a nice, dark green something-or-other— Lucy never could identify cars anymore—with a Springfield plate. And for some reason the name "Reba" should be ringing a bell . . .

So—big deal! If Will Evans's past occasionally came back on him, it certainly wasn't her affair.

Even so, the remainder of the books were shoved rather than shelved, and there was a little less zip to her step as she started for her car.

If only the woman hadn't been so—so beautiful! Part of it had been cosmetics and taste—but neither of those could disguise a lissome waistline, beautifully curved full breasts, and shapely legs.

Feeling very "run of the mill," Lucy parked in her drive, paralleling Vic Bonnelli's Toyota next door. She waved back at Tina who was perched on her grandmother's front step petting a very large, very serene tan Labrador retriever, and almost walked into wet paint although the warning sign was close enough to bite her.

Then she used the back door and was met by a waggy dog who not too subtly led her to an empty bowl.

At least Cutie knew what she wanted!

I am, Lucy admitted, more tired than I thought. My back aches. I could stop this silly nonsense in my head, use weariness as an excuse to Jessie, put on my night stuff, and fall into bed.

But I'm not going to do that.

I want to see Will. There. I've admitted it.

Permitting herself to think no more deeply than that, Lucy washed up perfunctorily, plugged in the curling iron, and looked at her limited wardrobe.

Now that the silk blouse smelled like a sewer, there really wasn't much choice. It boiled down to the pink sweater again or the "shit" shirt—and since Tina was obviously present, the pink sweater got the nod.

If Jessie'd wanted a fashion plate she certainly wouldn't have asked her neighbor anyway, Lucy thought, being a realist. Pulling on the sweater, she brushed and curled her hair as best she could, recalled momentarily her stylist back in Millard who charged thirty bucks a whack, and put on some more lipstick.

The neighborhood was sliding into the blues and grays of cloudy twilight with the street lamps popping on one by one as she let Cutie do her evening route, anointing each tree and bush. She didn't hear Will's pick-up pulling in behind Vic's car until suddenly he was just standing there, saying, "Hi" in the same hoarse voice.

"You don't sound any better!" She made her voice severe to disguise the sudden triphammer beat of her heart.

"But I feel better. Just seeing you."

"What Blarney stone did you touch?" she rejoined, avoiding the look she knew she'd see in the tired green eyes behind the glasses. "Hard day?"

"Worrisome. There's distemper going around—I

saw three dogs and a cat today. But don't worry—Cutie's had her shots. Frank was good about that."

At her name, Cutie trotted over to have her ears fluffled and stood obediently on three paws as he inspected the other ones in rotation.

"She's doing fine," he said, standing erect again and brushing leaves from his knees. "Are you out of salve?"

"Not quite."

"Remind me. I have some in the truck."

She nodded, opening the kitchen door for the dog to trot inside while he waited by the bottom step. He was looking at the backyard, dark and quiet in the twilight.

"Frank used to have his Scouts meet back here. When Tim was a kid. Say—did anyone tell you about that old well?"

"Jessie." She was locking the door. Let them think what they would. They weren't getting nasty phone calls!

"Good. Does Vic know? It really ought to be filled in. Frank hated to do it—water gets pretty short around here some summers and it's a live vein—still, I think the thing is damn dangerous."

"I know about it. But I'll tell Vic, anyway."

Together they walked through the break in the scruffy hedge, their feet scuffling leaves as a light wind swirled around them. There was a huge, venerable old elm tree at the corner of Jessie's veranda, its soaring branches almost empty. As they passed the gnarled trunk Will said suddenly, softly, "Wait." His arms went around Lucy, holding her gently, rocking her a little against his chest, his cheek pressing her hair. She could feel his heart beating steadily against her real breast, and his hoarse voice reached her ears in a low rasp, "I won't kiss you. You don't need this damn cold. I won't—oh, the hell I won't!"

How could one man's mouth be so hard, so searching, so sweet? She felt her own arms go helplessly upward around his bent shoulders, holding him, hearing him whisper, "Oh, God, oh God . . ." and wrap her even tighter, closer—

Then they both heard something else: Jessie's voice at her front door. "I know I saw 'em comin'—where in the world—"

They sprang apart like guilty children. But Will took time to whisper, "Later, hon . . ." before calling back cheerfully, "We're coming, Jess! Hold the biscuits!"

"Keepin' Vic and Pa off 'em is the problem," the little aproned lady said, pushing the screen door wider. "It's gettin' chillier! Maybe put on our storm windows tomorrow. Leave your jackets there on the couch with Vic's. Everyone to the table. Lucy, have you met my husband? Calvin, this is Martha's niece—you know—Frank's—"

But whatever else she said was totally negated by a sudden harsh coughing spasm from Will.

"Damn!" he said shakily, still choked up. "I was hoping I'd get by without that, too. I'm okay, Jessie. Just let me get a drink of water . . ."

Eileen, her face sober above her Bunny Burger top, was already handing him a glass. He drank it and said, "There. Better."

"Good!" That was Calvin Murphy, a short, stocky

man with a crewcut and crinkles around his eyes. He'd already nodded at Lucy Maud, acknowledging her presence. "Whatever you gave my boss's cat last winter, Doc, you'd better try some yourself. It sure worked on her."

" 'Physician, heal thyself,' " Will murmured as their host herded them all toward the bright dining room.

It was a round table beneath a stained-glass chandelier, heaped with food and smelling redolently of pot roast. Jessie bustled, seating them all, and her husband started passing dishes.

"Ignore the silly lights," he said to Lucy Maud across the table. "The damn chandelier is what sold Jessie on the house ten years ago, but I still can't get used to pink mashed potatoes. I hear tell you had a little flood, Doc."

"You heard right." Will cleared his throat, and Jessie said, "Don't make him talk, Cal. Ask Lucy—she was there."

"Getting distemper shots, no doubt," grinned her host and Lucy found herself—incredibly—almost blushing.

"Of course," she answered. "And mercy! It did smell. I spread files out to dry and some other gentlemen helped lug stuff upstairs, and—well—it was an interesting experience."

So, as a matter of fact, was the rest of the meal. Everyone bantered back and forth in a cheerful give-and-take almost like—like family. Or what she'd heard was like family. She'd certainly never known. The men carried the dishes to the kitchen while Jessie dealt out absolutely sinful pieces of apple pie which they all took back to the living room to eat while the ten o'clock news was on TV and Vic rocked a sleepy Tina.

Lucy Maud felt as if she was living a Laura Ingalls Wilder novel.

Will had gone out to his truck and dosed himself with something that lessened his coughing, and when Calvin proposed a round of gin rummy, he said, "Sure we will. I'm not in any hurry. Are you, Lucy?"

Lucy wasn't either—especially if her phone was ringing next door with that nasty voice on the line. But she'd never played gin rummy and said so.

"I'll watch," she smiled—a firm smile, and Will recognized it.

"Sit here so you can see Calvin's hand," he said.

Actually what Lucy ended up doing was rinsing dishes for Jessie to put in the dishwasher. Eileen carried Tina up to bed then joined them, sitting down at the small kitchen table and getting out a cigarette.

Her mother said promptly, "Don't you light one of those nasty things in here!"

"Oops. Forgot." Amiably, Eileen put them away. "And that from one of the three-pack-a-day folks," she said to Lucy.

"Four years ago," Jessie added proudly. "Ain't had a one since. And I don't want one. Lots of folks say they do." She was raising her thin eyebrows at Lucy, who shook her head as she sat down across from Eileen.

"Not me," she said and left it at that, thinking only that quitting smoking was one of the few problems she hadn't had.

"Coffee?"

Eileen held her cup out to her mother. Lucy shook her head. Jessie poured another for herself and sat down on the third chair.

She said to her daughter, "You hear about Leona Wilson?"

"Yes. That's a shame. She was a nice lady—always thanked the Bunny girls and left a tip, never complained—and never filled her purse with sugar packets. We had to stop putting them out on the table," she said to Lucy. "Some of those old ladies would clean the rack. And funny—it wasn't the poor women; it was the rich ones."

"Well," said Jessie, stirring sugar into her cup, "from what I'm pickin' up, that sure wasn't Leona. They're saying she was broke."

"Leona?"

"S'what I hear."

"I thought the bank was managing her money."

"If they were, they managed it right into the ground. I want a cookie. You girls?"

They shook their heads. Jessie reached far back to the counter and said, "Ouch—darned shoulder!" She got up and took the lid from the cookie jar. "Good thing you don't," she said, bringing out one cookie.

Eileen asked, "Tina?"

"Your dad."

"I should have guessed. Hey, Mom, you'd never guess who was in Bunny Burger today."

Jessie frowned, munching. "Who?"

"Reba."

Then the frown deepened. Noticeably. Lucy Maud,

whose attention had been caught sharply by the name, sat very still.

Jessie said, "Lookin' for Doc, I suppose. What the hell's she doin' in town?"

"Beats me."

"He sure don't need her."

Lucy said carefully, "Very—pretty woman?"

"Probably. Got a modeling agency over in Springfield. Why—did she come in the library, too? Sure she would—checkin' to see if Dottie was still there."

"Yes. She came in."

"That figures. She don't want him but she don't want to let him loose either. Doc's ex," Jessie added grimly. "Tim's mom. Only good thing she ever did."

"Except leave Doc."

"That, too. Poor man. Think we ought to warn him?"

"Maybe he wants to see her."

"Doc doesn't know what he wants. That's the damned problem."

This conversation between mother and daughter was settling a cloud on Lucy Maud. That beautiful woman was Will's former wife. And he didn't know what he wanted?

If she were a man—she'd know!

Twenty-five

They heard the sound of "Gin!" in the dining room, then raucous laughter and chairs being scraped back.

Vic appeared in the doorway, buttoning his collar and tightening his tie. "I have to drive to Penfield tonight," he said. "Better get goin'. Thanks for asking me, Jessie."

"Any time. You know that." Jessie was looking over his vast, bulky shoulder at Will. "You, too?"

"I won three hands in a row. Beginnin' to feel a bit unwelcome," Will grinned. "Maybe my luck is turning." He was looking right at Lucy Maud. "Want me to stop and check Cutie's paws?"

Jessie said severely, "If that's all you're checkin'."

"You're my chaperon?"

"Too late for that. I'm Lucy's."

"Negative," said Calvin, putting a burly arm around his wife's shoulders. "You ain't got time to chaperon nobody. I've been gone ten days, lady. We have some catchin' up of our own to do."

Vic Bonnelli whistled, "Wow! What was in that pie? Hey, Eilly, maybe you're in the way. Want to go to Penfield with me?"

"I'll lock my door," Eileen answered, laughing. "My

shift starts at four tomorrow morning. Good night, all. See some of you tomorrow."

As the cool night air swept in, another small car pulled up beside Vic's Toyota, and Dilanna Lewis climbed out.

"Hi, she said. "Can you take in a refugee? Mom and Dad are at it again and I just had to bail out."

"John's not here."

"I know. He's in Penfield, doing a job—won't be back until tomorrow. But Mom bought a new car—she always gets one for her birthday but Daddy didn't buy it this year so she bought it herself last week and wrote a check and the check almost bounced and Dad is positively livid—" The girl was rattling, her round face miserable beneath the porch light, her chubby hands clutching a coat half thrown across her shoulders. Jessie reached out and gave her shoulders a squeeze.

"Okay, hon, no problem. Just turn on the TV and hit the couch like you always do. G'night, everybody."

"G'night!"

It was a chorus. Vic went to his car and Lucy Maud felt herself being guided firmly back through the break in the hedge. Getting her key out, she said a little breathlessly, "You've checked Cutie's paws."

"Damn! You remembered!" But he was chuckling softly behind her, reaching around to push at the door that had started sticking since all the rains. "May I do it again?"

"I suppose!"

She put a pseudo-weary sound in her voice, thinking the light approach might not be too apropos.

Cutie was already greeting him, her tail a blur. Lucy

moved ahead, snapping on the living room lights, tossing her coat in through the door at the bed, and turning to the television. He was following her, the dog a furry shadow.

"Channel 10 okay?" she asked.

"Fine. And I promise not to go to sleep."

"Coffee?"

"Got it made?"

"It doesn't matter. That's what microwaves are for."

Calm. Practical. Prosaic. That's what she must be— all of those things. A friend. Watching the news. Going on home, shortly.

When she returned with two steaming cups, he was sitting on the couch, but Cutie, looking a bit miffed, was on the floor.

"Looks fine." He took the coffee and gestured at the couch beside him. "Sit. Share the feeling I have— that Frank and Martha are smiling down at us."

"I never knew Frank. I realize now that I—I hardly knew Aunt Martha."

But she was obeying! She was sitting down. On the worn couch. Next to Will Evans!

Lucy Maud Marshall, ex-head librarian for Millard, whose previous experiences, excluding Howard Lewis, had been basically laughing at the unreality of paperback romances—was sharing a seat with a man who had just put his arm around her shoulders.

He had also kicked off his shabby boots and was resting stockinged feet on the warmth of Cutie's back.

The socks matched.

"I dressed up," he said, grinning sideways.

"I'm complimented."

"You should be. It took me ten minutes to find a pair."

She took one finger and drew an imaginary star in the air. Then she sipped at her coffee. It was almost boiling but she would have sipped if it had been liquid fire.

His was on the end table at his elbow, along with a small pot of ivy Lucy had bought at the grocery store.

"Pour it hot, drink it cold," he said. "Used to drive Tim's mother insane. But real hot hurts my teeth. Always has."

His eyes were straight ahead, casually watching the newsman on the tube describe the latest governmental upset in Asia. The arm about her shoulders was motionless. But the fingers were turned, casually stroking the soft hair behind her ear.

He sighed. "Nice," he said. "Wow. I feel a hell of a lot better. Something took effect—the antibiotic, Jessie's cooking or—or you."

He wasn't looking at her. She almost wished he'd turn his head. At least then she'd have a clue from his eyes!

"It's me, of course," she answered lightly. "Hey—I never thought—want some cookies? There's a package of Oreos in the kitchen."

"No, thanks. Dottie was the cookie person. Since she's been gone I've finally shed a few pounds and want to keep it that way."

But he'd felt her stiffen.

And he did turn, those green eyes looking at her levelly. "Whoa," he said. "Hey. No, no, don't watch the damn television—look at me. What have the local ladies been telling you about Dot and myself?"

Struggling for equanimity, she said, "It's really not my business."

"That's a moot point. Since it is my business, did they tell you Dot's husband had been my partner? That he lay in that nursing home three years dying of cancer while I did what I could to help his wife? That when he died, she moved to her kid's in California? Did they bother to mention those things at all?"

"No." All anyone had ever said was what a nice lady she'd been and how everyone missed her! The additional allusions had mostly been in Lucy Maud Marshall's own small mind! "No—they—they just probably assumed I knew. She was—was very well liked."

"Don't throw sops at me. Just get things straight."

She made herself smile. "It's hard. I've been away from a small town a long time. I forget that people assume you know the—the important things."

"They do that. Because they're seldom interesting. They're facts. It's the other stuff that draws attention. Now. Since you've heard the facts about Dottie and myself—want to hear another one?"

"Another what?" He had relaxed, his lean fingers stroking her hair again, and she needed to buy a little time.

"Fact."

"Okay."

"I like you. I like you lots."

"I'm complimented."

"Good. But that's not quite what I was hoping to hear."

Parry. Thrust. Parry. Thrust.

"What were you hoping to hear?"

"That you liked me, also."

"I do." Or I wouldn't be sitting here on this couch with you, numbskull!

"Lots?"

"Define 'lots'."

"More than a little. Equivalent to a bunch." But he was laughing. "At least enough for me to want to keep you here in town indefinitely."

"I may be here indefinitely."

It just came out—she hadn't meant to say that at all. Dismayed, she added hurriedly, "I—I just don't know how things will go. You know. The—the house, and all."

"I figured that was Vic's problem."

"It is. Really. But I—" She stopped, bit her lip, closed her eyes. Then very quietly, she went on, "I just had to get away from Millard a while."

"Burnout?"

"Would that it were."

He was waiting. And she confessed. The new library. Kathryn MacClane. The job she had in store if she *did* go back.

At the end, he said angrily, "What a bitch!"

She didn't dispute that. "But a bitch going to bed with a senator."

"Which one?"

She told him. His silver brows rose like two croquet hoops. "Then you haven't really got away from her yet, hon."

"Why? What do you mean?"

"I mean that's the senator whose son just married

Dilanna Lewis's sister. He'll be here in Crewsville Saturday, staying with the Krueshanks. They're giving a big, fancy reception for him. He's forming a cultural delegation to visit Europe, and Dilanna's mother wants to go so bad she can taste it."

"I shall certainly avoid the Krueshanks this weekend."

"Oh, I don't know." His lean face was elfin. "He's bringing his wife. The Krueshanks have quite a bit of political pull—and they're good Christian folks."

"And you have a devious mind!" She could already envision the senator's distinguished face should he glimpse her chatting with Mrs. Krueshank.

"He'd know you."

"Oh, yes. We've sat on a number of panels together. But he thinks I'm a hundred miles away."

"Then let's do it. I can get invitations. He needs someone to blow the whistle on him anyway, the bastard. And understand me, hon. This isn't so you can leave Crewsville. This is just to dish a little back. Okay?"

She'd have to buy something elegant to wear. It would probably break her bank balance. Why in the world hadn't she packed the new outfit meant for the library opening? Who could send it to her? Maybe Pam would manage something . . .

"Earth to Mars!"

Will's laughing voice finally penetrated. She said, "Oh—sorry! I was trying to think what I'd wear."

Then he did laugh, throwing back his head, his broad shoulders shaking, making Cutie prick up her ears.

"My God! Women are wonderful! This guy and his

girlfriend screw you good! You have a chance to screw back—but by all that's holy you're damn well going to be dressed right for it! Oh, Lucy, Lucy—"

He put both arms around her then, pulling her over against him, holding her tightly. And his laughter stilled as his mouth found hers, then left it to kiss her eyelids, then went back to the sweetness he'd found on the soft lips she had no power to deny him.

He murmured against them, his voice thick, "Oh, Lucy, how I've been needing this, how I've been needing you . . ."

And the phone rang.

And again.

Again.

"Damn it all to hell!" Will muttered, giving her one last kiss before he released her from his warmth, his desire, the incredible haven of his stroking hands. "It's the damn vet in me," he said as she slipped away and went unsteadily toward the hall.

She had a suspicion she'd have let it ring until hell froze over.

"Hello."

No answer. Oh God! Not one of those!

"Hello!"

Then harsh breathing. And words—words pouring out, of indescribable filth and anger. Then a click. And silence.

Will saw her face and was up from the couch, going to her instantly, taking her hands. "Honey—what was it?"

Swallowing hard, she told him.

His arms were around her in a different way now,

rocking her, murmuring comfort. "Not kids? You're sure it's not kids . . ."

"I'm—I'm sure." She wasn't naive enough to say that kids didn't know those words. But the disguised voice was not young. Who? Who?

Then suddenly something came back to her in a searing flash . . . *you one-boobed whore!*

And she knew. She knew who.

But she couldn't tell Will. Or, she wouldn't. This was one affair she would have to take care of herself.

Besides, Will's pocket was beeping.

Twenty-six

Will said a few well-chosen words, scrabbling with one hand in his pocket. Behind the wire rims his eyes were rueful but honest.

"Honey," he said, "you may as well understand—if I'm lucky enough to win you over—this is one thing I can't ignore."

Then he was talking on the thing, saying, "Damn. Sure. I'll be right there."

To her he said, "Mrs. Beasley's rottweiler is whelping, and things aren't going well." Then he repocketed the beeper, putting his other arm around her once more, and hugging her close. In her ear, he murmured, "Prelude for beginners," and laid that hard, tender, warm mouth on hers again. "Dream about me," he added, and let her go.

What do you say to a man who has been the first to hold and kiss you lovingly in almost twenty years? Have a good day?

"I'll call," he said from the open door. "You answer. And lock your damn door!"

As the noise of his truck backing from the driveway came to her, she looked down at Cutie.

"This can't be me," she said. "This can't be Lucy

Maud Marshall! Not the one I've known for fifty years!"

But of course it was. And the bottom line was that whatever was going on, Lucy Maud Marshall had to deal with it: filthy phone calls; no job; short of cash; and one aging vet who made her heart race. Damn! Which one first?

None of the above. Not yet. Lock the doors, go to bed, and deal with everything in the morning.

She didn't dream of Will, as she hardly slept. But by morning she had come up with something of a plan.

As far as Howard Lewis was concerned, if he confined himself to disgusting phone calls, the hell with him! And she thought he would—he was too much of a local public figure to risk exposure just to get at her. The job situation was critical, but she could get by a little while, particularly if Vic sold the house. As for Will—if something was trying to happen there, the minute he found she had just one breast it would all be over, anyway. She'd be left with nothing but pain again.

The immediate thing she could do—and what her less meritorious being wanted to do—was screw the senator! Screw him good!

So she'd better call Pam, ask her to express that new blue outfit, and tell Will she did want to go to the Krueshank bash.

This resolved, she got out of bed, got into the tub, got dressed, went to Bunny Burger for breakfast, and ran into Howard Lewis.

Actually, she saw Miss Warpington first, sitting in

a sunny booth sipping coffee while a waitress in a ghost costume took her order. Oh, yes. Halloween.

"Please, dear, do sit down," Miss Warpington said, patting the seat beside her.

Lucy Maud did, because she was shocked again at how pale and drawn the elderly teacher looked above the immaculate blouse, the routine string of pearls, the careful make-up. Mostly it was the eyes, half-lidded and tired behind the glasses.

"I think dear Howard has decided I'm not capable of doing for myself," she said ruefully. "And I'm not sure he isn't right. My lunch is brought in, and for dinner I dine with friends, but I've always done my own breakfast—until now. I—I am just so upset about Leona. He says he found I'd put mustard sauce on my toast this morning, and I don't even recall making toast! Of course, he's very upset about her, also. It was a dreadful experience, finding her that way—wasn't it, dear?" The latter directed itself to the man in person as he placed a tray on the table and glanced with some uncertainty at Lucy Maud.

Or—was that what it had been? Uncertainty? Displeasure? He smiled, although his sunken eyes did not, and said, "Well, this is nice. Good morning, Lucy. May I get you something?"

"I've ordered. Thank you."

Then he sat down across from them, easing that paunch against the edge of the table and straightening his necktie—a gesture that Lucy Maud recognized from a hundred years ago as one he made when nervous.

Fine. She'd like him nervous.

"Yes, it was a bad experience," he said. "She was a very nice lady. Oh—excuse me. I see my daughter's just come in."

His daughter had also just gone out. He caught up with her in the parking lot, and Lucy could see very well over Miss Warpington's shoulder that they were not pleased with each other. Miss Warpington, however, was absently breaking toast into bits and saying, "I—I just don't understand. So many things. You know, I told you, dear, that Leona had just shown me her balance sheet on her investments and they were more than adequate. I'd been intending to chide dear Howard because he hadn't done as well for me—I'd even had Leona make a copy of hers so I could show him what I disliked—it's around the house somewhere I'm sure—but I kept forgetting. And now they say she was absolutely penniless. I just don't understand!"

Lucy Maud had paid very little attention, her eyes on Dilanna who was walking to her car with stiff shoulders. Howard, sliding back into his seat and grunting as the table edge cleaved his stomach, asked, "You don't understand what, my dear?"

"Oh—nothing to concern yourself about, Howard. Later, perhaps. Eat your breakfast."

"Then eat yours."

"I—I just don't seem to be hungry—and you brought me a double marmalade, Howard; I do appreciate that—I'm such a marmalade eater—but—but, Lucy Maud, why don't you have some?"

Howard's hand shot out as though from a cannon. "I'll take it," he said. "I—I suppose Lucy's on a diet. All pretty women seem to be."

"Well, well, I do thank you," Lucy Maud murmured, thinking what a contrast between this fat punk who smiled with his mouth and Will Evans who smiled with his eyes. Later, she realized a curious thing—Howard had swept the marmalade container into his pocket. At the moment, she was torn between wishing she was elsewhere and concern for the elderly woman beside her.

Miss Warpington was toying with her quiche. "I was just lamenting Leona's death to Lucy," she said. "And just at Halloween. Curious. Leona always loved Halloween when we were teaching. I found it a bore—or so I said. Recently I've realized that some things the children did really frightened me. An overdose of *Dracula* when I was young, I suppose."

"Dracula?" The question was from Howard, chowing on cheesy eggs.

"The novel, dear. Not the movie. Oh, yes—it gave me nightmares. That's one classic you don't need to bring me from the library, Lucy."

"Then I won't. I'm not even sure they have it, anyway."

"Oh, they do. I gave it to them. I think. Oh, dear, how things do leave your memory when you're ninety. However—if you will stop by, Lucy, I'll return the book I have."

"You're done?"

"I'm not sleeping. Reading is preferable to tossing and turning."

"I agree," answered Lucy wryly as she balled up her napkin. "I must run. Nice to see you, Miss Warpington."

She didn't mention that it was nice to see Howard, and he didn't seem to notice. Her predominant sense was that he felt very relieved at her going.

Well. He was no delight to her, either.

Her intention was to go back to Martha's and do some more furniture shifting—anything to make the place look better—but the cheery workmen waving from the roof were banging away at such a rate that even Cutie indicated a desire to go anywhere else that was quieter. Jessie, hanging wet, white sheets on her clothesline, said, "Poor puppy. Come on over here. It's all right, Lucy, I'll mind her. Say—Vic was by with two folks lookin' for a starter house. They seemed to like the place a lot—Vic said he'd catch you later." Her speech was a little muffled by two clothespins clenched in her teeth. "They would want the old well opened. She's got a thing about chemicals in the water. And that might be good for everyone—seems to me that old top is really sinking down. Rotted, probably. Want a cup of coffee?"

"Just had one, thank you." It was good news about the selling prospects; however, she did need to call Pam. Having Jessie listen in on the conversation didn't seem too diplomatic—but talking through that din at Martha's would be impossible. "I'm going to run down to the library."

"Okay. I'll tell Vic."

"Thanks. I'd appreciate it."

Little towns, she mused, backing out again and heading for the main street. You certainly don't need an answering machine . . .

The shabby library door was unlocked. Dilanna

Lewis sat on the high stool behind the desk, checking in a stack of books.

"Hi," she said, a little wearily. "Hope you don't mind. I needed something to do until my dad gets involved in the morning paper work. We're not—too happy with each other right now."

What do you answer to that?

Wisely, Lucy Maud said nothing, only gave the plump shoulder a pat in passing. As she put her handbag in the storeroom, she noticed a container of yesterday's coffee in the microwave, punched it on, waited, poured two Styrofoam cups and went back out into the main room again.

"Oh—thanks." Dilanna accepted hers gratefully. "I need it. I need something. I tell you, Miss Marshall, since my sis got married it seems everything's going down the tube! Mom yells at Dad, Dad yells at Mom— Mom is set on going on this excursion thing with my sis's father-in-law, Senator Porfield, and I don't think Dad can afford it though he doesn't say exactly that— there's just a feeling—you know—and then she threatens him with something—I'm not sure what, but he really gets upset—and she bought that new car—oh, it's just the pits around home! If I didn't know for sure I'd lose my job if I ran off and married Johnny, I'd do it in a flash—but he doesn't make very much, and we'd probably have to move away, considering how my parents would feel, and honestly! Honestly! Sometimes I feel I'll just go nuts! Oh—oh—almost forgot. Give Doc Evans a call."

"All right." What a casual reply disguising the heart

in her throat! "I've another call to make, first. Then I will."

"And I'd better run. It's almost nine. This stack is checked in, I can't find the cards for this stack, and this copy of Danielle Steel's new book is a 'gimmie.' Mrs. Burkiser at the grocery—she donated it. See ya!"

"See ya," Lucy Maud echoed, not even hearing herself, but adding automatically, "Thanks." She was revising her agenda. First, call Will. Then call Pam—there was no use sending a dress she wouldn't need, if Will's string-pulling hadn't worked.

But she strongly suspected that it had.

She was right.

"Hi, hon!" said Will's voice, echoing a little hollowly on his portable phone. "Get your trottin' rig ready for day after tomorrow at eight. Mrs. Krueshank was delighted. I think she has visions of my donating a hundred or so toward her senator's little overseas excursion. She doesn't know the only excursion I'd like to see him take would be into a hoglot after a big rain. Hold on, dammit, Spot! Fred doesn't want to eat you— he's just trying to figure out where to wind you up!"

The Spot bit had Lucy Maud a bit bemused, until Will went on, laughing, "Sorry—I'm in the middle of a confrontation between a Westie and a Great Dane. There we are. Cages closed. Anyway, sweetie—" and now the voice was clearer as she heard a door slam. "Any more phone calls?"

"No."

"Know who it is?"

"A—"

"All right. Be a lady. But I think I know, too. Want me to take care of the situation?"

She tried to sound amused. "Throw him in a hoglot after a big rain? No, Will. Thanks. I'm not losing any sleep over it. Truly. I'm a big girl."

"Among other things. Nice things. Need any books from Karen's place? I have to run down there tonight. There's another darned seminar at the ag building."

"No. I think we're fine."

"Okay. See you about seven-thirty. You may not even recognize me—they say I clean up pretty good. Lucy—"

"Yes?"

"You do want to go through with this? At the Krueshanks', I mean."

"Well—if I welch, no one will ever know."

"True. And we'll get a free buffet. Nothing like eating off the local aristocracy if you're a peasant. Take care, hon—thanks for calling back."

She hung up, feeling warm, indefinably happy—and turned to face Howard Lewis.

He was half inside the doorway, hesitant, the bright morning sun gleaming on the metallic hairspray. A tag of shirttail stuck out of his fly zipper.

"Good morning, Howard. You mean you've learned to read?"

"Dammit, Lucy—"

Then he stopped, cheeks empurpled, obviously choking back hasty words.

"All right, Lucy. I probably deserve that."

He was looking at his watch—a handsome thing. Rolex, probably. "I just have a minute. All I wanted to say was—was don't pay too much attention to what Miss Warpington might tell you. She's—this thing with Leona Wilson has been bad—I'm afraid Miss Warpington is—is losing it. Don't worry. I'll look after her. But just ignore her—her wild tales."

"I'd like to help."

"Oh, you can. She loves to read. Just don't believe all she says. Okay?"

Lucy shrugged. "I may not even see her again."

"You mean you're—leaving?"

Was that hope in his eyes? Who would he make nasty phone calls to?

Calmly, serenely, she asked as much.

"Lucy, you surely don't think that I—"

His voice was so hurt she almost laughed. But he was taking a step nearer, saying, "Lucy, I'd like to be—be friends."

"Boobs don't matter anymore?"

He flushed. "I've made a lot of mistakes. That was one of them."

It was, in a sense, an apology!

There was still too much hurt, too much anger.

She said stiffly, "I'm busy, Howard. Go run your bank."

He turned and left.

But she would remember the look on his face for a long, long time. And she wondered what might have been changed if she'd accepted his apology. Even then it had probably been too late.

But she had no awful phone calls that night.

Twenty-seven

Truthfully, she slept rather well. It surprised her. But she had learned to adapt her frame to the rather curious contours of Aunt Martha's mattress. However, if she did stay in Crewsville, a new one was going to be close to first on her agenda . . .

Then she was amazed, also, at having such a thought about staying in Crewsville!

Doing what, Dumbo? Living on part-time pay from that Ice Age library? Getting her kicks from carrying large-print novels to elderly patrons whose biggest daily thrill was watching a neighbor hang clothes on the line? Dodging that walking head louse, Howard.

Seeing Will Evans every day . . .

She was almost appalled at the sudden surge of warmth through her body, at the memory of his mouth, his gentle hands. Oh, God! She must be out of her mind!

He was a friend. That was it. "Good-bye, Will. Thanks for everything, but I have a new job in Timbuktu."

Slowly she slid bare feet to the cool floor and stood up, cautiously flexing that arthritic right shoulder. Her reflection in the dresser mirror caught her eye and she looked at it, not so much to see herself—she was familiar with that sight—but wondering again what other scenes it had reflected. Aunt Martha.

Frank.

In her vaguely remembered childhood, Aunt Martha had favored fluffy little nighties with blue ribbon run through eyelet lace. Is that what she'd worn for Frank?

But no other images would come—neither shy, smiling little Martha nor any sort of shadowy Frank. Just Lucy Maud, in a rather creased sweatshirt with tousled hair and a few wrinkles on her cheeks she'd swear hadn't been there yesterday.

An hour later, with a face somewhat restored if a little greasy, she sat down at the kitchen table with a cup of coffee. While Cutie happily lap-lapped up at her water bowl, Lucy turned up the blank side of a lumber company invoice and stared at it intently, trying to organize her day.

Cautiously sipping, she made an honest effort. She called the realty office and got the answering machine. So much for Vic. It was too early to call the bank about her balance, and unfortunately she thought she already knew. Bologna, cheese, and cheapo sandwich bread, stand ready! The two job contacts she held even dim hope for would not respond favorably to being pressured.

So what now?

Get down to that little punk library and do something useful. Put up some more Halloween stuff. Pick out a book or so for Miss Warpington.

The sound of ladders sliding over the eaves of the house moved both Lucy and Cutie to action.

Cutie's ears went up. She stopped lapping and looked at Lucy questioningly. The thought was almost readable: Well—do I have to stay here, or do I get to go over to Jessie's again?

"I'll have to ask Jessie," Lucy said in reply, and was once more astonished that she was actually talking to a dog! But catching the operative word "Jessie," Cutie's ears went to rest and she sat down patiently to wait.

"Honest to God!" Lucy said to herself in dismay, but went back to the telephone.

Jessie said she'd be glad to have Cutie. No problem. *No problem!* The catch phrase of Crewsville, along with "See ya!"

"Thanks, I appreciate it," Lucy said and hung up. She opened the back door, and the dog bounced happily down the back steps, pausing only for a morning pet from one of the carpenters before disappearing through the gap in the hedge.

The carpenter said, through two nails clenched in his teeth, "Mornin', ma'am. We should be through racketing today."

"No problem."

Good God! She was doing it, too!

Her purse was by her bed. A bit more wide awake in passing through the front room than she'd been previously, Lucy Maud saw something she'd missed before—Will Evans's flowers strewn over the floor, their vase fallen from its place on the old bookcase.

"Oh!" she said in distress. "Oh, dear!"

She'd bent and was picking up the limp and dying roses before something struck her almost like a physical jolt.

How could they have fallen? There was nothing to make them fall! Cutie couldn't reach that high. There was no way a draft of air could have done it.

And they'd been there in the vase last night before she'd gone to bed.

Puzzled and with a sober face, she reluctantly dropped them in the garbage, noting that the splat of water on the carpet was almost dry. So. It hadn't just happened . . .

Strange. Very strange.

The vibrations from the carpenters' pounding? That must be it.

Certainly not anything she needed to ponder at this point.

Remembering the old rhyme about "Ghosties and ghillies and long-legged beasties and things that go bump in the night," she soberly retrieved her purse and went out the door, locking it behind her. She also inspected her car rather carefully before she slid onto the seat. If someone was trying to carry Halloween a bit too far, she didn't want to be the victim!

But the car seemed fine, and the young carpenter called down cheerfully, "See ya!"

The sun was shining brightly, but there was also a chill in the air. Had she been a believer in esoteric things she might have said the bed of marigolds down the main strip held a sense of doom in their brave orange blossoms.

The carry-out boy at the grocery waved his broom; she waved back. The chubby lady unlocking the laundromat called, "Hey—tell 'em if they want to wash today, bring their own soap. The vendor's out until to-morrow."

Lucy Maud nodded. Surprisingly, the library door was also locked. She fished for her key and stepped into a warmth that said someone forgot to turn off the kerosene heater, and scooped an armload of books from the floor beneath the door slot.

Once more she felt transported back forty years. An illusion, she reminded herself grumpily.

There were lipstick-stained butts in the ashtray beneath the desk. Dilanna. That explained the stack of novels ready to be shelved.

Poor child, Lucy thought, mechanically alphabetizing them. Would she have to be at her mother's *soirée* with the senator tomorrow night? Probably. But not with John . . .

And I'll be there, she went on to herself, with Will. Will! Once more the wave of warmth surprised her. What was it with that man? Other guys had green eyes, wide shoulders, a pleasant laugh . . .

But they'd never held her close, never said in her ear, "Oh, Lucy, how I've been needing you—"

The library door opening was like a jangle on her nerves. The form framed in it didn't help matters.

Will's ex-wife was back, standing just inside, long-lashed eyes sweeping the premises.

"Oh. You're alone?"

It took Lucy's every defense mechanism to present a blank face. "I just opened. It's a little early. May I help you with something?" Self-strangulation would be nice.

"I guess not. I was hoping to catch Will."

"Will?"

"Dr. Evans. He's not here?"

"I haven't seen him."

"Do you know where he could be reached?"

Good God, woman, you were married to him! Not me! Lucy thought bitterly. "Have you tried his clinic?"

"Of course." Now she sounded calmly amused. "But Will has always been casual about his routine. I'm sure you've learned that." But before Lucy Maud could totally assimilate *that* interesting piece of inference, the lovely, melodic voice went on calmly, "Oh. I'm Reba. His ex-wife. Tell him I do *so* want to see him—and I'm at the Riverfront Motel."

"If *I* see him," Lucy Maud answered, her own voice a masterpiece of disguise. This gorgeous bitch must not know about the lump of pure ice that had just encased her heart.

Reba smiled. "Thank you," she said. "I'll be in town all weekend."

Even the tapered fingers shutting the door behind her were graceful!

It wasn't fair! Lucy Maud said that through her teeth, staring at the portico. It wasn't fair! How could any man resist a woman who looked like that? Particularly a man who'd been married to her.

She didn't sit on the tall stool behind the desk. She plopped. And the eyes still on the now-closed door were dreary.

What sort of evil star was she under? When in the world was it going to end?

Dealing with Will Evans on her own had been simple. Her choice. Suddenly feeling herself in competition with Venus de Milo was a different proposition. And Lucy Maud didn't like it one little tiny bit!

On a more practical basis, when Will learned his ex was in town and wanted to see him, would he still be available for the party with Senator Porfield?

Damn! It was only nine-thirty in the morning and everything was already screwed up!

She slid dully from the stool and shelved the armload of books with almost blind instinct.

The girls at the Millard Library would never believe this, she thought. Lucy Maud losing her entire sense of priority because one elderly vet kissed her!

Worse, she'd wanted him to do it!

When in a mental muddle perform something positive and concrete. Years with Verna Marshall had taught her that. So—dig out some more Halloween decorations. Find a pair of novels for Miss Warpington and take them to her. She'd deal with everything else later. When she had to.

In a back closet filled with holiday mishmosh, coverless books, dried up glue bottles, and mismatched children's galoshes she'd noticed a skein of orange and black streamers. It was wound around a blob that turned out to be a tatty, old, and rather horrid Dracula mask with one fang broken.

Lucy Maud shuddered and ditched it. She could almost sympathize with Miss Warpington's horror. But the bright crepe paper twists went around and around the desk very satisfactorily, augmenting the dancing cardboard skeleton. The kids should like that.

Now. Books for Miss Warpington. She hesitated over a new John Grisham, then went for a known quantity with an old Michener, and for nostalgia pulled out *Rebecca of Sunnybrook Farm*. Miss Warpington had looked as though she could use a little brightening.

Then, leaving a "Be right back" sticker on the entrance, she went out to her car, observing that the golden sun had warmed things up a bit. The rain-washed facades of the ancient buildings across the street positively glistened. Tom Burkiser waved. He was taping a "Ground beef—99¢ Sale" on his window with the help of a small boy. He also called something to Lucy. Assuming it was only a pleasant banality, she nodded, waved back, and drove away.

What will happen to this old place, she was wondering as she turned into the parking before the elegant old house, its brick cornered with stone and laced with scarlet ivy. She doubted if Miss Warpington had much family except for a few nieces or nephews . . .

The elderly lady answered the dignified door chime herself, looking—if possible—even more worn than the last time. But her smile was warm as she ushered Lucy Maud into the flickering cheer of a blazing fire and bade her sit in the same comfortable chair.

"Oh, my," she said, glancing at the titles of the books Lucy Maud handed over. Holding up *Rebecca*, she said, "How thoughtful of you, my dear—probably just what I need: a good antidote for the blues. I am just so—so *down*, Lucy. Nothing seems to make sense to me just now. Do you know that yesterday they were saying—some of the ladies—that when the mortician people dressed Leona for her burial they noticed a strange circular bruise on one ankle—as though she'd been hooked, or something! I do wish people would stop talking—it's a puzzle enough without more being added to it! Would you drink some tea, dear? I think the pot's still hot."

"That would be lovely."

Actually it was the last thing for which Lucy felt a need, but she had the sense this elderly gentlewoman was in desperate need of someone to talk to.

A pale, pungent brew was poured into a thin cup, and she tipped gently—then appreciatively.

"My—this is good, Miss Warpington. What is it?"

"As I said the other day, it's Earl Grey, my dear. But I have it sent from England—a good friend over there mails me a package every six months or so. It's blended differently from what we can buy here, you see. Lucy Maud—"

Miss Warpington was frowning into her own cup, tracing the delicate handle with one long, frail finger. The eyes she turned to Lucy were perplexed behind the wire frames. "May I—may I ask a favor of you? I—I just know no one else to whom I may turn—and I find I can't countenance alone anymore the—the terrible—and possibly unjust—thing I am thinking."

"Of course. If I can help."

"I don't know." The finger was now curling and uncurling, and the eyes seemed glued to it. "I may be so mistaken. I do hope I am. My thoughts are so—so dreadful."

"Whatever I can do."

"There's a—a paper I want another opinion on. I'd so appreciate it if you'd—oh, dear. The door. Excuse me a moment."

It was not only the door, but it was Howard Lewis.

And the way he said in surprise to Lucy Maud, "Well—good morning!" somehow conveyed to Lucy that it was really no surprise at all. Was the damned man following her?

"Tea, Howard? Lucy and I were just enjoying a cup."

"That would be fine."

Miss Warpington went to the inner door. Lucy noticed that as she passed through, she steadied herself with one hand. Howard, watching also, shrugged, and said, "Poor gal. I'm afraid she's really failing. Don't you notice it, too?"

"Howard, I've been around the lady perhaps four times since I came back to Crewsville—this morning just to deliver a couple of books. I'm no judge."

He shrugged heavy shoulders inside the dark serge suit. "I suppose. But everything seems to upset her now. And her imagination tends to—to run wild."

Sensing his eyes on her, and not even wanting to know what was on his mind, Lucy sipped her tea again. Casually she replied, "Oh—elderly people are worriers. Mother certainly was." "Mother" had been a few other things also, but that was really none of this overweight clod's affair.

"She seems to be unduly upset by Miss Wilson's death."

"Howard, for heaven's sake—they were best friends! And other women keep telling her things! Like some sort of circular bruise on the poor woman's ankle."

Howard jerked. It seemed to be spasmodic. But his voice was derogatory. "Oh, for cryin' out loud!"

"Don't come at me. I didn't say it." Lucy put her

cup carefully on its saucer. Haviland, she'd guess. Or Limoges. On Miss Warpington's demise this place was going to be a veritable antique lover's heaven! As the elderly lady reentered, carrying both a pot and a heavy book, Lucy stood up to help, murmuring, "Here—let me take that."

"That" was the book because Miss Warpington handed it to her. "Thank you, dear. It was in the kitchen, and I didn't want you to forget it. I've been remiss, I'm afraid. It should have been returned last week."

Lucy started to say, "But it doesn't—" then stopped. She remembered that narrowed look in Eleanora Warpington's eyes from forty years ago! Saying aloud that the book did not belong to the Crewsville Library was obviously not desired by her hostess.

"And your tea, dear," the lady was going on, turning to pour the amber liquid into the cup on the tray at Howard's elbow. "Oh—must you be going, Lucy Maud? That's right—you said you had an engagement. Well—do drop by again. Soon."

Lucy Maud, who suddenly realized that she was being dismissed, also caught the "soon."

"Of course," she answered. "Don't bother. I'll see myself out."

She made herself walk calmly across the velvety carpet, past the Belgian tapestries, on to the marble entry floor, then down the stone steps. She even drove her car away from the entrance out of sight before she pulled to a stop beneath the crisp yellow leaves of an old and tattered sycamore tree and picked up the book.

What in the world was going on?

Was Howard right?

Could Miss Warpington be losing it?

The book was an old 1940s Pillsbury cookbook, very faded and somewhat food-stained.

Puzzled, Lucy flipped the pages. Then she found it: a folded sheet of paper, with her name on the plain side.

All right. Miss Warpington had said something about a paper and here it was.

Frowning, Lucy pushed aside a yellow leaf that fluttered gently down on the thing, and opened it up.

What she had was a copy from a machine, a little dim and smeared. Leona Wilson's name was on the top. The rest seemed to be a summary of investments.

Things began to filter back to Lucy Maud—voices saying, "And they say she was broke!"

This summary certainly didn't bear that out. It showed a balance that Lucy Maud would like to see in her own account just once.

And the date was only two weeks ago.

Twenty-eight

Strange. Of course it was strange.

But Lucy Maud was feeling a strong sense of futility burgeoning inside her.

As if she didn't have enough on her plate with her financial problems, those spilled roses, Will's damned ex-wife bugging her, Howard Lewis's nasties—the list was almost endless!

Maybe for once Howard was right—perhaps the elderly lady was losing it, worrying where there was no cause to worry . . .

But—what if she wasn't? What if there was cause?

Lucy didn't even want to think about that, the ramifications were enormous.

Yet—she had to. She'd been asked and she'd said she would.

Later. That was it. Later, when she had time.

Lucy folded the paper and, on an impulse, stuck it in her wallet with the scant store of bills—at least it wouldn't get lost there as it might in the midst of lipsticks, Kleenex, grocery store receipts, note pads, antacid tablets, and the rest of the junk inhabiting the compartments in her purse!

And she would call Miss Warpington back. Of course she would!

With this virtuous resolution, she put the Ford in gear and drove on toward the library, a crackling skiff of yellow leaves scattering off the car hood before her.

This time the door was unlocked, the senior citizen bus stood before it, and five elderly patrons happily disheveled the book stacks while the driver perched on the high stool chatting cheerfully with a small boy.

"Hi," he said, as she entered. "Glad to see you. Can you come up with an old copy of *The Last of the Mohicans?* One of the guys couldn't make it today—he's sort of done a number on his ankle—but he's seen the movie, and now he wants to read the book again. I'd appreciate it."

"I'll look."

Lucy smiled at the small boy who was almost staring at her with dark eyes under lowered brows. "Hi, there. May I help you, too?"

"Oh." Her words seemed to distract his chain of thought. "Yes, ma'am. My Uncle Tommy sent me over with this."

"This" was a furled umbrella with a crooked handle. At Lucy's uncomprehending look, the driver chuckled and said, "Tom found it. Mrs. Mase has a shelf over there for Lost and Found."

So that's what that pile of junk was supposed to be! Grateful that she hadn't quite got around to tidying it, Lucy smiled down at the small, upturned face and replied, "I see. Fine. Would you like to put it there for me?"

He nodded, trotting off. Lucy turned to stamp dates on three Emily Lorings and a tattered Stephen King.

"Now there's a contrast," she said to the elderly lady taking them.

The little lady laughed, poked her glasses into their case, and dropped the volumes into a shopping bag. "The Lorings are for my sis," she said, her smile exhibiting an awesome set of dentures. "The King is for me. I read in bed, and when I get scared my husband comes to protect me. He—uh—protects real well."

The woman behind her giggled. "Maybe I ought to try one," she said, handing over two recipe books and a magazine. "My Ernie goes to bed before I do, though."

"Give him the King, and you do the protecting," the first lady said. "We're ready if you are, Carl."

The bus driver slid off his stool. "Okay. Head 'em up and move 'em out. Thanks, ma'am. Oh—how's Mabel doing?"

Mabel? Then Lucy remembered: the woman who'd filled in after Dottie left. "Last I heard, it would be a month or so. Did she fall off a horse or something?"

"Yeah. John, dammit, did you have to clear the whole magazine rack?"

The old gentleman who'd just plopped a stack on the desk grinned over his sweatered shoulder. "Go on," he said. "I'll be right there. All of these are on D-Day fifty years ago," he said to Lucy. "You don't mind, do you? I—I thought I might see someone I know."

Or knew, Lucy said soberly to herself, glancing at the cover photographs of bodies washed up on Omaha Beach. She stamped them quickly, saying, "It's fine.

Take what you want. We know where they are if we need them."

As the last senior citizen filed out and climbed on the bus, she gave a grateful sigh at being alone again.

No—not quite.

The small boy was still there. Hands deep in shabby jeans, he was regarding her steadily. His look was puzzled.

"Lady?"

"Yes. And my name is Miss Marshall. You may call me Lucy if you like."

"Oh. Okay. Lucy—" Then it came out, "Where's your tunnel?"

"My what?"

"I don't live here. We're on a farm now, with ducks and pigs and it's real neat. My daddy threw his office keys in the pond. But—I've looked all over, I can't find your tunnel."

"I—I don't have a tunnel."

"Yes, you do. My uncle said so."

"Your—uncle?"

Puzzled, Lucy perched on the high stool, leaning an elbow on the one spot that didn't have returned books covering it. Gracious, the child had huge black eyes!

"Yeah. Uncle Tommy. You know—he runs the store."

"Oh. Of course." Tom Burkiser! "He said I had a tunnel?"

"Well. Something like that. But I thought so. I mean—if you have tunnel vision, you got to have a tunnel to look into. Don't you?"

Lucy almost gasped, but stifled it quickly. What she

couldn't stifle was the feeling of dismay that caught at her heart. Tunnel vision!

Tom Burkiser had said she had tunnel vision!

On the heels of dismay was something quickly approaching anger. But it wasn't this youngster's fault!

Very gently, almost pedantically, she answered, "Honey, you misunderstood—not his words, his meaning. To grown-ups, tunnel vision is—is not being able to see anything but what's straight ahead."

His small face fell. "Then—there isn't any?"

"No. Sorry." Then, because she couldn't resist, even though she was addressing a small child, she asked, "Why did your Uncle Tom say I had such a thing?"

" 'Cause you didn't listen. You just waved. He said you'd never listened. Even when you were little."

Lucy Maud's mental teeth ground. She didn't care for that a bit. Making herself smile, she said, "I'm sorry. I should have listened. What did he say?"

"Only that he'd found the umbrella. It fell out of a car, I guess, only the lady said it wasn't her husband's, so Uncle Tommy sent it over here."

"Oh. Well—tell him I'm sorry. I'll listen next time. I thought he was just saying 'hello.' "

That should do to jolt Tom a bit for his off-key remarks to a child—if this little fellow repeated her words, which she really thought he would. In restitution she reached behind her for the little goblin-decorated candy jar Jessie had filled earlier, found it empty. Instead, she handed him a half-dollar from the battered change drawer. "Here, hon. Tell your Uncle Tom to let you have a treat. From me. Okay?"

"Gee, lady! Thanks!"

"And say I'll try to find the umbrella's owner."

"Okay. See ya!"

As silence fell, Lucy Maud rested her chin on her hands and frowned over the haphazard book stacks at the skeleton who was doing a short dance in the draught from the closing door. She was even too bemused to rebox the crayolas, spilled in a worn rainbow on one of the cardtables, or notice the dust reflecting the sun's warm rays.

Tunnel vision!

The first time she'd ever heard of that had been from Fred's wife back in Millard, sighing about her ex-military husband's lack of involvement in other civic affairs. "Since the war, Lucy, I swear he doesn't notice anything that fails to affect him personally! I try to tell myself that he's seen so much that was awful and unjust and tragic that he just doesn't want any more in his old age—and maybe he will survive longer than some of the other guys. I certainly hope so!"

Now, months later, suddenly the key word came back to Lucy: survival!

Was that what *she* had done all her adult life? Was it the reason she'd never let herself be involved with anything out of her own periphery? Survival?

Or was a better word "cowardice"? Scared to be hurt again. Scared of more scars . . .

Lucy shut her eyes, shivering. How awful that idea was. How barren her life must seem to others. How selfish. No involvement unless there was something good in it for her!

No, no . . . she couldn't be like that. She had friends! Only—where were those friends when her world fell apart? There'd only been Pam and Mona and Fred—inside her periphery with her. No one outside. No one at all . . .

A scanty, struggling library facility was not a good place for soul searching, particularly as her next awful thought was whether God could finally be getting through to her after all these years—making the point at last that you had to give to get?

It was too much for Lucy Maud to handle in one lump.

She tried to shut off her mind, tried to lose it momentarily in the methodical routine of restoring books to shelves, cards to files. But it kept coming back.

And the bottom line seemed to be that despite whatever Lucy Maud Marshall had accomplished, basically she was a coward.

A coward with tunnel vision.

After forty minutes of turmoil while she put fiction on the non-fiction shelves and spilled a cup of water into the tape rack, she did get far enough back on line to smile. A little.

Viewing herself from a distance, she conceded there was truth in the tunnel thing. Also, perhaps, a warning. So what could she do? Did she even have *time* given the hard facts financially and professionally?

To whom did she have the courage to give a little of her*self*—just for starters?

On cue, the umbrella that had started this entire process toppled to the floor, a result of being placed on a high shelf by a short arm.

Lucy Maud stopped dead and stared at the old furled article, lying quietly on the ancient linoleum floor.

Miss Warpington. Who had been missing an umbrella.

Miss Warpington, who also, just today, had plainly asked for help—and whom Lucy Maud Marshall had already lightly kissed off until some time later. Lucy's time. Not Miss Warpington's.

Soberly, she picked the umbrella up and looked at it with blank eyes, slowly noticing the barely discernible "L" above the "W" on the old-fashioned crook handle. *Leona Wilson.*

This could be the missing one. Was it a sign?

Oh, come off it, Lucy Maud! Still . . .

She heard a large sigh of self-resolution, turned—and almost poked a hole in the middle of Will Evans's plaid shirt.

He said, "Hey, lady, watch it!"

His voice was still hoarse, but the smiling green eyes melted the ice around her heart. He pushed aside the umbrella, caught her in a tight hug, and kissed her nose. His body felt lean and warm, and even if it also emitted a definite effluvia of horsebarn, she didn't care!

She whispered, "Oh, Will—" knowing achingly that this man did *not* have tunnel vision, and *did* give to those around him. "Will, I am so glad to see you—"

"Then that makes my day! What's the matter, love? Are you having a bad one?"

She laughed shakily into the rough denim of his jacket collar. "Sort of. My own fault, probably. Things just—seem to crash in on me sometimes."

"Welcome to a large club." One hand was smoothing the soft gray hair over her ear, and warm lips touched the cheek so exposed. "However, mine hasn't been so bad yet—and you certainly are making it better! Mr. Skeleton—look the other way. I'm going to kiss this lady good!"

He did. His mouth was hard and warm and searching, his arms held her tightly against his body, his hands caressed her back, her shoulders, and he rocked her slightly in a sort of loving rhythm. Then she felt him catch his breath and say softly, "Whoa!" And he let her go, tilting her chin up gently so those green eyes could look directly into her own.

"Hey," he said in a soft whisper, "I believe we're making progress!"

"I think—I think we are."

Was that a tunnel vision answer? Or just the ill-considered maundering of a lonely woman too hungry for love to remember the consequences?

Lucy hid her face against his jacket, hearing the thump-thump of that strong heart against her cheek, knowing only one thing clearly—she'd needed him, and he'd come!

Above her head, he chuckled hoarsely, saying in her ear, "Attagirl! However, what I want, and hopefully what you want, takes being alone—and I think two ladies are advancing on us from the grocery store. Behind the desk with you, hon, and check my Tom Clancy back in. If there's no one waiting, Tim would like to have it."

He let her go reluctantly, but was thumbing a magazine in perfect innocence as the door opened and the skeleton did his dance.

One of the ladies had been in earlier on the senior

bus. She advanced on Lucy, smiling ruefully and holding out a plastic bag of Halloween candy.

"That darned Ernie," she said. "He was handing your jelly beans out to everyone! Big deal! Too cheap to buy his own. Here, hon—treat the kids especially."

"Why—thank you!" Lucy was uncertain what else to say.

"No problem. Got to run—Mary's driving me home. See ya."

"See ya."

Will was shaking his graying head, the eyes behind the wire rims amused. "I know Ernie," he said. "Used to do his Jersey cows every year. Never spent a dime in his life if nine cents wouldn't do as well. Hi, Vic!"

The second skeleton dance heralded the bulk of Vic Bonnelli, entering and unbuttoning his car coat at the same time.

"Hi, Doc. Hi, Lucy—what have you got turned on in here, a blast furnace?"

"I gather it's warmed up outside," said Lucy, smiling. She had learned: you had to smile back at Vic.

"You want to sell your house?"

"Vic, dammit!" This was Will, frowning. "I'm just making my pitch, and *you* want to make her leave town? Think, man!"

"Then make another pitch and have her move in with you. Simple."

As they were grinning at each other, Lucy felt a bit off center.

She said, "Hey! How about consulting me?"

Vic leaned on the counter, grinning at her. "Why complicate things? Anyway, lady, I think these folks are really interested. I promised to bring them back when the eaves are done and the stuff is painted. I believe we can deal. Okay?"

"Have they seen the inside?"

"Yes. They don't like the bathroom, but that's their problem."

"Welcome to the club. Neither do I."

"Get yourself another. Try Doc's."

"Will you cut it out, Bonnelli!" The vet was smiling again. "You'll ruin my pitch! I told you!"

"I thought I was simplifying it." Vic pulled a face that was supposed to be chastened. "Anyway—it will be about a week before we have to take steps. Think on it. And I'll show some more people. Close at twelve and I'll buy you a Bunny Burger, Lucy—we can talk some more."

The room seemed vastly empty as he left it.

Will looked across at Lucy, and now the smile was warm again. "What a guy!" he said. "Even if he is taking my girl to lunch. I have to go, anyway—I'm due at a farm up north in about ten minutes. Give me a quick hug to last until later."

Halfway around the desk she remembered.

Reba. Her message.

She stopped cold. "Oh. Oh, Will—your—your ex-wife was in. Looking for you. She said she—she really wanted to see you and that she was at the Riverfront Motel."

"Oh, for Pete's sake," said Will, and shook his head. "What garbage. I don't want to see her. Are you listening, Lucy? I don't. I hear she's divorcing the poor sot she married after me, so she probably wants a shoulder to cry on. But it's not going to be mine. Okay? Got that?"

"I just deliver messages," said Lucy, hoping her lips weren't shaking.

It didn't matter, because he swiftly covered them with his own—warm, tender. Brief.

"This 'prelude' stuff has to end," he said over his shoulder, going out the door. "It's nice, but it's also like a classy *hors-d'oeuvre*. It makes you hungry for something substantial. Right?"

Did she answer? She really didn't know. She just remembered the length of him, waving, smiling with those green eyes, the door shutting, the skeleton flapping, and her heart thumping in her breast.

The smell remained, also, and she didn't mind at all. Perhaps she was setting herself up for another disaster. But at the moment the pain was overcome by longing—longing so deep it was making her hands shake.

Tunnel vision wouldn't be so bad if Will Evans was at the end of it. And if she could measure up to his expectations.

But she couldn't! She couldn't—not when he'd had a beautiful wife with an exquisite body like Reba's!

Closing her eyes against pure agony, she went like a blind person and picked the umbrella up off the card-table where she had dropped it. When Will kissed her.

Do something positive, Lucy Maud Marshall. Something for someone else.

Take Miss Warpington's umbrella back to her.

At least it would be a start.

Twenty-nine

It was not quite eleven-thirty. Half an hour ought to do it at Miss Warpington's—plenty of time to go to Bunny Burger with Vic.

Wryly conceding that there was really very little point in locking the door, she exited into the street.

At the back of her car was a ladder. On the ladder, perched precariously, was a city street man, stringing a fluttering white paper ghost with toothy smile over the top of the light pole.

"High school kids made 'em," he grinned down at her. "They'll look real neat tonight, I bet. Hang on and I'll move m' ladder."

"You're okay. I'll pull straight out."

She did, noting the breeze orchestrating a waving ghost dance like a chorus line all the way down the main drag.

Remembering that Aunt Martha used to decorate the Water Department window with black cats and pumpkins, she craned her neck to look as she turned the corner for Miss Warpington's.

They were there, a few things do *not* change.

To her astonishment tears came to her eyes.

Blinking them back, she thought perhaps she should put up something at the house. Just for Martha—

Unless it had been a damned ghost who'd dumped Will's roses!

However, some old goat calmly pulling his pick-up truck out in front of her distracted those thoughts, and by the time she'd arrived at the Warpington home, she'd already mapped out her procedure: return the umbrella; be patient as the lady reminisced; apologize for not having had time to go over Miss Wilson's financial statement yet; plead a lunch date and go.

Surely that would be at least a good start out of her "tunnel!"

The senior citizen delivery van was at the door, and the man was just following Eleanora Warpington inside with his tray. Depositing it on the wooden table of a very old fashioned kitchen, he said to them both cheerily, "See ya," and departed.

Lucy Maud said, "Please—do eat. You don't want it to get cold. I just came to return this."

Miss Warpington looked up from lifting Styrofoam lids and making a wry face at the contents thus revealed. The eyes behind the gold rims widened.

"You found it! My dear, I am so glad!"

"It turned up at the library. In the Lost and Found."

"For heaven's sake! How in the world—? Oh, well. Thank you, dear. And please sit down. I'll share."

"No, no. Just eat." Lucy was glancing at her watch. "But I do have about ten minutes. I will sit." She pulled out an old spindled chair, sitting on the bright calico cushion. "Is it good?"

The lady made a face. "Anything that has to be

cooked at four in the morning in order to make deliveries isn't going to be *haute cuisine,* dear. And of course they can't season because everyone is on some sort of a diet. But it's nutritional food. So I eat it. My mother would say I was a good girl. Is the sun in your eyes, Lucy? You may pull the blind."

"No, and it feels good. There. That's better." Lucy shifted so the bright glow through the ruffled curtains was re-aligned. "But you say you go out for dinner?"

"Mostly. It makes a break in my day that is, I fear, becoming very structured. Old age can be the pits, Lucy dear. Be forewarned. Have you—" She hesitated, forked what appeared to be limp broccoli, and touched the tidy gray chignon in its neat net at the back of her regal old head with the other veined hand. "Have you had a chance to—to look at what I gave you?"

"I'm sorry. Not yet. I want to take some time with it."

"Please do. I'd so appreciate your doing just—that."

Miss Warpington sighed, dabbing at sauce on her patrician chin with a paper napkin. "We had such plans, Leona and I. May I tell you, dear—in confidence? Because I've decided I am going to do it anyway."

"Of course. If you wish."

Miss Warpington put down the fork, the exquisite silver filigree flashing in the bright sun. She took a deep breath, stirring the crisp white jabot around her throat.

"Leona and I have—had no close heirs. All right? Old families do run out. Both of ours have."

Lucy Maud nodded, feeling speech would be super-fluous.

"So—she and I decided last month to—to endow a public library. For Crewsville."

Lucy's mouth gaped and her eyes widened. But it was nothing to the transformation of the lady's face across the table. Her eyes were shining, her lips softly curved, and her cheeks flushed with the speaking of a fond enterprise.

"Oh, we've been planning it, Lucy! A new building on the lot I own across from the lumber company. A substantial sum of money invested with interest not only to buy new books but to support the establishment for years! And we were gong to call it The Warson Free Public Library! See how Leona combined our names? Wasn't that clever? And that's what it will be—even now! The Warson Library! I decided last night. I decided that if Leona's money is indeed gone, then I will personally take up the slack, but retain the name—for Leona, bless her memory. What do you think, dear?"

Lucy Maud was gasping, fluttering her hands, say-ing at last, "I think it is sensational! What a fantastic-ally lovely, generous thing to do! Have you told the city?"

"No!" That word came out like a whip. And Miss Warpington's lined old face sobered, the delight flee-ing, replaced by something Lucy couldn't define. Sad-ness? No reason for that. Caution? Why? It would surely make the newspapers all over the county! Every-one would be tickled to death!

The sunken eyes behind the glasses had returned to

the plate of food, and she stirred what appeared to be applesauce almost absently.

Then they shot to Lucy and fastened.

"This is the most strict of confidences. Do you understand?"

"Y-Yes. Of course. If you feel it's right to tell me."

"Lucy, dear, you've been gone for years. You have an outlander's point of view. You'll not be prejudiced by—by local feelings. Also, my dear, you are indeed a career librarian as well as being a very sweet child. How could I do better?"

Almost humbly, Lucy murmured, "Thank you," and meant it, even too bemused to question the "child" at fifty-five!

"Very well. Then I must say this: I no longer trust Howard. I—I have reasons. Be that as it may. The pertinent fact is that I have an appointment next week with an architect in Springfield. Also, in the same city, I shall see a young man whom I had in school and who has become a very astute financial advisor. I shall turn Howard's report on Leona's estate over to him. And go from there. Do the—the intimations shock you?"

Lucy Maud's first reaction was pity for poor Howard if this lady was on his tail. Then the entire insinuation hit her like a dash of icy water. Hardly getting out the words, she mouthed, "You suspect Howard Lewis . . ."

Miss Warpington nodded sadly. "Please pray that I am wrong."

"Oh, God . . ." Then she said before she thought: "Poor Dilanna!"

Unexpectedly, Miss Warpington laughed. "Dilanna

will survive," she said. "After all, she'll have John." At her guest's totally startled face, she continued. "I'm not blind, Lucy. It's Amanda, poor noodle, and the Krueshanks who will suffer. The Lewises are—nonentities. Your ten minutes are up, dear, and I believe in being on time. Remember—strict silence! Until next week, anyway. I have your word?"

"Yes. Oh, yes."

"Your father was trustworthy. I knew you would be, also."

A new library! How absolutely magnificent. Lucy rose, hardly knowing she was doing so.

"Oh—oh! One more thing, and I'll be quick."

"Yes?"

"There is another person who knows about my project in a general way. He negotiated the sale of the lot. His name is Victor Bonnelli. You know him?"

"Vic? Yes. He's selling my house for me."

"A very trustworthy gentleman, also. If you must rattle on, Lucy dear, rattle to him. It will go no further. And I do understand that some things are occasionally too good to keep." Miss Warpington was smiling. "Even I feel better at having confided. Run along. We'll talk later when you have reviewed Leona's affairs. Just remember—poor Howard doesn't have any idea Leona gave me a copy, and he certainly wouldn't think of you."

"So watch my mouth."

"I use a gentler phrase: Mum's the word."

On an impulse, Lucy bent and kissed the top of the soft silver hair.

"You're a princess," she said. "I'm very excited. A new library for Crewsville—you've no idea—well, of course you have, but—all right. I'll shut up. And go. But thank you, Miss Warpington. You've greatly improved what started to be an awful, day!"

It was five minutes after twelve. Vic Bonnelli was a block in a business suit, standing by the library door and looking at his watch.

"Say, lady," he began as she pulled in beside him. Then he stopped and stared. "Holy smoke! Who just appointed you president? You're fairly scattering rainbows! If Doc has this effect he'd better close in fast before it showers again."

"I—I had some good news." That would do for the moment. "My car or yours?"

"Mine. Getting me out of yours would take a can opener." He was holding the door on his Toyota.

Lucy slid inside, noticing something was missing. "Where's your dog?"

"Doc has him. Claw clipping and shot time. I said Bunny Burger. Is that okay?"

"In Crewsville?"

"Don't be snide. There's Bleaker's on the drag, but by now he's hangin' them on the wall."

"Bunny Burger is fine."

"Obliging woman."

"Hungry woman." Suddenly she was. How her day had brightened up! Miss Warpington. And Will. She had to count Will; her entire body gave her no choice.

Bunny Burger was hardly lacking customers. Vic sighed at the number of people, particularly women, "holding seats" and said, "Okay, let's order. Something will open. Hey, buddy—" he called to a young couple with three children slurping ice cream cones in a corner booth. "Sit there until we come back. Okay?"

"Sure, Vic. Glad to."

"Appreciate it."

"And he'll appreciate *me* if I sell his house at the price he wants," Vic murmured as they got in line. "Okay. What do you want?"

Lucy settled for cheese quiche, ham on the side, with black coffee.

The little waitress with frizzy hair murmured to Vic as she took their order, "Double coupon day at the grocery. Everyone's in town. Your fries will be a little late."

Vic nodded. "It's okay, Kooky. No sweat. We'll be back there with Ralph's tribe."

"Ralph's tribe" vacated as they approached, the harried-looking mother swiping at ice cream dribbles on the seat with a paper napkin. "Susie!" she said sharply, "watch it! Lick the other side or you'll lose the whole thing—right in someone's shoe," she added to Lucy Maud, grinning. "They're free to the kids today and I just couldn't say 'no.' "

Lucy nodded, sliding in cautiously, putting her purse against the window. Vic sat, also, pushing the table six inches toward her as Howard had done.

"Now," he said, sipping his soda and grinning across at her, "what lit your fire? You've dropped ten years since morning."

"Well, thank you, sir." She smiled back, but ruefully. "Did I look that bad?"

"You've heard the phrase 'the cares of the world'? We just can't let every little thing bother us, honey child. We're both too old."

"Speak for yourself!"

"I am. I looked at myself in the mirror this morning and saw my Uncle Stanislaus. On the other hand, he died when he was ninety-three, so perhaps that's not all negative."

Eileen brought their order, sans fries, and tousled Vic's silvery curls. "You need a cut, boy."

"I was thinking of a pony tail."

"Think again." She grinned down at Lucy. "Did Doc find you? He was in here about nine, but I haven't seen him since."

She was cutting her eyes toward Vic. "Reba was looking for him, too."

"Jeez! Poor guy, he really needs her!"

Impelled to say something, Lucy said, "She's—very pretty."

"That's it. That's the bottom line. Put new clothes on her, stand her in a window where everyone can admire her, and she won't move for days! She probably doesn't even make love because it would mess her hair!"

"Not Vic's favorite person," Eileen smiled. "Got to run. Enjoy. See ya."

"Definitely not *my* favorite person," he corroborated, munching on a six-inch burger. "What she put Doc through would fill a book. I just hope he's cured for sure. You can help," he added suddenly, giving Lucy a pixie look that had a dab of catsup on it.

"Thanks a lot. It might just be more fun causing than curing. Did you ever think of that, wiseguy?"

"Not in this case. Trust me. Also, pass the salt."

"You don't need the salt."

"It's my body—Mom."

She shrugged, passed.

He lifted the burger lid, salted, and returned the cellar. "It's the 'lo' stuff, anyway," he said. "Smarty! But to get back: what I was saying is that you're good for Doc, hon. I can see it. And we all hope he's good for you."

As a delaying tactic, she raised her brows. *"We?"*

"Me. Eileen. Jessie. John. Dilanna. Even Tim and Karen. Oh, Tim has his mother's number pretty pat. He says he thinks he was switched at the hospital. But the point is that in the last few weeks Doc is getting his confidence back—from you. We can all see it."

Lucy swallowed her quiche with difficulty. In a very sober voice she said, "Vic, I'm not certain I'm ready for—for anything with Doc. I—I may not be what I seem to you at all. Just at this moment *I* don't even know what I am. Look—I came here loaded with problems and now you guys seem to want to load on more. Something with Will could be more of a problem than a solution."

"Straight talk. Is there another guy?"

"Good God, no!"

"Then that's the bottom line. Other things can be worked out."

"You're an optimist!"

"I'm a survivor." He said the word more ruefully than she expected. "Honey, getting your private parts and most of your leg shot off is not a Sunday picnic. I've been through a bit, too. And I'm not backpatting. I'm just saying it can be done."

The truth of his scarred body was so close to the truth of hers that it clenched the hands now clasped together beneath the table top. "Oh, I wish I could believe that!" she forced herself to say calmly.

"You can." He grinned a little sheepishly. "Ask Eileen. Or do you want a list?"

But men are different. They feel things differently, she thought.

However, she couldn't say that. Not even to this gentle giant. Besides, the words were Verna Marshall's, spoken in bitterness for twenty years. She was not going to quote Verna Marshall!

Instead, she equivocated. "I'll—think about it. Along with everything else." The last part was so wistful he put out one enormous, warm hand and covered hers.

"We'll help."

"Because of Doc?"

"And because we like you."

There was a new one! She was liked—and beyond her librarian periphery! Perhaps she was getting somewhere after all!

"I like you, too," she answered, ending that part of the conversation decisively, "because I'm going to tell you what made me so happy this morning."

He accepted the change of direction. "Good. I'm listening. What?"

"It all happened because of the umbrella."

"Okay."

"It was Miss Warpington's. Actually, it had been Miss Wilson's but she'd given it to Miss Warpington; she loaned it to Aunt Martha, and because they'd been such good friends Miss Warpington wanted it back."

"Understandable."

"Now how it fell out of someone's car at the grocery we'll never know. That doesn't matter."

Something else that Lucy Maud didn't know was that the chubby, brassy-curled woman in a the booth behind her had suddenly stopped devouring a diet-forbidden banana split and had frozen to attention at the barely caught name "Miss Warpington."

Quietly she moved, leaning her stiff curls against the tall booth back.

Lucy Maud replied, "What does matter is this: you know the lot she owns across the street from the lumber company?"

"I got it for her."

"Right. She said so. You know what she's going to put on it?"

"I've guessed."

"What?"

"A new library building."

"Bingo! You're astute."

"As well as handsome," he grinned. "I think it's a great idea. She is going to do it, then?"

"Definitely. And soon. Vic, I was so pleased to hear about it that I—I could have cried! And she'll do it right! No one else has both the money and the acumen that Eleanora Warpington has!"

He was grinning ever wider. "And you get to run it."

"What?"

"Logical solution. She builds it. You run it."

"Run" was exactly what the woman in the other booth had in mind. Run and tell Howard! He'd have an absolute kitten! Whatever plans he'd had for

Eleanora Warpington's money, a library hadn't been one of them! There would go their trip to Las Vegas. Perhaps her own journey to Europe with the senator! No more loans that Papa didn't need to know about . . .

So much for cosseting dippy old ladies! Some of them lied when they were really broke, and some of them were do-gooders! If Howard had only listened—

Well. He'd better listen, now!

Very quietly Amanda Lewis gathered up her purse and jacket. She'd just slip out through the back where the restrooms were. Howard had to know, and know quickly! The senator was coming this weekend! If Howard wasn't back in town, perhaps she could get him on the phone . . .

Innocently, Lucy Maud had first not grasped the true value of Vic's words. *She builds it. You run it.*

Then suddenly she had to lean against the booth back, all the starch gone out of her spine.

A new library! Privately owned.

Who more logical to run it than a librarian with years of experience? And who was more logical than Eleanora Warpington? Could she possibly be the one chosen to do so?

"Oh!" said Lucy softly, almost in a dream. "Oh, Vic. Oh, Vic—do you think it would be me?"

"Who else?"

She shut her eyes and saw beautiful rainbows cascading against the black, breathtaking solutions to almost everything—a new job she'd love, a salary again—and close to Will Evans.

It was almost too exciting to believe.

Thirty

The fries came—an enormous, golden stack. Vic slid them to the middle of the table. "It's nice to have kitchen connections," he said. "Here. I'll share. To celebrate." Then crunching appreciatively, he went on, "Hey—perhaps I'm premature. Would you take the job?"

Would Noah build the Ark?

But of course Vic didn't know about Millard.

There seemed no point in confessions, either. Lucy skipped them. "Yes. I would."

"You're not under contract or anything?"

"No." How large that negative was he'd never guess in a million years!

"Great. Because I'll bet that's what Miss Warpington has in mind. If not—" and he was grinning across at her, "—then volunteer. Would you keep your house?"

"Oh!" She hadn't progressed that far, but of course she wasn't a real estate agent, either. "I—I don't know."

His wide grin had turned teasing. "Doc's place in the country is really nice."

"Victor Bonnelli, will you *stop* that?"

He put up his big hands. "Just trying to keep your options open!"

"Let me keep them open. Things are happening too fast for me just now."

"Good for the system. Keeps you sharp."

He had inhaled the burger, and was fast consuming the fries. Between munches he chuckled. "Going to tell Doc?"

"Oh, no! The project is very confidential. She said I could tell you because I think she figured you knew already."

"Which I did. Pretty much. But it's still hush-hush, then."

"Completely. At least until she—she gets some other affairs settled."

"Well, I still think it's great." He was balling up his paper napkin and fishing a bill from his wallet for tips. He glanced over at her from beneath heavy brows. "Does her buddy the banker know?"

"No. No, I'm sure he doesn't."

"He's not in on the scheme?"

"No. Not at all."

"Well. Isn't that interesting."

She said nothing in reply. He didn't seem to notice. "Fellow made my skin crawl, first time I met him," he said. "I don't know how he got a nice kid like Dilanna. Maybe she was switched at the hospital like Tim Evans says he was. Sorry to hurry you, kiddo, but I'm meeting with a contractor at one."

"I'm done." She pushed her plate aside. "Thank you for lunch."

"It'll be on my bill."

"It better not."

"You'd notice, wouldn't you? Hard luck, when I'm retained by a smart one."

They wended their way through the crowd to the door. Eileen called a cheery "See ya, guys!" from the counter. "If you see Mom, Lucy, remind her I'm on late shift today."

"Will do."

Vic opened his car door for her, laughing. "It won't matter anyway," he said. "Jessie always cooks for threshers."

"What?"

"Cooks a lot." He interpreted, sliding in on his side. "Threshing crews used to go from farm to farm. The housewife always had to feed 'em. Library?"

"Please."

As he drove away, she mounted the gritty steps on the lightest feet she'd had since that disastrous morning three weeks ago. A new library! From scratch! And—perhaps—she would really, honestly, have a part in it with no hokey-pokey, no double-dealings, no chicanery.

It was too good to be true, and she'd better keep telling herself that! Nevertheless, she turned at the door and looked down the street beyond the nodding orange of the marigolds to where blue chicory still bloomed in a weedy vacant lot.

Marvelous. The location was perfect!

Behind her, the door opened. She turned and saw Dilanna Lewis standing there, Styrofoam coffee cup in hand, a puzzled look on her chubby, frizz-framed face.

Dilanna said, "Hi. I'm a refugee again. My mom's

tearing the bank down trying to find Daddy. Did you see her?"

"No."

"Oh. As I came from home I saw you go into Bunny Burger, and that's where she'd been. I don't know why she's in such a damned toot. She knows he won't be home until tomorrow, and then probably just in time to get dressed for Grandma's big party. Oh, well. Hey—I hear you and Doc are going. Great. Maybe I'll have somebody sensible to talk to. Certainly not my sis. Since she married the senator's son she thinks she's in line for First Lady or something."

The girl was rattling on. Lucy was beginning to understand that's what she did when she was upset— which seemed to be most of the time, poor child.

Smiling, she said, "I'm looking forward to it."

"I'm not." Dilanna made a face. "I'm stuck with that skinny wuss Mom is trying to promote. She can't understand he just wants to suck up to the senator. Isn't life the pits sometimes?"

"Sometimes."

After watching the girl's chubby figure plod away in the too-full skirt that made her look like an apple barrel in ruffles, Lucy slid up on the high stool behind the desk. She looked back across the room at the door. In her mind she saw Will standing there, felt his arms going around her again. As her heart rate jumped the phone rang. It was Jessie.

"I'm signin' for a UPS package," she said cheerfully. "Want he should drop it off up there, or put it on the porch?"

Her dress! Bless Pam! And Jessie!

"Put it on the porch. I'll be right home. Thank you."

When she pulled into the driveway, Jessie's husband waved as he trundled a lawnmower across in front of her. His lawn was freshly cut. So was hers. How good of the man!

She sat still a moment and looked at the small property with an entirely new perspective. The workmen's ladders were gone, and it sat in the midst of a tidy grass plot, neat and white, its windows shining clean. The front porch no longer sagged and the steps were straight, bright with paint. Even the old mailbox had been cleaned and replaced, brass letter "M" glistening against black metal.

"M"? For Martha?

Probably. Bless her heart.

There's another lady you missed enjoying, Lucy Maud! But certainly the people of Crewsville hadn't! How great to have been so beloved . . .

Slowly she opened the car door, thrust out one foot, felt it licked. Cutie had heard her car and trundled across from Jessie's and was now preceding her up the steps.

Still half in, half out, Lucy paused again.

She'd said she didn't believe in second sunrises. But—was it possible to have one after all? Here?

Could yesterday's disaster-ridden woman possibly find herself in a pleasant little house, not only tolerating but keeping a dog, going to a new and rewarding job—and glorying in the companionship of a nice man who said he needed her?

Look out, Lucy Maud. Look out. There has to be a sticker in it somewhere!

She mustn't be that sanguine. Nothing was ever that easy.

But also—nothing said she couldn't try!

Full of hope for the first time in days, Lucy stood up and followed the dog, who was waving her silky tail at the door just a shade impatiently.

"I'm coming!" Lucy said. "Hold your horses!"

She picked up the large, flat UPS box, carried it inside, put it on the couch. Cutie sniffed it, decided there was nothing of interest to her, and trotted on into the kitchen from where the now familiar crunching sounds ensued.

Lucy opened the box.

Her dress was just as pretty as she remembered, pure silk and soft, shining blue. Pam had even sent the shoes, bless her heart.

Going into the small bedroom, Lucy shucked her slacks and shirt, shrugged the dress on, zipped it up, and faced herself in the hazy mirror.

Not too bad!

The dropped waistline ended with a soft side drape that flowed when she moved. The sleeves fell away from her arms at the elbow, and the vee of the neckline dipped low and pulled to the left in a shimmering, easy ruffle.

It's still worth the two hundred bucks, Lucy said to herself happily. And now I get to wear it, after all.

What will Will think?

Her heart caught at that question. She reprimanded herself for being a silly schoolgirl, but the reprimand probably didn't have any effect. She was on a giddy roll. Cloud Nine.

But what if Miss Warpington actually meant to entice Dottie Mase to come back? Or that woman who's out of the library because she fell off her horse or something. You don't know it's you. *Vic Bonnelli* said that. After all, she'd been planning this new facility long before you even came back to town. Perhaps she's had someone else in mind from the beginning . . .

Damn it! Just because Lucy Maud Marshall had been the librarian in Millard for a millenium, it didn't mean she was the same here. And worse—as far as Miss Warpington knew, Lucy Maud Marshall had a job!

Lucy sank down on her Aunt Martha's bed in all her silken splendor, fortunately finding it behind her when her knees gave. The damned tunnel thing again. Only seeing something as it applied to her.

How could she be so consistently stupid?

She'd had plenty of practice—and hadn't learned a thing when her world had caved in on her three weeks ago! Vic, wanting to be nice, had possibly almost done more harm than good.

All right. What could she do?

Let Miss Warpington know she was available! Now!

Miss Warpington's phone didn't answer.

Slowly Lucy went back to the bedroom, took off the dress, hung it up in the closet on one of her aunt's old wire hangers, and almost threw away the shoes with the UPS box.

Boy, was she brilliant today!

Turning around, she caught a glimpse of herself in the mirror again. A man who had made love to Reba Whoever was supposed to go all warm and mushy over *that*?

Get real, Lucy Maud. Back to earth. Get a job. Sell the house. Face reality with Will.

That hurt. More than she was willing to admit.

But there was tomorrow. She had tomorrow with Will. At the Krueshanks'. Hopefully scaring the everloving whatsit out of Senator Porfield.

After that? One day at a time.

How many times had she said that to herself? When was she going to learn?

"Hoo-hoo!"

That was Jessie, at the kitchen door.

Lucy took a deep breath and answered, "Come on in! I'll be out in a minute," and grabbed her slacks. Of course she tripped pulling them on and almost broke her rib on the corner of the bureau, but with Lucy Maud Marshall, that did seem to be par for the course.

A little grimly she gave her hair a quick brush, noted again that a cut would not be out of order, and went into the kitchen.

Jessie was sitting at the table, petting Cutie, who had put her head on Jessie's knee and was looking at her soulfully.

"The Caylors called," she said, then correctly interpreting Lucy's blank look she clarified: "Martha's friends. The ones who took Cutie to live with them in Quincy."

"Oh." Why the sudden empty feeling in her stomach?

"They couldn't get any answer here so they called me. They just got back from vacation. The boy they'd left Cutie with told them she'd broken loose and run away."

"Oh."

"They're really upset about it. Really sorry. And amazed when I told them she'd come back here."

"I can imagine."

Lucy Maud pulled out another chair and sat in it. "Coffee?"

"No, thanks, dear. I just finished the pot at home. Oh, all right then!" The last was to the dog who had given a last tail wag, trotted around the table, and transferred her attentions to Lucy. "Anyway—they said to tell you that if you liked, they'd take her back. Here's their number." She handed over a slip of notepaper torn from a Purina Feeds pad.

"Thanks."

Cutie was now leaning against Lucy's knee, eyes closed; as Lucy absently stroked her silken ears she gave a soft sigh of pure contentment.

Jessie was going on, "I told them I didn't know. I said having her back was almost like old times again. But it's up to you, of course. Well—I have to run. Calvin starts for Wisconsin with a load of dairy feed tonight and he wants to eat before he goes. Be a good girl, Cutie."

Cutie didn't move, but her tail wagged.

Lucy said, "Thanks."

"No problem. Oh—" and Jessie paused, half out the door. "Johnny says if you want that power pole back up, he can do it over the weekend. And Cal didn't mow very close around the old well—so if it looks too tacky to you, he'll take the weed eater to it when he gets back Monday."

"Okay. I'll ask Vic about the pole. And tell your

husband not to worry about the well. If I can borrow your weed eater, I'll do it."

"Okay, hon. See ya."

The door shut again. Now, as the sun had moved westward, its golden rays filtered through the glass and across the worn floor, showing not only the worn pattern but reaching out to Cutie's black and white fur, making it shine.

How empty this house would be without her!

"Oh, shit!" said Lucy, and put her weary head in her cradled arms on the tabletop.

Would things never stop piling up?

Wasn't there ever going to be an end?

The telephone rang.

She almost didn't answer it—then conditioned responses took over.

"Hello."

The voice was tinny but she knew it immediately: "Lucy? It's Will."

Okay. So something's come up, Will and you can't make it tomorrow. Is it okay, and you're sorry. Sure. Sure, Will.

But it wasn't that at all. He was saying, "Hon, I'm stuck up here in the corner of the county for a while. Could you pick up my suit at the cleaners before they close? I'd really appreciate it—and we'll reach some—recompensory arrangement tomorrow."

The extent of her relief almost did her knees in again. "Oh! Yes. I'll be happy to get it."

"And pick me out a tie somewhere. Mine are all pretty dated, and we certainly don't want to be upstaged by the senator, do we? Okay—oh, wait a minute." His voice muffled just a little. "Yeah—that's it, Bill. Hold her head up and stroke her so she'll stay still. I want that bleeding stopped. Still there, hon?"

"Yes."

"Good. A little problem here. Bill's mare challenged a Jersey bull and the mare lost. Anyway—I'll call you tomorrow. It'll be too late tonight. See ya, hon."

"See ya."

She hung up, turned, and leaned against her Aunt Martha's faded-flower patterned wall.

Tomorrow. Tomorrow.

And suddenly she was filled with a totally selfish resolution. Whatever else happened—tomorrow was going to be a good one! She was due. Her turn.

After that, the Millennium, perhaps.

Take it as it comes.

Right now, at a quarter of five, she'd better go pick up a certain suit.

Thirty-one

The tall, thin man in the cleaners said, "Good! I'm glad you're gettin' it. I was about ready to go over and hang the thing on his clinic door. Figured he wanted to look real sharp for the Krueshank shindig tomorrow and we'll be closed. Goin' t' Branson, we are. Got tickets for Garth Brooks and Charlie Pride."

Digging in her wallet to pay the bill, Lucy murmured, "Oh, that's nice."

Then she realized: tunnel vision again. And she made amends. Branson might be as far from her world as—as Gene Autry, but it obviously wasn't to this man. Show some damned interest, Lucy Maud!

She added quickly, "It sounds as if you're really looking forward to it."

"Sure are. They put on a helluva show. And it's our thirtieth anniversary."

"Well—congratulations. Have a good time."

"Oh, we will. I've already asked to have Charley sing to my wife. And he'll do it. Nice guy. Oh—no vest with the suit. Knowin' Doc, he probably wrapped a kitten in it."

Lucy nodded, realizing such a thing was highly possible. As she hung the plastic-shrouded garment in her car, she ascertained that it was dark gray, and went looking for a necktie to match.

Ties were going wide again, and the one little store in town didn't offer many options. Settling for a paisley in black, gray, and green, she took it to the counter, wondering with a now familiar warmth around her heart how it would pick up the green in those magic eyes . . .

So she was acting like a teenager with a crush! Fine!

Perhaps second sunrises were like that!

The aging clerk wrapped it briskly and took the rest of her cash. "Good choice," he said. "Hey—are you Lucy Maud? Damn. You turned out pretty good. Oh—I'm Ben Tults—worked with Martha in the water office until I retired. This is just part-time in here—got to do something to keep out of my wife's hair. Sure do miss Martha and old Frank. You really selling the house?"

"I—I'm not sure."

"Glad to have you back. Oh—and my aunt sure does appreciate getting library books again! That's one of the nicest things you folks do. Sure hope you keep it up."

"Someone will, I'm sure," Lucy murmured, starting to go then realizing she was doing it again—concerned only with her own affairs. "Which lady is your aunt?"

"Oh—the snappy one in the wheelchair—Room 4 in the nursing home."

"Wants the sexy ones!"

"That's her." He grinned. "Sure makes you wonder about m' uncle, doesn't it? Hey—have a good time tomorrow night. Big-city caterers and all that! All for a real nerd, in my book. Porfield's never done a damn thing for this town but let the freeway go south of us. Of course, Amanda's suckin' up to make that Europe trip with him. Can't figure if she wants in his bed or out of Howard's. Oh—telephone. 'Scuse me. Have a nice day."

"You, too," Lucy murmured and made her exit thinking that the freedom of speech certainly hadn't diminished in Crewsville!

Or was it advancing age that let down discretionary bars? Did being seventy-ish give one the right to say what one damned well pleased?

It was a power Verna Marshall had exercised all her life, and age had had nothing to do with it.

One more thing, Lucy thought, to put on her personal list of "don'ts."

She shared the rest of Jessie's meatloaf with Cutie, then took to the couch for a *National Geographic* special. Suddenly she noticed that one hand had been absently and pleasurably stroking a pair of silky ears.

Lucy Maud. With a dog! Petting it!

It not only brought back a mental picture of her mother's horrified face, it recalled another decision she would have to make eventually.

Should Cutie be sent back to Quincy?

As though aware that her future was in the balance, the dog cuddled closer with a contented sigh and licked Lucy's hand.

Thanks a lot, dog. You really make it easy!

She also meant to watch the ten o'clock news and weather, but instead awoke with a start at twelve-thirty, let Cutie out, then formally called it a day.

Next morning she surfaced with a list in her head. Wash her hair, do it as best she could, find some polish for her nails, make certain her eye shadow didn't clash with her dress, and—oh, yes. Of course. Go down to the library for a while.

She was so accustomed to workmen banging around that the knock on her door didn't even register until the kitchen screen opened and Will walked in.

"It wasn't locked!" he said, grinning. "My girl is finally beginning to relax. At least fifty percent."

Then he held out his arms and she went into them, almost forgetting to put down her coffee cup. His kiss was brief, but very warm. He whispered in her ear, "Got the storm window guy watching through your west screen, there. Mustn't disappoint him."

Startled, Lucy looked. The young kid nailing frames waved cheerfully.

She said, "For heaven's sake—"

Doc had released her and was pouring some coffee. He smiled over his shoulder, those green eyes crinkling.

"Accept it, sweetie," he said. "I'm public property in a sense. Everyone is my daddy, and there isn't any strange city girl going to bamboozle me if she doesn't measure up. I have five minutes to spend frivolously. Come sit."

She obeyed, taking the chair opposite and allowing her senses to revel in how "at home" he seemed: long legs stretched, denim shirt opened casually on a wide chest showing just the beginnings of a silvered mat, and—since he'd laid the billed red St. Louis Cardinals cap on the table—gray hair tousled almost down to the rimmed glasses behind which his eyes sparkled at her.

He sipped, saying, "I'll take my suit—unless you want me to get dressed here."

"No," she answered calmly. "You may take it."

"Shoot. Another possibility squashed. Oh, well."

"I got you a tie."

"Good. Naked dancing girls on it, of course."

"No. Sorry."

"The conservative type. Just my luck. Oh, well."

It was banter, pure banter, snapping back and forth. They did it well, she found herself thinking. As though they'd been friends for years. This man was—was pure magic.

He drank coffee, "Decaf, I suppose."

"If you can't tell, what does it matter?"

"Just ruins my macho image, that's all. Anyway, hon, I'll pick you up about seven. Okay? There's a receiving line, then cocktail hour, then dinner, then dancing. Big deal. We're only committed to staying as long as you want. I couldn't care less."

"Good. I'm glad to hear that. We'll—what do they say around here?"

" 'Play it by ear'?"

"That's it. I may find myself rather unpopular."

"Or an object of extreme interest. Remember, sweetie, I said Amanda's folks are very religious—and I'm not being snotty—they're doing this thing because *she* tells them he's such an upstanding character. He's coming because *he* needs the financing."

"And I'm going because I think there's a chance I can screw him good."

"Inelegant, but true. At least you can scare the wadding out of him. He needs a totally positive record to win this next election."

"And adultery with a state employee doesn't help that along?"

"No, ma'am. Not in Crewsville. They're still a bit torqued about the freeway. Got to go."

He was scraping back his chair, grabbing his cap. Beneath the brim, those green eyes smiled at her. He went on, "I hope the suit is hanging where Dennis, out there, can't watch."

It was. His embrace left her breathless.

"Damn," he murmured in her ear, his lean cheek against hers, "I'm getting real impatient." His one hand slid across her back, found the curve of a breast, caressed it gently. She stiffened, but he didn't notice, only sliding the hand on to squeeze her shoulder and turn his next kiss into a smack on one cheek. "Got to go! See you at seven!"

Then, swinging the plastic covered suit, he was down the short hall, through the living room, and out the door.

She said, "You forgot your tie—" Then she stopped. He'd be back. And somehow good sense told her it wouldn't be the wisest thing in the world to turn him around now. That hand had been too sensuous, his breath against her throat too warm.

What was she to do?

"Control the game, you idiot," she mumbled aloud as she returned to the kitchen. That was your falsie and he didn't even know it.

But she had known, and her heart had turned cold inside her.

Damn! Why couldn't there be love without sex? She understood the need for propagation in the young to preserve the species—but surely older guys should be beyond proving their manhood! Why couldn't holding and kissing and warm companionship be enough? Why?

Fortunately, the telephone ringing ended that bit of philosophy. With effort she made her greeting civil:

"Hello."

"Lucy?"

"Yes."

"Good. Oh, good."

The caller's mother was going up the wall. She'd already read the four books Lucy had taken to her Wednesday, and needed more just like those. If Lucy would choose some and leave them on the library desk a brother would pick them up on his way to the feed store about two.

"Of course," said Lucy, thus putting the balance of the day in motion.

Routine.

But at this point, blessed routine.

However, by five o'clock, Lucy had rationalized herself into a state of pseudo-calm, and went home determined to keep her priorities straight.

As she pulled into her drive, Jessie hoo-hooed across the hedge, asking if she could keep Cutie for the night. Eilly was on late shift, Cal was truckin', and Tina was at her other grandma's. Jessie was lonesome.

Lucy nodded that it was okay, and went on into the house.

With no waggy tail or soft nose to greet her, it was rather different there, too!

Amazed at herself again, Lucy heated a cup of coffee in the microwave, took it to the bedroom, and prepared to make herself as glamorous as possible in two hours.

And she had to be honest: the results, with fifteen minutes to spare, weren't too bad!

The blue dress, with the grace of good design, fit her beautifully, flowed as she walked, and dipped just enough from the curve of her throat to the swell of her natural breast. Her hair had curled obediently and gently into soft framing waves over nicely done eyes whose blue matched the gown. If her damned heart would quit hammering every time the leaves of the elm tree brushed against the porch, she'd be just fine!

The tap at the door was not elm leaves. Will stood there in his gray suit, so handsome it took her breath away, a nice white car parked in the drive behind him. He was also sans a necktie.

"Wow!" he said softly. "You look great! Beautiful, hon!"

"You look nice, yourself."

"A tie would help."

He was grinning.

She handed it over, and he turned to the mirror by the doorway, hoisting his chin and whipping the ends around. "Nice," he said, looking down his nose. "I like it. Now. How's that?"

He turned around. "Karen says I clean up good."

"Karen is right."

"And Tim's answering the beeper. Until tomorrow. I promise. Ready?"

"Ready."

"Then off to the royal court."

They went down the steps, and he opened the car door. "Can you curtsey in that dress?"

"Of course."

To prove it, she sank to the ground in a swirl of skirts, her head modestly bowed.

His laughter sent the starlings in the elm tree scattering.

"Excellent!"

"Nice car," she said, settling herself. Excitement was beginning to course through her veins. The waft of his aftershave as he slid in on his side made her almost heady.

"Oh, I thought perhaps the pick-up might be a little conspicuous," he grinned, starting the engine. One arm across the back of the seat, he backed it out and winked at her. "All set?"

"All set."

"Then off we go!"

The Krueshanks still lived, as they had for almost a hundred years, on the edge of town in an immense brick house surrounded by towering sycamore trees, playing fountains, and cement deer; the mandatory lions stood at the gate in stiff regal poses, and espaliered shrubbery lined the driveway. A shorn beanfield to the right was already crowded with parked cars, and people handsomely attired were mounting the steps to the open doors in twos and threes.

"My, my," murmured Will, sliding out of his car and winking at the uniformed attendant. "Park this thing where I can find it in a hurry, will you, Josh?"

"Right by the gatepost, Doc. I heard you were coming. Evenin', ma'am."

Lucy was pleased to note that the young man's glance at her reflected approval. Reassured, she took Will's arm and together they mounted the wide steps.

A rush of voices, chamber music, and warmth came out to greet them, challenging the crispness of the cool autumn air. The pilastered anteroom was fragrant with flowers, and rainbow-lit from overhead lights on stained glass. Beyond its marble-tiled floor inside mahogany double doors the receiving line began, with Alvin and Carolyn Krueshank standing there. Peering around the couple ahead of her, Lucy thought that they were much the same as she remembered from her childhood—then realized there were some changes. Not only were they older and stooped, but Alvin's angular face had the look of an automaton, and Carolyn's chubby block of a body was braced by a metal walker.

As Carolyn greeted the pair preceding Lucy and Will, her faded eyes fell on Lucy with no little puzzlement—until they saw Will.

"Ah," she said. "Miss Marshall, isn't it? How nice to see you. Alvin, dear, Martha's niece."

"Yes, of course," said Alvin Krueshank. His extended hand moved Lucy ever so slightly but inexorably on. Alvin was obviously not in the mood for small talk. "Miss Marshall, may I present Senator Porfield? The senator is—"

Lucy cut him off briskly. "Of course. Senator Porfield and I are old acquaintances. Jack, how—nice to see you!"

No one would ever guess how her heart was thundering as she allowed her eyes to slide by the bulky politician to rest—in wide surprise—on the elegantly clad collection of aging but fashionably assembled bones next to him.

"Oh!" she said clearly and distinctly, "I was expecting Kathryn! Who is this, Jack dear?"

"May I present my wife, Margaret," said the senator in grim tones. "Margaret, Lucy Marshall. We've been on a few panel discussions together."

"Ah," said Margaret Porfield, her icy fingers barely touching Lucy's. "How nice."

"And I'm Jack junior," said the hearty young man standing next to his mother, shooting her a slightly puzzled and definitely scared look. "And my wife, Audrina."

"How do you do," murmured Audrina, her pretty brown but narrowed eyes cold. "Please do help yourself. Drinks are right over there."

"And I can use a drink," said Will in Lucy's ear, guiding her through the press of chattering, milling people. "Wow. You scored, sweetie. He was shocked to see you. Absolutely shocked. It was the last thing he expected."

"I don't think his wife was too pleased."

"You're right. She didn't care for it, either. But even better—the Krueshanks caught the whole scenario. I saw them. The senator is going to have to think fast if he wants financing for this 'Save Europe From the Devil' crusade. What will it be, hon—soda or fresh apple cider?"

"You're kidding," she blurted inelegantly.

He laughed. "No, no. I can see you're surprised, and

believe me—so are a lot of other folks standing around here. But remember, the Krueshanks don't approve of liquor and they're in the apple business. And trust me—the dinner will make up for it. I know the caterers."

He was right. Lucy Maud hadn't dined so well since she'd come back into this land of fried brain sandwiches—not even at Jessie's. The prime rib was prime, and the gossipy noise of a hundred diners diminished noticeably as they set to.

Seated between Will and a city councilman, Lucy Maud was, however, very aware of the covert glances she was receiving from the head table. The senator was not a happy diner. Down the line from him, Lucy also observed Howard Lewis and his wife. Amanda was clad in a frightful bit of frou-frou with her waist so tightly cinched it threatened to explode her ample breasts like cannon balls. The gentleman next to her seemed to be entertaining this hope, if his sidewise glances were any indication, but Howard appeared anything but amused. His face looked lined, weary. He seemed to have aged greatly. His eyes were bent to his half-eaten food—except once, when Lucy Maud inadvertently encountered them. Then, surprisingly, they'd seemed as poignant as a child's.

Fortunately, she thought, forking excellent asparagus, Howard was not her problem.

At the conclusion of the dinner everyone was escorted *en masse* to the vast living room, where a small ensemble was already playing music suitable for dancing.

Comfortably ensconced in a graceful Queen Anne chair by the door was Eleanora Warpington, clad in beautiful Valencia lace and patting the empty seat beside her as she waved to Lucy Maud.

"Come sit a moment," she said, adding calmly to Will. "Run along and bring me another Chianti, dear. I need to talk to this child."

"Chianti?" said Will, raising his eyebrows.

She laughed. "My dear, even Krueshanks cater to Warpingtons," she said. "Tell the man at the bar I sent you."

He shrugged, chuckled, and went off.

"Now," said Miss Warpington, lowering the voice which on occasion had carried too well, as Lucy remembered from her school days. "I'll be quick. I don't know where my brains were the other day. I forget so many important things if I don't make a list! What I meant to ask was—could you possibly consider staying here permanently and being my head librarian, Lucy? I do so dearly wish it. And I shall be sure your income is not reduced."

It was fortunate Lucy was sitting.

"Oh!" she said. "Oh, Miss Warpington—"

"Think about it, dear. I need no answer today. But be assured the position is yours if you desire. Yes, Howard?"

Howard Lewis had appeared, and the smile on his tired face reached everywhere but his eyes. "I thought perhaps Lucy Maud would like to—to dance."

"No, she wouldn't," said the person named calmly. "Thank you," she added, remembering her manners, but much too dazzled by the vista Miss Warpington had opened up to be concerned about Howard.

He hesitated, seemingly about to say something further, then abruptly turned and walked away through the circling couples. Amanda intercepted him. She seemed angry, frowning. He hesitated again, then put an arm about her bulging waist and joined the dancers.

Lucy didn't even notice.

She was saying to Miss Warpington, "Thank you. Oh, thank you. I will think about it." Native caution made her add that. "But—but it would be a project I'd enjoy enormously!"

"Good. Excellent. And one more thing—the copy machine at the post office broke down just as I made one more copy of that financial statement—you know. And I had to send it to the gentleman in Springfield. You do have yours?"

"Oh, yes."

"Good. That does so relieve my mind. All right, Will—stop hopping from one foot to the other. Dance with the child!"

Will had placed a crystal wine glass at the elderly woman's elbow. "Am I that obvious?"

"Only to one who knows you. As do I. Run along, Lucy. Dance while you may."

Will held out his arms. Lucy stood and went into them. She murmured against his shoulder, "I haven't danced in years. You may be sorry."

"I doubt that."

The music was slow, sweet—befitting senior citizens, Lucy thought, doubting there was anyone in the large room under forty-five—except Dilanna Lewis, who was sitting by a festooned and vaulted window looking extremely bored while the skinny young man at her side talked endlessly into unhearing ears.

The feel of Will's body moving against hers only added to the pleasure of her conversation with Miss Warpington. If she was on a dangerous high, so be it!

They circled the milling couples slowly, passing Margaret Porfield in the arms of her host whose dancing was obviously not one of his major accomplishments. In Lucy's ear, Will said, "We can leave whenever you say, hon."

Too late.

A grim voice said, "If I may cut in, please." And Lucy felt her arm removed from Will's shoulder by Senator Porfield.

Thirty-two

Porfield said again, "Please."

It was a request cast in iron. Lucy felt Will stiffen. She smiled at him.

"All right," she said. "We'll leave shortly, Will." The message between them was patent: I can handle this clod, she was saying, and he was replying, I'll be right here.

None of it pleased Porfield.

He began the motions of dancing. His voice was usually of such calculated mellifluity that it made her ill. Now it seemed downright sinister. "What the hell are you doing here?"

"This is my hometown. I returned when I lost my job to your girlfriend." If it was "calling a spade a spade" time then so be it. She sure as the world wasn't afraid of this guy; she'd dealt with a number of them and she knew how.

"The library job."

"Right."

"You want it back? You've got it."

The cold statement was like a bolt through her mind. She'd almost forgotten how frightening power can be.

"Kathryn won't care for that."

"The hell with Kathryn. You can screw up my whole deal here, and you know it. I know it. And I need that European trip. I need the prestige. Well?"

"I'll think about it. In the meantime, you'd better check with Kathryn."

"Hey. Look. She'd better do what I say or she'll never work anywhere again. She might even disappear. She knows that."

She stiffened. "Are you threatening me, Jack Porfield?"

"I can't afford to threaten you. There's too damn many people around who heard that jackass remark of yours. Now, what do you say?"

"I said I'd think about it."

She needn't tell this bulky sham that what she'd wanted she'd gotten: revenge. Revenge on them both. And now—now!—she didn't need the damned job! Kathryn would hear from him regardless, and he was going to hear from his wife. What happened from then on was simply not her affair.

She smiled, separated herself from him with hard fingers, patted his bulky shoulder in a mock show of sympathy, and went to find Will.

He was sipping Chianti with Miss Warpington, and rose at her approach. His green eyes were serious. "Score?"

"Totally. Dance with me a little more so he won't think I'm running."

"My pleasure," he said, and swung her out into the crowd.

She told him what Jack Porfield had said. He didn't care for it much—she could tell by his set jaw. And she realized that he was simply concerned about her. It was amazing. She'd never had a man just concerned about her in her whole life!

One could, she admitted wryly, get used to it!

But aloud she spoke only the amazing bottom line: "So, if I like, Kathryn is out on her ear. And I have my old job back."

He shifted so that his eyes could look directly down into hers. They were almost Christmas green with intensity. "Do you want it back?"

The only world she'd ever known. Her safe little hole.

Her tunnel.

The music ended. They both applauded politely, neither aware of doing so. Around them couples shifted with a whisper of skirts, and began to waltz. Suddenly realizing the conspicuousness of their standing still, Will moved, turning Lucy gently toward the edge of the floor. He repeated in her ear in that same intense voice, "Do you?"

"I—I'm not certain. I told him I'd let him know."

"When *you* know."

"Yes."

"So you don't."

"No. No, I don't. And—and please, Will—let me decide. It's—it's very important to me. I can't explain—just yet—because it's also rather stupid. But I need to be able to say—this is what I have made up my own mind to—to do."

He nodded, and briefly tightened the guiding arm about her shoulders. "Okay. But that doesn't mean I can't present an—an alternative."

"N-no."

Either the import of his words or the aftershock of her encounter with Porfield was suddenly making her knees weak.

She said, "I need to sit down."

"Eleanora just left. Howard's taking her home. We'll grab her seat."

Lucy sank into the higher end of the old Victorian settee, grateful for the tapestry cushions. Will took the other, smiling at her. He said, "Appropriate." At her look of confusion, he added, "This is a 'fainting couch.' You know—when delicate ladies used to get the vapors. Better now?"

"Yes." Then something struck her: "You call Miss Warpington 'Eleanora'?"

"She asked me to do it. A few years ago. I remember she said there weren't very many people left to do so. And now, with Leona Wilson gone, she's really feeling her age, poor lady. I like her very much, by the way. Oh—hi, Adele."

"Hi, Will," said a tall lady in crimson velvet, clutching a sheet of paper. "Darn. Has Miss Warpington gone?"

"Just. Why?"

"Oh—she was running off a copy of this at the post office when the machine screwed up. Oh, she said it was all right—you had one already, Miss Marshall— but she walked off and forgot the master. I thought I could catch her. Hey—Howard! Are you taking Miss Warpington home? Give this to her, will you?"

"Sure. I just came back for her gloves."

Then Howard Lewis looked at the paper in his hand.

"Where—" he cleared his throat. "Sorry. Where did you get this?"

"I didn't. Exactly. I was telling the folks here that she meant to run copies at the post office this morning but the copier screwed up. She said it was okay, though—Lucy already had one—then she went off without her original. It looks like a statement or something, so I thought I'd catch her here. If you don't mind . . ."

Howard was looking at the paper in his hand as though it might explode. He seemed almost to jolt himself back into the present. "Oh. Oh, sure. She's in the car. No problem. See ya."

"Gloves."

He paused, one polished foot in midair.

"Her gloves. Here." Will picked them off the small inlaid end table.

"Yes. Thank you."

Then he was gone, wending his way through the milling crowd. The woman called Adele shrugged. "I guess she'll get it," she said. "I'll call tomorrow. Have a nice time, guys. If you want to see a funny, lean back and look down the hallway."

The "funny" in the long hall was Dilanna Lewis, waltzing dreamily in the arms of a waiter.

Will chuckled. "Johnny," he said. "They'd better get a bit further out of sight or Amanda will have a cow. Well. What do you say, hon? Ready to blow this joint?"

For some reason Howard's lardy face was stuck in Lucy's mental vision. He'd looked, she reflected, as though someone had kicked him where it hurt—and it had happened when he'd glimpsed that financial statement.

Could Eleanora Warpington possibly be right in suspecting him?

"Earth to Mars!"

Will was smiling at her.

She shook her head ruefully, trying to clear it of anything but the moment. *Today* was going to be a tunnel of her own design. Remember?

"Would you like to go, Lucy?"

"Yes," she answered. "I think I would."

"Me, too. It's nine-thirty anyway—already half an hour past the Krueshank bedtime; I saw old Alvin yawn right in the middle of twirling the senator's frau. Let's do our polites and 'git.' "

Unfortunately, as Will arose, Amanda Lewis shot out a fat arm to detain him.

"But Willsy—you haven't danced with me yet!"

Will removed the arm firmly. "Sorry, Amanda, some other time," he replied and guided Lucy Maud toward the door. "Like when hell freezes over," he said from the side of his mouth. "Good evening, Mrs. Krueshank. We do appreciate your hospitality."

"So glad you could come." The cool eyes beneath floppy lids slid to Lucy. "And you, too, of course. Will you be with us long in Crewsville, Miss Marshall?"

"I really can't say." Now there was a profound truth, Lucy thought ruefully. "But—thank you for asking me. It's been such a—a rewarding evening."

"Do come again," the lady mouthed. Her fat hands were tight on her walker. "Perhaps we could chat sometime."

What was it Will had said? *When hell freezes over!*
"Perhaps. Good night."

As they went down the outside steps, Lucy noticed
that half the cars in the beanfield were already gone.

"Everyone's heading for the nearest bar," Will
grinned. She shivered in the cool night air and he drew
her closer, one arm warm around her shoulders. As
promised, his car was parked near the gryphon-topped
stone gatepost, dew-wet in the amber light. He opened
the door for her, then loped around and got in on his
side. "Let's sit a minute and get the heat on in here!
I'll bet it gets down in the teens tonight." Starting the
engine, he leaned back, arms locked behind his head,
and looked at her. "Will you come out to my place a
while? I had the gal who cleans for me pick up a bit
today—no four-day-old chili bowls in the sink—and
that fireplace is going to feel good. Besides, my boy
helped me build it and I'm proud of the sucker."

Despite the sudden thumping in her breast, she answered calmly, "I'd like that."

He eased the car around the pillar and they drove
back through town beneath a line of fluttering ghosts.

"I hear the high school kids made 'em," Will said.
"Makes the drag look festive, doesn't it? Tomorrow
the trick-or-treaters start. Remind me to stock up on
goodies."

They also noticed the line-up of cars clustered about
the local tavern and smiled at each other. Neither, however, saw the yellow Cadillac keeping a discreet distance behind them.

Will's house was right on the edge of town, gleaming white amid ancient, towering trees and embraced by a picket fence.

He maneuvered past a small green car parked on the shoulder, stopped, and slid out.

"Must have died on someone," he said of the car. "My electric's not working again. I'll open the gate manually and you drive in, will you, hon?"

Obediently she slid over, aware of the warm seat beneath her as she put the vehicle in gear and guided it inside.

"Fine," he said as she stopped beneath the sheltering limbs of a huge scarlet maple. "Leave it right there. And I won't push my luck and close the gate," he added. "Go on in, have a look. It's too cool to stand out here, and I want to check a cage. I'm babysitting my grandson's bunny rabbits and the damn 'coons keep eating their feed."

As he headed for a small rear building he had gestured toward the back porch, clean and tidy beneath its round dome light, although the adjacent garbage cans were so full their lids sat askew.

Smiling to herself at his speech about "the gal who cleans" and thinking the cans were probably a testimony to her, she went up the three steps and turned the knob on the door.

It was, of course, unlocked.

The light switch was right at hand. As she turned it on, she saw the kitchen was small, delft blue and white, and very functional. Cupboards, sink, stove, fridge, a table and four chairs. The only discordant note was a small saucer used as an ashtray, sitting on a counter corner with five butts in it.

One thing "the gal" had forgotten, probably. To her knowledge Will didn't smoke. Anyway, she smiled to herself, he'd hardly leave lipstick on them!

The kitchen opened into the short leg of an L-shaped living area with a vast stone fireplace fronting the long section, chairs and a sofa drawn up around it and its craggy expanse flanked by ceiling-high shelves of books.

Somehow, she thought, moving slowly toward the warmth of the smouldering embers, that doesn't surprise me . . .

She held out her cold hands as a log moved, sending a bright sparkle up the cavernous smoky-black chimney. She'd always wanted a fireplace.

She and Will were going to sit on that sofa. Before that fire. She knew they were . . .

And she had consented to coming here.

Suddenly breathless, she turned away, putting her purse on the sofa pillow, touching her hair, trying to bring reality back by prosaic thoughts such as which door was the bathroom.

The first one, near the kitchen?

Wrong. It was a small bedroom, lined with toys, and a purple plush dinosaur nodded at her from the bed pillows.

The second one, then. Will had said to look around!

She had that door half pushed before she realized there was a soft light inside.

Then it was too late.

From the puffy quilted cover of a double bed, a graceful form lay raised on one elbow, lustrous brown hair tumbled on naked shoulders, and a soft, sensuous voice murmured, "Well, it's about time you got home . . ."

Lucy didn't think she gasped. Or really made any noise. Still, the lashy eyes of the personage in the bed suddenly went wide. And Will Evans's ex-wife snapped, "Who the hell are you? Oh—my God! It's the old maid in the library!"

If Lucy Maud Marshall had had anything viable in her hands, she would have killed the woman. She knew it. However, matters were suddenly taken over by the angriest man she'd ever seen.

Will was standing by her in the doorway, his face a mask of fury, his fists clenched. Through set teeth, he grated, "What the hell do you think you're doing here?"

The soft voice cooed, "Waiting for you, lover. Wanting some pitchy-woo like old times." And the hand clutching the quilt lowered a trifle, showing the beginning swell of bare, silky breasts. "Send Miss Muffet back to her tuffet, sweetheart. She can't give you what I can. Howard says she's only got one boob—and you know what I've got—"

And she dropped the quilt, showing two beautiful, velvety breasts.

Lucy Maud wasn't sure what she said—if anything. She did remember a terrible strangling noise ripping from her throat before she whirled. And ran.

She thought she heard Will call, "Lucy! Lucy!"

She wasn't sure. She only knew no man would be fool enough to turn down what that beautiful woman was offering, and she couldn't deal with it!

His car was still in the drive, with the keys in the

ignition where she'd left them. Providence must have known.

Gulping back terrible tears, she backed it around, turned, and tore down the highway toward Crewsville.

She couldn't blame him. She mustn't blame him. She just didn't have to see it or listen to it.

She already knew the story too well.

He hadn't known Reba was there in his bed. It wasn't his fault.

It wasn't his fault.

It isn't, it isn't, she told herself through chattering teeth. Men are just like that. And I knew it. I knew it! Oh! What a fool!

She turned into her driveway and parked behind her own car, leaving the keys in his. He'd probably come back for it.

Later.

Much later.

Oh, God, she said to herself in the purest agony she'd known for years. Then she opened her own front door and went inside.

For a moment she just stood there, leaning against the old wooden panel, breathing sharp gasps of pain, her face twisted in the dark. And she wanted Cutie. She wanted someone who loved her—who didn't care how malformed she was!

But she was at Jessie's, and Lucy knew it.

Brutally she made herself obey her mind's command. Stop being an idiot. Get real!

Then she switched on the light.

And she saw another frightening thing: the house had been ransacked!

Drawers were pulled out, the small amount they contained dumped ruthlessly on the floor. Cushions were upended. Through the bedroom door she could see her suitcase on the bed, its scant contents tossed aside.

She was too angry to get scared. Here was a needless, senseless thing to wreak her rage upon.

In a furious voice she shouted words that her mother would never have even suspected she knew. They echoed through the small house.

Then Howard Lewis stepped through the kitchen door, saying, "All right, all right, shut up."

"Howard!"

"No. Santa Claus. What the hell are you doing home? You're supposed to be out screwing with the vet."

"Why are you in my house?"

"Looking for something, goddamnit!"

"What? Your brains?"

She couldn't see his hand closing on the brass Cupid vase on the table behind him, then unclosing. He took a deep breath, so deep it gaped the front of his disheveled white shirt even more. "Lucy, help me! That financial statement. From Leona Wilson. They said you had a copy."

"I do."

"Where the hell is it?"

Then she realized where it was—and almost laughed.

"In my purse. At Will's house."

"Oh, Christ!"

"Why do you want it. Howard? Enough to do this?" Her hand waved at the littered room. "Why didn't you just ask?"

"Because I don't know what's going on. What Warpington has said. She's losing it, Lucy—I've told you that. But I can't afford talk. Or anything. Not right now."

"*Have* you been taking her to the cleaner's, Howard? Did you take Leona Wilson?"

"For Christ's sake—do I look like that sort?"

"Looks have nothing to do with fraud."

His eyes narrowed and his breath caught. Through his teeth he said, "What has she been saying?"

Suddenly aware of being on thin ice, she said, "Go on home, Howard. Let's talk about it tomorrow."

"Home!" And he laughed—a bitter, derisive laugh. "Some home I've got—with a bitch of a wife on the make for everything, who's spent enough money this year to match the national debt!"

"But she has two boobs," said Lucy Maud sweetly. "Now get out of here. I have to pick up your mess."

She should have left it at that. He probably would have gone. But she was still too much the Woman in Charge, the Head Librarian. And she needed to hurt somebody as she'd been hurt. She added, "You always did leave stuff around. And you haven't changed. You're probably the one who lost Leona Wilson's umbrella."

"What?"

"The one Miss Warpington was looking for. Oh, don't concern yourself. She's got it back."

He put a hand on the end table, almost to steady himself. His voice sounded strangled, "She's *what?*"

"She's got it back. It fell out of someone's car and ended up in the library Lost and Found. I took it over to Miss Warpington's the other day."

His face startled her. It was sickly gray. Over an old

umbrella? A ragged thing with an obsolete, crook-ended handle?

Then something awful clicked: the circular bruise on Leona Wilson's ankle.

But she didn't have time to pursue that thought.

She only saw his arm rise, then caught the flash of the brass Cupid.

Then everything was dark.

Thirty-three

First she knew her head hurt.

Then she knew her arm prickled, and weakly opening her eyes a slit, she saw a strange man giving her some sort of shot. Next, she realized Cutie was cuddled up against her on Aunt Martha's sofa, and there were a lot of other people around. Lastly she recognized Will Evans, on his knees at her side, disheveled and dirty with a bruised cheekbone, but holding her hand.

She said, "What in the world—"

Around her, everyone said in a chorus, "Yea!" and she realized they were Vic Bonnelli and Jessie and Eileen and a strange young man in a policeman's shirt.

"She'll be okay," said the shot-giver, standing up and turning away with his empty syringe. "Just a lump and a headache."

Will said, "Thanks, Doc."

"How about you?"

"I'm fine. He just caught me with that slab of wood before I was ready for him."

Vic said, "He didn't catch you much. You were giving him hell with that right fist before Cutie bit his leg."

Lucy said a little wearily, "I hate to interrupt this, guys—but what's going on? What's happened?"

Then she remembered part of it. "Oh, Lord. He hit me, didn't he?"

Then all eyes swiveled to her. Will's hand tightened. He said, "He did *what?*"

"He hit me. With something. I was standing right there in the door telling him to go home. And—that's all I remember."

The young policeman asked in a very quiet voice, "Why did he hit you? You're talking about Mr. Lewis, I presume."

"Of course." She frowned; it was hard to think cogently with hammers inside her head. Slowly she went on, "I think—I think he suddenly realized I was putting two and two together and—and knew what he'd done. And I had. Just then. I did know."

"Know what?"

Something else caught her attention. Cautiously she rose on one elbow. "Where is he?"

It was Vic who answered. "Howard? After they separated him from Doc they sent him home."

"Home!"

"Isn't that what you were trying to do? Before you say he hit you?" The young officer didn't use the word "alleged" but the tone was in his voice. "Now, please, ma'am. What had he done—that you suddenly realized?"

If she was meant to feel like a doddering old lady, he was succeeding in doing it. His gentle voice and raised eyebrows were having their effect.

What did she know that she could prove? Nothing. Yet.

"How do you think I got this bang on the head, for Pete's sake?"

"Mr. Lewis says you fell down the back steps."

"I fell—" She stopped. Two things had just impressed her—Howard's audacity, and the reverence in the young policeman's voice when he said Howard's name. There was nothing to be gained here.

She looked directly at him. "I think I need a lawyer."

"That's your privilege, ma'am. Is she okay, Dr. Martin? If she is, I'll be going."

"I think she'll be fine. I'll run along, too."

"Then I'll bid you all good evening."

Lucy made frantic gestures to hush everyone until they both were out the door. Then she said, "Vic, please. I'm perfectly sane. Call Miss Warpington and make sure she's all right. Get someone in to stay with her."

Will's hand tightened again. He said, "Lucy—" and she rode over him, "I'm perfectly all right, dammit! I'm also scared silly."

In a vacuum of silence, Vic went to the hall and made the call. Lucy hated the strange looks she was getting but doggedly kept her silence until he returned. His broad face looked puzzled and he was frowning.

"She's okay. She's fine, Lucy, so cool it! But she wanted to know if you were all right. What the hell is going on?"

"Can someone stay with her?" Lucy asked.

"She'd already thought of that. The folks who do her yard work are there."

Lucy relaxed back against the pillows with a sigh

of pure relief and stroked a furry ear as Cutie nuzzled her.

She said, "All right. Now we can talk. First, tell me how you all happened to get in on it."

Vic half-grinned, hunching his big shoulders inside the "Missouri Tigers" sweatshirt the size of a tent and said mildly, "Okay. I'll start. I was out in Jessie's backyard with Cutie. She started to growl. And crouch. You know how she does—heading for the hedge. I saw Doc in his pick-up truck, turning hell-for-leather into Martha's drive, then jumping out and running into the house." He threw Will a knowing grin. "—Then Cutie broke through the hedge. I followed, yelling at her. And there stood Howard. The top of that old well was smashed in and he was just standing there with a board in his hand looking down at it. You were lying on the grass, Lucy, still as stone. Then here came Doc out the kitchen door at ninety per, down the steps and right into that chunk of board because Howard was swinging it at him. Doc staggered, then caught ol' Howie by the shirttail and whopped him back pretty good. Then Cutie made one lunge and sank her teeth in Howard's leg. He yelled and went down, Doc on top of both of them—and—well—I guess I sort of got into it then." He grinned as Eileen patted his thick shoulder. "Anyway, the bottom line is that Jessie called the police because she thought it was burglars. The police came pronto and sent Howard home. Then Will carried you in here, Lucy, and Dr. Martin came. Now—" he shrugged, "here we all are, wondering what the hell it's all about. But if it's none of our damn business, sweetheart, we'll leave."

Lucy had caught one item that stopped her breath. "The—top of the well was smashed in?"

"That's right. Howard said you were afraid Cutie had gone in the well, that you fell hurrying down the steps."

"But I knew Cutie was at Jessie's." She paused a moment. "Howard didn't know that. He was lying. Don't you see? He was lying." The entire scenario abruptly sank in, turning her icy cold. She caught her breath. "Oh, God!"

"What?" Will asked, his eyes suddenly hard.

"He—he meant to drown me. And have it look like an accident." And she knew that was true, as sure as God made green apples.

Everyone was staring.

Eileen said incredulously, "He meant to do what? Why?"

"Because I knew too much about him. But by sheer coincidence."

"What did you know?" Will asked calmly, his eyes concerned. She realized with a horrid jolt that she must sound as if the bang on her head had affected her brains.

"Listen. It all goes back to Leona Wilson's death—when they found out she was broke, her money gone."

They nodded like a Greek Chorus. She was catching their attention.

She continued quietly, "This puzzled Miss Warpington, because Miss Wilson had just shown her a financial statement from Howard's bank that said her assets were multiplying. Miss Wilson was not supposed to show it to Miss Warpington—it was supposed to be kept very confidential; but they were good friends, so she did it anyway. Howard didn't know that Miss Warpington had seen it."

She saw eyebrows go up. Good. Perhaps she was making some points. She went on, "Because neither of them had close relatives, both ladies were planning to put their money into a new library for Crewsville. Howard didn't know that, either. At Miss Wilson's death, Miss Warpington was electing to go on with it by herself—but Miss Wilson's lack of funds still bothered her and she has already, at this moment, contacted a financial investigator in Springfield. She also made a copy of Miss Wilson's statement and gave it to me. Howard just found that out tonight. It—it spooked him. Bad."

"Because he's been into Miss Warpington's money, too."

That was Vic, and it was a statement, not a question She *was* making some points!

Nodding, Lucy went on, "Probably."

"That's why you were scared for Miss Warpington."

"Exactly. How easy it would be to fake another death."

Everyone froze. Jessie croaked, "Another?"

"Miss Wilson, first." She told them about the umbrella. "And when I mentioned it to him, he freaked. That's when he hit me. Dammit, guys, I know this sounds like something from Perry Mason, but it's all true!"

At her suddenly indignant voice, Will put out his other hand and patted her cheek. "Calm down, hon," he said. "I believe you."

"So do I," said Eileen, shaking her head. "We've

all heard about Amanda's spending, about their arguments, about the rumors of Howard being personally in debt. And what you've said, Lucy—it's awful, but it makes sense."

"So—what do I do?"

"Tomorrow—follow Miss Warpington's lead and get a lawyer," said Will, not letting go of her hand. "Tonight, get some sleep. I'll be here; I'm not leaving this place. If the bastard comes back he'll get another surprise."

"And right now," said Vic, "let's count our lucky stars that you're okay. We kind of like you, lady."

The ice in Lucy's chest was melting, warmed by the eyes around her—and the feel of Will's hand. "Thanks," she said, her fingers curling around Will's.

"Although, somehow," Vic went on, getting his bulk up off Martha Hauser's old armchair, "I don't think he will. I think he'll realize he has enough problems and coming back here would only make them worse."

Jessie was thoughtfully pleating the edge of her cotton apron. "Do you think the Krueshanks will bail him out?"

"If he's been stealing money, they may try. He'll give them a good story. But if Eleanor Warpington charges him with murder, no. Those folks won't stand for that."

Jessie shivered involuntarily. "Poor Leona. I liked her. She didn't deserve such a death. And poor Dilanna—this will be awful for her."

"As a matter of fact," said Vic, stretching to his full height, "this could work for Dilly. In the end. Howard's daughter working in the bank might be a bit uncomfortable for everyone else there. Hey!"

He had literally frozen in mid-stretch. He said, "Hold on, everybody."

Taking his handkerchief from his hip pocket, he unfolded it, knelt, and fished an object from beneath the sofa.

"Looky, looky what I found," he said, and stood up. He was cradling a brass Cupid. "Could this be what hit you, Lucy Maud?"

Lucy swallowed hard and shuddered. "It—it might be."

"I think it was. See—there's gray hair caught on Cupid's bow."

Lucy turned her face away into Will's shoulder. Over her head his tight voice asked, "What are you going to do with it, Vic?"

"Whatever Lucy wants. But I don't think this should be ignored."

"I damn *well* don't think it should!" Will said sharply. "Can you take the thing home and put it in your safe?"

"You bet. Right now. Okay, guys, let's move out. Maybe Lucy can get some sleep. You're stayin', Doc?"

"You bet I am."

Will gently eased his arm from beneath Lucy's head, got up, and followed the three to the kitchen door. Lucy heard muffled voices receding, then the sound of a lock. Will came back in, winked at her, and—incredibly—turned the bolt on the front door, also.

"I may be blind, but I'm not stupid," he said.

"You—you're staying? You mean it?"

"Just try to pry me loose."

They were both startled by the telephone ringing.

Lucy's gray face wrenched Will's heart. She faltered, saying, "Surely it's not—not him! But he's been making those nasty calls—"

Will glanced at his watch. "Ten-thirty," he said. "I'll answer." And the "Hello!" he barked could have cut through steel.

Then he said, "What? Oh. Just a moment." His wide, rigid shoulders relaxed and he handed the phone on its long cord to Lucy. "Someone called Pam."

Pam! From Millard?

Lucy took the telephone and tried to make her voice calm. Will was rewarded by seeing her gray face turn pink.

"Oh, Pammy, shut up," she said into the phone.

Figuring that the caller was non-lethal, he went into the kitchen and put two cups of water in the microwave. On his return with the coffee, he found Lucy Maud lying back on the pillows, the telephone re-cradled.

She said to him, "You'll never believe this. When has there ever been such a day?"

He handed her the cup and sat down beside her. "What now?"

"Kathryn MacClane just called Pam. In Millard."

"That's the senator's bitch."

"Right. Kathryn. Not Pam."

"So?"

"She told Pam that the Millard Library was a real mess, she was tired of fighting it, fighting the staff, fighting the public, and she was bailing out. As of tomorrow. And if I wanted the damned job back, I could have it. Also tomorrow."

Will took a deep breath and stretched out his long legs. He petted Cutie absently, but did not look at Lucy. "Do you?"

"Want the job back?"

"Yes."

She shut her eyes. She was hurting now with something else besides the bang on the head.

Back to the tunnel? Back to being Miss Millard Public Library? Back to straight lines in an office she'd designed, to be an insulated cage?

Her lip trembled and she closed her eyes against the traitorous tears. "I told her I'd call her later."

"Why? Why not a straightforward answer? Yes, I'll be there. It's exactly what I want!"

She almost yelled across that harsh voice, "Will, shut up! Shut up a minute! Just—give me an answer." Then she stopped, made her voice calmer, but still didn't look at the gray-haired, green-eyed man at her side with the purple cheekbone and the grass-stained pants. "Vic said—said you tore into the driveway and ran into the house—here—yelling, and making a—a—"

"Big hoo-hah. Vic is nothing but descriptive."

"Why?"

"Why? Because I was madder'n hell, that's why!"

"Mad? At me?"

"You're damn right! Making me look like a real wimp!"

"A wimp!"

"Or a jackass. Or a pretty damned poor excuse for a human being!"

"I didn't do that!"

"You did them all! Running off like that, leaving me with a half-naked paper doll I can't stand the sight of! And worse—" Now he turned, and his green eyes were blazing. "Worse! Letting me know by your running that you thought I was only another stupid macho idiot looking to make out with Miss America! Damn it, Lucy. That hurt!"

She'd caught her breath and was staring at him in amazement, tears running down her pale cheeks unnoticed. "Hurt!"

"Of course it hurt! It's a pretty poor sort of human being who has to have two breasts or even *one*—or he won't play! My God! Don't you think there's more substance to me than that?"

"Will, I—"

"Haven't I tried to show that I liked your company? That I wanted to be with *you*—not Venus de Milo?" Then his voice softened and he reached out both arms, muttering, "Scram, dog," and—as the dog obeyed— gathered her fast, hard, into his arms, rocking her against him, saying in her ear, "I knew, dammit! I knew about your mastectomy—a long time ago! Howard was in the tavern, half-crocked, spouting off about his old girlfriend—and you know his problem? He was jealous—jealous, because you'd turned out to be a hell of a woman and he was married to a fat frump! Lucy, damn it all, I didn't think it was important enough to even mention! And I certainly didn't stop coming on to you! Now, be fair! Did I?"

Her heart was thundering. She whispered, "No . . . no . . ."

"No, I didn't."

"No, you didn't."

She shook her head. He'd swung his legs onto the sofa and was stretched beside her, murmuring in her ear, "Let me demonstrate that one breast is just fine— let me show you, sweetheart . . ." His warm fingers were pulling down the silky ruffles at her throat, slipping inside, cupping on the satin ball there, bringing it lovingly to his gentle mouth, kissing its tip with a heat that made her dizzy.

"See, sweetheart," he murmured against the softness, "see? There's no problem—oh, God, there certainly isn't—" And she could feel, then, his male hardness against her thigh, pressing, desiring.

Then he stopped, making himself stop, gently sliding the round breast damp with his kisses into its blue abode, and half sitting up again, holding her tightly, so she could feel the strong heart banging through his chest. " 'Not tonight, Josephine,' " he said huskily in her ear, mimicking Napoleon Bonaparte, trying to be light but yet not able to still either of their hearts. "Too much has happened today. I don't want your love as a reaction to something else—even if you don't think it is! I want it all—undistracted, uninfluenced by weirdos or jobs or—whatever. Later, hon. When it's just you— and me. And understand, sweetheart—" His voice had gone deep, steady in her ear, "—that either you throw me out on my ear right *now!* Or it *is* going to happen sometime soon—like I said."

"Just—kiss me . . ."

"No. Not now!" He was almost laughing, but it was pleased laughter. "Kiss is Step One. Step One leads logically to Step Two. And I said, not tonight! Tonight, hon, you need to get yourself off to bed alone and rest. Sleep! I'll be right here, never fear—and tomorrow may just be one hell of a day. So—scoot. Before," he added, "I lose all my good resolutions."

He was lifting her to her feet, spanking her silky fanny lightly. She said, almost laughing, "May I drink my coffee?"

"Take it with you. Good night, Lucy Maud."

"Good night, Dr. Evans."

Lying in bed, listening to the slight noises in the front room, catching the flicker of a muted television on the far wall, she heard him pacing the floor.

But she didn't call out.

This was a strong man, trying to be stronger. And she owed it to him to be strong also.

Amazingly, she did go to sleep. The human frame does have demands of its own, separate from the mind, and this time the human frame won.

Thirty-four

Crisp autumn sunlight streamed from the window across the tatty stitching of Martha Hauser's old quilt, reflecting back from the mirror and spraying the bed with gold.

Lucy opened her eyes to the dazzling light and closed them again. At first she was content to lie still, supine.

Then reality dawned—all the tumbled, incredible events of yesterday—and the day before—and the day before that! She'd come to Crewsville distraught and frantic—but she'd also come smug, condescending, and convinced of her own superiority. Now, what, Lucy Maud?

Have you learned anything? Will you use what you've learned? Or are you going to take the easy way out and go back to being Miss Marshall in your cozy, closed-in library tunnel world—until the next crisis.

And there will be one. Bet on it. Heaven knows what—but it will come. And then do you want to do a solo again? Fight everything by yourself?

Solos are lonely.

If she'd learned one thing, she'd learned that.

But she had learned a few more things, also. Or—
she hoped she had—

Her mental meanderings was suddenly halted by a
strange sound. A buzzing noise. What in the world—

Then she knew. She knew with a start, then a smile,
and a settling back among the disheveled quilts.

An electric razor. That's what it was.

Will. Shaving.

And that brought on more assessment, quickening
her heart, putting involuntary hands to a mussed head.
She swung her feet to the floor and reached for the
pink robe flung across a chairback.

Just in time.

The razor stopped. There was a gentle tap-tap on
her door, and on her answering, Will stood there, smiling, polishing his wire-rim glasses with a handkerchief, wearing jeans and a white tee-shirt.

"Emergency kit in the truck," he said. *"Be prepared*—the motto of the country vet. Good morning,
hon. You look beautiful. Sleep well? As well as possible, I mean."

Sheepishly, she nodded. He put on the glasses and
held out his arms. She went into them. There was no
question, no hesitation.

"Oh, golly," he said gently into her hair, "How I've
been waiting for this. Wanting this." Tilting her face
upward, he kissed her gently, murmuring, "How's the
aching head?"

It wasn't aching. She said so. "How's the cheekbone?"

"Sore as hell." But he laughed softly, rubbing his

face against the top of her head. "But this will make it feel better."

Over his shoulder she'd just caught a glimpse of the clock. Eight-thirty!

She said, "Sorry I'm so late getting myself up."

"That's not all you're getting up, lady." Then when the remark sank in and she gasped, turning pink, he laughed, and stepped back, releasing her. "However, Jessie called, and wants us over for breakfast. Okay? It doesn't," he added, smiling at her, "leave much time for hanky-panky. I assume you take rainchecks."

At this point she'd take anything he offered. But of course, he didn't need to know that.

He was going toward the kitchen, saying over his shoulder, "I'll let Cutie out. Get moving."

"Will—"

He stopped, half turned, then saw her eyes shut as she remembered that horrid, gaping well in the back. She said tensely, "Out front? Take her out front?"

"You bet. Don't worry. Run get dressed."

She'd need to do laundry soon. Such mundane, ordinary thoughts kept her on an even keel as she creamed her face, took her pills, did her teeth, pulled on slacks and the same heavy sweater. Her hair was awful. It just wouldn't brush into shape. Perhaps if she parted it on the other side . . .

That was better. Now a little lipstick . . .

Suddenly aware of voices in the front of the house, she hurriedly blotted her mouth, closed the door on an unmade bed, and stepped into the living room.

Will could be glimpsed on the porch, watching Cutie water the last of the marigolds, his shoulders hunched against the chill. Bundled into a heavy blue sweater, Eleanora Warpington was just closing the door behind her.

So she was all right! On a note of thankfulness, Lucy said, "Well, good morning!"

"Good morning, dear. I was just telling Will how noticeably this house has changed since you've been here. It's marvelous what a coat of paint, a few flowers and plants, and a little rearranging can do." She was unbuttoning the sweater and glancing around appreciatively. Lucy realized with a start that everything strewn about had been put back. How well had Will slept last night if he'd had time to do that?

Miss Warpington was going on, "Martha, bless her, had no grace with furnishings. But your father certainly had. A touch here, a picture there, a chair repositioned. Oh, yes, indeed. And my heavens—whatever did you do to your hair? This morning you look exactly like him!"

Lucy Maud was having difficulty dealing with the first part of Miss Warpington's casual pronouncement. The second part almost made her reel.

She said hoarsely, "My—my father?"

"Of course, dear. Frank."

Then Eleanora Warpington looked closely at Lucy's face. Her own pinkened in dismay. "Oh, dear. Oh, dear! Whatever have I said? You can't mean that—that you didn't know—"

She sat down in Martha's armchair, oblivious of the fine dog hairs that almost rose in a shower to coat her dark blue skirt.

Her head literally whirling, Lucy Maud sank into

the other chair—the one she'd decided had been Frank's. Aunt Martha's *amour!*

But—her father? Her own father? The shadowy figure who had done nothing right? Who had disappeared when she was not even a year old?

Making her voice steady, trying to soothe the aghast old face across from her, she said, "Please. My mother was—very short on facts. She was not a—a happy lady, ever. Tell me about him. As a favor."

"You do wish it?"

"Oh, yes. Yes. You see, everyone in Crewsville assumed I knew. And I—I didn't." But talk about tunnel vision! Anyone else would have picked it up! She knew that. Now.

Miss Warpington took a deep breath, folding thin old hands on crossed knees. "He was really a fine man."

"I know. I hear it from everyone."

"It's true. But you see—years ago, he drank. A lot."

Somewhere Lucy remembered hearing that. She nodded.

"Unfortunately, your Aunt Martha and your mother both fell in love with him. He really loved Martha—but Verna—I'm sorry, dear—"

"I understand my mother. Go on."

"Verna—so the story goes—got him drunk. She always said he seduced her, but I'm afraid no one believed it. Anyway, she was pregnant. And they married."

"And he left."

"Yes. He did. It was an intolerable situation—married to Verna and loving your aunt."

"And my mother never divorced him."

"No. She wouldn't. She refused. I've always

thought—" Miss Warpington hesitated, then went on wryly, "that her attitude was a deliberate revenge on Martha. However, my personal attitude is not always a generous one. Be that as it may, in a nutshell, dear, when you and your mother left town Frank returned. He was sober. He was sober the rest of his life, but unfortunately the damage to his liver had been done."

"And he lived here. With my aunt."

"Yes. The finest, most generous, most civic-minded couple there ever was. I am trying not to negate your mother, dear. Frank's rejection was the tragedy of her life. But he and Martha rose above it. I—I hope she did, also."

Never. Not for a day. And she tried to perpetuate her hatred in me!

Anger rose inside Lucy Maud, and she tried to still it with sympathy, a better understanding. Later. Later she could—when the revelation she'd just received was not so new. Later she'd school herself to pity. Later.

Just now she was remembering that worn little album of her childhood pictures. And understanding whose they'd been. Not Martha's. Frank's.

A slow warmth began to seep up from her heart. She had had a father, after all. A fine man. They all said so. One who had loved her enough to carry her image with him.

Lucy smiled at Eleanor Warpington. She said softly, "You have no idea what a gift you've just given me! What a wonderful gift! How can I ever repay you?"

Miss Warpington smiled back. "Simple," she said. "Agree to take charge of the thing dearest to my heart—the library project. So even if something hap-

pens to me—I am, after all, in my nineties, child—
Leona's and my precious dream can still come true."

Lucy knew the answer to that—and suddenly, logically, she knew *more* than that. She knew what she was going to do if—if Will still wanted her around. He was standing just inside the door, Cutie sitting happily at his feet. And the look in his green eyes as they met hers gave her all the answer she needed.

"I agree," she said, and no reward could ever match the look on his face.

"Oh, my dear!" said Miss Warpington happily, holding up her hands. Lucy found herself embracing the elderly aristocrat in a swift, loving hug.

"However," Lucy went on, holding the frail old hands, "I still have to tie up some loose ends in Millard. There's my apartment—and they'll need someone in the library until they can find a replacement. It will take a week or so—"

"All the time you need," Miss Warpington was saying. "I have engaged an architect and I shall want your input on that. However, I know we can work everything out." Then she suddenly realized she was talking to thin air. The woman holding her hands had her attention fastened on the bespectacled man in the doorway petting a somnolent dog.

He was smiling, too, and nodding his head.

"Good idea," he said. "We can deal with a week or so, can't we, Cutie?"

Cutie!

Amazed at the hollow feeling in her throat, Lucy Maud said, "Jessie will keep her, won't she? While I'm gone? I can't take her, or I would." And she knew it was true. She *would* take her—but she didn't think the neighbor's Doberman wouldn't care for it much. Nor would Cutie.

"Sure she will," he was answering easily. "Look, Miss Warpington—we're due over there for breakfast. Won't you join us? I know Jessie would be delighted."

"Oh, no, no." The lady was gathering up her purse and gloves, buttoning her sweater. "My car is waiting outside, and I have a doctor's appointment. It's curious, and probably nothing—but on my annual exam last week he found strange traces of some sort of drug in my blood. He feels it might account for my being so— hazy—recently. Anyway, a friend is taking me. Not Howard," she added, looking directly at Lucy Maud. "I'm ending that association very shortly—when, in particular, my lawyer in Springfield discovers what I suspect he will."

Lucy Maud suddenly realized Miss Warpington knew nothing about the night before. She caught her breath, glancing at Will. "I understand you have some-one staying with you now."

"Yes. Temporarily. Although I find it so pleasant to have someone else in the house I may persuade them to make the arrangement permanent." She rose to her full, regal stature, pulling on her gloves. The eyes be-hind the gold-rimmed glasses were like a pleased child's. "I asked them because of Halloween," she said. "You've heard me say how silly I am about Dracula and that sort of thing." She shrugged, apologetically at Will as she passed him, and bent to pet Cutie who per-mitted it happily. Straightening, she went on, "And it's amazing how sometimes things happen right. With the proper timing, I mean. Would you believe that last night late my people heard a funny noise, opened the door, and were screamed at by somebody in a Dracula suit? Trick-or-treaters, of course, and they said the person then ran like a rabbit." She laughed. "I imagine he was quite surprised, too—seeing two strangers and probably expecting me! Some neighborhood child, of course. Good morning, dears. We'll chat more later. And Lucy, when you're ready to go on salary, we'll get a contract drawn!"

She went carefully down the steps, assisted by a stout man who sprang from his car to assist her. With a wave, she was driven away.

In the doorway, Lucy Maud and Will Evans looked at each other, seeking answers in each other's eyes.

"Howard," said Lucy.

"Probably. After he left here. We have to nail him, Lucy, before he nails someone else. That guy is getting scary. I get the feeling he's running on sheer ego, thinking he's done what *he* wanted so long he's invincible."

"He's desperate. Things are closing in on him."

"Poor baby," Will said sarcastically. "He's nowhere as closed in as Leona Wilson is in a vault in the cemetery."

"Hoo-hoo!" called Jessie, peering through the hedge. She added cheerfully, "It's ready when you are. Vic's already eating."

"Somehow I'm not surprised," Will answered, and laughed at Lucy. He took her hand in his. "Let's go. If," he added *sotto voce,* "you're not offering any alternatives."

"Not at the moment," she said and was again

amazed at herself. Could this be the staid Lucy Maud Marshall she knew?

Or was this Frank Marshall's daughter?

Warmth and the sound of laughing voices came from Jessie's kitchen as she held the old screen door open. To their surprise they saw Dilanna and John seated at the round table with Vic and Eileen. The air was redolent with eggs and cheese and hot toast. Dilanna held up her hand. A diamond flashed.

"See?" she caroled. "See? Oh, I'm so happy, guys!"

"I've had it for a year," John beamed, "but she wouldn't let me put the thing on until last night."

"It was so strange," Dilanna said, making room by scooting her chair closer to John's. "We were all still at Grandpa's, just sort of sitting around. Grandpa was half asleep. Then all of a sudden Daddy comes charging in. He'd gone to take Miss Warpington home, I guess, and we hadn't seen him since. That wasn't unusual. He's always doing that. Anyway—here he comes—and looking like he'd been in a garbage truck. I mean—he was a mess! Thank goodness the senator had already left. And he went right past us into the kitchen—and came out with Johnny!"

"I was putting stuff in the dishwasher," John said. "I make a little on the side part-timing with the catering service, you see. And holy smoke—here's Mr. Lewis, grabbing my arm, hauling me out where the family's sittin'. It kind of scared me for a minute."

"Me, too—but Daddy—he just stops and says to everybody in this loud voice, 'This is the young man who's going to marry my daughter! Does everyone understand that?' I thought my mom was going to have a cow! But Daddy just looks at her and says, 'Shut up. It's my wish. My decision. Okay?' "

"Then he leaves," said John, shrugging his wide, thin shoulders. "He leaves. Bang! The door!"

"And so do we," said Dilanna. "I mean—everyone was just sort of—looking at each other—"

"Now we're trying to get up enough courage to go back," John continued. "I won't let her go alone. And it doesn't matter, now." He smiled sideways at Dilanna. "We got married last night. I'd had the paperwork for days, but she just wouldn't do it."

"But Daddy'd said okay. He'd said okay! Oh, guys, I'm so happy!"

It was obvious in the glistening eyes beneath the frizz. Lucy Maud bent and gave the chubby shoulders a hug.

"And I'm glad for you kids," she said. "Congratulations! And all the best wishes in the world!"

"We'll have to give you a wedding shower or something," Eileen was saying. "Will you help us, Lucy?"

"Of course!"

Lucy sat down next to the glowing girl and felt Will's hand close on hers beneath the table. He and Vic had exchanged covert glances, and she knew what was in their minds: Where was Howard Lewis now?

Thirty-five

Jessie was loading a cheese omelet on her plate, flanked by a heap of bacon and crusty, buttered toast.

"The marmalade's right at your elbow," she said.

And suddenly a small memory slid into Lucy's mind: The little marmalade packages Howard had brought to Miss Warpington—but had quickly re-pocketed when she'd offered them to her. Now the doctor said Miss Warpington had appeared to have—what was the phrase she'd used? *Small traces of some drug in her blood.*

A chill swept through her. Was there no limit to what the man would do? Was Will right? Was he just running on manic ego? Or was she right—that he was panicked because everything had caved in?

What in the world could they do?

"Okay, kiddo," John was saying, standing up and reaching for his new wife's hand. "Let's go. It's 'face the music' time. Thanks for the food, Jessie. You're a doll."

"You're always welcome here, kids. You know that."

"We know it." Dilanna gave Jessie a swift hug. "See you all later!"

"Good luck!"

John said to Vic, "I've had it already. When I got this girl."

"Oh, boy!" murmured Eileen, watching them go down the back steps.

Vic said, "They'll be okay. John's a fine young man." He was wiping his broad face with a napkin. "Probably got egg in my ears," he went on, grinning. "I was hungry. Forgot to buy groceries, and didn't have anything in my apartment this morning but beer." He was leaning back to shut the door John and Dilanna had left open. "Damn. It's fall, all right. Got down to sixteen last night." Then he stopped, the door half shut. "Hey, Doc, one of us left his scanner on. Your truck or my car?"

"Not my truck. Mine's in the shop."

"Mine, then. I'll go shut it off. Don't want to wake the neighbors on Sunday morning—they might want to come over and eat, too."

He crunched down the steps and around the shrubbery. Jessie was laughing. "He's spotted the cinnamon rolls," she said. "You can't keep any sort of food away from that man."

Eileen was getting up. "I'll help stack dishes," she said. "Sit down, Mom. Your coffee's getting cold."

Jessie sat. She tasted her cup, made a wry face, and reached behind for the pot. Her eyes went to Lucy, then to Will.

"I must say," she smiled, "that both of you look a little better for wear then you did last night."

"We feel a little better than we did last night," Will answered, forking his eggs. "It was kind of wild around there for a while."

"What are you going to do about Howard Lewis?"

It was a direct question. Will chewed thoughtfully before he even tried to answer.

"We may not," he said, "have to do anything ourselves. Not when Eleanora Warpington does what she says she's going to do. If Leona Wilson's financial statement is as fraudulent as we think, and if they find Eleanora's estate has also been tampered with, Howard's up the creek."

Jessie sighed, puffing out wrinkled cheeks. "It's a shame, really," she said. "He has been good to a lot of old folks. They've really liked him."

"And trusted him," Will added grimly.

She nodded. "I know. It's kind of a sad commentary on the world, isn't it? I mean—so many people my age—they don't have anybody! No one who cares, I mean. Then when they do find somebody who takes the time to do nice things for 'em—look what happens. I'm so lucky, Calvin and I both—havin' you guys. All of you," she went on, reaching out to pat Lucy's hand. "It's just great getting Lucy in the house next door. Like old times, when Martha and Frank were there."

And I'm Frank's daughter!

Ruefully, sadly, Lucy wondered how many many times people in Crewsville had mentioned Frank to her, said how nice he was, assuming she'd known she was his daughter!

Someone with a wider, more sensitive ear would have picked up on it. But not Lucy Maud Marshall! Not Lucy Maud, trying to stay inside her little tunnel!

She said to Jessie, "I just wish I'd known him better. My father."

"Well, hon, that was your mom. You know how she

was. But Martha, she kept him up on everything you did—and he was real proud of you. I've heard him say so. More coffee, Will?"

"Sure."

Will held out his cup. "My hostess didn't get around to making any."

"I'm not surprised. With a head bonk like that, I'm pleased she even got around at all. Hey—listen. That's the ambulance."

A distant wail soared and died in their ears as Vic opened the door on a draft of chill autumnal air, then closed it behind him. His broad face was set. Of the ambulance receding into the distance he said, "Yeah," and sat down again, the chair creaking.

"What was on the scanner?" Eileen asked casually. Then as she saw his tight face she said, "Vic? What was it? What's going on?"

He closed his eyes momentarily, choosing words. Then opening them and looking straight at Lucy Maud, he answered, "Someone's car went off the bridge into the city lake last night. One of the groundskeepers just found it. The driver's still inside."

"Drowned?" Eileen asked sharply.

He replied in the same toneless voice, "Ten foot of water. I'd say so."

"Oh, God, poor man!" said Jessie. "Whoever—he must have lost it on that curve. They keep warning everybody—and the speed sign's right there!"

"Maybe," said Vic. His eyes went to Will, flickered, and went back to Lucy Maud. "The car's a yellow Cadillac."

She'd known that. She'd known before he said it. Now they all knew. Howard.

"Well," said Eileen, drawing her breath in sharply, "I guess he took the easy way out."

"The coward's way," said Will harshly. "The damned son of a bitch. The coward's way! Leaving the hard stuff for his family to do!" He had reached out and taken Lucy's cold hand in his. "Personally—God forgive me—I think we're all well rid of the bum!"

"God will forgive you," said Jessie softly, "but will He forgive Howard? Oh—poor Dilanna! What she's walking into! But now at least she has John. Probably the one good thing her father ever did! Try to relax, hon. I'll warm your coffee. You look as if you could use it."

That was just like Jessie, bustling, doing what she did best, Lucy realized. Helping people. Helping someone beside herself. Could she learn to do that? Oh, she'd try! She was really going to try!

She turned her hand and closed her fingers on Will's. She had a sense of one day ending, another beginning. Perhaps there was such a thing as a second sunrise, after all. For her.

Then Will's beeper went off.

He rolled his eyes, loosened his hand, said to Jessie, "Don't let her get away," and went out the door.

Jessie looked at Lucy. "You want to get away?"

Lucy shook her head. "No."

And everyone smiled at her. Everyone!

Will was coming back in. He'd pulled on one of his denim jackets and handed another to Lucy. "Nothing much," he said to her, "just a guy in the bend of Bee

Creek, wants me to take a look at his Walker. Thinks she might be gettin' ready to foal."

"Tennessee Walker," said Vic to Lucy's blank face. "A horse."

"She'll learn," Will grinned. "I'll see to it. Look, Lucy—I seem to have two cars in your drive. Why don't you follow me home in one of them, then we'll—"

"—Check on the Walker?" Eileen finished for him, winking at Vic and her mother.

"Eventually. First, I have to throw a load of sheets and a blanket in the washer. Something dirtied my bed yesterday."

And that was a message that Lucy received.

She took a deep breath and smiled at them all. A "Frank Marshall" smile. From his daughter. Among friends. Where she belonged.

"I need to feed Cutie."

"Good land, I will!" said Jessie. "She thinks she owns this place, too. She always did. Run along. And don't forget—there's cinnamon rolls for later."

Lucy stood, letting Will put the jacket on her. They went back down the steps and through the hedge, not hearing Vic in the kitchen behind them saying, "Oh— one more thing. Sort of odd. Out at the lake there was a Dracula mask and a sheet on the bank. That's what first caught the groundskeeper's eye."

"Kids," said Jessie, dismissing it. Her eyes soft, she was still watching the pair walking toward Martha's house. "Think she'll still sell the place, Vic?"

"After a while. Don't push, Jessie."

"Doc's got that awful nice house on the edge of town."

"He said—don't push, Mom!" But Eileen was smiling. "Pour me some coffee, too. I have to wake Tina up in five minutes."

"Goin' to church?"

"I think it's a good day to go," said Eileen.

Both Vic and Jessie nodded.

On the other side of the hedge, an interested dog was watching as Will Evans held Lucy Maud Marshall tight in his arms, moving his cheek rhythmically against the top of her head. The sun was warming Will's broad back, a light, rustling breeze was cascading crimson maple leaves down on them both, and high above on a bare branch a black, fierce-eyed starling was cursing them both roundly because they stood on the best place in the yard for bugs.

Neither noticed.

"One step at a time, hon," Will was saying into her ear. "Back to Millard is the first one. And I understand. But the second is back here. To stay."

"And the third?"

One strong finger found her chin and lifted her face to those green eyes beneath that soft fall of gray hair. What she saw there made her heart stop.

Second sunrise. It could happen. It was happening to her.

And she helped, raising her hand, bringing that loving, wonderful face down to hers, rejoicing in his male warmth, the thud of his heart, the press of his long body against her own.

He was whispering in her ear, "It doesn't take long to rip off dirty sheets."

She whispered back, "Mine are clean already."

"What will the neighbors say?" He was chuckling in her ear, that deep sound she'd learned to love.

"That—that Martha Hauser's house is a happy one again."

It was an excellent point.

They went to make it true.

Cutie, ever insouciant, padded back to Jessie's to have a cinnamon roll.

Look for these new *To Love Again* novels
next month:

ANYTHING FOR LOVE—a super release from
Zebra's best-selling romance author,
Janelle Taylor

and

COUNTRY LOVE SONG by Charlotte Sherman

and coming in August . . .

THE BEST MAN by Phoebe Gallant

and

CALL IT PARADISE by Mary Jane Lloyd